# Advance Praise for *The Kids Are Gonna Ask*

"Going viral takes on a whole new meaning in this wry and humane look at the unintended consequences of inviting the world into your private life. *The Kids Are Gonna Ask* is a touching, wonderful novel about the discoveries we make when the simplest questions spark the most complicated answers."

**—Abbi Waxman, bestselling author of *The Bookish Life of Nina Hill* and *Other People's Houses***

"Totally original, filled with quirky and heartfelt characters that leap to life off the page. *The Kids Are Gonna Ask* explores the complexities of familial love and the search for a biological father that quickly escalates into a national controversy. Gretchen Anthony has her pen on the pulse of today's social media culture and delivers a page-turning novel that could very well go viral."    **—Renee Rosen, author of *Park Avenue Summer***

"A smart, engaging send-up of our modern age wrapped up in a story too delicious to put down. With a lovable matriarch, a pair of insightful kids, a spot-on villain and even a ghost or two for good measure, plan to get totally sucked in to the tweets, texts, and podcasts that pepper this funny, heartfelt exploration of what makes us who we are."

**—Kelly Harms, bestselling author of *The Overdue Life of Amy Byler***

"Not your typical family saga… *The Kids Are Gonna Ask* is a quirky tale that puts a new spin on the ancestry.com and 23andMe craze by putting one set of siblings' search for their biological father into the limelight. Anthony captures millennial fervor perfectly in this thoroughly modern story. I truly enjoyed it!"

**—Elyssa Friedland, author of *The Floating Feldmans***

## Praise for *Evergreen Tidings from the Baumgartners*

"[A] funny, affectionate debut… Part social farce, part family drama, this openhearted, entertaining novel shows an often wrongheaded, annoyingly intrusive but caring matriarch and her family willing to have the difficult, honest conversations needed to work through their misunderstandings and reach harmony."                    —*Minneapolis Star Tribune*

"Anthony's debut successfully mixes reali~~ life events with a sense of humor, prevent~~ becoming a victim or a villain."      —

# THE KIDS ARE GONNA ASK

## GRETCHEN ANTHONY

PARK
ROW
BOOKS

PARK
ROW
BOOKS™

Recycling programs
for this product may
not exist in your area.

ISBN-13: 978-0-7783-0874-4

The Kids Are Gonna Ask

This edition published by arrangement with Harlequin Books S.A.

Park Row Books
22 Adelaide St. West, 40th Floor
Toronto, Ontario M5H 4E3, Canada
ParkRowBooks.com
BookClubbish.com

Printed in U.S.A.

To Mom,

who set a magical table for our family.

# July

The house had become an aquarium—one side tank, the other, fingerprint-smeared glass—with Thomas McClair on the inside looking out. There had been a dozen protests outside their home in less than a week, all for the McClairs to—*what*, enjoy? Critique? Reject? There was no making sense of it.

Tonight, Thomas pulled his desk chair up to the window and kicked his feet onto the sill. He'd been too anxious to eat dinner, but his mind apparently hadn't notified his stomach, which now growled and cramped. He was seventeen. He could swallow a whole pizza and wash it down with a half-gallon of milk, then go back for more, especially being an athlete. But that was *before*. Before the podcast, before the secrets, before the wave of national attention. Now he was just a screwup with a group of strangers swarming the parkway across the street from his house because he'd practically invited them to come.

He deserved to feel awful.

The McClairs had been locked in the house for a week, leaving Thomas short of both entertainment and sanity. He had no choice but to watch the show unfolding outside. Stuck in his beige bedroom, with the Foo Fighters at Wembley poster and the Pinewood Derby blue ribbons, overlooking the front lawn and the driveway and the hand-me-down Volvo neither he nor Savannah had driven since last week. There they stood—a crowd of milling strangers, all vying for the McClairs' attention. All these people with their causes. Some who came to help or ogle. More who came to hate.

Thomas brought his face almost to the glass and tried to figure out the newly assembling crowd. Earlier that day, out of all the attention seekers, one guy in particular had stood out. He wore black jeans, black boots, a black beanie—a massive amount of clothing for the kind of day where you could see the summer heat curling up from the pavement—and a black T-shirt that screamed Who's paying you? in pink neon. He also held a leash attached to a life-size German shepherd plushy toy.

Some of the demonstrators had gone home for the night, only to be replaced by a candlelight vigil. And a cappella singing. There were only about a dozen people in the group, all women, except for two tall guys in the back lending their baritones to a standard rotation of hymns. "Amazing Grace" first, followed by "Jesus Loves the Little Children." Now they were into a song Thomas didn't know, but the longer he listened, he figured hundred-to-one odds that the lyrics consisted of no more than three words, repeated over and over. They hit the last note and raised their candles high above their heads. *By daaaaaaaaaaaaayyyy.*

"No more," he begged into the glass. "I can't take any more."

A week. Of this.

Of protests, rallies and news crews with their vans and satellites and microphones.

Of his sister, Savannah, locked in her room, refusing to speak to him.

Of his grandmother Maggie in hers, sick with worry.

Of finding—then losing—his biodad, the missing piece of his mother's story. And his own.

Thomas was left to deal with it all. Because he'd started it. And because he was a finisher. And most of all, because it wasn't over yet.

# BOOK ONE

Two months earlier

# ONE

## MAGGIE

If every home has a heart, my family's beats at our dining room table. Broad, sturdy and claw-footed, it has been the McClair family gathering place for more than a hundred and twenty years.

My great-grandmother was a baby at that table. She learned to pray there, and keep her hands in her lap, and listen more than she spoke. Later, when my grandmother became a mother, she painted the bland maple wood a vibrant red and, in a quiet act of rebellion, told her daughter, "Growing up, I was taught that men carried the conversation, and women carried the dishes. We're going to do things differently."

Many years after that, when my mother brought the table into our house, she repainted it, but kept the striking color. "Brown would match the cupboards better," I suggested. My mother shook her head. "We keep it red for a reason," she told me. "It's a reminder. That everyone has a voice, and every voice deserves a place at the table."

Elizabeth (Bess) McClair
Excerpt, college entrance essay

The day her family's lives would change forever, Maggie McClair passed through the door from the kitchen and glanced at the dining room wall. Wouldn't you know, Bess's essay was crooked again. She walked over and ran a finger down the side of the glass-framed paper, nudging its corners to a perfect ninety degrees. *There.*

In Maggie's mind, Bess laughed. *Really, Mom? It was only slanted a few degrees. You couldn't let that be?*

*Oh, you hush*, Maggie scolded, but she was smiling. She continued on her way to retrieve the mail from the front door mail slot.

Maggie loved her house and everything in it. A classic example of Italianate architecture on Lake of the Isles Parkway in Minneapolis, the McClair house was a Fitzgeraldesque treasure. A Gatsby among its peers. Windows tiled like dominoes across the front, living room to dining room. The wooden floors creaked. There was a sunroom circled by lead-glass windows and hallways lined with heavy oak doors and brass doorknobs exhibiting the wear of generations. Only the kitchen had changed and that—with its new appliances and upgraded sink—was merely a face-lift on the house's Roaring Twenties aesthetic.

The dining room, though, was by far Maggie's favorite. More than any other place in the house, it's where her memories lived.

She thought back to the day, twenty-some years ago, she'd hung Bess's essay there.

"I can't believe you," Bess had scoffed, Maggie being an infinite source of amusement to her daughter. "It's not like I'm Harper Lee or something." She watched her mother ascend their worn stepladder, hammer in hand.

"You wrote a beautiful testament to our values," Maggie explained. "And I love it." She drove a nail into the plaster with a swift *one-two*.

George had been there, too. Before he was only a memory, back when his heart was still pumping, and he could stand as he always did with his feet wide and his hands on his hips. "I think it's terrific," he'd said. "It's a reminder about the importance of family. Like I always say—" he thrust a declarative finger in the air "—we McClairs will always have enough—"

Bess groaned, but chimed in anyway, joining her father for the chorus. *"Because we have each other!"*

Maggie descended the last rung of the stepladder and examined her work. The frame tilted a bit to the left and she straightened it. "There. Now it's perfect." The three of them stood, shoulder to shoulder, admiring.

"Neither this essay or the red table are to leave this house until I do," Maggie had proclaimed. "Which is not to happen until I'm toes up and ass down."

"We know, Mom."

"Yes, we do," George said, kissing her cheek and patting her backside. "Nor shall I ever forget how glorious your ass looked up there on that ladder."

Maggie smacked him playfully on the chest and gave him a kiss.

"I can't wait to move out." Bess gagged as she fled the room, leaving her parents alone to coo at each other like teenagers.

Back when they still could.

Maggie sighed and looked at the red table. After her mother died, Maggie brought the table into her own dining room, vowing never to dull its vibrant presence. By then, Maggie and George had owned their house for nearly a decade. Along the way, they traveled and shopped and filled its rooms with treasure. But Maggie had kept the dining room purposefully empty, knowing that someday her family's table would take its rightful place there.

Bess had learned the state capitals by laying flash cards on the table's red surface. Her Brownie troop had spread Elmer's glue on Popsicle stick crafts there and debated the individual merits of every Girl Scout cookie type. The table had held Bess's birthday cakes and her mugs of hot chocolate on days when snowstorms canceled school. It hosted her group of high school friends as they gathered for a final farewell dinner before flying away to new lives. *Pepperdine. Dartmouth. Michigan. Northwestern. Minnesota.*

When George died, Maggie and Bess laid the table thick with offerings for his funeral guests. Prime rib and pasta Bolognese and crab-stuffed mushrooms. More and more, until Bess whispered, "That's enough now, Mom. We have enough."

*How?* Maggie wanted to know. *How would she ever have enough without him?*

Maggie snapped to when she heard a car pull into the driveway, followed by two slamming doors. Thomas and Savannah were home from school.

She had become a grandmother just over a year after George died, and the work of helping Bess with her twins buried Maggie's sorrow under piles of spit-up-stained laundry and school permission forms and spelling tests. Bess had given Maggie two tiny McClairs to love—a family of four—which meant that even in Maggie's quiet moments, when life without George didn't feel like enough, it was at least plenty.

Until one Thursday afternoon, just after lunch, when Bess died. The accident took her swiftly, when Thomas and Savannah were thirteen. Old enough to have known her, but too young to be without a mother.

Maggie's friends stepped in where she could not and filled every inch of the table's red surface with foods meant to reflect life's joys, rather than its tragedies. White chocolate rosebuds. Buttercream-frosted tea cakes. Salads dotted with lavender and blue pansies straight from the fresh, spring soil.

Maggie had stood at her table that day, not eating, her arms around an inconsolable Thomas and Savannah. But she still believed in the table's power. In its ability to nourish, and foster, and delight. Even when life, as the McClairs knew it, had ended.

*You're getting maudlin again, Mom,* Bess whispered, catapulting Maggie out of her memories into the here and now.

Maggie waved her daughter's accusation away. Bess had been gone for four years, and still, she had a knack for sharing her opinions whenever Maggie least needed to hear them. And she wasn't getting maudlin. There was something, some *thing* missing from her relationship with her grandchildren. It hadn't always been gone. Not when they were small, not even after they lost Bess. There had been a time when they were a unit, when they'd flourished under the unbreakable bond that is family. Only now—

Savannah burst through the kitchen door, followed closely by Thomas.

"Welcome home," Maggie chirped. "Tell me all about your days."

The rush of air as her grandchildren blew past was so strong it mussed her hair.

"Fine!" came their reply in unison, then they were gone to their rooms.

*Oh well.*

Maggie wiped at a smudge on the red table and tucked her shirt back into her pants. She didn't have time for a walk down memory lane. She had to get Thomas to the orthodontist and Savannah was out of deodorant. Chef Bart would return soon to start cooking, and they were hosting a guest for one of the famous McClair Friday dinners. A woman named—what was it? Maggie tried to jog her memory. She'd met her on the parkway while walking Katherine Mansfield, their standard

poodle. The woman had been in the airline industry. Negotiated with hijackers. What was her blasted name?

In the aftermath of Bess's death, Maggie had struggled
to fill the silence that swallowed her family. Some days she
heard little more from her grandchildren than the scrape of a
fork at dinner. She tried reading aloud at mealtime from the
pages of once-favorite magazines—*Rolling Stone* for Thomas
and *Variety* for Savannah. When that brought little reaction,
she encouraged them to invite their friends over, but after
several awkward dinners it quickly became clear that middle
school children didn't know what to do or say in the home
of the recently deceased.

Maggie believed in the power of silence. She also knew
that too much became a poison.

One morning, Maggie had looked up from her oatmeal and
asked, "How would you like to meet some of my friends?"

"All right," answered Thomas.

"Friends are good," said Savannah.

Maggie and George had been people collectors together,
and for more than twenty years, their house hummed with
new acquaintances. There was Officer Priestly, who'd helped
Maggie retrieve the contents of her purse from the lanes of
Interstate 35 after she'd driven away with it on the roof of
her car. And Richard Endres, who'd developed the "Cough
it up for Lung Cancer Research" advertising campaign back
when George was on the board of the Minnesota Cancer
Foundation. They'd met Alice Overberg, who raised money
for the Minnesota Orchestra, and Tilley Thillis, who styled
the blunt, silver-white bob for which Alice was so famous.
The McClair house was a revolving door.

Throughout it all, the McClairs prioritized one thing:
interesting conversation. Maggie hoped her once-beloved

dinners might just be the antidote to a silence, a sorrow so hungry it threatened to devour her family whole.

There at the red table, with the help of her acquaintances, Maggie offered the twins all the riches on which she herself had been raised—food and conversation and laughter and debate.

Little wonder that the quest to find Thomas and Savannah's father would take root at the red table, as well.

It all started with that night's Friday dinner. Chef Bart bustled in the kitchen with preparations, cooking something that smelled of nutmeg and apricots and anise. "I'll pay fifty dollars to anyone who correctly guesses the mystery spice!" he called from the kitchen.

Chef Bart had come to Maggie's and the twins' rescue four years ago, soon after Bess had passed. Maggie'd met him in the produce section of the co-op near her house when she had started to cry while holding a pomegranate.

"They're so sweet," she wept to the kind stranger. "But almost too difficult to eat."

He took her next door to a café, bought her a cup of coffee and taught her how to seed a pomegranate right there at the table.

"I understand grief all too well, myself," he'd confessed. "Good food is my favorite medicine." She offered him a job on the spot as her personal chef.

These days he arrived in time for lunch and stayed through dinner, bringing with him fresh produce, heirloom recipes and a bottomless good will. He also brought his sixteen-year-old daughter, Nadine. Strangers sometimes bristled when Maggie mentioned having a personal cook, but friends never did. They knew Chef Bart allowed Maggie to put her attention where it needed to be—on her grandchildren. And she could afford it. George had left her with plenty; real estate development was a good game in the eighties. She had a bookkeeper for the bills, a handyman on speed dial and a cleaning team every Monday. But she counted her lucky stars for Chef Bart, a gentle soul, who was to Maggie what Vitamin D was to one's diet—good for the heart and the mind.

Nadine, Savannah and Thomas sat at the red table, flipping through Maggie's ancient collection of church basement cookbooks. Katherine Mansfield lay at their feet sporting a neckerchief awash in spring colors, waiting for a scrap to fall from Chef Bart's chopping block.

The twins didn't go to the same high school as Nadine—Minneapolis had ten—and they didn't socialize outside of the McClair house. But Maggie believed that sometimes, fate works on people like a warm morning breeze. They might not have known it, but they needed each other.

"Oooh, here's a good one," said Savannah. *"Unusual Tuna Loaf."*

"How about *Beefy Bunwiches*," laughed Nadine.

*"Mother's Helper Hot Dish."*

*"Lazy Daisy Cakes."*

"Let's hope Mother's Helper doesn't turn out to be Lazy Daisy," said Thomas.

"True. That would make Unhappy Father," agreed Nadine.

"With a side of Disappointed David."

Maggie sat, content, waiting for their guest to show up. She'd been gathering friends to her home like this for years. Decades, really. All the way back to when Bess was a child and George was busy building his real estate business, the period of their lives when she made a pot of coffee every morning for her husband, sent their daughter off to school and got to work doing her part for the common good. "I'm a people gatherer," she liked to say. "Life is best lived *among*, don't you think?"

The doorbell rang, and Maggie sang cheerily, "That must be her!"

She would look back on this as the moment the course of their lives changed. If they hadn't opened that door, hadn't allowed that guest to walk through, perhaps nothing would have gone awry like it had. But they didn't know this yet.

"Would you please answer the door, Thomas?" Maggie said.

Thomas did as he was asked.

# TWO

## THOMAS

Thomas opened the door to find a brick of a woman in a brightly hand-knit tam and matching knee socks on the front stoop. She was wearing massive clogs, practically the size of shipping crates.

"I'm Eugenia Banks," she said. "Maggie McClair invited me for dinner."

"Right, of course—Maggie is my grandmother. I'm Thomas." As he held the door and ushered her inside, Thomas extended his hand, but the woman didn't shake it. Instead, Eugenia stepped through and passed him her shoulder bag, also hand-knit. Two wooden needles poked out the top.

"So, it's you and your twin who do the podcast, then?"

"My sister *Savannah* and I, yes." Thomas hated when people substituted the generic *twin* for their names. "Are you familiar with podcasts?"

Eugenia grunted. "Does it matter?"

And that's when Thomas knew. This was going to be one of *those* dinners.

It had been Savannah's idea to start the *McClair Dinner Salon* podcast in the first place. It was last year when they were in tenth grade and she needed a project for her Modern Broadcasting class.

"Maggie's always bringing interesting strangers home for dinner—what if we record the conversations and edit them down into a podcast?"

"What do you mean, 'we'?" Thomas hadn't looked up

from his textbook. He was trying to finish his homework for World History, and he'd read the same boring paragraph about Hessian soldiers three times. If he looked busy, maybe she'd leave him alone.

Savannah kept up her pleading, anyway.

"I only need one episode, two at the very most. And you're great at audio stuff. Every class presentation you do has some multimedia component."

Thomas put his pencil down on the text to mark his place and turned. "But I don't know anything about podcasting."

"Neither do I."

*Typical Savannah.* "So you want to fail your project, is that what you're saying?"

"No, silly—"

Thomas braced for the coming charm offensive. His sister only ever called him by one of two nicknames—"dummy" when she was mad, and "silly" when she wanted something.

"I want to do something incredible, something no one else in the class can do. Think about the people Maggie brings over for dinner—remember the guy who invented Count Chocula cereal? She met him at the vet's office."

Thomas smirked. "True, but that's also where she met the lady who talked about her cat who loved to eat lipstick, tube and all."

Savannah flashed him her most inviting smile. Thomas was close to being convinced, and she knew it. "Don't forget the woman who worked at the Sound 80 studio back in the seventies. Remember her? She told us all those stories about meeting Prince."

That lady had been especially cool, regaling them with stories of meeting other celebrities like Bob Dylan and Cat Stevens. And that was enough to get Thomas to agree to help.

They still had to convince Maggie, though. "Why on earth would we do that?" she'd asked.

"Because," Savannah said, "I need a final project. Plus, you're always telling us to do something *worthwhile*. A podcast is the perfect match of our skills. Thomas can handle the audio and all the technical stuff, and I can do the writing and producing."

"It's pretty much just a few microphones and an audio file uplink," he said.

Maggie stopped them. "I don't even know what a podcast is, let alone a file updo—whatever you said."

"Think of your favorite NPR program," said Thomas. "Now imagine getting to listen to it on your iPod whenever you want."

"Like a DVR for my ears?"

"Um—sort of."

Maggie liked that idea, and she agreed to allow it in her home.

That was twenty-four episodes ago. Now the *McClair Dinner Salon* had three hundred-some loyal fans, and tonight's dinner with Eugenia Banks was set to become episode twenty-five.

Once Eugenia was inside and her knitting bag was tucked away in the front hall closet, Thomas directed her on the proper placement of her clip-on microphone.

"After a few minutes, you won't even remember it's there." He handed her the battery pack.

Eugenia examined the small black box. "I heard they wrap these in condoms before taping them to an actor's skin," she said. "I don't want mine in a condom."

Thomas did his best not to grimace. "Just…your pocket. That'll be fine."

Savannah joined them.

"Hi, I'm Maggie's granddaughter, Savannah." She extended a hand, but Eugenia recoiled like it was crawling with maggots.

"I don't shake hands. Germs. It's a perfectly logical concern, but pull out a bottle of Purell after meeting someone and they act as if you've slapped them across the face."

Savannah smiled politely and dropped her arm. "Uh, sure. Anyway, I thought I'd give you the rundown for tonight. After everyone is seated, Maggie will open the show. I wrote her a script for that, but you don't have to think about anything—just enjoy yourself and your dinner."

Thomas gave his sister a look that said, *Beware. We've got a strange one tonight.* She shrugged, clearly eager to get the podcast recording started.

Savannah's passions—writing, movies, podcasts, television—weren't uncommon. It's just that she was so weird about them. Obsessed, more like. While Thomas spent his free time with friends, she spent her weekends mostly alone, bingeing Netflix and writing down the names of every woman listed in the production credits. Then she'd hole up in her room clacking out letters to them on the ancient typewriter she insisted on using because it gave her correspondence a "brand." If he complained about the noise, she'd reply, "Unlike you, Thomas, us regular people have to work to stand out. I wasn't born with good-looking, white boy privilege."

Thomas and his sister were opposites in almost every way. She was short—five foot even to his six foot one. But unlike him, she looked like she belonged in their family. Savannah and Maggie were so much alike with their dark hair and eyes, their mom used to call them "the Hershey's Kisses twins."

And who did Thomas look like? Who'd he get his strawberry-blond hair from or the gap in his front teeth that the orthodontist was charging Maggie a few thousand bucks to fix? How come he could look down on his entire family by the time he was in sixth grade? Their mother had never told them anything about their father, and now that it was too late to ask her, Thomas felt the question of his father's identity burn brighter with each passing day. He had mentioned it casually in passing to Savannah the other day, like a test balloon to see how she'd respond. Which, of course, she hadn't. She'd ignored him, like always.

Some days, Thomas wondered if the only things he and Savannah shared were the podcast, a last name and the upstairs bathroom.

And Maggie. They had her, too. But she was a whole other bunch of weird.

For starters, their grandmother was always bringing home strays—people she treated like old friends, even though she'd just met them twenty minutes ago. Not that everyone was annoying. How else would Thomas have gotten to eat dinner with the former ambassador to Uganda if his grandmother hadn't met her shopping for fresh mung bean sprouts at the Vietnamese grocery? The problem was, Maggie thought almost everyone was fascinating, which meant they'd also had to spend an entire dinner listening to her podiatrist talk about foot fungus.

And now, here they were with another strange one, Eugenia Banks.

The four of them sat down at the red table and Thomas gave Maggie the thumbs-up to begin recording.

"Welcome to this week's *McClair Dinner Salon*," she read. Maggie sounded stilted with a script, but Savannah insisted on a written opening every week anyway. "Fix yourself a drink, find a comfortable chair and join us as we dig in to four courses of intellectual delight.

"With us at the table tonight is Ms. Eugenia Banks, who I met recently outside the architecturally renowned Purcell-

Cutts house in Minneapolis. We chatted about everything from Eugenia's interest in Icelandic knitting to our shared fascination with an odd little sleep disorder called idiopathic hypersomnia. Ms. Banks has lived a very full life, my friends. First as a stewardess and now, raising chickens in her backyard and selling the eggs out of her refurbished milk truck. Tonight, I sincerely hope she'll tell us the story of the time she successfully negotiated with hijackers. Last, but certainly not least, our dinner, as always, has been prepared by our fearless Chef Bart." She looked at Savannah. "Would you do the honors and introduce our family, love?"

Maggie and Savannah both knew that wasn't actually a question. Every week, Savannah found a new metaphor to explain their atypical family, and Thomas braced for her newest description.

"Think of our McClair family like a BLT lettuce wrap," Savannah began. "Thomas and I started out like your typical sandwich, a slice of bread for our two parents. But we never knew our dad, which made us an open-faced sandwich from the very beginning. Then, our mom died, and suddenly, we were like just bacon and tomato with nothing holding us together. So Maggie, the lettuce, wrapped Thomas and me up and she's the one who holds the family together now. A BLT, but with a lot fewer carbs. And if you hear a dog bark, that's our poodle, Katherine Mansfield."

Maggie was visibly trying not to laugh. "Thank you, Savannah. The three of us make a BLT lettuce wrap—I like it. Chef Bart has just served our appetizer course, tofu steak crostini with shiitake mushroom glaze. Please, let's dig in."

With that, they were off.

"Ms. Banks, tell us," Maggie said. "When did you start working for the airlines?"

"In 1969," she said. "Braniff. The one with the airplanes painted like jelly beans."

"Oh, 1969," Maggie said. "That was quite a year, wasn't it? I don't think I'll ever forget. Did you feel it on your flights? The social change? The simmering tensions?"

"Well, they made us stewardesses wear Pucci boots, if that's what you mean. We looked like go-go dancers. Ridiculous." Eugenia picked up her tofu steak with her fork and examined it. "Is this supposed to be gray?"

Thomas stifled a laugh. This was definitely one of *those* dinners. He heard Savannah's phone buzz against the dining room table, and immediately knew who it was. Savannah and her best friend, Trigg, couldn't go ten minutes without each other.

*Shut it off*, he mouthed.

She ignored him and thumbed out a text, laughing silently to herself.

These days, Thomas thought of Trigg as one of those girls you couldn't escape. She was everywhere, even when she wasn't. Like now, interrupting the *Dinner Salon*. Or in school. You might not see Trigg's head poking above the chaos at passing time, but you couldn't miss the sound of her.

Eugenia, meanwhile, brought her hand into the air and twisted it. "All this knitting lately has given me an issue with my wrist."

"What sort of issue?" Maggie asked, and Thomas could tell her voice sounded just a little too excited. He felt a surge of panic and glanced at Maggie, trying to gauge how close she was to heading off on a gross-out tangent. There was nothing his grandmother loved more than a good medical mystery.

Eugenia, turns out, was the one he should have been worried about. "Probably just a Bible bump. Nothing more than fluid collecting at the joint," she said.

Thomas frowned. This train was coming no matter what he did, and he couldn't look away.

"I get them when I overdo it. Mostly painless," she added. "Before modern medicine, people used to make the bump go away by hitting it with the heaviest book available. In most households, that was the Bible."

Thomas winced. Chef Bart came in from the kitchen carrying the main course, and Savannah, *thank god*, changed the subject.

"So, fun fact," she said. "In the original 1954 *Godzilla* they made the sound of his roar by running a mitt covered in pine tar over a double-stringed bass."

Thomas glanced around the table to measure the interest in this new topic. If Savannah was successful, the bodily ailments portion of their evening might—*hopefully*—be over.

"And did you know," Savannah went on, "that Alfred Hitchcock had his sound man *audition* different melon varieties for the stabbing sounds in the *Psycho* shower scene?"

Eugenia swallowed the last of her drink. "I once escorted Hitchcock to his flight."

"Marvelous!" Maggie clapped her hands. "Tell us all about it."

"He sat in first class."

"Then what?"

Eugenia shrugged and helped herself to another chunk of crusty bread and took an enormous bite, saying nothing more.

"That's not the flight that was hijacked, was it?" Maggie was obviously prompting. She really wanted to hear the hijacking story.

"No," Eugenia said.

Thomas glanced at his watch. This woman was a lot of work for a dinner guest.

"I'd like to fly first class someday." Savannah accepted

the freshly assembled cheese plate from Chef Bart and took a wedge of whatever he'd marked for her with a toothpick flag. She was lactose intolerant but did all right with hard cheeses. Something about the aging process.

"Don't bother," Eugenia said. "An awful lot of money for a whole lot of nothin'."

"Bummer." Savannah looked as crushed as if Eugenia had just dropped the bad news about Santa. "Still. Maybe some-day."

"Anyway, I don't know if I told you," Eugenia went on, ignoring Savannah's obvious disappointment. "My father was a twin."

Maggie slid a slice of Brie onto her plate. "Oh?"

Thomas couldn't figure out how they'd jumped from *Godzilla* to Alfred Hitchcock to twins. Maggie, though, didn't pause at Eugenia's non sequitur. "Identical or fraternal?"

"My dad said the doctors couldn't tell."

The look on Maggie's face said *one hundred percent intrigued*. "I take it your father and his twin were both male?"

The cheese plate came around, but Thomas passed it to Eugenia, who forked a slice of Havarti. He'd preemptively lost his appetite.

"Couldn't tell the other baby's sex, either." Eugenia laid the cheese onto another slice of bread and took a hefty bite. She had everyone's attention now, all of them wondering how it was possible to not know if a baby was a girl or a boy. Thomas looked at Maggie, who eyed her guest. He could see she was willing to ask the inevitable next question, but Eugenia didn't give her a chance. "My dad ate his twin. In utero. My grandmother claims he kept passing the teeth in his stool."

Thomas squeezed his eyes shut as tight as they'd go, try-ing to block out the room. It was his only option, since he couldn't exactly stick his fingers in his ears and begin to hum.

"Oh—dear." Their grandmother didn't sound flustered often, but she was flustered now. "I... I'm not sure how to respond to that."

"My siblings and I don't know if we believe it or not, but that was the family story. Never could get our dad to question it."

Conversation stopped for at least a full minute. Dead air that Thomas would have to edit out. He opened his eyes to see Chef Bart come in from the kitchen holding a second basket of bread, but, upon seeing their faces, silently backed out again. Savannah looked about ready to bolt for the bathroom, and Thomas wondered if he was going to have to beat her to it.

"Do twins...run in your family?" Maggie finally asked. She was usually pretty good at changing topics, but even she didn't seem to know where to steer this one.

"Not sure. Haven't had any since," said Eugenia. "That we know of."

"Oh my g—" Savannah choked on her cheese, and they sat for another minute while she tried to cough it up.

Thomas, meanwhile, thought he ought to be awarded some kind of prize. He thought about jumping up on his chair and declaring himself victorious—he'd known this was going to be one of *those dinners*. Eugenia Banks and her condom comments and germ phobia and her inability to maintain normal conversation. He'd spotted all the red flags, and he'd been right.

"Can we please just get through at least *one* dinner without our stomachs turning?" He realized too late that the words in his head were actually coming from his mouth. Everyone stared at him.

"Thomas!" Maggie scolded.

Savannah sniggered.

Eugenia Banks forked another slice of Havarti. "Well, I

didn't enjoy the grayish tofu, but the rest of the food has been quite acceptable."

Maggie began to nod vigorously, obviously stupefied. "Thank you, Eugenia. We are quite blessed to have Chef Bart feeding us."

Savannah's phone buzzed and she again began thumbing furiously. Stupid Trigg. Stupid Savannah. Stupid twin-eating-storytelling Eugenia Banks and stupid Maggie for inviting her.

"I've never met my father," Thomas said, looking directly at Eugenia. "But I'd like to."

The whole room stopped, as if all the air had been sucked out. Where had that even come from?

Then, Savannah. "Seriously, T! This again? It's like all you ever talk about lately."

"I said it once!" Thomas threw a leftover scrap of bread at his sister. He *had* only brought it up once to her lately, even if it had been on his mind every day. "How would you know what I talk about anyway? Your face is glued to your phone 24-7."

Eugenia Banks reached for the cheese plate. "Far be it from me to overstep my bounds, but I'm not sure that's appropriate dinner conversation, young man."

"Yeah, *young man*," Savannah mocked. "Way to throw a wrench into an otherwise lovely dinner."

"Shut it, Van." Thomas panicked and turned toward his grandmother, suddenly waking up to what he'd done. They never talked about their father. Maggie didn't seem open to it—as if she expected Thomas and Savannah to tiptoe around the subject of him, as if their father was Beetlejuice, or a ghost in the attic who would wake up by saying its name. As if they'd be fine, as long as they never let themselves need him.

"Maggie, I didn't mean—" He felt the weight of everything he'd just said settle in his throat. "I'm so sorry. I didn't mean you're not enough. You are. You're everything to us. It's just—"

"I know," Maggie finished for him. Spoke the truth of what he'd been keeping to himself for so impossibly long. "The reality is, I'm not nearly enough, at all."

# THREE

## MAGGIE

"Are you sure this is what you want?" Maggie sat with Thomas and Savannah at the kitchen table, the pendant lamp overhead wrapping them under a soft cone of light.

Chef Bart had cleaned up dinner quickly and left the three of them alone to talk. His daughter, Nadine, had heard everything from the kitchen and she gave Maggie and Savannah hugs, then hustled out behind her father. Eugenia hadn't been difficult, either. When the food stopped coming, she stood up and announced she had somewhere to be.

Now Maggie looked at Thomas's almost-man face—the sculpted cheeks, the blue eyes that had appeared so enormous as a baby, the whisper of a someday mustache. Bess had been gone for what finally felt like a long time. Thomas and Savannah were barely teenagers when she died, and now they were nearly adults. Legally, at least. Soon they would no longer need Maggie's permission for much, if anything.

"I'm not sure what I want." Thomas shrugged helplessly. "It's like, right now I don't know what I'm missing. He could be a great guy."

"Savannah?" Maggie said. It hadn't escaped notice that her granddaughter had said very little since dinner. "Are you curious about your father?"

"Of course I'm curious." She pulled at a strand of hair, some of which she'd recently dyed lavender, wrapping and unwrapping it on her finger. "I just—we never talk about him. Like, we're not supposed to. Or maybe Mom didn't want us to."

Maggie felt her stomach twist in on itself. "Is that what you think?"

Savannah didn't answer, just kept fiddling with her hair.

"I don't believe—" Maggie was about to say she didn't believe Bess hadn't wanted her children to find their father someday. But she stopped because, really, what did she know? She had asked, but Bess hadn't told. Then she died and left Maggie alone to improvise.

*That's not exactly how it went*, Bess whispered.

Maggie hushed her.

Savannah, still playing with her hair, put a few more thoughts together. "I've always been curious, but that's different than wanting to *find* him. What if he's awful? Like one of those idiots on *Cops* who tries to use a Super Soaker to rob a liquor store?"

"I doubt Mom would have been dumb enough to get involved with someone like that." Thomas looked to Maggie for confirmation. He always seemed to do that with her, even when he'd been young. Like he knew the real answers to his questions but didn't trust Maggie to give them. Once, he had asked her what time it was and when she answered, "Three o'clock," he'd said, "No, it's two fifty-five."

"Well," Maggie said to them now, "as her mother, I would hope not. But you know I can't say for certain."

"I will admit to wondering about him," said Savannah. "How Mom met him, whether they would have been good together, or if he was an awful human being."

She looked at Maggie with her dark, chocolate eyes. "You really don't know anything about him? Or them?"

Oh, how Maggie wished she did. Eighteen years ago, Bess had gone off on a ski trip her senior year of college. Two months later, she had driven home holding a diploma and a white stick bearing two pink lines.

"I want to keep it," she'd said.

"Trust your instincts, lovey," Maggie'd answered and hadn't pried further. Her daughter had seemed happy—that was enough.

Savannah sagged in her chair. "Anyway, I'm curious about all the random stuff, like the lactose thing. You guys can eat whatever you like. And Mom, too. Remember how much toasted almond fudge ice cream she ate? I'd love to do that, but I can't." She smiled. "And the way I look. Mom used to say to me, 'Let's imagine you're a tasty little chocolate drop and I eat you all up!' But you?" She poked Thomas's arm. "You're like the Jolly Green Giant."

"That's what I've been trying to say—" He stopped, the words refusing to come. This was the Thomas Maggie knew. Bold to a point, then suddenly fearful. The owlet who needed a push before leaving the nest to fly.

Savannah surrendered, quiet for a moment. "It's just…she never talked about him. It's like she was giving us a clue, or something. Like she was saying it's better not to know."

And there it was, Maggie realized. The key question in their puzzle, pulled from the shadows into the light. *Was it better to know, or not?* There would always be pieces of Bess's story that Maggie wished she hadn't learned. Maggie was no ostrich, not one to bury her head in the sand to avoid hearing the truth, and yet what good had knowledge done her back then? It hadn't changed the trajectory of her daughter's fate.

Sometimes, the answers just led to more questions.

Maggie reached for Thomas's hand and he let her take it. "When you were little," Maggie said, "we spent our mornings watching *Sesame Street* and eating bowls of Cheerios. Do you remember?"

Thomas gave a half smile.

"And they'd sing that song about one of the things not being like the other, and you and Savannah would shout and try to beat the other to point out which one it was—like the red balloon or the baseball hat."

Savannah laughed. "I nailed that game. It's my directorial eye."

Maggie nodded but kept her eyes on Thomas, desperate not to lose the connection with this unhappy, searching boy. "And do you remember the day I found you looking at our family pictures and singing the same song? We'd just gotten the proofs back from the photographer and I was trying to choose one for our Christmas cards. I left for a minute to do something and came back to find you there, holding up a photo and singing."

Thomas said he remembered.

"Do you know what you pointed out to me? Which one you said was not like the others?"

"Me." He paused, tripping over the memory. "I said me, didn't I?"

Yes, that's exactly what he'd said.

Maggie had long forgotten that moment, tucked it away with so many other anecdotes from busy days filling busy years. When it had happened, she'd assumed he was merely pointing out that he was a boy in a family of girls.

Now, though, it struck her.

"I suppose it feels as if you've spent your entire life as the odd man out."

Thomas turned his face to the ceiling, as if not wanting to consider anything but the white expanse above. "Yeah," he whispered. "Maybe."

"Being different is difficult." Maggie gave his hand a reassuring squeeze. "I know how important it is to belong,

Thomas. But before you decide anything, I want you to consider this—sometimes it's easier to settle with a little bit of mystery, than to not like what you discover when you dig."

The decision to find their father wasn't, as it turned out, entirely theirs. Eugenia Banks's twin-eating anecdote exploded like a bomb through their small podcast audience. Listeners told their friends, who listened and told their friends, and suddenly, Eugenia's cannibalistic father went viral. From listener emails to friends on the phone, everyone wanted to know where Maggie had met a character quite as unique as Eugenia Banks. It was all Maggie was hearing about. The previous episode, number twenty-four, had three hundred-some downloads. Episode twenty-five had over four thousand.

As if that weren't surprising enough, just two weeks had passed and already Thomas and Savannah had taken to spending their family dinners trading anecdotes about what the internet was now calling the Zombie Baby. Even people who never had any intention of listening to the *McClair Dinner Salon* knew about Zombie Baby.

"I can't believe it," Thomas said. "Something that happened in this very dining room has become a meme."

"Did you see the one of Zombie Baby eating Tide PODS?" Savannah said.

"Yeah, saw that. You see Dancing Zombie Baby?"

"Yep. Unicorn Zombie Baby?"

Maggie cleared her throat—to no avail.

"Puppy-Monkey-Zombie-Baby?"

"Nadine showed us that one."

"Right. Forgot."

Maggie clanged her spoon against the side of her plate.

"What if Zombie Baby became a Super Bowl commercial?" Thomas said.

"What if Zombie Baby became a Super Bowl commercial with Betty White?" added Savannah.

"That would be awesome."

"I could finally die happy."

Maggie clapped her hands—*one, two*. She waited, then clapped again—*one, two, three*. They finally looked at her.

"The two of you will be eighteen in less than six months. And it's gotten me thinking about our recent discussion." She paused to ensure she still had their attention. "Legally, once you hit adulthood, you can do whatever you like about your father. So, I want you both to know that I'm behind you. One hundred percent. Whether you start your search now, or in six months, or six years."

It hadn't been an easy decision to come to. But ultimately, Maggie believed her most important job as guardian was to help Savannah and Thomas grow into confident, independent adults. To fix them with all the skills they needed, and then get out of the way. But this puzzle before them, of from where they came and from *whom*, was never going to disappear. It was a house of cards built on existential questions. Questions of genetics. Of connection, similarity, difference. Questions of missing pieces, and about the people who held them.

Questions they would ask, regardless.

She really didn't have any choice.

Thomas and Savannah exchanged glances, a sign of something they weren't telling her.

*What now?*

"Well—" Savannah looked at Thomas, who raised a single eyebrow, reminding Maggie of Savannah's truly impressive ability to read the myriad subtleties of her brother's nods and shrugs and blinks. "We weren't sure whether to bring this up yet or not."

Thomas slid a sheet of paper across the table.

"We got this email through the *Dinner Salon* website."
Maggie picked it up and read.

Dear Thomas and Savannah,
My name's Sam Tamblin and I'm the cofounder of Guava
Media. I listened to your most recent episode. I'll admit,
it was Zombie Baby that got my attention, but I'm also
intrigued by your desire to find your biological father. I'd
like to help you. I want to make sure you find him.

As I write this, Guava Media is producing eight medium-
busting shows with more in the works. I want to talk the
two of you into conducting your search with us via podcast. You have just the sort of story we're looking for.

If you're intrigued, reach out. My details are below.
Let's call this email a small beginning to a huge success.

Regards,

Sam Tamblin
Creator and Producer, *It's Only Murder* and *Sex Upended*
Guava Media

"That's quite an offer." Maggie took a breath to buy herself time to think. She'd accepted the risks of searching for a
man who could exist anywhere on the human spectrum between Warren Buffett and Harvey Weinstein. But this letter
suggested they do their search in public. That was an entirely
different equation.

Maggie tried to circle her thoughts around this new set
of hazards. If the past two weeks had shown her anything,
it was just how quickly the trivial could explode into a phenomenon. Her dilemma, however, remained fundamental.
Today, her grandchildren were minors and still under her
care, but in six months they'd be free to do as they pleased.

Today, at least, she could simultaneously influence and encourage their independence.

"Are you interested in the producer's offer?" she finally said.

Thomas held up a finger, his mouth full of Chef Bart's dinner. Maggie looked to Savannah for an answer.

"Kind of. We've talked about it."

"But?" Maggie prodded.

"Well, for starters, I looked into this Sam Tamblin guy and there's not much information available. The only real information we have to go on is the success of Guava Media. Which I have to admit is pretty impressive."

Savannah paused to exchange glances with Thomas. "On the flip side, though, it feels like we might be betraying Mom."

"Like she'd be hurt that we're going against her wishes or something," Thomas added.

Maggie knew the conundrum all too well.

The table went quiet for a bit, each of them lost in their own thoughts. Maggie knew there were risks to the proposal before them. Plenty. But, in what context should they be evaluated? On the one hand, looking for a biological father was a very private subject, a question of who their mother had slept with and when. But on the other hand, Thomas and Savannah couldn't find him on their own. They needed all the information they could get, and that would only come from reaching out.

And what about the publicity of it all? If Zombie Baby had gone viral, who knew what else could happen. Then again, they'd hosted the *McClair Dinner Salon* for a year and still had only three hundred regular listeners. Zombie Baby was hot now, but she doubted it would prove to be much more than a blip. Certainly, no guarantee that their new podcast would garner the same attention.

*Tell me*, she pleaded with Bess. *Tell me what to do.*

Bess didn't answer.

Savannah broke the room's silence. "What sort of producer uses a phrase like 'medium-busting,' though? Sounds iffy."

"He's probably a millennial." Thomas scooped a mound of crab stuffing onto his fork. "He produces podcasts—that's mostly a millennial thing, right? I bet he's twenty-five years old, tops. Probably has a beard, too."

He held his plate out to Savannah. "If you're not going to eat your crab, load me up."

"If I can have your fish."

"Deal."

"And his flagship podcast," Savannah went on. "*It's Only Murder*? Seriously. It's only murder on the ears. Have you heard it? That host has a major case of vocal fry."

"True," said Thomas. "But then again, the show averages a half-million downloads per episode. Pretty impressive."

"What is vocal fry?" Maggie interjected.

"It's the term internet trolls have given to people who let their voices slip to the back of their throat," Thomas explained. "It makes the sound sort of crackle. Like they're sitting on their vocal cords instead of projecting through them."

Savannah demonstrated. "I'm an internet troll and I can't use my brain to think for myself."

*Awful.* "You sound like the last peals of a deflating balloon."

"That's a good way to describe it." Thomas nodded.

"And most of the time," said Savannah, "the accusations of vocal fry are totally misogynistic. Mostly young women broadcasters are accused. Which, of course, conveniently overlooks the fact that just as many men exhibit vocal fry as women."

Thomas shrugged. "What she said."

"And I know what you're thinking, Maggie," Savannah added. "But no. It's neither the result nor cause of any gory medical conditions."

Maggie mock-scowled. "You ought to be kinder to me. I *am* your elder."

She suddenly remembered the day she first met George. It was May 1978. At the stoplight at Twelfth and La Salle. He stood directly in front of her, apparently fresh from the barber's chair because the skin on the back of his neck turned from bronze to pale in the narrow space between the old hairline and the new. There was also a heart-shaped freckle behind his right ear, and she found it nearly impossible to resist touching it. She'd said, "I've always loved a man who smells like Barbasol and talc."

They married eight weeks later.

Maggie didn't believe in living life small. She believed in living. Period.

"Trust your instincts, loves," she said finally. She looked at each of her grandchildren in turn. Savannah. Then Thomas.

*Too afraid to stop them, huh?* Bess whispered.

*Oh, perfect*, Maggie replied. *Now you show up?*

**Trigg:**

OMG!!!!! [screaming cat face emoji] You're gonna be famous!!!!!!!!!!!!! [microphone emoji] [dancing woman emoji] [fireworks emoji]

**Trigg:**

You totally have to do it. I don't know why you're even thinking twice about it. [thought cloud emoji] [thinking face emoji]

**Trigg:**

Your dad is going to be so normal. Like, normal normal. Norm. We'll just call him Norm. Normal Norm. [Caucasian male face emoji] [geek face emoji]

**Trigg:**

Plus, this is what you want, right? Big time producer. OMG!!! What if you get discovered and they make your story into a movie?! That could totally totally totally happen. [popcorn bucket emoji] [movie ticket emoji] [movie camera emoji] Can I be in the movie?

**Savannah:**

Nobody is even going to care, stupid. Settle down.

[yoga pose emoji]

# FOUR

## SAVANNAH

The next day, Savannah sat in her eleventh-grade English class, her favorite. Most of her classmates were morons, but the books their teacher, Mrs. Thornbird, assigned were great. Plus, she gave them writing projects every week—and on those, Savannah excelled.

The bell rang and Mrs. Thornbird instructed the class to *pipe down*. She'd graded their one-act plays and she wanted to read an example aloud.

"I won't say whose work this is, but I want you to listen up for how the student uses dialogue to craft the story. It's really well done." She cleared her throat. "This is titled, *Midnight Visit*."

Savannah panicked. She sank down in her seat as low as she could, though even if she could have sunk all the way to the school basement, it wouldn't have been deep enough to hide from what she knew was coming.

"We open on a young woman in bed," Mrs. Thornbird read. "She's dressed in her nightgown and has obviously been sleeping. An elderly woman sits on the side of the bed, looking at her."

ELLIE: Oh! I was hoping you'd come tonight. I've missed you so much.

Parker White piped up from the back row. Because of course he would—he never had anything better to do than mock Savannah. "Oh," he purred, his voice all churlish and high-pitched. "I was hoping you'd *come* tonight." Then, growling, he responded to himself and said, "Oooh yeah, me, too, baby."

"Parker White!" Mrs. Thornbird barked.

Parker mumbled an insincere apology at the teacher while flashing Savannah a Cheshire Cat smile.

*Idiot*, she mouthed.

Mrs. Thornbird continued.

[Ellie moves to prop herself up. The elderly woman smiles at Ellie but does not speak.]

ELLIE: There's so much I've been wanting to tell you. Where should I start? School isn't very much fun, so that's nothing new. And life at home is just, you know, life at home. But I'm still glad you came.

[Ellie moves as if to hug the old woman but stops.]

ELLIE: To be honest, I've been sort of sad lately. Okay, maybe that's obvious. You probably already know how I feel.

[Ellie waits for the visitor to respond. When she does nothing more than continue to smile, Ellie speaks again.]

ELLIE: Is that why you came? Because I'm so sad? Did I summon you? Did you feel how much I needed you? Because, I've thought about it a lot—A LOT— and I don't really understand what you can see and hear and feel of me. I mean, why can't you

come visit every night? I want you with me all
the time. Mom says you are. She says that we can
talk to you whenever we want. That even though
we can't see you doesn't mean you aren't with us.
But I don't know how to feel you, except during
times like now, when you visit me.

[The elderly woman moves a hand to Ellie's back.]

Mrs. Thornbird dropped the script to her side. "The play
goes on for several more pages, but that gives you a good example of what I'm talking about."

She moved across the room, dropped Savannah's script
on the pile of assignments, and perched on the corner of her
desk. "After hearing that, what do you think the author did
particularly well?"

She waited, but no one raised their hand. Typical. No one
in their class was dumb enough to intentionally make themselves vulnerable to the endless cycle of ridicule that was life
at Lincoln High School. At least Savannah had an excuse to
keep her hand down, given that she wasn't about to compliment her own work.

"Ms. Westlund." The teacher pointed to Carrie Westlund,
who was more famous with her Instagram followers than
anyone they were in class with. "What do you think the author did well?"

Carrie tilted her head and stared at the ceiling. "Well, it
sounded pretty real. Is that right?"

"It's your opinion, Ms. Westlund—there are no right and
wrong answers."

"Okay, then, yeah. The dialogue sounded real." Carrie sat
back in her chair, looking relieved to have that over with.

Then, in a move that seemed to surprise Mrs. Thornbird as
much as anyone, Savannah's best friend, Trigg, raised her hand.

"I think it was cool that the author only wrote dialogue for one of her characters. Like, there are two characters, but only one of them is speaking. The other one doesn't say anything at all, but you sort of know what she's saying just from what she does, physically. Like when she reaches out to rub Savannah's back. You know she's being kind."

Savannah stifled a scream—Trigg had just told everyone the play was hers! She tried to sink farther into her seat, but her butt slipped off the front of her chair and she nearly landed on the floor.

Mrs. Thornbird put up her hand. "Let's please leave names out of our discussion, Ms. Kline."

"Sorry, Mrs. T. I meant to say Ellie."

Savannah put her forehead on the desk. *When was this torture going to end?*

"Anyway." Apparently, Trigg wasn't done yet. "I think the play says a lot, even with only one character talking. Especially because it's such a mysterious topic. I mean, I know lots of people would like to see their dead loved ones in dreams, but like, Savannah's mom actually came to her. And Savannah captures that in the play. I'm super jealous of her talent."

There was no choice now. Savannah had no choice but to curl up and die, right there at her desk. She hadn't even lifted her head, and already she could feel a whole classroom of faces turning to look at her.

"Is that true," the girl in front of her whispered. "Do you see your mom's ghost?"

*No*, Savannah moaned and rolled her head from side to side. *No, no, no.*

She'd written a play. A stupid, *fictional* play—about a grandmother, no less. Not a mother. What was Trigg thinking? Savannah had told her about her mom once, in confidence, in the middle of the night during a sleepover. But now, thanks to her best friend's big mouth, Savannah was about to become the social punching bag of the entire school.

Parker White leaned over and wailed like a dying teenager in a slasher film. "Help me! I see dead people!"

Savannah kept her head on her desk. "You're an asshole, Parker."

None of these idiots understood—what it was like to lose your mom, to have to live with your grandmother because there wasn't a single other person in your entire family left to take care of you. The closest any of her stupid classmates came to losing a parent was divorce—but even then, they still got to see their mom and dad. Savannah's mom was dead. Gone. Never coming back. And she'd never even known her father. For all practical purposes, she was an orphan. A pitiful orphan who missed her mother so much she conjured her up in her sleep.

Maybe Thomas hadn't been so wrong about wanting to find their biodad, after all.

# FIVE

## THOMAS

"A fully produced, commercially sponsored, episodic search for your biodad. The whole package." The following afternoon, Thomas sat clustered with Savannah and Maggie at the kitchen table while Sam Tamblin's voice echoed through the speakerphone.

"More and more, podcast audiences are clamoring for a good mystery. Not only that, they want an active role in solving it. Listeners want to dig their fingers in, find clues, debate conclusions. Do you know how many hours the average podcast überfan will spend on a discussion thread? It's crazy. You don't even want to know. Point is, give the audience a regular dose of cliff-hanger crack and those superfans will step in and do half your work."

Savannah reached over and pressed Mute. "Are we sure this guy's for real?"

Sam Tamblin carried on, unaware. "We're thinking, start out with the cast of characters. Introduce the could-be daddies. Give the audience just enough info to believe any one of these men could be the needle in your genetic haystack. We spend a few episodes exploring each father's potential, only to inevitably uncover the one irrefutable piece of evidence that forces him off the list. By the end, we have maybe two or three viable candidates left and *BAM*! We hit the world with a DNA-slash-final episode superreveal."

The three of them stared at the phone in disbelief.

"Just so we're clear," Savannah said to everyone but Sam, who was still muted, "I don't want to do that."

"Of course not," said Thomas. "But let's get a contract first." He unmuted the line. "Hey, Sam, sounds interesting. Tell us more."

Savannah hit the Mute button again. "Don't tell him that! He'll think we like the idea."

"I know. I'm just humoring him."

"Don't."

"Well, you're not saying anything at all."

"Yeah, but at least I'm not saying anything wrong."

Thomas heard Sam Tamblin now going on about the evolution of criminal versus familial DNA. He unmuted the line.

"Hey, Sam," Thomas interrupted. "Let's discuss all that. But before I forget, I'd like to have a role in engineering the audio for whatever we do. We have a fair bit of equipment from our *Dinner Salon* podcast and I'd like to build it out into a full studio setup."

He smirked at Savannah. Let her argue that was the wrong thing to say.

"Oh, uh, cool. Excellent," said Sam. "We'll have to test the sound, all that. But if it checks out, we'll run with on-site recording. Save some money on studio rental."

Thomas smiled, and a flush of pride ran up his neck.

Savannah muted the line again. "If you get to engineer, I want to produce."

"All right," said Thomas. "Tell him that."

"He's going to say no."

"No, he won't. Just tell him." Thomas unmuted the line. "Sam?" Then mouthed *tell him* at Savannah.

She scowled but took a run at it. "How do you determine who gets to produce? Is that just one person, or more than one—"

Thomas gave her a *good grief* look and pointed at the phone, urging her to try again—this time for-real asking instead of hinting.

As for Sam, he met Savannah's questions with silence. Nothing. They waited for him to respond, until finally, Maggie spoke up. "Has Savannah's question taken you by surprise, Mr. Tamblin?"

"I don't know what she's asking."

Thomas felt a small surge of *I told you so* but kept it to himself.

"I'm sure you're aware of my granddaughter's career ambitions and skill."

Another moment of silence, and Sam said, "Savannah, I can let you write some of the scripts."

Savannah's mouth fell open, but no words came. After a pause, she hit the Mute button again. "Seriously? He said yes to Thomas's requests without a second thought."

"You didn't actually ask to produce, Van. And he's giving you a chance to write."

"Yeah, but—" She deflated into her chair. "Oh, whatever. Fine, I'll write. But it just goes to show how women always start out two rungs below their male competitors, no matter how good they are." She gave Thomas a pointed look.

He threw his hands up. "What did I do?" *Typical Savannah.*

Maggie studied her. "Are you certain?"

Savannah nodded. Then Maggie, their guardian and the only one at the table who could legally agree to a deal, unmuted the line one last time. "Mr. Tamblin? I believe we've reached an agreement."

"All right," said Sam, sounding more Matthew McConaughey than media executive. "Oh, one last thing, actually. GenePuul is ready to sign on as our leading sponsor.

But they won't do it without a guarantee you'll use their product for testing."

"What is GenePuul?" asked Maggie.

"Genetic testing. Like Ancestry.com or whatever. Anyway, this is the first podcast GenePuul has ever offered to sponsor. It's a major coup."

"And we just have to agree to use their product for DNA testing?" Thomas asked.

"Truth," said Sam.

Thomas smirked. Even if their search went nowhere, Sam Tamblin's hipster persona was at least good for a few laughs.

Savannah hit the Mute button. "Of course we'll do DNA tests, right? To make sure we have the right guy. But I mean, only after we've learned what we can about him. Where he's from, how he met Mom, all that stuff?"

Thomas nodded and shot a look at the phone. "Tell him."

Just as before, Sam Tamblin had gone on talking. "By using GenePuul's science from the start, the story is so much bigger, with so many leads to pursue. That's how they caught the Golden State Killer. You know that, right? Because his relatives researched their genealogy through DNA testing? You'll never know who you could be related to without it."

"He makes it sound like our podcast should be called *To Catch a Killer*," Savannah whispered.

"We're making a big mistake if we don't tap the forensic science fans. Think about it—all the top-rated TV shows for the past *decade* have been forensic crime dramas. People. Dig. DNA. This opportunity we're sitting on is huge. Think Team Jacob versus Team Edward. But bigger. Think *The Bachelor*, but with biodads—"

"Sam, we don't want to turn our experience into a game show," Savannah interrupted.

"Game show? This isn't a game show! This is drama! The Divine effing Human Drama!"

Savannah whispered, "He just described a DNA rose ceremony—we're not doing it."

Sam moved on to talking about episodes on location and the challenges of outdoor recording.

"Mr. Tamblin…" said Maggie, but he continued to talk over her. She waited about a breath before: "SAM TAMBLIN!"

Thomas and Savannah snapped to attention. Even Sam went silent.

"Think about this from our side. The reality is, we don't know if this search will be successful. Even if we do locate the biofather, my grandchildren don't know if they'll like him. And what's more, we could learn a few things about their mother, Bess, that we wish we'd never known. Are you following?"

Savannah wrote *goal: learn more about Mom* on the slip of notes Thomas was taking and underlined it twice.

He nodded, and underlined it, too.

Sam stayed silent, then finally said, "If you won't go the DNA route, that leaves us with the *Serial* model."

Savannah punched the air with a triumphant fist. "That's exactly what we're talking about."

Thomas smiled and nodded. *Serial* hadn't just been a breakout success, it had become a cultural phenomenon. Over the course of several episodes, it explored the 1999 murder of a young woman, Hae Min Lee, and tried to answer a fundamental question: Did the man in prison for her murder actually commit the crime? *Everyone* listening seemed to have an opinion. And they didn't just have opinions, they got involved. They did their own research. They started podcasts about the podcast. They made websites to track the theories that then got discussed on other podcasts.

Even more amazing, with all the attention and evidence the show shook loose, the defendant in question had been awarded a new trial. *Serial* was the listener-engagement Holy Grail, and every podcaster was chasing its success.

"Do you know how much work that type of show requires?" Sam no longer sounded quite so enthusiastic. "Taking the DNA route would cut your work in half. Three-quarters."

"But," said Savannah, "it probably wouldn't tell us a thing about our mother. This is about her as much as it is about our father."

She and Thomas exchanged smiles, and Thomas felt a lump in his throat he couldn't swallow down. He said—quickly, since he could hear the note in Sam's voice that said he was ready to call this discussion history—"We're doing this to learn our story. Not to ambush our dad. We want to find him and hopefully meet him. And the only way that will happen is if we act like decent people. Like the sort of people he'd be proud to meet."

"Are we in agreement, then, Mr. Tamblin?" Maggie said.

"Crystal."

A few days later, Thomas and his best friend, Nico, made their way from the track to the locker room. Together, they made up one half of the varsity team's 4x200 relay. Pete Biehl, along with Roger Rostenkowski—who they called Ro— made up the other half. Track practice went until five o'clock, which meant Thomas and his friends spent two hours every afternoon pushing their metabolisms to the brink. Their first stop on the way home was at Burger Mania, just around the corner, for to-go vanilla shakes.

"Dude, you've added eight-tenths of a second in your two hundred," Nico said.

"You better drop time," Pete said. "Or they'll put Soltis in for you."

"Slow-tice," said Ro.

Thomas unwrapped his straw and smirked. "Soltis is way too slow to replace me."

"He's running two-tenths faster than you right now," said Pete.

"No way." Thomas was fast, a born sprinter. His times couldn't have taken that much of a hit.

"Coach writes it all down, stupid," Nico said. "Which means, you're either getting slow or Soltis is juicing on steroids." He looked at Thomas's shake. "You sure you should be eating that, fatty?"

"Shut it, Nico," Thomas said.

*"Shut it, Nico,"* mimicked Nico.

Such an idiot. Nico's dad was a radiologist and his mom was a neurosurgeon, and between the two of them, they'd raised a kid with a foot permanently implanted in his mouth.

"We've only got a few qualifying meets left before the State meet in June." Pete excelled at ignoring the Nico-Thomas dynamic. "Wayzata is running three-tenths faster than they did last year when they beat us out for the title. Which means we've got to hit the training hard if we have any hope of winning this year."

Ro examined his half-empty cup and threw it in the trash without finishing it.

"No rest days," Pete said. "I say we even meet up Saturday morning for a long run."

"Can't Saturday. That's the podcast launch party," Thomas said. "I promised Maggie I'd be around to help set up."

"Party's not until that night though, right?" said Pete. "Plenty of time to set up between a.m. and p.m."

Thomas took a final pull on his shake. He was starving, but maybe they were right. He was running the slowest time on the team, and he never ran the slowest time. When it came to running track, he didn't want to just be good—he ran to catch the feeling of what it was like when he *excelled*.

"Fine." He threw the remainder of his shake in the trash. "See you tomorrow, then."

*"See you tomorrow, sweetie,"* said Nico.

Thomas turned at the corner and headed for home, finally alone. Maybe the idea of finding their dad had him a little preoccupied, but Maggie'd made sure their contract said they weren't supposed to do any work until school ended, and that was still a few weeks away. He wasn't going to think about it yet.

Still. He couldn't help but wonder.

At a minimum, his dad was athletic. He knew because his mom told him once. They'd been watching the summer Olympics when she'd said it. The sprinters. Thomas said that was the track-and-field event he liked best.

"I'm not surprised," she'd answered. "You've got the long legs of a sprinter."

"If I'm fast enough, I can get a college scholarship. Then you won't have to pay." Thomas felt a constant awareness that their mother had one salary paying for two kids: two mouths to feed, two closets to fill, two tuitions to pay.

"That would be great. But you know you don't have to worry, Thomas. We are plenty blessed."

"I know," he said, like he always did, telling himself to believe it. "But if I got a scholarship, then I'd be on the team, and that's my best chance for real training." He hooked a thumb toward the television. "You know. Like if I ever wanted to make it to the Olympics, or something."

His mom smiled, her brown eyes crinkling at the corners. "Let's hope you're as athletic as your father, then."

*As athletic as.* He hoped he remembered that correctly. *As athletic as* meant he stood out somehow. That his athleticism was notable. That people noticed it. Maybe the same way you'd remember an athlete by name.

Thomas turned the words in his head the whole way home. *As athletic as...*

That night, while reminding himself not to think about the podcast until school was out, he got to worrying about living up to his athletic potential. *As athletic as...* What did that mean? How was he supposed to know how far his potential could take him? How hard he should be pushing himself?

He didn't know a single person who could give him the answers.

But there might be someone who could. And Thomas might just be able to find him.

# SIX

## MAGGIE

Saturday afternoon, Maggie opened the door to a man with drumsticks tucked behind each ear. "Come in!" The podcast wasn't due to start for a few weeks, but why wait to throw a party? Celebrating was more fun than waiting. "The party's in the front parlor, but I'll have you set everything up in the sunroom."

A crew of four began to cart a full complement of electric keyboards, drums, vibraphones, cymbals and electric guitars into the house. They were going to record the podcast's theme song tonight.

By seven o'clock, the pianist Maggie had hired for the evening was at the piano with a list of Gershwin favorites, and Katherine Mansfield sat by the front door, a lovely violet silk scarf around her neck. The doorbell began to ring.

Savannah's best friend, Trigg, arrived first. "Hey, Maggie."

"Welcome!" she said. Trigg Kline had always struck Maggie as a young girl in a woman's body, something she feared would follow the girl long after her calendar age caught up to her looks. Emotional and physical maturity were such different things.

"Hey, Van," Trigg said, glancing over Maggie's shoulder.

"Trigg," answered Savannah. "That the photo booth thingy?"

Trigg had arrived holding a cardboard tube nearly as tall as she was. "Obviously."

Maggie noted an icy chill in the air between the two girls

but put a pin in it. She'd have to ask Savannah later, when the doorbell quit ringing.

Their neighbors, Stan and Tabby Melby, arrived next, as did the owners of the local Vietnamese grocery, Trang and Tina Phan. There were Mayor Pennypiece and Samuel, who ran the airport shoe-shine stand, and a woman named Blue, who Maggie had never met but who sported a billowy, boho-chic style that few could have pulled off.

The house was full to bursting, and so was her heart.

A house full of people was medicine to Maggie, always providing exactly what she needed—laughter when she was down, hope when all felt lost. A means of crowding unwanted thoughts from her head. She loved how George used to say, "When doom strikes, fill the ice trays and throw open the doors. Pain is no match for a party."

Sometimes, though, with George and Bess both gone, Maggie found herself wondering why God made the math work out so evenly. He took her husband and daughter and gave her Thomas and Savannah in return. Maggie shook the equation from her mind.

Chef Bart served a buffet of appetizers and created a new cocktail called the "Truth Hurts"—one part whiskey, three parts Fireball, and served in a glass rimmed with habanero pepper oil.

"You get it?" He handed Maggie the inaugural glass. "You're either swallowing fire or breathing it."

"Talk about foreshadowing." She took a sip and felt it burn all the way down. "Yikes."

Over in the corner near the piano, Savannah, Trigg and Bart's daughter, Nadine, had begun to hang an oversize sheet of vinyl—a photo backdrop—to help kick off the podcast's social media campaign. When they unrolled the sheet, there wasn't much more to see than a Guava Media logo and the text, *#McClairTwinsMystery.*

Maggie set down her drink and headed over to help.

"That's not even the name of the show," she heard Savannah complain.

"I could've had the guy put the right name on there if you'd answered my texts," Trigg replied.

Nadine got to work, saying nothing.

"I was a little bit busy today, Trigg."

"Oh yeah? 'Cuz it sorta felt like you were just being—"

"Girls?" Maggie interrupted. "Having some trouble?" Savannah and Trigg sounded about one syllable away from total meltdown. Plus, the tape Trigg brought was too flimsy, and the heavy vinyl backdrop drooped feebly on the wall, ready to fall. Nadine plastered on strip after strip, trying to secure it.

"It's just a play, Savannah. You need to calm down. It's not my fault Mrs. Thornbird read it out loud." Trigg's face burned with the hot splotches of anger, like she was battling scarlet fever. *"Poor Savannah. The star of the class again."*

"Oh, very nice! Is that why you told everyone what I'd said to you *in confidence*? Because you were *jealous*?"

Trigg didn't answer, but instead, let go of the vinyl sheeting and walked away. It broke loose from the wall and landed on Nadine.

Chef Bart hustled across the room. "Let me," he said. "I'm sure you've got something in the pantry heavy-duty enough to hold that up."

Maggie mouthed a silent *thank you* at him and quickly helped Nadine guide the vinyl off her shoulders and onto the floor. Then she took Savannah's hand and led her into the kitchen.

"What is happening with you and Trigg?"

Savannah was now burning as hot as her friend had been.

"It's this dumb one–act play I wrote for English class. It's about a girl who sees her dead grandmother in her sleep and Trigg had to go and tell everyone that sometimes I see Mom."

Maggie stroked her cheek. "Did you have another dream?" Bess regularly antagonized Maggie, but she treated Savannah differently, stepping into her daughter's sleep to soothe her when she needed it most.

Not that Maggie believed in supernatural hoodoo-voodoo nonsense.

"It's nothing." Savannah huffed. "I mean, whatever. It's just a few idiots. They'll probably get so stoned this weekend they won't even have enough brain cells left to remember on Monday."

Maggie studied her granddaughter. "You have the right to feel hurt, Savannah."

Thomas then burst through the door with Nico, Pete and the other member of their relay team whose name Maggie could never remember. "Hey, Maggie! Nico just bet Ro he couldn't eat a dozen raw eggs. Do we have any?"

Maggie pointed toward the back door. "Take it outside, boys. I don't even want to see."

As the evening went on, the crowd began to thin. Trigg, who was supposed to sleep over after the party, had gone home, which perhaps had been a blessing. Savannah's mood had improved significantly.

The remaining adults sat around in clusters of threes and fours, finishing drinks and the last of their stories, tired and nearly chatted out. Thomas and his friends, along with Nadine, huddled in the sunroom, laughing and recording theme songs.

Finally, Thomas emerged and hushed the group. "Listen

to this." When it was quiet, he clicked a button on his remote control.

Everyone waited.

First came the sound of children laughing, followed by the
circus-like pipes of a calliope. For a moment, it sounded like
a day at the park, the happy noise of a children's playground.
Then, even as the laughter and the pipes carried on in the
background, there came a confused mash-up of bells and vi-
braphone and drum—audible chaos. That continued for a
few confusing moments until suddenly, the loud *CRASH* of
a gong. As the sound drifted away to silence, Nadine's wisp
of a voice broke through. "You know what they say... *The
kids are gonna ask.*"

The room was still for no more than a beat, then thun-
dered with applause.

Nadine blushed. Thomas beamed. His friends ran around
the room slapping high fives with guests.

Even Savannah couldn't help grinning. "That. Is. *Cool!*
Nadine, you could do voice-overs, I swear."

The piece, every part of it, was unexpected. Maggie felt
as if her heart were about to leap from her chest, racing and
jumping, her entire circulatory system applauding the music.
"Play it again!" she shouted.

Thomas fiddled with the remote control. "Hang on, lost
my place."

He paused just long enough for Maggie to notice that her
heart hadn't slowed. It wasn't racing as it had been a moment
ago, but neither had it calmed. Instead, it seemed to have es-
tablished a new rhythm, like an excited, dancing child. Not
arrhythmic, and yet, entirely unique.

She stood, thinking she might just slip out to the kitchen
for a glass of water, when Thomas hollered, "Got it!"

Again, the room filled with sound—the children and the pipes and the chaos and the crash.

Followed, note-for-note, by Maggie's pirouetting heart.

*How absolutely fascinating.*

She brought a hand up under her ribs, far enough away from the undulation of her lungs to get a better feel for what was happening. She wasn't frightened. The ol' girl was still ticking, pumping blood where she needed it. But it was telling her something. It was beating in time to the music.

*Seems fishy*, Bess whispered.

A heart was never something to ignore. And Bess was right—it might be worrisome.

It could also be...*utterly magical.*

# SEVEN

## THOMAS

"Do you have my keys?" Savannah ran through the kitchen. She was dressed for school, but nowhere near ready to leave.

"Did you look on the hook by the door?" said Thomas.

"Of course, I looked on the hook." She threw her backpack down on the table and ripped open the pockets. "I swear. Why do we even have keys? As soon as they put everything I need on a microchip, I'll be the first guinea pig in line."

Thomas heard the keys jangling at the bottom of her bag.

"Have you even eaten yet?" she said, still rummaging. "We don't have time for any drive-through stops this morning."

"Not eating breakfast today."

Savannah stopped digging and eyed him. "You never skip a chance to eat."

"And we're never late when it's my turn to drive." He walked over to the table and punched the bottom of her bag, rattling the keys. "Let's go, Sherlock."

*"Seriously?"*

A few minutes later they were both in the car and headed down the driveway. Savannah glanced at him out of the corner of her eye. "You don't have, like, an eating disorder or anything, do you?"

Thomas shook his head. "We're supposed to be dropping time in our relay. But the last three meets, we've actually gained."

"So?"

"What do you mean, *so?* We nearly took the state title

in the four-by-two-hundred relay last year. As sophomores. That's a big deal."

"I'm not saying it's not. It's just—train hard, do your best, you know? Starving yourself won't help."

"I'm not starving myself." He'd stashed three protein bars in his backpack. He wasn't *not* eating; he was just trying a different approach. He'd also run three miles and done fifty push-ups before Savannah had even gotten out of bed.

Traffic was slow enough for her to turn and face him, but Thomas kept his eyes on the dashboard clock, watching the minutes melt away.

"All right," she said. "Just cut yourself some slack. You've been a little distracted."

The sentiment hit with the swift punch of accusation. "Why does everyone keep blaming the stupid podcast? I'm not distracted. If anything, I'm working harder than ever."

Nico and Pete had been all over him at practice last night. *Get your head on! Focus!* All of their complaints rained down on him, even though Ro had been slowest at the last meet. Only by two-one-hundredths of a second, but still.

At one point, Nico even yelled, "Hey, look, Thomas, your daddy's at the finish line! *Run!*"

*Stupid Nico.*

He fought the sudden urge to tell Savannah to pull over and get out of the car. He didn't care about being late, he cared about being trapped in one more discussion about something he didn't know how to fix.

"And anyway," he said, "what about you? How come nobody's accusing you of being distracted?"

"Ha!" Savannah snorted. "Shows what you know. I have been distracted, just not about our biodad."

She pulled to a stop at the last intersection before school. "Crap!" She sank down into her seat, trying desperately to melt below the windshield. "Is that Carrie Westlund in front of us?"

Thomas twisted, trying to get an angle on the driver ahead of them. "Maybe?" He rolled down his window, preparing to lean out for a better look.

Savannah slapped his arm. "Don't! Don't show her your face!" She slapped him again.

"Stop hitting me!" Now he had to lean out the window just to get out of her reach.

"Get in here!" She hit the automatic window button, propelling him back inside. The window rose, pinching his arm between the glass and the door frame.

"*OW!*" Now he was rubbing both arms. "What is *with* you?"

"Just—" Savannah pounded the steering wheel with her fist. "Put it this way—I basically became an Instagram meme last weekend. No more Zombie Baby. Now it's my turn."

"'#SavannahSeesDeadPeople'?"

She flashed him a shocked glance as the traffic started to move. "You saw it?"

"Don't worry, Van. Everybody knows Carrie Westlund is just in it for the attention. And Parker White has always been an ass."

"He tagged me alongside about a gazillion ghost hunters."

"Ghost hunters don't use Instagram."

"Everyone uses Instagram!" Savannah swung wide into the school parking lot, avoiding Carrie up ahead by opting for a spot in the farthest corner from the entrance.

They had one minute before the bell.

"Wow, thanks, Van. Now we're definitely going to be on time."

"Save your anger for the track, dummy." She slammed her door and sprinted for school.

"*Have a good day, sweetie!*" Thomas called.

★ ★ ★

That afternoon, Coach pulled Thomas aside at practice. "I'm taking you off the four-by-two and swapping in Soltis. You're a good sprinter, but I've got to give your relay the best chance of getting to State." He lifted his chin, looking for confirmation.

Thomas felt a shock of panic up his spine. "I just had a few bad days, is all." He'd been tired, but he would come back. He'd rest hard and train hard. Isn't that what Coach was always telling him?

Coach shook his head. "I don't know what's happening, T. You always come out of the blocks strong, but you're slowing down too much before handoff. Like you don't know how to do it anymore. This week you dropped more batons than you handed off."

"No problem!" If it was just the handoffs, Thomas could fix that. "I'll run drills every practice. I'll get over it, get my rhythm back."

"Too late for that, bud. We're deep into qualifiers." Coach scuffed his toe along the rubber track surface. "You seem—off, lately. Anything going on at home you want to talk about?"

Thomas said no. Because there wasn't. "I understand, Coach. You've got to do what's right for the team." The words came out easy but ran cold all the way to his toes.

"Keep coming to practice, though. Don't quit working."

"I dunno. Maybe."

Coach's face said he already knew Thomas wouldn't be at practice Monday. "Think about it over the weekend." He gave Thomas a soft punch to the shoulder, then turned and walked away.

Thomas didn't take his eyes off him until he disappeared into the school. If he had, he would have been forced to admit that Nico, Pete and Ro had stood by and watched the whole thing.

**Trigg:**

Ok, you just need to settle down. [yoga pose emoji]

**Trigg:**

Some people actually think it's cool you have powers. [angel emoji] [praying hands emoji]

**Trigg:**

Taylor Parks lost her grandma a few months ago and she says she's going to visualize her every night before she goes to sleep until she shows up.

**Savannah:**
OMG I DON'T SEE DEAD PEOPLE!!!!!

# EIGHT

## THOMAS

"Thomas?" He should have been sleeping, but he wasn't. Neither was his sister. She knocked again. "I know you're awake. I can see your light under the door."

"Come in." He sat up and noticed he hadn't bothered to change before going to bed. His sweatshirt and shorts both screamed *Lincoln Track and Field*. As if he wanted the reminder.

Savannah walked in wrapped in her quilt. "I heard about the relay. I'm sorry."

He shoved to the side of the bed and made room for her. "That news traveled fast."

"Nico's got a big mouth." She leaned into him, trying to nudge out a laugh. "In case you were unaware of that fact."

He surrendered a weak smile. "He does have an awesome video gaming setup, though. Makes him worth it." Then he did laugh. "Mostly."

Thomas may have been cracking jokes, but they weren't working on his mood. He couldn't believe Coach had taken him off the relay. It was humiliating. He'd had the second-best time on last year's team behind Pete. He'd beaten Nico and Ro, both.

But now, *Soltis*? He hadn't even learned to tie his shoes until middle school. He forgot his uniform once and wore jeans to a meet. Coach wouldn't let him on the field—and rightly so. The guy was farm league.

Several minutes went by, neither of them talking. Savannah sat back against his headboard. He ran his fingers along the raised stitching on his bedspread until the sensation all but numbed his fingertips.

"Sorry I wasn't very sympathetic about the Instagram thing," he said.

Savannah groaned. "Carrie Westlund is the worst. Remember in eighth grade when I had that cast on my leg? She asked me what happened, so I told her, 'I fractured my tibia.' And she goes, '*Oh my gawd, why can't you just say you broke your leg like a normal person?*'"

"Seriously?"

"I know, right?" Savannah wiped a tear from her eye and Thomas couldn't tell if it was the laughing or crying kind. "I guess I'm learning what Nora Ephron meant when she said, 'Everything is copy.'"

She loosened her quilt, freeing her arms. "I was thinking, though. Since you won't be at track practice every night and I'm currently social dog food—" She watched him for a reaction. "Do you know where I'm going with this?"

Of course, he did. "You want to start working on the podcast?"

Her entire face broke into a grin. The same way Maggie's did when she met an interesting stranger, or the way their mom's had done after finding a fresh pint of toasted almond fudge ice cream in the freezer.

"How does tomorrow morning sound?" she said.

"Early." He smiled back. "But okay."

At least he could quit thinking about his humiliating track failure.

Savannah took the lead on the first few episodes.

"Episode one is going to be a game of balance." They were in the dining room the next morning, the whole red table piled high with notes and podcast research they'd downloaded. "On the one hand, we have to explain why we're doing this and what we already know."

"Right." Thomas nodded.

"But it also has to be the hook. If the audience doesn't care after the first few minutes, they won't keep listening. And without an audience, we don't stand a chance of finding anything new about Mom or our sperm daddy."

Thomas scowled. "Can you quit calling him that?"

"What, does the word *sperm* make you uncomfortable?" Savannah smirked.

"You're disgusting."

She laughed. "And you're a prude. Which you should probably get over before you get a girlfriend."

Thomas knocked her stack of papers off the table.

"Hey!" Savannah protested. "That just proves you're a prude *and* a bully."

He knew she was trying to sound indignant, but making him squirm was one of Savannah's favorite hobbies. He waited for her to reassemble her notes. "You were saying?"

She stuck her tongue out at him. "Anyway, dummy, episode two is when I think we should bring in Maggie."

Yeah, Thomas figured that sounded about right. He added, "Do you think we should call her Grandma or something? Just for the podcast?"

"Why?"

"Won't people think it's weird we call her by her first name? I mean, we're trying to sound mostly normal."

"She's the one who told us to call her Maggie." Which was true. When they were little, she said the name Grandma made her feel old. Later, she called it old-fashioned. Eventually, she said that anyone who disliked that they called her Maggie was surrendering to antiquated patriarchal beliefs. Whatever that meant.

Savannah paused for a moment. "Mmm, no. I still think we call her Maggie. That's her name. Let's just not make a big deal about it."

Thomas eyed her. "Is that going to be your answer to everything?"

Savannah didn't bother to look up. "If it works, yeah."

Finally, they were almost ready to record the first episode. Savannah scribbled a note on her script. Thomas scanned the settings on the monitor in front of him.

"I just want to test your audio level again," he said.

Savannah sat up and leaned into her microphone. Her head looked double its natural size thanks to the heavy padding on their studio headphones and she had to work to keep her balance. "Testing. Testing. Mary had a little lamb. Because she was doing keto again and she was sick of chicken."

Thomas raised a hand, telling her to wait. He notched up the bass in Savannah's voice and equalized the output of their microphones.

"One more time."

Savannah obliged. "Testing. Testing."

Thomas flashed her the *Okay* sign and nodded. He ran a finger down the checklist he kept in his clipboard. Everything looked good.

*Ready?* he mouthed.

She smiled and gave him a thumbs-up.

Thomas moved the mouse across his screen, clicked Record and pointed at his sister.

"'The Kids Are Gonna Ask. Episode one,'" Savannah began. "Here's what we know. Bess McClair had just turned twenty-two when she and three friends flew from Minneapolis to Colorado. It was spring break, March 2002. The four women—"

"Van—" Thomas waved his hand in her face and paused

the recording. "Try that again. You're coming across like one of those crime show hosts."

"I'm not trying to."

"All right, let me reset." He marked the end of the first take on his screen and clicked Record again.

*Go.*

"Here's what we know," Savannah began a second time. "Bess McClair had just turned twenty-two when she and three friends—"

Thomas stopped her again. At this rate, they'd be recording all night. "You're still doing it."

"What?"

"The crime show voice." He pushed his voice deep into his chest. *"Here's what we know…"*

"I'd have to go through puberty four more times *and* grow a penis if I wanted to sound like that."

"Gross, Van—"

"I'm just sayin'."

Thomas leaned back in his chair, trying to find the best way to explain. Whenever he tried to verbalize his thoughts, Savannah had a habit of responding like a jackhammer, smashing his words to bits as soon as they came out of his mouth. He had to be careful. Had to be exact. "Just…" he said, finally. "Try reading the script without making it sound as if Mom and her friends are all about to get murdered."

Savannah's face flashed red-hot. "Oh my god, T! Did you seriously just say that to me? As if I would *ever*—"

Thomas threw up his hands. "Oh right. Savannah McClair is *perfect*. How could I forget?" His sister's diva act was so predictable it was almost boring. This time, though, Thomas had proof he was right. He moved the digital slider on his screen back a few seconds and pressed Play. Savannah's voice rang through his headphones. The recording sounded as clear and resonant as if they'd made it in a professional studio, and not in their basement, with their grandmother just above their heads in the kitchen, loading the dishwasher.

"—*Minneapolis to Colorado. It was spring break, March 2002.*"

Thomas clicked Stop. "See? I'll play it for you again if your delicate ego needs convincing." He realized he was shouting, trying to hear himself above the noise cancellation of the headphones and pulled one ear free. He needed to bring the argument down a notch.

He took a breath. "You sound…" The words came slow and deep. "Like…this."

Savannah crossed her arms across her chest and glared at him. Then she leaned into her microphone and articulated her next words very carefully. And loudly. "It's called *projection*, dummy. Google. It."

Thomas stood, walked over to Savannah's chair, and knocked her headphones off.

"Hey!" she yelled.

"You practically busted my eardrums!"

"You nearly punched me in the face!"

"I did not!"

Savannah smacked him in the chest with the back of her hand. "Now we're even."

He smacked her in the shoulder. "No, *now* we're even!"

"What the—" Savannah stood up to go in for another strike, only to get yanked back in her chair by the cord on her headphones. She squealed and rubbed at her thighs where her bare legs had ripped from the vinyl seat cushion.

Thomas laughed so hard he had to double over. He couldn't help it. And she deserved it.

The door at the top of the stairs opened and Maggie called, "Everything okay down there?"

"*Yes, fine!*"

<<EXCERPT>>

The Kids Are Gonna Ask
*A Guava Media Podcast*
Season01—Episode01
Tuesday, May 26

**SAVANNAH**
Here's what we know: Bess McClair had just turned twenty-two when she and three friends flew from Minneapolis to Colorado. It was spring break, March 2002. The four women were college seniors, due to graduate in two months. It was their last vacation before they'd move on to the next chapter in their lives.

**THOMAS**
They could have headed to the beach like so many spring breakers their age. Minnesota winters are long and cold. But Bess loved to ski, had been doing it nearly as long as she could walk. So she and her friends rented a two-bedroom condominium in the resort town of Breckenridge, packed their bags and boarded the plane.

**SAVANNAH**
The women spent six days in Breckenridge. At the end of the week, they all flew home. Two months later, Bess graduated from the University of Minnesota with a bachelor's degree in marketing, moved out of her campus apartment and back into her parents' house in Minneapolis where she'd grown up. That's when she found out she was pregnant.

**THOMAS**
Bess's father had died of a heart attack the year before. So it was just Bess and her mother, Maggie, in the big house the afternoon she told her mom the news. She said it happened on spring break. She said he was a nice guy, but there was no relationship. No

reason to involve him. She didn't tell her mother his name. But she did say, "I want to keep it."

**SAVANNAH**
There's one other thing we know about Bess from that day: she wasn't pregnant with just one baby. She was carrying twins. And we are those kids. Our mother passed away before we could ever find out who our father is.

[pause]

My name is Savannah McClair.

**THOMAS**
And my name is Thomas McClair.

**SAVANNAH**
And this is the story of our search for our biological father.

[pause]

Over the next several episodes, we'll do our best to interview anyone and everyone who can tell us more about our origin story. The friends who traveled together, the people they encountered, those who heard the stories of their time in Colorado. We'll also ask you, our listeners, to help us in our search. One of you out there may know something—no matter how small—that helps us put the pieces of our history together.

**THOMAS**
Why do we want to do this? The reasons are both huge and obvious. We want to understand the other half of our DNA. We want to learn more about ourselves. We want to learn more about our mother, Bess. We may even get to meet the man who helped make us.

**SAVANNAH**

There's also the question, "Just what do we expect from this adventure?" Do we expect a relationship with our biological father? Do we expect him to even want to be found?

**THOMAS**

And do we expect to like what we find?

**SAVANNAH**

To be honest, we don't know. We don't know what we'll find. We don't know what to expect.

**THOMAS**

But we do know we want to try.

**SAVANNAH**

We know one more thing, too. We know our mother, Bess, isn't here to help us. She can't answer any of our questions.

**THOMAS**

Our mother died in a car accident four years ago. We spent enough of our lives with her to know how much we loved her. And we believe she'd support our efforts to solve this mystery.

**SAVANNAH**

But she's not here. And that means, this journey is ours to start.

**THOMAS**

We don't have any idea how long it will take us to find our dad. To be honest, we don't know if we even will find him.

**SAVANNAH**

That's why we're going to need all the help we can get. From the people we know. And from people we've never even met.

**THOMAS**
So to those of you listening right now, thanks. We're glad you're here.

**SAVANNAH**
Really. So glad you're here.

**THOMAS**
And, we're hoping you'll stick with us. All the way to the end.

<<END EXCERPT>>

# NINE

## THOMAS

The day after their first episode aired, Savannah, Maggie and Thomas sat in the basement studio sporting headphones and surrounded by blankets on the walls as temporary soundproofing. They agreed to interview Maggie before any of their other potential guests because she was the most readily available.

"Bess figured she was about eight weeks along by the time she graduated."

Thomas monitored the soundboard. Savannah asked the questions.

"Two months is far enough along to believe a pregnancy test, but too far along to not have seen a doctor, so I scrambled to find a good ob-gyn for her. I didn't have one of my own, of course. I was in my late fifties by that point and my lady parts were well beyond their *use by* date—"

"Ew, Maggie," Savannah interrupted. "Boundaries."

Thomas shook the image of—*whatever*—from his mind.

"Apologies—" Maggie held up her hands in surrender. "My point is, Dr. Maher's mother and I went to high school together, and she was the only woman in our class to go all the way through to a PhD. So, I knew her daughter came from smarts."

Savannah jotted notes on her script. "All right, so you've got this appointment for Mom. What happens at the doctor's office?"

"That's when we learned there were two heartbeats, not just one."

"Right," Savannah prompted. "But paint the picture for us. How did you find out? What did you experience?"

Maggie nodded. "All right. Well, your mom—"

Savannah interrupted again. "Remember, you're telling this story to the audience, not us. Call her Bess."

"Of course. *Bess*—" she paused briefly and gave them an accommodating smile "—wanted me to go into the appointment with her. So I did. And it had been over twenty years since I'd been pregnant, so I didn't realize until the procedure was already underway that, in the early stages of a woman's pregnancy, ultrasounds aren't done by scanning the top of the belly. They're performed with a vaginal wand that looks like an electronic penis with its own special condom and everything."

"Maggie!" Thomas swatted the headphones from his ears.

"You told me to paint a picture."

"Can you at least leave Mom's veejay out of it, please?" Savannah didn't look like she was ever going to be able to peel the disgust off her face. "It's not like Thomas and I want to picture that."

"You do know how babies are born, yes?"

Thomas decided to step in before he got nauseous. "Maybe just stick to the basics. Okay?"

"Good grief, you two." Maggie scowled. "All right. So the doctor is there with Bess and me, and we can see a grainy black-and-white image on the ultrasound. We have no idea what we're looking at until Dr. Maher says, 'Do you see what I see?'"

Thomas felt his face flush with preemptive panic about the image Maggie was about to conjure.

"And the doctor must have seen the confusion on our

faces because she smiled and pointed at a tiny flutter along the curved outline of what she told us was the uterine wall. 'This is Baby A.' And your mother—" Maggie caught herself. "Sorry. *Bess* sat nearly upright on the table. 'That's my baby?' she said. I couldn't tell if she was amazed or dumbfounded or happy or all three."

Maggie stopped and sat back in her chair. She smiled, and Thomas could see that her eyes were set on memories made eighteen years ago.

"The doctor replied, 'That's one of your babies, yes.' Then she pointed at a nearly identical flutter on the opposite side of Bess's uterus and said, 'This is Baby B.'"

*Holy cow.* Thomas had never thought about the two of them like...*that*. Before they had names. Before he was the boy and Savannah was the girl. Before he was big and she was little. Before she was the artist and he was the scientist. Back when they were blank screens, just waiting to be switched on and start running their code.

Where had his code originated? That was what he had always wondered. He knew only half of himself, at best. Half of his data set, of his inputs, his variables. His bugs. The rest of it—of what made him—came from a whole group of people he couldn't even picture. Ghosts in the machine.

And Thomas had never liked ghosts.

Maggie's interview was interesting, but if they were going to get anywhere, they needed to interview the three friends who were there in the very beginning—the women on their mom's fateful spring break trip to Colorado.

"Don't call it *fateful*," Savannah argued. "That implies something bad happened."

They'd moved all their work from the dining room down to the desk in the basement studio.

"Decisive?" Thomas said.

"Oh, because Mom purposefully went hunting for a sperm daddy?"

She'd *promised* to quit using that term. "Fine. *Momentous.* That better?"

"Pivotal," said Savannah. "In fact, that's got to be our focus for this whole search. Focus on the pivotal moments. That's where we'll find the most important stuff."

Her logic actually seemed to make sense. "Okay, but what's another example of a pivotal moment? Besides the one that made us?"

Savannah looked at him like she'd just caught him counting to ten on his fingers. "For starters, her decision to keep us?"

*Oh, that.*

"And who knows what else," she went on. "Maybe Mom had conversations with Maggie or her friends that we don't know about. Like, what if she asked one of them whether she should tell us about our dad? *Or—*" She slapped her hand on the desk. "What if he tried to get in touch? What if he actually knows one of Mom's friends?"

No way. Thomas didn't have any more proof than the sick feeling in his stomach, but he knew what Savannah was implying couldn't be true. "She wouldn't have hidden him from us, Van."

She wagged a finger. "But we don't know that *for sure.*"

An icy feeling swept him from top to bottom, fast and chilling. *Their mom would never have done that.*

Maggie opened the door to the basement and clomped downstairs. She appeared around the corner holding a wicker basket overflowing with mail. "I have the addresses for your mom's friends in here somewhere. I thought you might need them." She dropped the basket onto the desk and began to rummage. "I don't know why I keep all this, but I guess it's coming in handy now." She flipped through the pile of torn envelopes and holiday cards. "You know the names of the three women who were in Colorado with her, right? Kristen, Elise and Brynn. They still send us Christmas cards every year."

"There's one of them." Thomas grabbed a picture from the basket of a young family, all smiles and L.L. Bean sweaters. He looked at the mother's face, where the soft crinkles formed around her eyes—his mom would have had those now. She would have been just old enough.

"Ta-da!" Maggie pulled a second card from the pile. "You have Elise there, and I found Kristen. Now, where is Brynn?"

When they'd found all three addresses, Thomas and Savannah wrote to the women, asking if they'd be willing to be interviewed. Kristen and Elise agreed within a few days.

Then, there was Brynn. Thomas and Savannah were shocked to listen to her terse voice mail on the McClairs' home phone later the next week.

*This is Brynn Reynolds. I'm calling in regard to the letter I received from Thomas and Savannah regarding their search for their biological father. In regard to your request to interview me, I am calling to say that I'm certain I have nothing of value to add in regard to what happened during that spring break trip. Thank you.*

So many *regard*s for zero cooperation.

That night, Maggie requested Chef Bart's miso noodle soup for dinner, and the three of them sat down to discuss the Brynn dilemma over brimming bowls.

Thomas didn't feel like eating. His *former* 4x200 team had dropped a whopping nine-tenths of a second in that day's meet. He'd stood in the bleachers watching while they'd celebrated the victory he'd wanted so badly.

"That's good news for Lincoln, folks," the announcer had said over the loudspeaker. "Our four-by-two-hundred relay team of Bratakos, Biehl, Rostenkowski and Soltis have qualified for conference finals."

The implication could not have been clearer: he had been the team's problem all along. The realization sat in his stomach like a rock.

"Brynn clearly doesn't want to participate," Savannah said. Thomas snapped back to attention. "Maybe we should draft a list of questions for Brynn and drop them in the mail. If she doesn't want to talk to us in person, she might answer in written form. Might be better, anyway. She sounded uptight."

"Did you hear her say no?" Thomas said. "All I heard was lots of blah-blah-blah about whether or not she has anything to *add* to our search. How does she know? Why does she get to decide what we do?"

"Thomas?" It was Maggie's *something's wrong but I'm not going to push* voice.

"What's with you, all of a sudden?" Savannah never had a problem pushing. "All I'm saying is that Brynn reminded me of Mrs. Borstrup." She'd been their third grade teacher and was so mean that, on the days Savannah didn't come home crying, Thomas did.

Maggie looked up at the mention of her name. "Awful woman."

Savannah nodded. "Dead inside." She looked back at Thomas. "Maybe we should steer clear."

Thomas again fought the urge to escape another conversation with no answers.

"Or—" Maggie paused to consider. "Brynn already received one letter, and that didn't work. But a phone call could help. She might find it reassuring to speak with you personally. And how harmful could a call possibly be?"

<<EXCERPT>>

The Kids Are Gonna Ask
*A Guava Media Podcast*
Season01—Episode02
Tuesday, June 02

**SAVANNAH**
What questions did you ask Mom about our father? I mean, you had to be curious about him, right?

**MAGGIE**
Sure I was curious. But, when the two of you came along I didn't have time to wonder. Let's be honest, you don't get many quiet moments to think when you're raising twins. And when Bess first came home and told me she was pregnant and she wanted to keep you, I mean…it was enough to just try and take that in. You have to remember, I'd just lost my husband. My best friend. I was still in shock, trying to find my bearings. Some days it was still hard to get out of bed. But I was looking forward to Bess's graduation. I had it circled on the calendar with hearts and stars. It was the first happy thing to happen in a year, ever since we lost George.

[pause]

So when she said, "Mom, there's something else, too," I admit, maybe it was selfish, but I was overjoyed! It was all I could think about. A baby! And I mean, I threw myself into Bess's pregnancy. Making sure she was healthy and eating right and happy. And that her baby—the two of you, come to find out—were healthy and safe and happy, too.

**THOMAS**
Did you ask anything about him? Can you remember anything specific?

**MAGGIE**

Well, I know I said something like, "What about the father?" And she said, "He's not in the picture" or "There's no reason to involve him." I don't remember, loves. I'm so sorry. I really wish I had more I could tell you.

**THOMAS**

But it was for sure on the trip to Colorado? It wasn't someone she went to school with or anyone like that?

**MAGGIE**

No, she was clear about Colorado. She said something like, "I met him on spring break when we went skiing." No question.

**SAVANNAH**

You and Mom were close, though, right? She would've told you more about him if you'd asked, wouldn't she?

**MAGGIE**

[pause]

Bess and I were close. Always. As a little girl, she'd make me sit by the side of her bed and she'd yammer about her day until she fell asleep. Even when she was in college, we talked two, three times a week. So, when she came home and said she wanted to keep her baby, I didn't have to ask more. Because we were so close. After all, being close to someone means, I guess, that you don't always need the words. You don't need to explain to the other one because they just know. They understand.

[pause]
[sigh]

All that, and do you know what the last thing I ever said to her was? She called me. From her office, as she was leaving for her friend's funeral. You know there was a funeral for one of her colleagues that afternoon, right?

**BOTH**
We know.

**MAGGIE**
She called to say she wasn't sure how late she'd be home, that she might not be back in time for dinner and not to wait if the two of you got hungry.

[pause]
[sniff]
[pause]

And I said, "Just be home to give the kids their bedtime kisses."

[pause]

Which, of course, she wasn't. As it turned out.

<<END EXCERPT>>

# TEN

## THOMAS

Thomas stepped through the back doors of the school and headed for the student parking lot. There was only a week of school left and between now and then he had two papers to write and finals to study for. He'd intentionally gone straight outside after the last bell, ducking any chance of running into Nico or Pete or Ro on their way to the locker room.

*"Yo, T!"*

Only, he'd forgotten that the bus taking the track team to Conference Finals would be parked right outside.

"Hey, Nico," he called back. The *revised* 4x200 team each had a window seat. "Hey guys. Leave 'em in the dust today, all right?" The enthusiasm in his voice sounded fake, even to him.

"You should come." Nico had his window open and was hanging halfway out. "Coach'll let you on the bus. Right, Coach?"

Thomas heard Coach holler at Nico to get his head back inside.

"Text me! Send me results," Thomas hollered. He fingered his phone in his back pocket. Maybe, with any luck, the battery had died while he was in class.

Summer vacation couldn't come soon enough. He didn't have time for track, anyway. Not really. Except if that was true, why did watching the bus pull away suck the breath out of his chest?

Savannah came up behind him. "Hey, let's go. Hurry."

"What's happening?" Thomas turned, looking past her in the direction she'd come. He saw Carrie Westlund, along with Trigg. "Ugh."

"Just go, dummy." Savannah was shoving him toward the parking lot with her shoulder.

"Van!"

Carrie and Trigg caught up anyway. "So, you two are famous. First Insta, now a podcast."

"Hey, Carrie," said Thomas. He eyed her shirt, which read #Famous in glitter-gold lettering. "Looks like you're the famous one, though."

"Crazy, right?" She held up her phone, mock-posing for the camera. "The company just sent it to me hoping I'd post some selfies."

Thomas turned and started walking again. Running into Nico and the whole track team had been enough. Now, Savannah was going to obsess about Carrie and Trigg the whole drive home.

"Sorry, guys," Savannah called, doubling her pace to catch up to him. "We've got to run. We have an appointment."

He remembered that was true. A phone call for the podcast with their mom's best friend, Elise. They were hoping to get her advice on how to break through to the third woman on the ski trip, Brynn, who still refused to talk to them.

"Bye, Van!" chirped Trigg. "Text you later!"

"I can't believe Trigg is hanging out with her," Savannah said, once they were out of earshot. "She knows how mortified I am."

Thomas kept walking. They weren't even to the car, and Savannah was already starting in.

"If it were just the Insta hashtag, I could ignore it. But Parker White asked me in class today if we'd ever held a séance. A séance! He said it all hush-hush with this look of phony concern on his face. As if he wasn't just being an ass."

"I told you, Parker White has always been an ass."

"Yeah, but why does he have to do it in my face?"

They reached the car and Savannah threw the keys over the top of the roof to Thomas. "You drive. I'm too pissed off."

They switched sides and got in.

"Did I tell you I got called into the guidance counselor's office yesterday? Mrs. Adams wanted to make sure I wasn't getting *cyber bullied*."

"Well, you sort of are, right?"

"Of course I am, but what's Mrs. Adams going to do about it? She can't even remember her login half the time. I'll be in her office like, *Are there any film schools coming to the college fair next fall?* And she has to pull out this Post-it note she keeps in her top drawer with all her passwords written on it. Then she can never find her reading glasses… It's a whole thing."

They were five minutes from home and Savannah could go on about her hashtag drama for hours, if he let her. Thomas changed the subject to focus on the call they were about to make.

"Do you think Elise will be willing to help?" They'd left several unreturned messages on Brynn's voice mail and even sent her another handwritten note. So far, none of it worked. Now they were calling their mom's other friends, asking if they might be willing to intervene on their behalf.

"Hope so. Working the friends angle was effective for the *White Lies* reporters, at least." They'd been bingeing investigative reporting podcasts. In a mutual favorite, *White Lies*, two reporters for National Public Radio investigated the 1965 murder of Reverend James Reeb who'd been down in Selma, Alabama, registering voters when he was attacked on the street and killed. Three local men were tried for the crime soon after, but their acquittal had long been considered a sham. Fifty years later, when the two NPR reporters took up the case, they worked the tight-knit Selma community person-by-person for three years and, thanks to their tenacity, identified a fourth man who'd been there for the attack that night. They were even able to record the man discussing his involvement in Reeb's attack on tape—just a week or so before he died. It was an extreme example, Thomas had to admit. But if those reporters could find their guy, he and Savannah ought to be able to find their father.

"All right," Thomas said, "so the plan is to ask Elise to appeal to Brynn on our behalf. Try and convince her to at least take our phone call?"

"Right. With the hope that once she gets to know us, she'll be willing to talk."

"I mean, it's not like we murdered someone. Or our father did."

"No," Savannah agreed. "Unless he did. And then that's a *whole* other podcast."

When they got home, they dialed Elise. She picked up right away and got to the point.

"Look, guys. Brynn is a good person. Smart, committed, the whole bit. It's just—"

She was obviously weighing her words carefully.

"So, you know how your mom was always like, *People are just who they are!* Bess never got too bent out of shape about anything. But Brynn, she's your mom's exact opposite. She has an opinion about *everything*. She's black-and-white, right versus wrong. Which isn't always bad. I mean, we choose our friends for a reason, right? If your mom and I had been left to plan that trip to Colorado, we might have flown out there without even knowing where we were going to stay when we landed. But Brynn's a planner. And that's good sometimes. She likes things done right and she has high expectations. Kristen and I still go with her on girls' weekends every year. She can be a total pain in—" She caught herself. "Well, let's just say, she knows *all* the great places to eat, stay and shop. Last year, we got an entire four-course meal in Sonoma *comped* because one of the dishes was overcooked."

"Do you think it's even worth us trying to talk to her?" The more Thomas heard, the less he was sure.

"Absolutely!" Elise's answer came quickly. "Kristen and I remember the highlights about the trip, but if anyone remembers the details, it'll be Brynn."

<<EXCERPT>>

The Kids Are Gonna Ask
*A Guava Media Podcast*
Season01—Episode03
Tuesday, June 09

**SAVANNAH**
So, Kristen and Elise. You both remember our mom meeting and spending at least one night with the guy Elise told us she called "the hunky bartender."

**KRISTEN**
[laughter] Yes! Is that what you called him, Elise? That's too funny. He was super cute, though. Oh my gosh. We laughed because Bess came all the way out to Colorado and hooked up with a guy who looked like he was straight out of a Minnesota catalog. You know—tall, blond, cheekbones. The Nordic god. Which fit—oh, yeah, I should mention this—because he had one of those stereotypical Scandinavian names. Bjorn or Thor or whatever.

**THOMAS**
Loki?

**ELISE**
Ha! God no, thankfully it wasn't Loki. I remember that much.

**SAVANNAH**
But you don't remember his name?

**KRISTEN**
No, sorry. Wish I did.

**ELISE**
Me, either.

**SAVANNAH**

All right, so we've got this guy you both remember as a Nordic god bartender with a name to match. You both remember that Mom spent at least one night with him. Can you tell us more about how they met? Was she flirting with him for free drinks? Did he ask her to stay around until his shift was over?

**KRISTEN**

No, we all met him, like, one of the first nights we were there. He was the bartender at one of the smaller places in town. I don't know how we wandered in there—I think it was close to our condo or something. God, it was so long ago, sorry.

**ELISE**

Remember? The bar he worked at was on the street level, just below our condo. Like, storefronts all along the street and condos above that. You could only get into our place by going up those awful wooden stairs in the back alley.

**KRISTEN**

Yes! The stairs were always covered in ice. Didn't Bess totally wipe out on those stairs? Or was it me?

**ELISE**

We all wiped out on those stairs. I'm surprised Brynn didn't file a lawsuit. Probably would these days.

**KRISTEN**

Ha! She probably would...

**SAVANNAH**

So, the bar. The place our dad worked was on the same street as the condo you stayed in? Or even just below it?

**KRISTEN**

That's right. And anyway, the first time we went in there, I don't think it was very busy, so we were all just chatting with him, the bartender. You know, where should we go when we're in town, how's the skiing been this year, how to avoid the lift lines—that sort of thing. And I remember because the next night, we walked into this other place and he was there with some friends of his. Not townies, exactly, but guys who worked at the resorts all season long.

**ELISE**

Not tourists, like us.

**THOMAS**

This was a different bar?

**KRISTEN**

Yeah. He was just there with friends. Having a beer. And Bess, your mom, was like, *Oh, hey! Must be fate!* And then they talked forever. They definitely were into each other. They clicked. They laughed and talked and it seemed really easy—I mean, god, not *easy*, easy—

**ELISE**

Kristen!

**THOMAS**

We get it. They clicked.

**KRISTEN**

Exactly!

**SAVANNAH**

And they went home together?

**ELISE**

Not that night. He came skiing with us the next day. Didn't we tell you that?

**THOMAS**
No.

**SAVANNAH**
No!

**KRISTEN**
Oh yeah! I forgot that part.

**ELISE**
He was really good. Of course, being a Norse god and all. Bess
was, too, and so after a few runs they just went off on their own.
Kristen, you were a good skier but not as good as Bess...sorry.
Brynn and I were both just lucky to keep up.

**KRISTEN**
Right...they went off and we didn't really see them again until
Bess came sneaking into the condo the next morning.

**THOMAS**
Did she see him again, do you know? That week, at least?

**KRISTEN**
Um, maybe? Elise, do you remember?

**ELISE**
No, sorry. But I guess, probably? She really liked him. And we
should say, too, that he didn't seem like one of those resort guys
who just hits on all the out-of-town women. I mean, maybe he
was, what do I know, but he didn't seem that way to me.

**SAVANNAH**
So you finish your trip, you fly home, you get back to school.
When did you find out Mom was pregnant?

**KRISTEN**

A few months later. At least, that's when I found out. It was spring by then, I remember. It was our senior year and we had so much work to do but the weather was finally nice, and I kept asking your mom if she wanted to come study outside. On the hill behind the library. I remember looking at her and she was so pale, and I was teasing her and said, "You could use some sun on that pale face of yours, at least." And she was like, "Yeah, pale because I can't stop puking." And I remember thinking, *Oh my god, when do you possibly find time to party with finals coming up,* and she blurted out, "I'm pregnant."

**SAVANNAH**

Morning sickness, in other words?

**KRISTEN**

And then some, from the look of her.

**THOMAS**

You must have been surprised, right?

**KRISTEN**

Uh, yeah!

**ELISE**

Your mom had boyfriends, but she didn't sleep around. And she didn't have a boyfriend when we graduated. I remember because I did and all we did was fight about what was going to happen to us after school ended.

**KRISTEN**

So, anyway, I was confused. I said, "How did you get pregnant?" And she said, "Remember that guy in Colorado?" And I said, "What are you going to do?" Because, that was just a fling. If she was keeping in touch with him, I had no clue. I couldn't even imagine being in her position. And she didn't know what she was going to do yet. But I do remember her saying, "I'm going to graduate. Then I'll figure out what comes next." Because that was totally Bess, right? First things first.

**ELISE**
Like, *I'll cross that bridge when I come to it.*

**SAVANNAH**
Did she say anything more about the father? Do you know if she even told him about us?

**KRISTEN**
I don't know for sure. It was so crazy at that point with finals and graduation. Plus, she said she didn't want to talk about it, so we didn't. But at some point—I don't remember if this was before we graduated or after—she was conflicted. She used to say she had a honey jar stuck on her nose, you know, like Winnie the Pooh? It was her way of saying she had a problem she didn't know how to handle.

**SAVANNAH**
She used to say the same thing to us.

**THOMAS**
But she posed it as a question. She'd ask, "Got a honey jar stuck on your nose, Thomas?"

**KRISTEN**
Exactly. I remember thinking, um, appropriate comparison? Winnie the Pooh and not knowing what to do about a pregnancy? Anyway. We got to talking about the father, you know, could she expect anything from him? And if I remember right, I thought she ought to tell him. He had a right to know. But her point was

sort of, *I don't expect anything of him, and I really don't want to have to consult a stranger on how to raise this kid.* Plus, I think he had plans to big-time travel to like South America or Australia or something for a long time. I don't know exactly what, but I do know she thought it was complicated enough to be single and pregnant, let alone with a guy she didn't really know and who was about to be halfway around the world—

**ELISE**
New Zealand! That's where he was going! We talked about it that first day at the bar. Oh my gosh, I can't believe I just remembered that. He was going backpacking in New Zealand. Which I guess makes sense since half of the lift operators at the resort that winter were from Australia and New Zealand 'cuz, you know, their seasons are the opposite of ours.

**KRISTEN**
Yeah...everyone called them the Kiwi Crew—

**SAVANNAH**
Okay, stop. So what you're telling us is that, one, we're looking for a guy who—at least seventeen years ago—looked like a Norse god and, two, had a name to match. Three, he worked at a bar in Breckenridge in 2002. Four, he spent a few months backpacking in New Zealand, and five, he may or may not know about us?

**ELISE**
Mmm-hmm.

**KRISTEN**
[audible sigh] That about sums it up, yeah. Dollars to doughnuts, that guy's your biodad.

<<END EXCERPT>>

# ELEVEN

## MAGGIE

"Are you all right?"

Maggie was in a state, sitting on a park bench with Katherine Mansfield at her feet, sweat pouring from every surface and a hand pressed to her heart. Strangers had good reason to wonder if she was okay, but so far, only one of them had stopped—the woman bobbing from foot to foot in front of her now, dressed in the sort of running gear reserved for the young and very fit.

"Yes, I'm fine—"

"Are you sure? I saw you clutching your chest. My grand-dad died of a heart attack and it freaks me out."

Nothing more reassuring to a woman in distress than to be compared to the elderly and dead.

"I think I've simply overheated," Maggie said. "I forget that I shouldn't leave the house past eighty-five degrees." Which was true. George used to accuse her of being part earthworm—always making her way into the sun but forgetting how easily she wilted. "What am I going to do the day I come home to find you all shriveled up on the sidewalk?" he'd say. Then he died and left her on her own to never find out.

"Here," the jogger said. "You need to drink something." She pulled a water bottle from the belt around her waist and wiped the mouthpiece with her shirt. "I'm not sick. I promise."

Maggie reached for the bottle and realized, to her surprise, her hand was shaking. "Oh—"

"Are you sure you're okay?" The woman plopped down

on the bench and urged the bottle to Maggie's lips. She took several long sips.

Maggie hadn't been able to stay in the house, not even one more minute. Nothing was happening, and that nothingness was a problem. Chef Bart hadn't arrived yet and she'd hardly seen her grandkids at all recently—they'd either been at school or locked away in their rooms studying for finals, and when all that was done, they stomped downstairs like a herd of elephants into the basement studio and shut the door behind them.

The house was too quiet.

Ever since the podcast began, Maggie's head had been swimming—with the questions Savannah and Thomas wanted answers to, as well as the questions she kept asking herself. And the question she'd been asking her daughter for the past four years: *Why, Bess? Why?*

She felt her breathing go shallow and she forced herself to take deep, steadying breaths.

Her heart was on her mind lately, too. The odd instance at the launch party hadn't been a onetime hiccup. Last night her heartbeat matched itself to the pressing rhythms of the evening news theme song and the day before that, to *All Things Considered* on NPR. It had also taken to jumping out of her chest every time the doorbell rang, which meant that now she had a full-on conundrum: How could she fill the house with happy noise and people if she couldn't handle the sound of the bell at their arrival?

"Thank you for the water." Maggie tried to hand the bottle back to her young jogger friend, but the woman refused to take it.

"May I?" She took Maggie by the wrist and found her pulse. She counted, timing the seconds on her watch. "Your pulse is all over the place. I can't even get a heart rate."

"I'm dehydrated. That happens."

"Maybe, but if I leave you here and you keel over—no offense—I'll never be able to forgive myself."

Maggie surrendered by way of taking another long sip of her water.

"Not that it's any of my business, but have you had a checkup lately?"

Maggie considered the best way to answer. She hadn't physically been in a doctor's office since the last time Thomas or Savannah got sick—which, thanks to Chef Bart's careful attention to nutrition, didn't happen often. She was, however, more attuned than most to the intricacies of the human body. In fact, few things fascinated her more. She'd maintained a subscription to the *New England Journal of Medicine* since 1982; purchased an updated *Physicians' Desk Reference* every year; kept a detailed journal of her weight, energy, mood and physical state; and read Sandra B. Goodman's "Medical Mysteries" column in the *Washington Post* regularly. So, while she hadn't been in a doctor's office recently, it also wouldn't be accurate to say she'd been ignoring her health.

"I pay careful attention, yes," she told the woman.

*You sure?* Bess whispered.

Maggie ignored her and took another sip of water.

Because Maggie had, in fact, been paying attention. She'd been at her laptop several evenings this week researching the possible causes and concerns related to her mysteriously magical heart. Given that George's overburdened ticker had given up on him entirely too soon, Maggie took cardiac issues seriously. Her research into her own symptoms, however, had given her cause for optimism. From what she'd gathered so far, it seemed that issues like hers tended to be electrical—highly treatable when necessary and not entirely malevolent.

For example, she found a white paper online about a

woman named Sarah Adelbaum in Poplar Springs, Idaho, who had EKGs documenting her ability to match her heartbeat almost identically to "Battle Hymn of the Republic" and "Yankee Doodle." Ms. Adelbaum's quality of life was virtually unaffected and, even more, the only complaint she listed was that her heart didn't have a wider catalog of music.

A second study assessed the health of a woman named Marietta Van Kleef of Dallas, Texas, who had to quit attending funerals because the somber music slowed her heart rate so much, she fell asleep. As long as Ms. Van Kleef avoided certain categories of music—lullabies, adagios and something called "New Age Soundscapes"—she was able to go about her days as normal.

Maggie took a final, long sip of water from the woman's bottle. "I'm feeling much better, thank you. I just needed a moment to gather myself." She put the water on the bench between them and stood. "In fact, your neighborly concern has reminded me of just how lucky I am. I have my family, my friends, my dog. An interesting life. And that's all anyone needs, isn't it?" And with that, she pushed every worry about Thomas and Savannah and their podcast as far out of her head as she could manage.

<<EXCERPT>>

The Kids Are Gonna Ask
*A Guava Media Podcast*
Season01—Episode04
Tuesday, June 16

[voice-over]

**THOMAS**
Not everyone was embracing the search for our father with the same enthusiasm as Savannah and me.

**SAVANNAH**
Mom went with three friends on that pivotal trip to Colorado. You've already been introduced to Kristen and Elise.

**THOMAS**
But remember Brynn, the woman who didn't want to be interviewed? We finally got the chance to speak.

[phone call]

**BRYNN**
I didn't want to talk to you because I can't support what you're doing.

**SAVANNAH**
Finding our father?

**BRYNN**
That's your private business. Which is how it ought to stay. This isn't a conversation that should be had in public.

**THOMAS**
What do you mean?

**BRYNN**

I mean, your mother's choices are her private business. I have young children at home. How can I teach them right from wrong if I turn around and talk about this sort of thing? Not to mention that you stand a very good chance of disturbing an innocent man's life.

**SAVANNAH**

Innocent? We're not trying to shame him.

**THOMAS**

We're just trying to find him.

**BRYNN**

And I'm saying, I want nothing to do with it.

[voice-over]

**SAVANNAH**

We didn't call her again. Kristen and Elise would have to be enough.

<<END EXCERPT>>

<<EXCERPT>>

The Travis Stephens Show
Where America goes for answers
*A TalkNation Syndication*

June 17

**TRAVIS**
Folks, if you're just joining us, we're talking to Brynn this afternoon—and just so you know, we're choosing not to tell you Brynn's last name to protect her privacy.

Our good friend Brynn, here, has a story I think is important for every one of you out there to hear. See, our wonderful guest, through no fault of her own, just happened to get featured on a podcast. Two kids who lost their mother in a car accident, looking for their father. A man they never had the pleasure of knowing.

Sounds tragic, doesn't it? Truly, truly tragic.

[pause]

Except, what happens when those kids start looking for their dad, in public, on a podcast available to anyone in the world?

You see, that's where our friend Brynn comes in.

Now, Brynn, you say their mother was a friend of yours? How well did you know her?

**BRYNN**
It was college. We were young. Everyone is trying to find their way during those years, and I think some people make different choices than others.

**TRAVIS**

I take it you're referring to the fact that she got pregnant while she was in college, correct?

**BRYNN**

Yes. And that there are some things Bess and I didn't see eye to eye on.

**TRAVIS**

Well, to be totally transparent, I should say before we go any further that I know I, myself, made a few *different* choices back in the day. Am I right, listeners?

[laugh track]

But in all seriousness, if you knew their mother—may God rest her soul—what made you hesitate? Two young kids, calling you up, just trying to find out a little bit of their history—

**BRYNN**

Well, that's just it, isn't it? They're kids. Asking very *personal* questions about a very *private* matter. How am I supposed to know what they're really up to? Or that the man they're looking for doesn't have young children of his own at home now?

Travis, you have to understand that I am a mother. I hold that job dearer than anything else in my life. So there was no way I was about to risk ruining a man's life. A *family's* life. I just couldn't. And *especially* not for the sake of a podcast.

Not to mention, I don't want to be forced into a conversation with my children about premarital sex thanks to a podcast, either.

**TRAVIS**

Well, I have to say, Brynn, you could be absolutely right. The whole situation is just the tiniest bit fishy. I mean, let's lay out the facts here. Two kids, no mom, calling up strangers and asking for names.

Am I right?

Let's imagine I pick up the phone tomorrow and some kid's on the line saying he thinks I'm his father. What's he really asking for? Money? Attention? You've got to wonder.

[pause]

Hey, TravisTalkers, we need you all in on this discussion. Give us a call. Get busy on Twitter. You've got the info, you know it all by heart. Let's get some debate going, can we?

Caller, you're on the line.

<<END EXCERPT>>

# TWELVE

## MAGGIE

The Brynn interview changed everything. Download numbers for the podcast more than doubled. Subscriber numbers went up even more than that. And Brynn started hitting the talk show circuit—because even though she didn't want to talk *to* Thomas and Savannah, she didn't have any problem talking *about* them on live radio.

And the talk shows' hosts, it turned out, had incredible listener armies. Brynn's complaints about invasions of privacy brought *The Kids Are Gonna Ask* nothing but publicity.

Sam Tamblin began emailing Maggie with interview requests within the week.

"Brynn is setting the world on *fire*, Maggs. I'm telling you."

Maggie wondered if she'd ever get used to him speaking with the cadence of a Sondheim song. "And what does that mean, specifically, Sam?"

"It means, we have an audience. It means, people care—they're taking sides. #McClairWonderTwins versus #PaternalLivesMatter. #SpermDaddy is trending on Twitter, by the way. Have you seen it? Mad crazy traffic."

Facebook was as far as Maggie ventured in the electronic world—Twitter sounded like the social equivalent of a New Year's Eve in Las Vegas, unbridled and unmannered. "Brynn's interview was productive because it was provocative? Is that what you're saying?"

"Precisely." Sam laughed. "Did you hear that? Alliteration."

Oh dear. Sam was on the verge of distraction. "You're not at all concerned about Brynn's allegations?"

"We've got a signed release form. That's all I need."

Her grandchildren, as it happened, were being accused of not telling Brynn their phone conversation was being recorded. Although, as also happened with so many other issues of outrage and debate, the situation was murky with gray. According to Thomas and Savannah—and the recording— they said, "We're calling you from the recording studio. Are you okay with that?" Assuming, of course, Brynn understood the implication.

Brynn, however, claimed she did not. Though, only after she'd signed Sam Tamblin's aforementioned release waiver. "I thought it was simply for use of my name on the podcast, not for using my interview."

Thus, the explosion of attention. Depending on one's view of the world, Thomas and Savannah were either innocent kids just trying to discover a history that was rightfully theirs. Or they were conniving, overprivileged products of a whole generation of children who never heard the word *no* and who were willing to compromise other peoples' privacy in exchange for fame.

Maggie had been out of the house when Thomas and Savannah called Brynn. She had walked Katherine Mansfield down to the dog beach for a swim and then stopped to share a cup of vanilla bean ice cream on the Sebastian Joe's patio. It was summer, after all, and the patio wouldn't be open indefinitely. Curious how life worked, she thought. If she and Katherine Mansfield hadn't stopped for ice cream, would events have unfolded differently? Perhaps she could have prevented the misunderstanding, ensured Thomas and Savannah handled the finer details of consent more effectively. Then again, with the recording happening downstairs in the studio, how would she have even known?

Maggie promised Sam Tamblin she would discuss the interview offers with Savannah and Thomas as soon as she could.

"Theoretically speaking, there are lots of great options," Savannah said when Maggie broached the subject. It was nearly dark, and Maggie had finally coaxed the kids out of their studio hole for a bite to eat. She hadn't seen more than flashes of them since school ended last week. "But if I were producing," Savannah continued, "I'd have us start with public radio interviews. This podcast is told as a story, and that's an NPR specialty."

Thomas nodded and chewed a mouthful of Chef Bart's chilled farro salad—a menu Maggie had ordered because it was rich in fiber, zinc and iron for the young cave dwellers. "It'll be great to take advantage of the recent attention. You never know who could be listening. A podcast is one thing, but radio? That's a whole new level of reach."

Maggie's grandchildren were beginning to sound like Guava Media executives themselves. She agreed that a sizable audience increased the chances of finding the man they sought, but she felt uneasy that the recent surge had come as a result of a woman shaming Thomas and Savannah for their methods. There was something eerily disquieting about the power of public humiliation.

"And you're certain you're comfortable with the level of attention that may come as a result?" she asked. "Like you said, a podcast is one thing. Radio is quite another."

Thomas and Savannah exchanged what was becoming a familiar knowing glance.

"I know where you're going with this," Savannah said. "And I was skeptical, too. I mean, why should we have to go on the radio to justify ourselves? The podcast speaks for itself—and *we* speak for ourselves *on* the podcast. But then Thomas reminded me that if we're really going to do this right, if we're really going to find him, then the wider the audience, the better. You know what I'm saying?"

Maggie did. But that hadn't been her question. She started to say something, but Savannah went on. "Plus, we made a deal. Thomas is going to do most of the talking."

"Sort of my fault we're in this situation, after all," Thomas added. "I'm the one who wanted to start this search in the first place."

"Of course, but—" Maggie spoke quickly, trying to squeeze herself back into the debate. "Don't forget that you both stand to benefit if you do find your father. No matter who does the majority of the interview, you'll both be affected by the results. Good and bad."

Maggie raised her water glass to her lips to buy herself time to consider. If she'd looked into the future when the kids were little, she would have predicted with full confidence that Savannah would be the one now grabbing the microphone. They were both smart, but Savannah was quick with her words. Until middle school. Puberty is hard enough on any child, but send an outspoken, smart girl into the war zone that is the female middle school experience, and even the most confident kid can come home believing herself to be the ugliest, stupidest creature to have ever been born. Then kill her mom in a gruesome, front-page-news accident and see what happens. The child can't speak for herself, that's what.

One evening a year or so after Bess died, Maggie had gone downstairs to overhear Trigg on the phone in their kitchen. Savannah had been there next to her, scribbling words on a scrap of paper.

"We know you're spreading gossip about Savannah," she'd heard Trigg say. "Everyone says so. And we just called to tell you you're a—" There was a whispered exchange and Trigg said, "An insecure gory hound."

*Whispering.*

"*Glory* hound," Trigg clarified.

So, that was it, Maggie'd thought. Bess's daughter still had her words, but the confidence to put her own voice behind them had vanished.

She closed her eyes. *Help me*, she pleaded to Bess. *I can't do this alone.*

Nothing but silence.

"Savannah," Maggie said, snapping free of her thoughts. "The interviewer is certain to ask you some questions, too. You may not have the choice to give Thomas the lead."

Savannah scowled with the ferocity available only to teenage girls. "*Duh*, Maggie. They're going to expect Thomas to take the lead. Because he's a *dude*."

"That doesn't seem to me as *duh* territory, at all. In fact, I'd expect quite the opposite. Think of the lead you've taken with your guests on the podcast."

"There's a difference between asking the questions and having to answer them. Plus, it's not like I'm going to sit there and *not* say anything."

Where did they go from here? From all indications, Savannah and Thomas had thought it through together, and decisions like these were ultimately theirs to make. "Well, then," she said, "I guess I have no choice but to trust you to trust your instincts." Which, Maggie had to admit, was what she always said when she had worries, but no answers.

Savannah and Thomas beamed, while Bess *tsk-tsk*ed in Maggie's ear.

Thomas and Savannah recorded an interview with *Mid-Morning* radio the following week.

"You two have become a bit of an overnight phenomenon." The segment host, Blaise Elliot, had a voice as soothing as warm milk. Very public radio. "Why do you think the podcast has become so popular?"

Thomas answered, as planned. "I think there are lots of Thomases and Savannahs out there—people just like us who want to find out the rest of their story. Our lives feel like an unsolved mystery."

Maggie was at the kitchen table with Chef Bart listening live on the radio. The kids were right below their feet, calling into the interview from their basement studio, but they sounded so grown-up, so confident and calm, they may as well have been a thousand miles away.

*"They're doing great!"* Chef Bart whispered.

Maggie held a finger to her lips.

"You're not the first podcast—or show, for that matter—in which people are looking for their biological parents, though. Why do you think yours is the story that's broken through?"

Thomas again. "I think it's because of how we're telling it. When we first started working with Guava Media, we discussed the fact that true crime stories are, historically, the most popular genre on television. And that has translated to the podcasting world. True crime podcasts have proven to be really popular."

"Yours isn't a crime, however."

"No," said Thomas. "But it *is* a mystery. And because we don't know how the story ends—even as we're telling it—it engages our audience in an entirely unique way. They get to participate in solving our mystery."

"Has the sudden attention affected the podcast? Or either of you?"

"Well, that's just it. That's the point," Thomas said. "The more attention this search receives, the higher the chances someone can lead us in the right direction." Then he added, "To be clear, it's not about the attention so much as increasing the odds we'll get somewhere."

Yes, yes, Blaise could understand that. She asked, "Why now?" Then she asked why the kids thought Bess never involved their father.

"Well, you know—" Thomas stopped.

Maggie waited for him to finish his thought. When nothing came, she leaned in, knowing he couldn't hear her but urging him on just the same. "C'mon, T," she whispered. "You're doing fine. Don't let your nerves get the best of you."

Savannah finally jumped in. "You'll have to keep listening. That's the question we dig into next."

"Oh," Blaise said. "I love a good show tease."

"It's important people understand…" Savannah continued slowly, as if giving Thomas a chance to jump back in. He didn't. "Well, I guess we want people to know that we're not on the hunt for a replacement parent. But we do hope to meet our father, especially now that our mom is gone."

Blaise hmm'd and went where Savannah was taking her. "You understand, of course, that there's a fair bit of debate on how you're going about your search. That doing it in such a public fashion may prove harmful—to your biological father, and to your subsequent relationship with him."

"It is remarkable, though, isn't it?" said Savannah. "We had decent listener numbers when the podcast was just about two kids trying to find their dad. It wasn't until one of the women we interviewed publicly scolded us that the podcast really took off."

There. That was exactly what Maggie had been thinking. Savannah had nailed it. The bitter truth in a guileless endeavor. The controversy made them vulnerable, while also promoting their cause.

"How do you respond to the argument that such a public outing is unfair?"

"I say, what gives a man a level of privacy that our mother—or any woman—wasn't granted? They were equal partners in conception. Why not in responsibility?"

"Though, of course," said Blaise, "critics have compared your podcast as something akin to an episode of *The Jerry Springer Show*. Especially since your existence may very well blindside a complete stranger."

"We don't know that to be necessarily true," Savannah said. "The way Thomas and I see it, there are only two people who know for sure what happened when Mom discovered she was pregnant. And one of those people—the one we knew—is gone."

Thomas finally stepped in. "I think we should also be careful to say that just because we're looking for our biological father doesn't mean he has to become a public figure. We don't have to release his name. How he chooses to associate with our search is up to him."

"But some would argue," Blaise said, "that being a public figure isn't the only consideration when it comes to privacy. There is the issue of his personal and family life. What would you say to those who feel it's potentially harmful to his family? What if he has children?"

"Who's to say that he wouldn't welcome us?" Savannah answered. "Or that his family, if he has one, wouldn't want to meet their half siblings? Heck, one of his kids could be in desperate need of a kidney transplant right now and we could be the perfect matches."

"You have to admit, though," said Blaise. "You've gotten a lot of people asking whether you have the right to disrupt other lives."

"Well, that's not—" Thomas stammered, sounding desperate to pull his thoughts together. "It's just—people need to remember what our mother did not do. She didn't terminate her pregnancy. She raised us, had a career, gave us a good life. To us, it's a matter of biology. Savannah and I are here, and we share his DNA. We just want to understand what that means."

Blaise hmm'd again and ended the segment with a velvety, "We wish you well."

Sam Tamblin called the house as soon as the interview aired, raving, "We'll take the wave this creates and spin it into a hurricane of press."

*Isn't it the hurricane that creates the wave?* Maggie wanted to say.

# THIRTEEN

## THOMAS

"Why did you have to be so—" Thomas searched for the word. "Combative?"

Savannah scoffed at him. "What are you talking about? I just answered her questions."

They'd barely hung up from the interview and already, they were at each other. Which was weird because they'd been arguing slightly less lately. Working on the podcast, they'd fallen into a decent balance—Savannah did her stuff and Thomas did his. Thomas figured they'd split the load just right, fair and square. Being fair was a huge deal to Savannah.

And by huge, he meant *huge*.

In third grade, Thomas got invited to his first sleepover birthday party and Savannah threw a fit, crying all through dinner how it wasn't *fair* she'd never gotten to sleep over at any of her friends' houses.

Then later, Thomas was the first to buy his own laptop with money he'd saved from two years of birthdays, Christmases and mowing Mrs. Tellison's yard down the street, but Savannah complained it was unfair because no one ever considered having a girl mow their lawn.

"The wage gap starts the day we're born!" she wailed.

Maggie barely looked up from whatever she was doing. "There's always babysitting, love."

Which only made Savannah scream, "Oh right, because all girls love babysitting!"

With the way they'd planned the podcast work—research-

ing and interviewing together, then splitting up the production tasks—Thomas and Savannah would learn the same
information at the same time, which was about as fair as he
could imagine. And the balance had been working. Mostly.

"I thought we agreed—I was going to take the hard questions."

"Me, too. But then you had some sort of brain fart and
couldn't finish your sentences." She gave him a smirk, then
lifted the screen on her laptop. They still had a thousand calls
to make today and the to-do list ran off the bottom of her
screen. Then, her cell phone buzzed with a text and she had
to waste the next eight thousand minutes going back and
forth with Trigg.

*"Savannah!"*

She slammed her phone down. "Oh my god, Thomas! I
don't know why you're griping at me. The interview went
*fine.*"

*Fine.* Sometimes he wondered if Savannah could hear herself. Or if anyone had ever told her there was a major difference between the words you say in your head and the way
they sound coming out of your mouth. His answers hadn't
been perfect, and yeah, he'd had a hiccup or two. But at least
he'd done everything possible to sound reasonable. Level-
headed even on the hard questions. Taken his time, measuring
his tone. Isn't that what they'd agreed on from the very beginning? That they wanted to come across as the kind of people
their dad would be proud to know. Savannah, though—no
wonder she had the reputation she did at school. She answered
every question in class like it was stupid the teacher even asked
it. Today, she did exactly the same thing.

"You know why everyone gives you a hard time, right?
Because you're such an easy mark. You blow everything way
out of proportion."

"Ex-*cuse* me?"

"Like for the chemistry final—Mr. Philpot said we could prepare one note card to bring with us on the day of the test and you had to get all weird about it. *But people can use that to cheat, Mr. Philpot!* Like he doesn't *know* that? Everyone just wanted you to *shut up!*"

"Why should I study if all those morons are just going to write the answers on their note cards?"

"How can you cheat if you don't even know what questions are on the test?" His voice cracked and his head felt like it might split open, full enough to burst. "Van! You're smart, we get it. That's cool. But you don't have to make everyone else feel stupid when they're around you." Being so honest made his stomach knot, but someone had to tell her.

Savannah gave him a look so blistering she could've shot lasers out her eyes. "I didn't say anything you wouldn't have said."

"You got all uppity about our dad not taking responsibility!"

The lasers were suddenly hot enough to burn a hole in the wall behind his head. "Did you seriously just call me *uppity*?"

"No, I said you got all—"

"Uppity. You said I *got all uppity*."

"And?"

"*And?* You may as well accuse me of getting all *emotional*, too."

"Well, yeah. You kinda were." How had this become his fault?

Savannah, though, was slamming her laptop closed and pounding up the stairs. "I can't believe that you, of all people, have turned into a sexist pig!"

"You're the one who said his kids probably needed a *kidney transplant*!"

Savannah slammed the door behind her, ensuring, as always, that she got the final say.

**Trigg:**
Guess who just texted me and said he'd been listening to your ittle wittle podcast? [microphone emoji]

**Trigg:**
His name might rhyme with Lyle Karson. And he might have just broken up with Olivia Jenkins. [broken heart emoji] [laughing emoji]

**Trigg:**
Oh, and did I forget to mention he asked if you were single? [screaming face emoji]

# FOURTEEN

## MAGGIE

Chef Bart poked his head into the family room one evening soon after the kids' radio debut. The podcast was
rapidly gaining attention and Sam Tamblin called more and
more frequently with what Maggie had begun to think of as
"Hype Updates."

"Got a mention on Marc Maron. I'm talkin' Marc Maron,
Maggs! The number one podcast in the whole effing U-S-
of-effing-A!"

"Really, Sam. Must I remind you?" He apologized for the
language and hung up, only to call back a few minutes later
with another Hype Update.

Tonight, Maggie had the TV on and a magazine in her lap,
but her gaze was at the windows, staring out. Meteorologists
were all over the airwaves warning about several days of op-
pressive heat on the way, and she was preparing herself for
the reality she and Katherine Mansfield wouldn't be leaving
the air-conditioned house to walk for more than a few minutes at a time until it was over.

"Looks to me like you might need an escape," Chef Bart
said. "I'm done for the day, Nadine is at a friend's house and
it's perfect weather to put the top down."

Chef Bart owned a convertible gold Volkswagen Beetle,
circa 1970-something, that he drove only in the summer and
only when the sun was out. Maggie loved going for drives in
his little gold bug. She batted her eyelashes and clasped her

hands at her heart, the best Scarlett O'Hara she could muster. "My hero."

"How about a quick spin around the lakes and then I'll bring you back and mix you up a sour-plum manhattan?"

"Perfect." There was no better cocktail in the upper Midwest. Chef Bart watched the farmers markets closely for the few days every summer when sour plums were available, then bought as many as the vendor would sell and spent the day canning the plums in a rich syrup laced with ginger and some other spice that Maggie could never identify and he wouldn't tell.

"I hope you don't expect me to drink alone, though."

"Never!"

Maggie left a note for the kids and refreshed Katherine Mansfield's water dish. Thomas and Savannah had each been squirreled away in their rooms all day, separately, no podcast. She'd checked in with them, tried to engage, but Thomas seemed to be working something out by exploding imaginary video game worlds on his laptop, and Savannah was either legitimately asleep or pretending to be every time she peeked in.

She could only imagine the quicksand pit of emotion they were trying to avoid.

"They'll probably appreciate having the house to themselves for a bit." She grabbed her purse. "Plus, you're right. I could use the escape."

Bart pulled away from the curb and they zipped up the parkway, convertible top down, making a loop around Lake Bde Maka Ska but opting not to turn right where the parkway connected to neighboring Lake Harriet. There was a concert at the Harriet Bandshell, and traffic had all but stopped.

"A shorter excursion than I'd planned," Chef Bart said, already turning back into the neighborhood. "I guess we weren't the only ones needing an escape tonight."

"Oh well," Maggie sighed. "I guess we'll have to drink two cocktails, instead."

They pulled back to the curb and made their way up the walk. Moments later, Chef Bart placed a chilled glass in Maggie's hand, and swung his lanky legs across the piano bench. "Classical or heathen tonight?"

"I'm feeling positively heathen." Maggie took a long sip. Chef Bart hadn't been wrong. She had needed a change of plans.

"I call this my 'All Things Rocky' medley." Chef Bart turned toward the keys and started in on "Dammit Janet" from *The Rocky Horror Picture Show*. He wasn't a terribly precise pianist—Maggie would never pay him to play the way she paid him to cook—but he made up for his lack of skill with some surprising creativity. He transitioned from the *Rocky Horror* tune into John Denver's "Rocky Mountain High" followed by—what else?—"Gonna Fly Now," the theme to *Rocky*.

"Bravo!" Maggie cheered, pouring herself a second manhattan.

Chef Bart changed decades. "Chantilly Lace" and "Peggy Sue" and "Eleanor Rigby" and "Octopus's Garden." Maggie's heart began to dance along, thoroughly entertained.

At the start of her third manhattan, Maggie topped off Bart's nearly untouched drink and motioned him over to the couch. The cocktails made her feel just free enough to take a chance with the truth. "You are one of my dearest, most loyal friends, so I'm going to let you in on a secret. Or, not exactly a secret so much as…a magical mystery. A magical *medical* mystery."

Chef Bart gestured as if he were putting a lock on his lips and throwing away the key.

She paused, gathering her thoughts. There wasn't any way to put this that didn't sound a bit batty. "Here's the thing. You know I've had an unusual amount of time to myself lately. Savannah and Thomas are home, but rarely aboveground—down in their studio until well after I'm in bed."

She took another moment to arrange her words. "And... I've noticed a strange phenomenon with my heart. The first time it happened was at the launch party. The kids were playing their new theme song and *BAM!* I felt it. Then last week I had the radio on during breakfast, and there it was again. Yesterday, when Katherine Mansfield and I were on the parkway, I was listening to Carole King on my iPod and *it happened again.*"

"What happened?"

"My heart can match itself to music."

He said nothing and took another sip of his manhattan.

"No, listen to me. At first, I thought something was horribly wrong, but before leaping to conclusions I decided to do some research. Obviously, everyone has a heart that speeds up and slows down with music. Others, though, can adapt to rhythm. Like a conductor. That's what mine does—like it's listening. Do you see what I'm saying?"

He frowned.

"I'm not crazy." She swatted his arm.

"You are crazy, but that's not what I'm worried about. You're talking about your heart—your *heart*, Maggie."

He shook his head, then cleared their drinks to the kitchen.

She followed him, a hand on her still-swooning heart. "I know you think I'm just being crazy or imagining things or worse but I'm telling you, this is happening."

"I'd drive you straight to the hospital if I didn't think you'd jump out of the car at the first stoplight." He turned on the faucet and rinsed the glasses before loading them into the dishwasher.

"In all of our years of friendship, Bart, have I ever been wrong?"

Turning back to her, he arched an eyebrow. "You believe you can lose five pounds by eating nothing but cucumbers and ginger slices."

"How else do you think I'm able to wear those velvet pants every Christmas? I bought them the year Bess graduated from high school and I'm still wearing them."

"Make a doctor's appointment," Chef Bart said. "Tomorrow."

<<EXCERPT>>

The Kids Are Gonna Ask
*A Guava Media Podcast*
Season01—Episode05
Tuesday, June 30

**THOMAS**
Mr. Miller? Abe Miller?

**ABE MILLER**
Speaking.

**THOMAS**
Mr. Miller, hi. This is Thomas McClair calling. I sent you an email last week, and you said you'd be willing to speak with us about a bartender who used to work at your place?

**ABE**
Yuh.

**THOMAS**
I have my sister, Savannah, here with me and we're recording, if you'll give your consent?

**ABE**
Not sure how much I can tell you. But, sure. Shoot.

**SAVANNAH**
That's your consent, correct? That you know we're recording?

**ABE**
Yuh. Something else to it?

**THOMAS**
All right, so like I wrote in my email, we're looking for our biological father, and we have a podcast where we've been broadcasting our search. We're following a lead that one of your former

waitresses—Andi Benson—sent us after listening to the show. Not sure if you remember her?

**ABE**
Andi was around for a few years. A waitress, I think. Long time ago, though.

**THOMAS**
Right. She said she was there from '99 to 2002.

**ABE**
Yuh. Sounds like that could be right.

**THOMAS**
Great. So, like I said, she contacted us because we're looking for a tall, good-looking blond guy who talked about wanting to save money for a trip to New Zealand and she said that sounded like a guy she used to work with at your bar, The Mine.

**ABE**
This town is full of good-looking blond kids. You know his name?

**SAVANNAH**
Andi said she thought his name was Thor. Does that ring a bell?

**ABE**
Well, could do.

[pause]

That's a lot a years back for me to remember a blond kid.

**SAVANNAH**
We realize. But we thought maybe you had employment records you could check? Tax statements? That sort of thing?

**ABE**
What year did you say?

**THOMAS**
2002-ish. We know it's a long shot. I'm sure you probably hire a lot of folks every year.

[transition music]
[voice-over]

**THOMAS**
It was a long shot.

**SAVANNAH**
One we didn't expect to overcome.

**THOMAS**
Until, out of the blue—

**SAVANNAH**
Abe called back.

[phone ringing]

**THOMAS**
Thomas McClair, here.

**ABE**
Yuh. This is Abe Miller. You called me looking for a bartender named Thor?

**THOMAS**
Yes! Did you find something, Mr. Miller?

**ABE**
No. I didn't. Well, not me, I didn't. I just happened to mention it to Cindy, the manager here. She's been around near as long as I've had this place.

**THOMAS**
And she remembered Thor?

**ABE**

Well, sorta. But she got real curious and went back through the files there in the office. Found a W-2 from 2001 and a forwarding address from about a year later.

**THOMAS**

Incredible! Can you send that to us?

**ABE**

Well, not sure if I'm s'posed to do that. But I can tell you I doubt he's there anymore. The address was for a big resort outside of Bend. You know, Oregon. Big resort.

**THOMAS**

So you think he left Colorado to go work at a resort in Oregon.

**ABE**

What it looks like. Yuh.

**THOMAS**

I see.

[pause]

Any chance you can at least give us his last name?

**ABE**

Sure. Says here it's [beep].

[transition music]
[voice-over]

**SAVANNAH**

Sorry, folks. We're choosing not to broadcast Thor's whole name. You're just going to have to trust us on this one.

<<END EXCERPT>>

# FIFTEEN

## THOMAS

The morning a few days before the fifth episode was scheduled to air, Thomas knocked on Savannah's bedroom door. "Van! Are you ever going to come back to the studio?" She was in there with Trigg, which he knew because he'd heard them laughing all night long. "C'mon, Van. I want to call the list of resorts in Bend."

She opened the door just far enough to peek her face through. "Geez, T. Don't get so *emotional*."

"Yeah, T," Trigg teased from behind the door. "Quit acting like such a chick."

Stupid Trigg.

He ignored the bait. "The next episode drops in two days. We've got a ton of work to do."

Seeing her face-to-face, he could tell Savannah hadn't slept much. There were dark circles under her eyes and her hair looked greasy, even in a ponytail. She knew the deadlines as well as he did. Why was she goofing around when he was the one making all the sacrifices?

"I could've gone to the end-of-season track party last night, but I didn't. Because *we have work to do*."

"Oh, is that why you didn't go to the party?" Savannah's voice dripped with phony concern.

"Shut it, Van."

She rolled her eyes. He wanted to slam the door in her face. He'd intended to go to the end-of-season party last night.

Nico and Pete came by to pick him up. Only, they were early, and Thomas hadn't showered yet.

"Give me a few minutes," he'd said, and left them in the kitchen while he ran upstairs. When he came down again, Nadine was there, too, helping her dad prep dinner.

Chef Bart and Nadine were busy chopping. And Nico was busy making an ass of himself.

"Thomas is fast," he was saying. "But he probably needs to stick to individual events. We lost four-tenths of a second every time he passed the baton."

"That so?" Thomas figured he'd walked in just in time. "What other theories you got?"

Pete flushed, but Nico shrugged like he wasn't embarrassed at all. "I'm saying, you ought to run individuals. The two hundred. The four."

"Hmm." Thomas brought his hand to his chin as if he were actually interested. "And I'm saying, you better leave."

Nico scoffed. "Whatever, drama queen."

"Hey, Thomas—" Pete started. But he must have figured there was nothing more to say, because he just stood and motioned toward the door. "C'mon, Nico. And shut your mouth for once, will you?"

Nico shook his head but followed. "I didn't say anything Thomas doesn't already know."

Pete turned on their way out, holding the door open as he leaned inside. "You should come anyway, T. If you want to." Then he turned back around and let the door slam behind them. But even with it closed, Thomas, Chef Bart and Nadine could all still hear Nico continue to justify everything he'd said on their way to the car.

"I didn't even ask him about any of that, Thomas." Nadine's face was plastered with pity. "He was just trying to show off."

Thomas retreated, turning to head back upstairs to his room. "Never mind," he said. "Doesn't matter. We have an early morning in the studio, anyway."

Now, though, Savannah wasn't even coming out of her room.

"Listen, Thomas," she said. "My best friend is here. And unlike you, I like hanging out with friends. I'll come down as soon as we're done with girl time."

"Yeah, Thomas," Trigg called from inside the bedroom. "We *chicks* need our time to bond. And to talk about boys!"

Savannah's face went suddenly red. "Shut *up*, Trigg, oh my god!"

This was too dumb to tolerate any longer. Thomas waved Savannah back from the door and pushed it open. "Go home, Trigg. Savannah has to work."

"Rude!" yelled Trigg.

"Bully!" hollered Savannah.

*Idiots!* thought Thomas.

A half hour later, Savannah opened the basement door and came downstairs to the studio with damp hair and smelling like Irish Spring from her shower. "Brought you a present." She handed him a bagel with cream cheese.

"Thanks." He took it, even though he wasn't really hungry.

"Don't get too excited," she said. "It's really just to show you that I'm a *big girl* and I can *take care of myself.*" She took her finger and shoved it deep into his food.

"Dammit, Van!" he hollered, and before he knew it, he'd grabbed the bagel and smeared its cream cheese all down the front of her shirt.

"*Idiot!*" she screamed, holding her arms out and scanning the damage in horror.

"*You're* the idiot! We agreed to be in the studio by ten o'clock this morning!"

"Oh, who are you? My *teacher*? It's summer break!"

The door to the basement opened and Maggie called downstairs, "Everything all right?"

"*Yeah!*" they answered.

The moment broken, they retreated to their corners. Savannah grabbed a stack of leftover Jimmy John's napkins and tried to wipe the cream cheese off her shirt. Thomas watched, hoping it didn't work.

"Do you know how pissed *you'd* be if I took off with my friends?" he said.

She scoffed. "You have friends?"

"Funny." He returned her sarcasm with a scowl. "I'm just saying, you don't have to do everything Trigg does."

"How about you mind your own business? Or better yet, *get a life of your own.*"

"I'm the one who was in the studio on time!" *Great.* Now they were shouting again.

"That's not what I mean! I mean, go find some people who aren't going to drop you when you're no good to them anymore!"

He kicked the corner of the desk and immediately regretted it, the pain ringing from his toes all the way up his shin. "*Agh!* My team didn't drop me, *Coach* dropped me!" *Shit.* It still made his throat pinch to say it.

Savannah stopped yelling and was quiet for a moment. "Thomas," she said finally, "Nico's mean to you. He's mean to everyone."

Thomas stood and slowly circled the studio, trying to walk off the pain. "Yeah, well. You're no picnic, either."

Savannah huffed. "Oh yeah? Try telling that to Sam Tamblin."

Sam Tamblin had taken to practically smothering them with praise. Thanks to the *Mid-Morning* interview, discussion traffic on the show's Facebook page now required its own dedicated Guava Media moderator. Crazy numbers of people suddenly cared whether they found their dad or not.

There were even camps forming. The biggest camp was made up of casual detectives—the people who loved a missing person challenge and wanted to have a hand in helping solve it. Last time Thomas went online, he read a comment from a woman named Allison Braxton who wrote, "This is like stepping into a real-life Nancy Drew mystery."

*Not really,* he wanted to write back. *This is my life.*

The Detectives, though, were way better than the other two camps. Thomas thought of them as the Brynns versus the Besses.

The Brynns were all puffed up about protecting "the innocents." Mainly, their camp griped about the invasion of men's private lives, much like the real Brynn had done. But a good portion of them also took a child advocacy tack. They were the ones who loved to attack Maggie for exposing her grandchildren to public risk and ridicule, while claiming that Thomas and Savannah, as minors, couldn't possibly be mature enough to understand the implications of their actions. As if they were seven, instead of seventeen.

The Besses, on the other hand, were like the caped avengers, always ready to defend Thomas and Savannah. He knew it was wrong to think of his mother as their namesake, but he couldn't help making the association. They just acted so maternal, so unconditionally supportive. Like they were willing to hold back the Brynn attacks, no matter the cost, as long as doing so allowed Thomas and Savannah to keep going.

They were still nutty, though.

One woman, Alexis DuVrey posted a bedtime blessing for Thomas and Savannah every night at the same time. He only knew this, of course, because Sam Tamblin thought it was hysterical.

"May the energy of the universe overwhelm those spirts that would do you hard," she wrote one night. It was obviously an innocent and unfortunate series of typos, but ever since, Sam couldn't resist calling on the "the spirts" to do him "hard."

Thomas, meanwhile, was just trying to keep their priorities straight. Today, they had a list of nearly two dozen cold calls to make. And neither he nor Savannah had even sat down yet.

Savannah licked a bit of rogue cream cheese from her finger. "You keep accusing me of being snotty or—*whatever*—but I don't see you standing up when Nico gives me a hard time."

Thomas scoffed. They'd been through this an obnoxious number of times. "I've told you. He's just kidding with all that."

Admittedly, Nico was a jerk, but he was harmless. A basic smart-ass. Whenever Savannah raised her hand in class, he had to make a big show of mimicking her from the back row. When he got called on and didn't know the answer, his default suggestion was, "I'm sure Ms. McClair knows."

If Nico hadn't grown up knowing Savannah since forever, or if he'd said something nasty about her when they were alone, it would be different. But he was just an idiot.

"You know he doesn't mean it, Van."

"Do I?" she said. "Better yet, do you?"

Thomas shook his head and tried to get back on track. She was sucking him into an argument, and he didn't want to fall for it.

"Just—here." He handed her a copy of the phone numbers they'd gathered, every resort in or around Bend, Oregon, circa 2002. The info gathering hadn't been hard—it was just a few hours on the library public records database. But the list was long, and the day was getting shorter with every wasted minute.

She grabbed the list and scanned it. "Fine. But I'm leaving to meet Trigg for a movie at one."

# SIXTEEN

## MAGGIE

The morning after episode five aired, Maggie finally found her grandchildren in the kitchen—Savannah studying the label on a bottle of green tea, Thomas eating a slice of Chef Bart's leftover mango-prosciutto pizza.

"Maggie, do you know how much caffeine there is in green tea? I can't decide if I need to cut back or drink more."

Maggie took the bottle from her hand and poured its contents into a glass. "What I do know, love, is that everything liquid is better on ice." Then she hugged Savannah tight. It felt like ages since she'd seen her grands. Life had gotten so lonely.

"Sit down and tell me everything." She poured herself a cup of coffee, gathered her morning kimono around her knees and scooted into the corner chair between the kitchen table and the wall. "No excuses. Come, come."

Savannah sat first. "Well, I think we're on the verge of a breakthrough. Really, really close."

Maggie looked at Thomas for his take on the situation.

He shook his head. "I thought we were closer yesterday. Our leads in Oregon went nowhere."

"Yeah, but think of all the people we talked to there—we got them thinking and they're going talk to people and those people will talk to people and then it's going to be just like the—" She snapped her fingers, looking for the words.

"Like the Fabergé Organics commercial?" Maggie winked. On the ever-shortening list of pastimes she and her grandchildren still enjoyed together, one of her favorites was watching the classic commercials available on YouTube.

"She told two friends, and she told two friends…" Thomas hinted.

"Very funny. No, I was going to say it would be just like what happened when Abe told his manager, Cindy."

"So did you really learn your father's full name?" Maggie asked.

Savannah nodded, swallowing her iced tea. "It's not Thor at all—that was his nickname. His given name is John James Thorson. Thor, for short."

Maggie sat with the name for a minute, hoping it would ring a bell. It didn't. Nor did Bess care to step in with a reminder. Silent when Maggie needed her, as usual.

"I'm sorry," Maggie told them, disappointment piercing her. She had so little to contribute to their search. "I was hoping I'd hear it and realize that I'd met him or something. But John Thorson, or John Jack, or Thor—I can't remember your mom ever talking about anyone like that. And you're certain about the name?"

Thomas wiped the last crumbs of pizza from his hands and sat down across from her at the table. "Pretty certain. I mean, we're not detectives, right? But the dots seem to connect. He was in Colorado at the right time, he worked as a bartender, he fits the description, people remember him, and if it's true that he went by a nickname, I mean—yeah. It seems to add up."

"Nothing's settled until we find him, obviously," added Savannah. "I mean, will we look like him? Will the DNA tests check out?"

Maggie was surprised. "You've decided to go ahead with the DNA tests Sam offered?" She thought they'd vetoed Sam Tamblin on all DNA fronts.

Savannah shook her head. "Only after we find the guy who seems to check all the boxes."

A moment of quiet fell, each of them lost in their thoughts. Maggie could see circles forming under Thomas's eyes and Savannah's hair looked like she hadn't brushed it in a dog's age.

"I'm proud of you both." She reached for their hands and didn't let go until, eventually, as she knew they would, they pulled away and drifted off into their own lives once again.

<<EXCERPT>>

The Kids Are Gonna Ask
*A Guava Media Podcast*
Season01—Episode06
Tuesday, July 07

[voice-over]

**SAVANNAH**
So, we made a list of all the resorts in and around Bend, where Colorado Abe told us Thor had listed as his last forwarding address. Then we started calling.

**THOMAS**
For any of you thinking of launching a search like this yourself, a word of warning. This is what most of your time will sound like.

[ringing phone]

**SAVANNAH**
Hi, I'm calling in reference to a man who may have once been an employee at your resort in or around 2002 by the name of [beep]. Do you, by chance, have a record of him working there?

**WOMAN #1**
2002? We didn't open until 2010.

[hang up]

**WOMAN #2**
Nope. I asked around. Nobody's heard of him. Sorry.

[hang up]

**WOMAN #3**

I don't remember ever hiring a [beep] but if he did work here, those files are long gone. We had a flood that wiped out pretty much everything a few years ago.

[hang up]

**MAN #1**

Who did you say you're with? You need to submit that sort of request in writing.

[hang up]
[voice-over]

**THOMAS**

It was several days of the same.

**SAVANNAH**

But we figured, this is what research is, right? Lots of dead ends mixed with a few leads that look promising but are really just a looping route to yet another dead end.

**THOMAS**

We're no detectives. We don't claim to be experts at this. Do we even know what we're doing?

**SAVANNAH**

Maybe not!

**THOMAS**

But, we are McClairs. And what's the McClair family motto?

**SAVANNAH**

Trust your instincts!

**THOMAS**

So, we kept calling. Until we'd dialed every last Oregon lead. And then?

[phone ringing]

**SAVANNAH**

Hi, I was given your name by Mary, who does your seasonal hiring? She told me that you may remember a man we're looking for, that you have a knack for hiring good people away from other resorts? Anyway, this was back in 2002. His name is [beep].

**WOMAN #4**

2002. [restates name]. 2002. [pause] Are you talking about Thor?

**SAVANNAH**

Yes! At least, that's the name we're told he went by.

**WOMAN #4**

Well, if it's the same one, yes, I remember him. Who could forget him, really? Gorgeous. Cheekbones. He was a bartender in Colorado. Breckenridge. My husband and I own a place there. He skis, but I just like to wear tight pants and cute boots.

**SAVANNAH**

Is that where you met Thor?

**WOMAN #4**

Exactly, at The Mine. It's a bar, kind of a dump but it's been there forever, and we've been in Breck for so long that it's just sort of a tradition—between us and all our friends. Better than having to fight the tourists for a table, anyway.

**SAVANNAH**

And Thor? What's the connection with Bend?

**WOMAN #4**
Well, I hired him! Poached him, really. For our resort. We own Sky River.

[voice-over]

**THOMAS**
We did some research. Turns out, the Sky River Resort and Spa is one of the largest luxury resorts in Oregon. Fifty thousand acres of secluded mountain retreat. Two hundred rooms. A going summer rate of more than four hundred dollars a night. In comparison to Sky River, Savannah and I had basically been calling roadside motels looking for Thor. That one of the owners of this multimillion-dollar property remembers him personally is nothing short of impaling ourselves on the needle buried in the haystack.

[phone call]

**WOMAN #4**
Mary—who you talked to—does the hiring. I just steal people from time to time. The ones I like. The ones who make an incredible martini and are lovely to look at.

**SAVANNAH**
Like Thor. Is that what you're saying?

**WOMAN #4**
Exactly like Thor. I had him all set up to run our best bar here on property, The Haze.

**SAVANNAH**
How long was he at The Haze, then?

**WOMAN #4**
Exactly zero days. That's what I'm saying. I had him set up to run it. Only he never showed up.

[voice-over]

**SAVANNAH**
So, that was the Oregon story. Thor was all set to leave for Bend. He had a good job, a personal invitation. But he never showed up. We called Abe back at The Mine in Breckenridge to ask if the address he would have had at Sky River matched what he listed on his forwarding address form. It did.

**THOMAS**
See what we mean about dead ends?

[phone call]

**SAVANNAH**
So, you're saying you hired him, but he never showed up? Do you know what happened? Like, did he have a car accident on the way to Oregon or something?

**WOMAN #4**
I got a postcard. Some nonsense about having had a change of heart. Bullshit, really. Left us scrambling for a new manager at the last minute. And for all I know he's living in one of those— what do you call them…like in Mongolia?

**SAVANNAH**
A yurt?

**WOMAN #4**
Right. For all I know he's off somewhere living in a yurt.

[voice-over]

**SAVANNAH**
I honestly worried when she said he didn't show up that she was going to tell me he died or something.

**THOMAS**
That we were suddenly a podcast about our unknown father's mysterious death.

**SAVANNAH**
Or that he was in prison. Something.

**THOMAS**
Do we know he's not in prison?

**SAVANNAH**
Oh my god. No, we don't.

**THOMAS**
See what we mean about the looping research?

<<END EXCERPT>>

# SEVENTEEN

## THOMAS

"Do you really think we're getting close?" Thomas and Savannah were in the kitchen raiding the refrigerator. They'd just finished cutting episode six and they were exhausted and starving. Savannah grabbed a package of peppered turkey slices, oven-roasted chicken breast, and the jar of Chef Bart's homemade chipotle mayo, then kicked the refrigerator door shut. They stacked the sandwich fixings on the counter and dug in.

"What do you mean?" Savannah asked.

"The other day. You told Maggie you thought we were getting really close. I'm wondering if you believe that."

"Yeah, I do think we're making progress."

"But do you think we're close?" He could hear the pinch in his voice, part midnight fatigue, part anxiety. He hoped Savannah wouldn't notice.

"I don't know what to tell you, bud. Maybe, maybe not."

Of course, she couldn't be any more definitive than that. He understood. But lately, it seemed like every discovery they made ratcheted his mood, pulled his nerves tighter and tighter until now he couldn't sleep and couldn't sit still. Right this minute, he was exhausted but knew he wouldn't sleep more than a few hours thanks to his hypervigilant brain.

Obviously, Savannah didn't know anything more than he did and it probably wasn't fair to ask her for assurances. But she was the other half of this puzzle, the only other person who really had any idea what it felt like to look for a man who'd had almost zero influence on your life, but without whom you wouldn't even be alive.

If he didn't have Savannah, he didn't have anyone.

"It's like I told Maggie," Savannah said. "We're getting people talking. I think of what we're doing sort of like that scene in *101 Dalmatians* after the puppies are stolen. Their parents go outside and bark, trying to sound the alarm to all the other dogs in town. As soon as the neighbor dogs hear it, they pass the SOS to other dogs, who pass it on, and eventually the call makes it all the way out to the country, where the puppies are hidden."

"So, the podcast is our form of the twilight bark?" Thomas wanted to be skeptical of his sister using a Disney movie as a real-life comparison, but right now, he needed something to grab onto.

"I guess, yeah." Savannah slapped the top slice of bread onto her sandwich. "Which means, we'd better be ready."

Knowing sleep would elude him, Thomas didn't bother to lie down. Instead, he sat by his window and watched the few joggers on the dark parkway below. During the summer, people didn't stop running just because the sun had gone down. June was already over and he'd barely noticed, always in the studio, oblivious to the scenery beyond their basement walls.

Not that he cared. They were starting to get somewhere.

He grabbed his laptop and opened his email. Sam Tamblin had taken to sending them a daily email summarizing any decent leads that might have come in via the discussion groups or email. It was another protection Maggie'd insisted on.

"I don't want Thomas and Savannah exposed to the crazies and nasties online," she'd said during negotiations. "If Guava Media wants to broadcast this story, it also needs to be responsible for filtering the noise it kicks up."

The answer to her request came in the form of Sam's daily email, which he called the "Nightcap." Thomas opened tonight's edition.

s.tamblin@guavamediausa.com
To: t.mcclair@guavamediausa.com; s.mcclair@guavamediausa.com; m.mcclair@guavamediausa.com

Subject: Nightcap—July 07

Hey all, online chatter mostly nonsense today. Here are a few things worth noting.

LEADS
1.   Discussion on Facebook forum re: woman who claims to contradict Sky River's story that Thor never worked there. Says she worked with him at Sky River for a period of at least six months and offers to provide photos. Requesting via email; Sam to follow up.

2.   Two new paternity claims via website. Justin Mathers of Dayton, OH and Ray Nguyen of Fort Collins, CO. After investigating, the claims are false and will be disregarded.

MEDIA COVERAGE
🎬 Podcast mention: "Ten Things I'm Loving Right Now" interview with Bradley Cooper (#6), PowerPlayerz.com

FOLLOW-UPS
Taxi driver claiming to have spoken with Thor on recent trip from LAX deemed not credible.

Sam

Thomas had learned to quit expecting much from Sam's emails. Whatever leads came in mostly got disproven within the next day or so, and he'd begun to skim the Nightcaps rather than read for substance. The only meaningful information had come through interviews—the ones he and Savannah had conducted themselves.

He cleared the rest of his inbox, flipped through a few *BuzzFeed* articles, and still, he wasn't the least bit tired. The clock in the corner of his screen read 3:13 a.m. He didn't have any idea what he was going to do with the next few hours. Even Nico, who he normally would've pinged for a video game or two, was offline.

He could send a thank-you email to the woman at Sky River, but Savannah claimed email carried less impact than mailing a letter and insisted on using her typewriter. Apparently, ancient equaled earnest.

He could also go back to searching public records databases for John James Thorson, but experience had quickly taught them they didn't know how to decipher meaningful hits from junk. Searching his full name, John James Thorson, generated 1,200 records, but add in searches on John Thorson or John J. Thorson and the records climbed into the hundreds of thousands. They needed professional help, a private detective or a paid researcher or some resource they hadn't thought of yet. But that was a discussion that needed to include Maggie and Sam. And it called for money.

He sat back in his chair, deflated. He was seventeen years old. He wasn't supposed to be sitting at home in the middle of the night without anyone to talk to. Yeah, he had Savannah, but a sister didn't count. At a minimum, he needed someone he could talk to *about* his sister.

The email icon on his screen lit up, indicating a new message. He reopened his email and took a look. His heart stopped when he saw an email from John James Thorson.

thorJJ1979@gmail.com
To: mcclairinfo@mcclairsalonpod.com
Subject: Hello

Dear Savannah and Thomas,

This is an email I never expected to write, but I'll get to the point—I think I'm your biological father. My name is John James Thorson. For a long time I went by the nickname, Thor. Now I go by Jack.

I know you're probably getting a lot of these letters. I've been listening to your podcast and I know it's really popular. I know I probably should have contacted you through the Guava Media site, but I worried this might not get to you if I do. So I'm sending it through your other podcast website. Don't know if that's any better.

Anyway. Why don't I just tell you what I can?

I grew up in Colorado and moved to Breckenridge in 1999. I needed a break from college and thought I'd see how long I could make it as a ski bum. Turns out, about two and a half years. I skied most days but got a job bartending at The Mine during the summer of 2000. I worked there until I moved in 2002.

I don't want to tell you everything right now, like where I live and what I do for a living. It's kind of a shock (no offense) that I have kids. Well, if I do. I guess we don't really know that for sure.

I'm really sorry about your mom, Bess. I remember her. She had a small "and" symbol tattooed on one of her fingers...you know, the & sign. I think it was her right hand, but I could be wrong. When I asked her about it she said she got it after her dad died. I guess that would be your grandfather. She wanted it to remind her there's always more to the story. That's what I remember really liking about her. She was smart and thoughtful. Kind of outgoing, and really interesting, too. We talked a lot. I told her I was thinking about spending the summer in New Zealand traveling and she encouraged me to do it.

I don't know if you know this, but your mom was a really good skier. I remember that, too, because she had this thick Minnesota accent and there aren't any mountains there. I think I even asked her if she was Canadian. Anyway, she teased me for assuming Coloradans were the only people in America who could ski. I probably deserved it. Anyhow, I hope she was able to teach you.

If anything in this letter sounds not too crazy, you can email me back. I guess, though, I'd really appreciate it if you don't put this in your podcast or give my name away yet or anything. I know I can't stop you, but if I do turn out to be your biological father, I think I'd rather meet you in person. I'm not ashamed, in case you're thinking that. I'm really impressed with you both. Amazed, actually. I'm not a big talker and so if this thing does prove to be true, you didn't get any of your podcasting talents from me.

Wow, this email has gotten really long. Sorry. Hope I don't sound like one of the crazies.

Jack Thorson

# BOOK TWO

# EIGHTEEN

## JACK

It started with a nibble. A nudge. A string of clues even Jack had the good sense not to ignore.

The evidence piled up. It was loose and circumstantial, but it added up to what seemed like a believable story. Like, in episode two. Thomas teased Savannah about being a public hazard in flip-flops. Jack couldn't wear flip-flops, either. Which wasn't groundbreaking—they obviously weren't the only two people in the world with footwear restrictions. But the more details he heard, the more it all made sense.

Bess, included.

Especially Bess.

He remembered saying to her, "Let's imagine you stay here in Colorado with me. Or you go home, graduate, and we leave for New Zealand together when you're done. Sleep on couches at night and ski all day."

She'd said, "Let's imagine we just call this the incredible week that it was."

She hadn't stayed. And they hadn't gone to New Zealand. And they hadn't kept in touch. And now Jack found out from the podcast that Bess was dead.

He wondered how things might have been different if he had tried harder to be with her. But it wouldn't have worked. Not in the long run, anyway. Bess had a future planned. And Jack had made himself unwelcome in every place he'd ever tried to call home, including where he was at now—working as a fishing charter guide on Tybee Island near Savannah, Georgia.

Jack had discovered the podcast thanks to an obnoxious kid from the family on his boat that morning—a family of four down from New York or New Jersey, he hadn't cared which. He'd seen plenty of their kind before. The mother couldn't do anything for herself. The father didn't have a nice thing to say about anyone. Daughter didn't talk about anything except getting off the boat. And their son was on his way to becoming a clone of his dad—a full-on loudmouthed bully.

"Hey, Gilligan. Any part of this boat that don't stink like fish?" The kid sneered. "Bet your girlfriend makes you shower twice before you even touch her."

*Asshole.*

The kid was trying to goad him, but Jack wasn't interested. He knew it was just a game for the attention he didn't get from his parents. Jack was going on more than fifteen years as a fishing guide, getting paid to take people out to where the fish were biting. If clients wanted to catch redfish or flounder, he packed the bait buckets with live shrimp on ice and turned inland. For sheepshead, he packed crabs and anchored under the bridges or near the embankments. That was Jack's job—to know the waters. It was the one thing he was good at. He watched the weather and the seasons and the tides. He baited hooks and taught people how to get a feel for their lines and to predict just the right moment to start reeling in. He sent clients home with full coolers and loaded cameras.

Jack didn't owe any of them any more than that.

"You checked your bait?" Jack nodded at the kid's line, which he'd been ignoring all morning, his face stuck in his phone. He was in that awkward thirteen- or fourteen-year-old phase, and Jack told himself to cut him some slack. He'd been a perfect little prick at that age, too.

"You mean boner bait?" The kid thrust his phone in Jack's face. "Check out the tits on her."

Jack pushed the phone away and waited for the parental smackdown. No parent would let their son say that sort of thing.

But no rebuke came. Dad was standing in the bow babbling to no one about the time he'd caught a shark off the coast of South Carolina and Mom was arguing with her daughter about putting on a hat.

They hadn't heard, or they hadn't cared, or both.

Jack was about ready to pick the kid up by the neck and throw him overboard. "You're on my boat, you show some respect."

"Don't get your tidies in a bunch, old man." The kid flashed his phone in Jack's face again. "I'm just admiring my favorite twins."

What Jack saw stopped him cold. He grabbed the phone and stared at the picture on the screen, the first time he ever saw Savannah and Thomas, side by side, smiling. Savannah with the off-center cleft in her chin and Thomas with the gap between his two front teeth.

He'd seen these people before. Not actually *seen* them, of course, and not even known of them. But the moment was instant, a recognition—known and unknown at once.

"Who are these kids?"

Tybee Island was a lifestyle. It's barely twenty minutes from Savannah, Georgia, but once a person crossed those bridges, the island shed Savannah's dark, eerie shadows. Jack liked to believe that tourists went to Savannah for a good haunting, the ghostly lore that drips from the historic district's brick and iron homes like Spanish moss from a magnolia tree. After they'd had enough talk of death, they headed to Tybee for a few days of good island living.

Jack chose Tybee for a reason.

Compared to Savannah, life on Tybee was like wearing

swim trunks to a cotillion. The island didn't get all up in family lineage and historic preservation boards of review. On any given morning, half of Tybee looked hungover—even the buildings. It boasted about being the worldwide headquarters of fish art. It hosted an annual pirate festival. To visitors, Tybee looked like one long, salty party from morning to night.

Jack had lived there for seventeen years, moved to Tybee not long after a man who introduced himself as Ford wandered into the bar in Breckenridge, ordered a Jim Beam and Coke and swore he was "never goin' up that summa'bitch mountain again." Business was slow that day, so he and Jack got to talking. About how Ford had booked the trip to Colorado after his soon-to-be ex-wife accused him of being a *boring old coot*. About his real life as a fishing guide off the coast of Georgia. About the difference between saltwater catch and the freshwater varieties Jack had grown up fishing in Colorado.

Jack proved himself decent company, and when his shift ended, Ford handed him his card. "You ever feel like tryin' your hand at bein' a saltwater fishing guide, you come work for me."

Ford had changed Jack's prospects all those years ago, altered his trajectory from near-certain disaster. He'd been making decent money as a bartender and even had plans to leave Colorado for a big resort in Oregon. His new boss had offered him a cash raise, plus a steamier sort of compensation as a bonus, and he'd come within a razor's edge of falling for her proposal.

Ford's offer woke him up just in time.

Now, anchored in the South Channel of the Savannah River beneath the shadow of Fort Pulaski, Jack's Colorado past loomed unexpectedly before his eyes.

"They're looking for their biodad," the kid from the boat

had told him. "S'posed to be some guy their mom met skiing in Colorado."

If it had only been a picture of the girl, Savannah, Jack probably wouldn't have even paused. Thomas, though. He could've been his twin, the face of a younger Jack.

He binged every episode of the podcast that night. He listened again the next morning. Again that night. And when he couldn't stand it anymore, he played a game with his head, the kind you play when you wake up from a dream and tell yourself none of it really happened.

No way he was the guy they were looking for. And still, it had to be him—their story tracked his.

It wasn't complicated.

Jack had left his hometown of Hartwell, Colorado, for college and made it about eighteen months—his second year more blur than recollection—until the University of Northern Colorado memorialized his brief tenure in a letter stating that his time as a UNC student was officially over.

"I need a break anyway," he told his roommate.

"Got an opportunity I can't pass up," he told his landlord.

"I'll be back to school. Six months, tops," he told the girl he was sleeping with when he couldn't make it the five blocks to his own place because he was so drunk.

Getting kicked out of UNC seemed like a favor for a while, woke him up to the fact that he had higher priorities than the classroom. The mountains, he hoped, would be just the distraction he needed. He found his way to Breckenridge and got a job bartending at The Mine. His first night he made more money than he'd ever held in his pocket, and it was easy. He liked hearing people's stories. Life in a ski town narrows conversation to a handful of topics. What slopes you skied today and what you're going to ski tomorrow. The snow conditions today and the snow conditions expected tomorrow. The mountains you've already skied and the mountains you hoped to ski before you died. Everyone comes down the mountain at the end of the day with an experience all their own.

The most consequential thing about a ski town, though, is the impermanence. Only the mountain itself is there to stay. Everything else is fleeting—the weather, the stories and especially the people.

He didn't have a lot of flings, but he had a few, and like everything in a ski town, the romance melted with time. As soon as the women went back to where they came from, Jack moved on—to work or to hit the slopes. He rarely had any more expectation of seeing a woman again in the morning than he did of seeing the same flake fall from the sky.

But he'd never forgotten Bess. He wouldn't have talked about her to anyone. They weren't destined to be together. But he remembered her the way land remembers a flood, her mark brief but indelible.

The morning episode six dropped, Jack was in his truck on the way to the landing. The sun was just breaking, the mist clinging to the marsh, all quiet, the edge of eerie.

"You're going to have to excuse my brother," Savannah said. "He's a zombie today. I'll translate when he's not making sense."

"Shut it, Van. You know I can't sleep when there's lightning."

Jack slammed on the brakes and pulled over to the side of the road under a sign warning drivers to watch for crossing turtles. No one else reacted to thunderstorms the way Jack did—until now. After what he'd just heard, there was no doubt he was the father these seventeen-year-old kids were looking for.

t.mcclair@guavamediausa.com
To: thorJJ1979@gmail.com
Re: Further info

Jack,

Thank you for writing. We appreciate you listening to the podcast.

You're right that we have been getting a lot of emails like yours, though you did include a few details that haven't been in the broadcast. Like your full name and our mom's tattoo.

I hope you won't take my skepticism personally, but it is conceivable that someone could dig through public files for the name John Jack Thorson. And most people my mom used to meet noticed her tattoo and asked about it.

Even so, I'd like to hear more. Are there any personal characteristics you can tell us about yourself or your time with our mom that other people wouldn't be able to claim?

Feel free to email back. And, no, we won't put personal details into the podcast.

Thanks,
Thomas McClair

# NINETEEN

## SAVANNAH

Savannah looked at her phone to find a text from Trigg.

What do you want me to tell Kyle?????

No emojis. Meaning, Trigg wanted an answer now. Savannah texted back.

I don't know...just tell him you haven't been able to get ahold of me.

She was standing in the kitchen. Maggie was down a rabbit hole on her laptop. Nadine was flipping channels on the TV and Chef Bart had his head in the refrigerator.

Can't. He knows I'm texting with you right now.

*What?*

TRIGG!!!!!

Only when Nadine turned did Savannah realize she'd said this out loud.

"Sorry." Savannah felt herself flush. "Just—stupid Trigg." She put her phone facedown on the table and pulled out the chair next to Nadine. "So, how's your summer so far?"

"Pretty good. I'm taking driver's ed."

"Oh, nice."

Everything about Nadine was nice. Not extraordinary. Not awful. Just nice. A nice person with a nice dad and a nice, *whatever*. They laughed and talked when she came over. Mostly about stuff like YouTube and music and movies. Funny stuff. Nice stuff.

Savannah, though, could do with some cute. And Kyle Larson, who Trigg was all over her about, was definitely cute. But was he nice? He was a friend of Carrie Westlund, which meant nice seemed unlikely.

"Trigg's bugging me about this guy at school," she said, explaining her earlier outburst. "Says he's been asking about me."

"Yeah?" Nadine said. "Is he nice?"

*"See?"* She threw her hands up. "You *totally* get it."

Nadine was what Maggie would've called *wise beyond her years*. Savannah knew this because that was the other thing they talked about, the awful something in Nadine's past. Thomas didn't know what that thing was, only that the one time they asked Maggie why Chef Bart brought his daughter to work with him, she said it was because *life can be cruel*. Then Maggie turned and left the room before they could ask any more questions, which Savannah and Thomas both knew was code for, *that's all I'm going to tell you about that.*

But Savannah wasn't as strong as Thomas and Maggie. One night, late, when Chef Bart was cleaning up and Nadine was half-asleep on the couch waiting, Savannah gave in to temptation. She'd felt dark all day, and she couldn't help herself.

"Why are you always here?" she'd said, knowing how cruel and ripe with accusation she sounded. But dark people, she also knew, were willing to ask such things.

Then Nadine told her, and for a long time Savannah wished she'd never asked. Eventually, though, she grew to appreciate the reminder that she wasn't the only member of the Dead Mother's Club.

And now, here they were. Chef Bart cooking, Maggie lost in her own world, Thomas up in his room, and Savannah and Nadine watching TV. Savannah was about to offer to take Nadine out driving when Nadine grabbed the remote and spiked the volume.

"These McClair dupes," said a woman with blond streaks and incredible cheekbones, "are an obvious demonstration of blatant hypocrisy. Because here we have a mother and a grandmother who *conspired* to rob these *children* and their *father* from ever having any sort of relationship. And, yes, I mean it when I say *conspired* because can there be any other way of looking at this tragedy? It's more than a conspiracy. It's a conspiracy of angry women."

Savannah couldn't believe what she was hearing. "Is she kidding me? Is she seriously talking about us?"

Maggie was alert now, too. "What in the world?"

Maggie grabbed her glasses and read the news crawl at the bottom of the screen aloud. "'BREAKING NEWS: Minnesota twins caught in the middle of paternity mystery of their own mother's making.'"

Savannah, for a moment, couldn't decide what was more ridiculous—the assertion of malicious intent, or the fact that their story would be considered breaking news on this planet or any other.

"Hand me that." Savannah pointed at the remote and Nadine surrendered it. She flipped channels. Every cable news program seemed to be stuck in the same vortex.

Channel 813 asked viewers, "Paternity privacy pickle or podcasting stunt?" She didn't know what that meant and didn't stop to find out.

Channel 814 was giving uninterrupted camera time to the

hour's host—the woman with the blond hair and the cheek-bones, Kristian Caldwell. She was working herself up into a righteous glow over what she was calling an "angry feminist conspiracy." Savannah knew better than to stop and listen to whatever this woman had to spew, but she couldn't help herself.

"And hear me when I tell you—this outpouring of public sympathy for these McClair dupes, let's be honest here, folks, unduly glorifies the horrific choice made by their conspiring mother and grandmother all those years ago. Seventeen years, to be exact, that they could have been benefiting from getting to know their father, from gaining a balanced influence, a balanced perspective on life—female *and* male. Yes, she chose to keep these babies. *But at what cost?*"

Savannah's stomach lurched. She wanted to puke, then scream, then cry, and for sure laugh. What was happening? She was either going to have to break for the bathroom or tuck herself into a ball until she could function again. Luckily, Chef Bart saw what was happening and brought her a glass of water.

"Take slow sips," he said.

Maggie, meanwhile, was just getting started, fighting back as if all those talking heads could hear her. "Horrific choice? You're the horrific choice!" she hollered. "We don't see any outpouring of public sympathy. You don't know what you're talking about!"

Chef Bart clicked off the TV, and the room went blessedly silent.

Something awful was happening.

"I don't get it. The podcast is doing great." Savannah dropped her head and felt the world tilt. "Sam told us we're getting *mind-bending numbers*. They monitor all the chat rooms.

I mean, we know there are haters and trolls. But—is this because of our interview? They told us we did great."

Everything she'd said was true. They did have excellent audience numbers, and that always came with haters and trolls. But according to Sam, they had just as many, if not more, fans who cheered them on and wanted to help. Their interviewers pressed the hard questions, but never—

People must have misunderstood. These broadcasters couldn't be talking about them. Their tiny podcast couldn't be on cable news. The jump was too big.

Maggie pointed a finger at the dark screen like Kristian Caldwell was still there. "You," she said. "I see your game. You think you are the Red Queen."

Savannah shot a questioning look at Nadine, but then it hit her. The Red Queen. From *Alice in Wonderland*. The one who cried, "Off with their heads!" The one who said, "It is far better to be feared than loved."

Savannah didn't know what'd brought her and Thomas to the attention of the nation's cable news producers, but she did understand what Maggie was trying to say. The horrible fact that their story had been widely appreciated when it was about love and family and connection. But it took off when it became a story about anger.

Seconds later, the house phone rang, and Maggie picked it up to find Sam Tamblin on the other end.

"Hang on," she said. "Let me put you on speaker so Thomas and Savannah can both hear."

Savannah bolted out of the kitchen and up the first few stairs, hollering at Thomas to come quick.

"What?" he yelled back. "I'm trying to finish something!"

"I *mean it*! Come now!" Savannah heard her voice break, and she couldn't tell if she was excited or scared or both.

"This coverage is a harvest we have to reap," Sam said,

coming through the speakerphone. "We've got Saj in NYC working the gears on at least a dozen different angles right now. We need to be in front of this. Dale Earnhardting the debate."

Maggie asked him to back up and explain.

"The podcast has been gaining attention since its inception—which we knew—but this was a total turn of events. Bryce Sawyer. Big on talk radio. Turns out, his daughters listen to the podcast and talked about it at dinner one night. They'd also heard a bunch of Brynn's interviews. Next morning, Bryce does a full segment on the show's *incipient* dangers. That's the word. Incipient. Had to look it up. Anyway, *BOOM*! That's all it took. The jaws of the nation's top culture warriors snapped shut and now won't let go."

Sam's metaphor reminded Savannah of the stories Maggie always told them about her dog, Elga, catching squirrels and shaking them to death, then dropping their dead bodies at the door like offerings. *Oh god.* Were they the squirrels?

"Who is Sage?" said Maggie.

"Who?"

"You said there was a Sage in NYC."

"Oh, Saj. Pronounced like 'Madge.' She's our PR guru. Her name's really SaraJane but everyone calls her Saj. Like I said, she's taken this on personally. And that is *huge*. She's like a horse whisperer. Only better."

Savannah looked at Thomas, who raised a tentative eyebrow. He didn't seem to have any more idea what Sam was proposing than she did.

"So," Maggie continued, "you trust this Saj woman to manage something like this?"

"Manage? No. Exploit? Abso-freaking-lutely."

Savannah began to feel blobs of skepticism stick to her every thought, like the commercial illustrations of cholesterol in your bloodstream. All the excitement she'd felt following the first round of interviews was gone. This felt heavy, impossible and dark.

Maggie pressed the mute button and looked at them. "You don't have to agree to this, you know. You can keep going, just as you have been. Do the podcast without the publicity."

Thomas looked at Savannah, and she was surprised to see she'd misinterpreted him a moment ago. He was red and antsy, obviously coming to very different conclusions than she was. Angry to her wary.

"They're out there telling lies," he said. The words flew like he was spitting out poison.

"So? That's been happening all along. The trolls have been after us since we started." Given other circumstances, Savannah would have laughed, hearing herself. They sounded like characters in a fairy tale, twins being chased by the creature under the bridge. But this wasn't a story. The troll army really was on the loose and they were outnumbered. "No matter what we say, they're still going to hate us. Still going to believe they won."

"Maybe. But—" Thomas stopped, struggling for words. He wouldn't look at her. "We said we were never going to do anything that might make our dad think any less of us."

"We don't even know him yet!"

"Exactly! If we don't say anything, they'll be free to say anything! Trash us, trash him—" Again, he stopped short of a full thought.

Savannah felt an ever-escalating panic in her throat. Thomas wasn't going to back down.

"I get that," she said. "But what is Sam even proposing? I don't know what he wants us to do."

Maggie unmuted the line. "To confirm, Sam, you're proposing another interview?"

"A full slate of interviews," he said. "Take our version of the story to TV. Saj can set 'em up and prep you here."

"In New York?" Savannah asked.

Thomas rolled his eyes at her question. "That's where all the cable networks are."

She glared at him. "I'm just checking."

"Yeah," said Sam. "Here in the city."

Maggie pressed the mute button. "Thoughts?"

"I don't think we have a choice," said Thomas. "We have to do it."

Savannah stopped herself before answering. She didn't want to contradict Thomas out of habit. That had always been their game—if one argued green, the other couldn't help arguing orange. Even so, there was some truth in what he was saying. Stories are shaped by the ones who tell them. As a writer and aspiring storyteller, she knew that better than anyone.

But really, who was she to be out there? On national television, talking to broadcasters that normally reported on war and the economy and natural disasters. She was just a random teenage girl from Minnesota looking for her dad.

Last week at the library, she went to use the restroom and a woman actually asked her if she'd lost her mother. Like she was an eight-year-old who needed help reaching the sink.

"No, I'm seventeen," she'd answered. The woman blushed and hurried off, embarrassed, and the real irony, Savannah knew, was that she could have embarrassed the woman even more if she'd given the other truthful answer to her question. "Yes," she could have said. "I did lose my mother. When a chunk of concrete fell off the 46th Avenue bridge and crushed her."

But that was just it. She didn't have her mom anymore. And she hadn't died because she drank too much and drove into a tree, or never went to the doctor and got too sick to be cured, or even made a few bad choices that led to disaster. The engineer or the cement manufacturer or the construction crew—they were the ones to blame for what Savannah and Thomas were doing now. If they still had a mother, they probably wouldn't be here at all. Kristian Caldwell and Bryce Sawyer would've had to find other people to pick on.

She suddenly felt very, very small compared to what Sam had already told them was becoming *huge*. Her heart felt like ice. Her breath stopped in her throat. Her body was literally fighting the choice in front of her.

"Let's go," said Savannah, taking herself by surprise.

"You're certain?" said Maggie. "You know this could be rough. I believe you can handle it if you believe you can. But I want you to be sure."

Savannah looked at Thomas, whose agitation had somewhat calmed. He finally allowed his eyes to meet hers. "We have to do this, Van."

She nodded. He was right. This was what they had to do. "It's true. We have to tell our own story. We'll practice it. We'll get it just right. And when we tell it, people won't have any choice but to believe us."

Maggie unmuted the line and informed Sam of their decision.

"Fantasti-licious."

Savannah wondered what in the world they had just gotten themselves into.

*Thank you for calling the McClairs. Please leave a message. If you don't hear back, you know where to find us. Or just stop by for dinner. Chef Bart always makes enough for a crowd.*

*[BEEP]*

*You have thirty-nine new messages.*

*[BEEP]*

*Hello, McClair family. This is Jonathan Skriff from Channel Nine News, hoping to connect with you about all the attention your podcast has been getting lately. I see I've missed you, so I'll try back. If you are interested in doing a live interview, please call me, here are my details...*

*[BEEP]*

*Maggie. Thomas. Savannah. This is Audrey Bristol. I'm a reporter for the Minneapolis/St. Paul Standard. Listen, I'm doing a piece on the meteoric rise of your podcast and I'd like to hear your end of the story. At a minimum, I'd like to check a few facts with you. My number is...*

*[BEEP]*

*Maggie, it's Saj in NYC. Call me. We've got several interview opportunities to discuss. It's time to strategize. You have my contact info.*

*[BEEP]*

*Hello, McClairs! This is an exciting time for you. Congratulations. I know I'm probably not the only one calling you, but I am wildly interested in your story. And so is my audience. Let's get you all on the show. We'd love it. Avril Holton, of course, from At the Moment on MSNBC. I believe my producer, Ashley Cane, has already reached out. Let's do connect. You can find Ashley at...*

*[BEEP]*

*Mrs. McClair. This is Ashley Cane. I'm a producer on At the Moment with Avril Holton on MSNBC. I called earlier, and it seems I've missed you again. We would really love to speak with you. Avril loves your story. So does the At the Moment audience. I'll try back.*

*[BEEP]*

*Maggie, dear! It's Saj in NYC. Call me!*

*[BEEP]*

*Maggs. It's Sam Tamblin. My phone is blow-ing up. Time to strike! Has Saj been calling you? Let's connect ASAP.*

*[BEEP]*

*Maggie! Do you text? Sam didn't send me anything except your home phone. Need you! Text me! Call me! Send me a candygram! Just get in touch, please. It's Saj in NYC.*

*[BEEP]*

*Mrs. McClair, this is Theodore Sykes. I work with Kristian Caldwell as a producer. We'd very much love to speak with you. Get your side of things. We could do a one-on-one thing with Kristian or you could be a part of a panel. Whatever you feel more comfortable with. I'll call back in a bit. Or if you're just picking this up, here's the best way to reach me...*

*[BEEP]*

*Maggie, this is Kristian Caldwell. I know this must seem overwhelming to you, but I want you to consider one thing: Who's telling your side of the story? There's a vacuum out there about what your kids are trying to achieve, Maggie. If you don't fill that vacuum, other people will. I have a platform. Two and a half million viewers every night. They want to hear from you. No bias. Just you and me. Talking. Theodore will get in touch.*

*[BEEP]*

*Hi, this is Angie up at Hiawatha Cleaners. We've got your order done and I was just going through some back inventory and I think we've got a suede jacket up here that's yours, too. It's kind of pale pink? Anyway, come look at it when you stop in to pick up. The tag got mangled somehow but I think it says McClair on it and, heck, it's so cute and it just looks like something you'd wear, Maggie. Again, it's Angie. Up here at Hiawatha Cleaners.*

*[BEEP]*

# TWENTY

## JACK

Jack pulled up to his apartment and found a pint-sized menace sitting on the front porch.

"You ever gonna let me be yer deckhand, Jack?"

Carter Allman was the runt of his siblings, probably fourteen years old, but looking a lot younger than double digits. Jack had never been able to keep track of how many brothers and sisters Carter had. Except that it was a lot. They all called him "Deuce" because of the two patches in the back of his head where his brown hair had no color.

"You owe me, don' forget. On account o' me savin' yer life. Two times." Carter spoke with the honey-tongued mosey of life in the Georgia low country. His words didn't hurry, but they didn't leave you guessing, either.

"You didn't save my life. Just found me passed out, is all."

"An' about to sleep on through yer charters. I saved you money, at least."

"That you did. And I already thanked you. Two times."

It wasn't that Jack didn't want Carter as a deckhand, he just didn't want one, period. Another person to account for and plan for. And pay. Most boats had them, doing all the stuff for the clients the other captains didn't want to bother with anymore. But Jack didn't mind the baiting or the teaching or all the other gritty jobs. And anyway, he never took more than four people out at a time. And he didn't want more.

"Story hasn't changed since last time you asked. Don't need a deckhand. Don't want a deckhand."

He reached into the bed of the truck and pulled out his toolbox. He made the mistake of leaving it there overnight just once before finding out firsthand there was a hot market for stolen Snap-ons.

"Cap'n Slush says he's just waitin' fer you to mess up so he can take yer clients."

"Captain Slush can say what he wants. It's a free country." Jack shooed him out of the way so he could reach the front door.

"Cap'n Slush says no Yankee from the mountains knows saltwater fishin' anyhow."

Carter was behind him now, watching Jack pull the keys from his pocket. Funny how the kid who wanted a job so badly didn't offer to help with the forty-pound toolbox or the plastic grocery bag slowly tearing under its own weight in Jack's hand.

"Sounds to me like you really want to work for Captain Slush."

"He says I ain't big enough. And anyway, yer the only boat without a hand."

That was probably true. Jack popped the lock on the door and stepped through. Carter let the screen slam between them, but it didn't stop his talking.

"If it's money yer worried about, you don't have to pay me rate."

Jack was already around the corner in the kitchen putting the sandwich meat and beer he'd just bought into the refrigerator. "Get on now, Carter. You've got my answer."

"I'm not always gonna be this size. My gran'daddy din' grow 'til he was in the Army."

He was still talking when Jack walked over to the door and closed it.

He cracked open the beer he'd pulled from the six-pack

and dialed his voice mail. Told himself to get it over with. He almost never answered his cell phone when he was out with clients.

Voice Mail Lady announced *First message*.

"Hey, Junior. It's your mom. I'm just sitting here thinking about my boy and how much I miss him. You know you don't get home nearly enough, but you never listen when I tell you that, so I've quit saying it. Nothing much to report around here. Dad's still pretending he's strong enough to be out in the fields all day with Telo, and I keep telling him he's not. But you know him. Always thinks he's smarter than everyone else. Anyway. I hope you'll consider comin' home. You know I miss you."

Jack pressed seven for Delete without waiting for Voice Mail Lady to prompt him.

*Next message*, she said.

"Yeah, this is Josiah Phelps down at National Union Bank. I'm calling for John Thorson. I left you a message, last week I think it was. We've received yer application for the business loan, but we need a few more pieces of information from you. Call me back and hopefully we can get to workin' on this real soon."

He left a number and an extension, neither of which Jack wrote down.

He pressed seven for Delete.

And again, Voice Mail Lady announced *Next message*.

"Johnny, it's your mama again. I missss you and—" He hit seven and hung up as soon as he heard the first note of a slur. Given the time change, it was still midafternoon in Colorado, and it had been a few hours since the last message. Meaning, barely past lunchtime and his mother was already sloshed.

"Surprises never cease," he said to the lifeless phone.

His mother had probably always been a drinker, but he

didn't recognize the signs until he started showing them himself. As a kid, he rarely saw her take a drink, so how could he understand that the truth about her wasn't always what it looked like—maybe she was extra tired, or feeling talkative, or really was that proud of him. Maybe she just naturally felt lousy in the mornings. And yeah, it did stink that his dad was always out in the fields.

When Jack really thought about it, though, he knew he'd never seen any other kid's mom crying in the grocery store, never seen any of them knock over a stack of cans with her cart. And no other kid ever talked about the sheriff pulling their mom over to the side of the road and threatening to call her husband "again." The older he got, the more he knew that sort of stuff didn't happen to every kid.

He thought back to the night he'd started drinking, with his buddy from a stolen bottle of rye in his grandfather's barn. That was the night it became clear what his mother had been doing all those years. The rosy feeling, followed by the slurring, followed by the disconnect from gravity. Being drunk meant leaving yourself behind, and that made more sense to Jack than anything he'd ever known.

Now, he couldn't escape all the people begging for his attention. Carter was on his front porch every day, and that had been Ford's bank on his voice mail, trying to close on the offer Jack had made for the two remaining boats in Ford's fleet. Ford was trying to retire after forty-some years in the guiding business, and Jack was trying to help him.

The way Jack saw it, Ford had done more for him than his own father. Sounded cliché when he said it out loud, but it was true. The math alone proved it. He'd started as Ford's deckhand, and they'd spent twelve to fifteen hours a day together for ten years until Ford's brother died of lung cancer and Jack became a captain in his place. As a kid, Jack was lucky to see his father just once, at dinner, listening to him grunt and eat.

He made an offer on Ford's business because it was the only way he could think of to show his thanks. Problem was, he didn't have the money. It wouldn't be long before the bank exposed him, and Ford became just another name on the long list of people Jack chose to disappoint.

thorJJ1979@gmail.com
To: t.mcclair@guavamediausa.com
Re: Further info

Thomas and Savannah,
Thanks for emailing me back. I get why you'd want further
information from me, so here's more of what has me curious.

Thomas, in episode 6 you said you hadn't slept well
on account of lightning. Was it because your ears pop?
That's what happens to me.

Savannah, in episode 2, Thomas said you can't wear
flip-flops. I can't wear them, either. Is it because you have
really shallow webbing between your toes and it's hard to
grip the sandal? That's my problem, anyway.

I won't make this as long as my last email. But I do want
you to know that I really hope you find your dad. And I
hope he's a good guy. Every kid deserves good parents,
but not every kid gets them.

Even if I'm wrong about the lightning and the flip-flop
thing, would you mind letting me know? This has me sort
of preoccupied lately. Hope that doesn't make me sound
crazy again.

Jack Thorson

———

t.mcclair@guavamediausa.com
To: thorJJ1979@gmail.com
Re: Further info

Jack,
I can't believe you guessed right about the lightning.

Though I suppose it's not guessing when it happens to you, too. Mine's more of a vertigo sensation, that's how the doctor explained it anyway. But I can see how you'd call it a pop.

Can you eat cheese?

Thomas McClair

———

thorJJ1979@gmail.com
To: t.mcclair@guavamediausa.com
Re: Further info

Thomas,
I can eat some cheese. Not ice cream, though.
Jack

# TWENTY-ONE

## SAVANNAH

A few days after Savannah and Thomas became national news, Saj had a car waiting at LaGuardia to take the Mc-Clairs to Guava Media's headquarters in midtown. They sat three-across in the back, with Maggie in the middle. Savannah put her forehead to the window and whispered, "This is so wild." She meant all of it—The City, capitalized. History and future. Grime and glitter. Destitution and destiny.

To distract herself from her nerves, she'd spent the morning researching. Now she had landmarks to watch for. If their driver took the Queensboro Bridge, she'd be able to see the sign for Silvercup Studios where Cherien Dabis produced *Quantico*, Tina Fey produced episodes of *30 Rock* and Dawn DeKeyser produced *Ugly Betty*. If they went farther south to the Manhattan or Brooklyn Bridge, she might just get a glimpse of Steiner Studios from the Brooklyn-Queens Expressway, where Amy Sherman-Palladino—her writer god and showrunner hero—produced *The Marvelous Mrs. Maisel*.

The Statue of Liberty was somewhere down there, too.

Their driver took the Queensboro Bridge. And by the time they'd reached Guava Media's office, Savannah's head swirled, trying to take everything in.

The driver dropped them outside Saj's building and the McClairs walked into the lobby, all of it framed by floor-to-ceiling glass. They found the elevators and rode to the nineteenth floor. Saj was waiting for them.

"Welcome, McClairs!" Saj was itty-bitty, even shorter than

Savannah—and half as thick. Manhattan fashionable but like a bouquet of helium balloons might carry her away. When Savannah returned her hug, she worried she'd heard something snap.

"Do all of these people work for you?" she asked Saj. The office bustled with an army of twenty-somethings, and she laughed as if Savannah had just asked if the cell phone in her hand could also make coffee.

"No! Oh my god, that's so precious. No, this is a coworking space." Saj hugged her again for a reason Savannah didn't quite understand. "It's midtown. Meh. An absolute migraine. But I have to be here. I mean, of course, right?"

She phrased the last part not so much as a question, but as a chance to nod and agree. So, Savannah did.

"Anyway," Saj continued, "I've reserved a conference room for the whole day. Sam will join us. Lunch is coming at one." She turned to Savannah and Thomas. "Salads okay? I had them throw a couple of turkey sandwiches in, too, just in case. And Sam's roast beef. He's such a Neanderthal."

This was the first they'd met Saj in person, but she'd made clear from their very first call that she wasn't one to waste any time. They'd hardly set their bags in the conference room when she got to work.

"The schedule!" she said, passing each of them a printed spreadsheet of venues, interviewers, arrival times, segment lengths and a column titled *Key Messages*.

"Our number one goal is this—humanize, personalize, sympathize."

Savannah stopped herself from pointing out that was actually three goals.

"So far, the media has been characterizing you in a vacuum. To one side, you're champions of free speech. To the other, you're pawns in a manipulative scheme."

"And privacy advocates don't know what to make of us,"

Savannah added. "On the one hand, we're accused of invading a man's privacy. On the other hand, they get stuck when they come up against the first amendment and our right to information as a form of free speech."

Saj nodded. "And?"

The curtness of her response made the words stop in Savannah's throat. "Well, I mean—" Was Saj agreeing? Or telling Savannah she was wrong?

"Was there something I missed?" Saj prompted.

Savannah dropped her gaze, pretending to study a spot on her pants even though she really hoped her hair would fall in front of her face and hide the blush. "Um, I think maybe the privacy crowd? Should we address them?"

"Yes," Saj answered. "By looking beautiful and innocent."

Thomas and Maggie laughed just as a man of small stature wearing a pinched smile and curiously tight pants walked through the door.

"Sam Tamblin is in the hiz-ouse!"

Thomas had been right—Sam Tamblin did have a beard. A sparse, tangly one, but it qualified.

"Sam, great," Saj said. "I just started to explain the strategy."

"Listen to this lady, folks. She's the prez of press." He took a seat and scanned the room, the intensity of his radiant blue eyes matched only by the manic twiddling of his fingers.

Saj grabbed a marker and walked to the whiteboard at the front of the room. "Name the things people love to watch on YouTube. Seriously, just shout 'em at me."

"Cat videos, obviously," said Savannah, unable to resist her earlier urge to never speak again.

"Talking babies," said Thomas.

"Don't forget them puppies," added Sam Tamblin.

Saj started a list on the board. It took less than a minute to arrive at her destination.

"Puppies and babies." Saj wrote the words in enormous

letters and circled them wildly. "People can't resist them. They're cute and innocent and unexpected."

She dropped the marker into its tray and came back to the table. "You two need to become as lovable to America as puppies and babies."

"Word," Sam Tamblin confirmed.

Judging from the way Maggie began to squirm, though, she wasn't convinced. "You have *got* to be kidding me."

"Not in the least," answered Saj. "Because here's the bottom line—these two aren't advocating anything. They're not the Parkland students standing up to demand a change in gun laws. They're not—" She snapped her fingers. "Who was that woman who accused that senator of stalking her?"

*Too many to count*, Savannah wanted to say.

"Anyway. You're not trying to *change* anything. You're simply looking for your biological father. Problem is, you've caught the attention of the media, which not coincidentally, is controlled by very rich and equally powerful men. And you, my friends, have become a threat—to people who turn their cameras on others because they very much do not want them turned on themselves."

Saj paused to take a hummingbird-size sip of water from a crystalline mug, and Sam Tamblin took it as an excuse to jump in. "I told you this one was a smarty." He hooked a thumb toward Saj.

"This isn't a privacy issue, or a free speech issue, or a women's rights issue," she went on. "It's a fear issue."

Saj paused for effect, and amazingly, it worked. Savannah knew she was way less naive about the media industry than the average seventeen-year-old, but it hadn't hit her until just that second that men's power and money brought so much more than the ability to green-light projects.

"As long as the media can keep people afraid of you, that plays to their advantage. That keeps them in control of the issue. But—and this is a big one—we live in a world that heaps billions of dollars a year on a little company called Disney. That's consumer power. Our money is our vote. And we Americans throw heaps of cash at Disney for one very simple reason—we love a good Beauty and the Beast story."

She raised an eyebrow and looked at them. "We adore it when love overcomes fear. And you—" She pointed at Savannah and Thomas. "The media has made you out to seem scary, like Beast. But we're going to make America fall in love with you anyway, just like Beauty does."

Savannah recognized from Saj's tone that she'd expected this to translate into an *Aha!* moment for all three McClairs. Instead, Thomas said, "I thought you said we were puppies."

Saj gave him the same *aren't you precious* laugh she'd given Savannah in the lobby. "Exactly. Innocent. Nothing to fear. Worthy of our fascination and love."

Neither Savannah nor Thomas said anything, but sat, staring at each other.

"It's like the beetle costume all over again," Savannah said finally.

Thomas laughed. "Let's hope not."

The reference went all the way back to second grade when their class performed a play called *Farmer Friendly's Garden*, which was basically an excuse for parents to watch their children sing songs about vegetables while dressed as pea pods and tomatoes. To maximize fairness, their teacher, Mrs. Lace, drew each student's role from a hat. Thomas was cast as a carrot, Savannah as a beetle.

"I don't want to be a dirty old beetle!" She wailed all through dinner and all through baths. She wailed through homework time. And she was still at it when it came time for bedtime books.

Finally, her mother set whatever favorite Judy Blume book

they were reading aside and rubbed her back. "Savannah. I know beetles aren't pretty, but they are powerful. They drive away other pests and keep their garden fertilized. Wouldn't you rather be powerful than pretty?"

Savannah stopped crying, sat up and looked directly at her mom. "Why should I have to choose?"

Now here they were again. Given the choice between being beautiful or being strong.

Savannah was still in her head when Thomas asked, "What about Maggie? Shouldn't she be with us in the interviews?"

For the first time all morning, Saj took a seat. "We feel it's best you do the interviews on your own." She turned to Maggie. "We will craft a statement of support from you, Maggie, but we want the optics to be two kids, without a mother, looking for their father. That's the *sympathize* part of the strategy."

Savannah realized she'd never even considered that Maggie wouldn't be a part of the interviews. They'd done everything else on their own, but this was another creature entirely. It was TV. Prime time. And people seemed to hate them for real.

"Maggs," Sam asked. "Whatcha wanna do?"

"You're both capable of this," Maggie said, meeting their eyes. "But I obviously want you to trust your instincts. If you want me there, I'll be there." She did not break her gaze until they answered.

Thomas said, "You'll be backstage, right?"

Maggie nodded.

Savannah took a beat longer, then said, "No one ought to expect you to prove that you love us." She'd intended that as more opening statement than final answer, but Saj took it as a decision and handed them each a spiral-bound packet with a clear plastic cover. The title page read, "Savannah and Thomas McClair. July 17th. Messaging."

She had no choice but to get to work.

t.mcclair@guavamediausa.com
To: thorJJ1979@gmail.com
Re: Further info

Jack,
What about school? Were you a good student? Did you go to college? What did you study?

Thomas McClair

———

thorJJ1979@gmail.com
To: t.mcclair@guavamediausa.com
Re: Further info

Thomas,
When I was a kid, school was easy. Mainly because I grew up in a small town and my graduating class had 43 kids. I did go to college for a few years, though. I think I may have mentioned that. I studied engineering at the University of Northern Colorado. That ended pretty quick.
    Are you thinking about college?

Jack

———

t.mcclair@guavamediausa.com
To: thorJJ1979@gmail.com
Re: Further info

Jack,
Definitely. Hoping to, at least. I think my chances are pretty

good. My grades are decent, mostly As. Savannah's are better. She wants to be a Hollywood producer, but you probably already know that from listening to the podcast.

I've thought about engineering, since I'm pretty into electronics. Sound engineer, maybe? The guidance counselor at school is supposed to help us figure out what schools would be a good match for our interests but my counselor didn't even know what I meant when I mentioned sound engineering. But we've got a whole studio in our basement and I designed most of it. Maggie calls it our cave. What kind of engineering did you study?

Thomas McClair

————

thorJJ1979@gmail.com
To: t.mcclair@guavamediausa.com
Re: Further info

Thomas,
I guess if I'd made it further I would have ended up in mechanical engineering. I'm pretty good at taking things apart and getting them back together again. I have to do that a lot in my work. I'd tell you not to listen to your counselor, but I don't want to sound like I'm giving you any advice. So instead I'll just say, in my experience, it's best not to let people who are stuck in the past determine your future.

You can ignore that last part if you want to.

Jack

# TWENTY-TWO

## JACK

Jack was bringing in a group of four clients on his boat when he spotted Carter standing on the landing, waiting for him. The clients had hired Jack because they'd heard he was especially good at catching redfish, and he'd proven his reputation by helping them take in their daily limit within just a few hours.

That was good luck for Carter, too, since Jack was about to put him to work filleting every last fish.

"How'd you get yourself out here?" Jack called. He grabbed the bowline closest to him and tossed it to Carter on the landing. He nodded toward the cleat he wanted him to tie up on. "You can't bike all the way to the landing from your house."

"Can, so." Carter wrapped the line into a perfect hitch, then waited for Jack to toss the spring line. "But I caught a ride with Ford. He was here lookin' for you, but he's gone an' left. I said I'd stay 'til you came back."

Ford being at the landing made sense. But Ford looking for Jack while knowing he'd be out with clients? And Ford picking up Carter along the way? That didn't.

"Say what he wanted me for?" Once they were docked, Jack handed off the first of the ice-packed coolers.

Carter took it. "I asked if it was on account o' something you done, but he said it wasn't none of my business. And anyhow, he said you'd know, yerself."

Carter grabbed the next cooler and hollered over his shoulder at the disembarking foursome. "C'mon. I'll show yeh where we clean these."

Jack noted his use of "we." Couldn't accuse the kid of being a pushover.

He grabbed the last cooler and hauled it onto the dock and went back to tie the stern line. He tested his hitch, then the ones Carter had tied. He already owed Ford enough. Last thing he needed to do was lose one of his fleet.

When the boat was emptied and rinsed, he checked on Carter, who was up to his elbows in redfish guts. "These'r easy. It's the sheepshead I hate."

Jack glanced into the cooler. Half of the catch was already cleaned.

"Impressive." He grabbed a fish for himself. No client of Ford's ever went home without every bit of their catch ready to cook and eat, no matter how hard it was raining or how many fish you'd already cleaned or how tired you were at the end of the day. Filleting the catch was nonnegotiable.

He nudged Carter over a few inches to make room for himself.

"I thought maybe Ford was lookin' fer you 'cuz that guy who's been askin' around."

"Asking around about what?"

"'Bout you. Where you live an' such. He ain't asked me yet, but I heard Sandra Beals talkin' 'bout it down at the daiquiri stand. Said the guy was real curious."

A curious stranger asking around town about Jack. That didn't sound like anything the bank would be up to. He tore into his fish with his knife, almost slashing his palm open along with it. "Heard anything else about him?"

"Nah." Carter tossed a fresh fillet onto the ice and grabbed another fish. "Sandra Beals thought maybe you had a friend or family come to stay. But I told her no way. I ain't seen Jack with no one lately."

Carter ripped his blade down the fish's belly, swift and precise, then looked at Jack. "How come I never see you with no one these days? And why don' you date none?"

"I date." That's just what Jack needed—a kid who wasn't even old enough to drive giving relationship advice.

"No you don't."

"How do you know what I do or don't do?"

"I know on account o' I ain't seen you with no woman since you was with Lizzie Drummond. An' she's been gone from Tybee least two years."

Jack hushed him. He tossed a ragged fillet on ice and saw that the cooler was nearly full. The kid was outcleaning him two-to-one.

"May not seem like it now, but two years is only a long time when you're thirteen."

"I turned fourteen last month."

Jack didn't respond, hoping instead to let the conversation die. Point was, there wasn't anyone on Tybee he wanted to date, and he liked it that way. No questions. No demands. Until just a few days ago, he'd hoped to buy out Ford and then mind his own business. Figuratively and literally.

They were on the last of the fish when Carter said, "You know Sandra Beals said she'd marry you."

Jack resisted the urge to roll his eyes, forcing himself to focus so he didn't cut his finger off. "Sandra Beals is hardly old enough to own that daiquiri stand, let alone get married."

"Well yer practically ancient. An' you ain' got no family or kids or nothin'."

Jack dropped his knife and looked at the kid. He had a family. A messy, drunk, unhappy one, but a family. And now he likely *did* have kids.

All these people thinking they were entitled to an opinion. Same on Tybee as it had been in Hartwell and Breckenridge. No town different from any other when it came to nosing in other people's business. A hot flash of anger raced through him, making him sweat.

"Finish up." He reined in the urge to bark at the kid and took a deep breath. Wasn't Carter's fault he didn't know any different. Wasn't his fault Jack had a stranger on his tail. "Get these fillets over to the guys' trucks and I'll give you a ride home."

He had to get out of the sun.

t.mcclair@guavamediausa.com
To: thorJJ1979@gmail.com
Re: Further info

Jack,
I don't know if you work all day or whatever, but I thought I'd let you know that we're going to do a bunch of TV interviews on Friday. Morning shows, mostly. I don't exactly know, sorry. Just thought I'd tell you in case you're interested in watching.

Thomas

———

thorJJ1979@gmail.com
To: t.mcclair@guavamediausa.com
Re: Further info

Thomas and Savannah,
Wow, that's amazing. You're going to be on TV. Thanks for letting me know. I'll try to find a way to watch. Good luck.

Jack

———

t.mcclair@guavamediausa.com
To: thorJJ1979@gmail.com
Re: Further info

Jack,
Thanks. I don't know what you've seen or heard, but we've

sort of been all over the news lately. Anyway, don't worry. We're not going to out you or, whatever. The attention is just getting kinda out of hand.

Thomas

————

thorJJ1979@gmail.com
To: t.mcclair@guavamediausa.com
Re: Further info

Thomas,
Are you and Savannah ok?

# TWENTY-THREE

## SAVANNAH

Her mother was sitting there again, on the corner of Savannah's bed.

"Did I make you come visit?" Savannah asked.

Her mother smiled.

"I wish you'd visit more often. Every night, even."

Her mother's hair was perfect. Wavy but not wild. Brown without the gray.

"I guess I know why you're here now."

No wrinkles. Or maybe a few. The ones around her eyes when she smiled. The ones Savannah wanted to trace with her finger.

"At least I hope I do."

Her smile was all she said, and it warmed Savannah as it always did. Filled her chest with knowing.

"Thank you, Mommy. I miss you so much."

She was there until Savannah woke.

It was the morning of their big day of interviews, and Savannah was calm. Her mother had ensured that for her.

Thomas, Savannah, Maggie, Saj and even Sam Tamblin made it to the studio by their 6:00 a.m. call time and the day began in earnest. Hair. Makeup. Talking points review.

"This is the worst part, the sitting and waiting backstage," Saj said. "Once you get onto the set, it's much easier. For starters, you'll see how small the set is. That will help with your nerves."

"Like a hobbit house," said Sam Tamblin. "Only people sized."

Savannah bit down on her lip and took a sudden interest in her fingernails, knowing if she caught Thomas's eye, there'd be no way to keep from laughing.

Saj broke the moment for them. She touched a hand to Savannah's stylist, stopping her mid style. "Can we try her hair up?"

The stylist mumbled a crude reply that made Savannah snicker.

Unfazed, Saj continued. "Ignore the cameras. Ignore the lights. Just keep your eyes on the interviewer and let yourself engage. Remember, it's a conversation." She held up a copy of the messaging strategy. "With a few very important points to make!"

Savannah looked in the mirror. Besides her hair looking lopsided halfway pinned up, she didn't appear anxious. She wasn't frowning or wrinkling her nose. She wasn't flushed. Her heart raced in her chest, but not in the way that made her stomach want to follow.

She finally looked at Thomas. *How are you?* she mouthed.

He wasn't looking so calm, starting with the red that had all but swallowed the freckles on his cheeks. *Nervous*, he mouthed back.

Not ideal. Savannah didn't want to have to carry his weight again. He'd choked halfway through their last interview, and she'd had to step in. Yesterday on the plane she asked what the chances were of him doing that again, and all he'd said was, "Shut it, Van."

Now it struck her. Maybe their mother had known. Thomas was nervous and Savannah needed to be ready. Maybe that's why she'd come to visit.

A woman in a headset appeared at the door. "McClairs up next," she said to the room.

"We're ready!" Saj chirped, while simultaneously flicking at Savannah's stylist again. "No time to finish. Take it down!"

A minute or so later, headset woman hustled Savannah and Thomas onto the set, and the first interview began.

"Well, you two have made quite a splash!" The woman sitting on the couch across from them had blond hair that fell to her boobs and legs long enough to stretch into the next room. Her male cohost diverted attention from his balding head with a giant neon-toothed smile.

"What's next for you guys?" he laughed. "Finding the real D. B. Cooper?"

The woman smacked his knee and put on her serious face. "This is quite a personal journey for you, though, isn't it? Tell us how you decided a podcast would be the best way to go about your search for your father."

Savannah glanced at Thomas, who looked ready to bolt from the couch and hide. *Good grief.*

"Well, at first, we wanted to reach as wide an audience as possible," she started. "But as the search got underway, we realized we also wanted people to get to know our mother. At least enough to understand how wonderful she was."

"Why don't you tell us about her."

"I'd love to." As Savannah answered the question, she followed Saj's advice to keep smiling, no matter what. "Most importantly, Mom taught us to think for ourselves, to reach for our dreams. She'd say, 'You have everything you'll ever need, way down deep inside. Sometimes, you just have to dig.' She was always our biggest cheerleader."

"So, you believe she'd support your search?" the woman asked.

Savannah answered, "Absolutely. We *know* she does." Because Savannah did know, in her heart, in her whole being. She'd been reminded again last night.

She also knew, however, that these were only the windup questions. The tougher ones would come next. Her stomach knotted.

First, the interviewer broached the privacy issue.

"The podcast, though. There are so many stories of people finding their biological parents through DNA tests and genealogy sites. Why not use tools that don't present such privacy concerns?"

Thomas finally found his voice and jumped in. "I'll admit, that was my preference at first, too," he said. "I love science. But, where I love all that stuff, Savannah is a storyteller, and she pointed out that a DNA test wouldn't teach us anything about our mother. About her life before us."

Savannah added, "Mom would have answered our questions herself—she was always open with us. But we never got the chance to ask them. With the podcast, we can unfold a richer story than data alone can tell."

The woman nodded, smiling as if she agreed with all her heart. Then she said, "And yet you're doing this so publicly. Do you ever worry you're exposing other children to risk? What if you find that your father has a family of his own?"

And there it was, the trigger question—the one specifically designed to make it clear to viewers this wasn't any common fluff piece. This, Savannah realized, is where Saj's *humanize, personalize, sympathize* strategy had come from.

"Counter every defensive question by going on charm offensive," Saj had said before drilling the skill of the "charm pivot" into them. They'd practiced with question after question.

Savannah smiled at the interviewer. "Our mom used to say, 'More than anything, remember to be kind.' We hope our father—or any father listening to the podcast, really—would be proud of how we're trying to honor her advice."

"And if he is raising kids of his own," Thomas continued, "we hope he sees that we haven't lied or stretched the truth to fit our story. We don't curse or make nasty insinuations. We ask honest questions, but we don't believe it's fair to shame anyone…"

Thomas paused, and turned his face directly into the camera. The woman interviewing them cocked her head, waiting for him to finish. But he didn't. He just stared. Stuck, or confused, or trying to push something down that was threatening to break out.

The woman was about to interject when he snapped to.

"A-anyway," he stammered, regaining his footing. "It's not about fame or attention. It's about finding our roots. We hope that if our father is still alive and learns about us, he'll be proud to know us."

Savannah saw Saj offstage, grinning and punching at the air. Savannah, though, was still stuck on Thomas's weird glitch.

"What about the risk, however?" The interviewer hadn't taken the charm pivot bait. "What if you expose him publicly against his will?"

Thomas answered, sounding calmer. "Our policy is to never broadcast any identifiers that verge on the invasive. From the very beginning, we've aimed to conduct ourselves in a way that invites our biological father to reach out. We have no interest in outing him publicly. And if that happens, it will be because of others. Because of people with questionable intent."

"Are you asking people to back off?" Savannah was surprised to see this was the male cohost asking the question since, so far, he hadn't made any contribution but jokes. "Are you asking people to respect your father's privacy, if he's out there?"

Savannah leaned in and smiled, just as Saj had taught. "We are asking people to follow the lead we've set," she said. "Ask honest questions. Invite connection. Stay away from shaming."

The woman added that was a lesson everyone could take to heart, before thanking them for coming and telling viewers interested in listening to the podcast how to find it.

*And, we're out.*

# TWENTY-FOUR

## JACK

"Jack! You in there? What the hell you gone and done?"
Whoever had come to visit didn't wait for an answer. Not that it mattered. They could just go on and do whatever they were gonna do. And anyway, he didn't think he could get up off the floor.

He heard the screen door open and then slam shut. He heard the crunch of glass underfoot. He heard a pair of boots stop near his head.

He strained to sort his muddled head, trying to remember. He tasted beer. But the ground beneath him was steady, not spinning. He was home. And alone. And...

*Right.*

He opened one eye onto familiar weather-beaten pants.

"You do all this yourself?" he heard Ford say. "Or is there someone I gotta go chase down for you?"

Jack groaned and spit a piece of—*what?*—from his mouth. "Nah."

"You want to explain why your bathroom door is half-off its hinges then?"

"They found me." His throat felt like he'd been eating razors. "Them and him. All of 'em." He knew he wasn't making any sense, nor did he care.

Ford didn't respond. Instead, he walked across the room and returned with a towel. "Sit up." He knelt and pulled Jack half-upright against the side of the couch. "Put this on your arm. Yer bleedin'."

Sure enough, Jack looked down to find a gash across his

forearm. If he remembered right, he'd caught it on a broken beer bottle stuck down between the couch cushions. He held the towel to his arm, feeling it throb, thinking he'd got what he deserved.

"Doesn't look like you're in good enough shape to talk any," said Ford.

Seemed pretty obvious.

"Anything else bleedin'?"

He didn't think so.

"And yer sure there weren't anyone else responsible."

Jack swore there wasn't.

"All right then. Sleep it off. Take a shower. Make sure you show up on time for your morning charter." Ford walked across the room, ran the sink and returned once more. He handed Jack a glass of water. "I'm leavin' for Atlanta in the morning. I'll be gone a few days, but at least that'll be enough time for you to get yer head back on straight. When I get back, though, we've got business to discuss."

Jack felt his stomach turn and prayed he could keep everything down until Ford left. As soon as the screen door slammed shut, he balled back up on the only patch of floor not covered in glass and tried to do the math on how he'd gotten there.

It wasn't Thomas's fault, all this mess. But it had started with him. They'd been on a roll, emailing and answering within minutes. Almost normal. As if they weren't perfect strangers sitting in front of screens hundreds of miles apart. And the similarities. That kid's brain worked just like his. It wasn't enough to just call them both analytical. Jack could guess what Thomas was going to ask next.

Back and forth and again. Every day after work. Talk about college. And baseball. And Savannah. And Bess. It gave him something, those emails. Made the days on the water shorter, his charter clients less aggravating. The kid, even in electronic form, was good company.

Tonight, he'd stopped at Chen's Quick Shop on his way home from the landing. He planned to eat, shower off the day's salty grime and check his email. He bought a six-pack of Coors and a frozen pizza. Sara Chen rang him up and gave him a hard time for never eating anything healthy. He grabbed a banana from the basket of overpriced fruit they kept at the register.

Then he spotted the man raising a camera at him from behind the cardboard MoonPie display.

Carter's warning exploded through his thoughts. *"There's a guy been askin' around 'bout you."*

Jack grabbed his food and sprinted for his truck, nearly killing the engine as he threw the gear into Drive. He didn't think the camera guy had time to follow him, but he took every wrong turn possible between the Quick Shop and his apartment, just in case. He covered half the island, turning left and right, always keeping east of Highway 80, where the summer tourists would be clogging the crosswalks on their way to the beach, dragging traffic to a crawl.

He kept going for several minutes, south, then west toward the raised houses along Tybee Creek, and east again into the small nook of subdivided cement bungalows where his apartment was. He passed his driveway and parked on the street a block away, then hauled his beer, frozen pizza and his forty-pound toolbox up the road, Peter Rabbit–like, through the hole in old man Frederick's gardenia bushes and over Mrs. Truesdale's sagging backyard fence. He stopped just before turning the corner to his front door. He needed to catch his breath—his lungs were burning from the overloaded sprint—and sneaked a glance at the street. No sign of anyone. Not even Carter.

As if he weren't already on edge from his surprise at the Quick Shop, his water heater was on the fritz and he'd had to take a cold shower. He burned his pizza, and then his tongue, and washed it all down with lukewarm beer. Everything was suddenly wrong—cold was hot was cold.

At least there was an email from Thomas.

**We've sort of been all over the news lately. Didn't know if you'd seen any of it.**

So, they'd be on TV. That was great for them, no? Savannah had Hollywood goals. And Thomas must have found all the studio equipment interesting. Getting on the news meant the podcast was getting noticed.

Except. He was the guy they were looking for on that podcast. The guy a lot of people suddenly seemed to be looking for—his cold existence becoming suddenly hot. He took a long swig of his beer and rubbed at the patch of sand or dirt he'd missed on his face during his icy shower. Then kept reading.

**We're not going to out you or, whatever. The attention is just getting a little out of hand.**

What did that even mean, *a little out of hand*? He didn't watch the news and, most days, he didn't care. Then again, what did Thomas mean? Were he and Savannah in trouble? Getting hassled?

The realization hit him head-on: if he knew this kid the way he was starting to believe he did, he knew this was Thomas's idea of a warning.

The beer went sour on his tongue.

**We're not going to out you or, whatever.**

Jack had done enough living in his forty years to know that promises and outcomes didn't always match up. Keeping his life private might not be up to them. He was already on the radar of at least one guy with a camera.

Even so, the sentiment was enough to calm him, and he took a moment to think before he answered Thomas's email.

**Are you and Savannah ok?**

It was all he wrote because he knew, with swift clarity, that was all he cared about.

He clicked Send without allowing himself to rethink his choice and sat back in his chair. He'd said it. It was out there. They knew how he felt.

And then...

Thomas didn't answer.

Nothing.

Silence.

All Jack could do was sit, waiting. The accumulating beer bottles counted the hours for him as they passed.

That was the problem with waiting. For Jack, waiting always turned to thinking, and thinking turned to another drink. And finally, after enough beer, he realized, *this is total shit*. There he was, hanging on, staring at an unchanged screen like some sucker, hoping to hear from a kid he didn't know and hadn't cared about.

As if Thomas was his responsibility.

As if Jack should even care whether he'd freaked the kid out or pissed him off.

Or if he was even for real.

**The attention is just getting kinda out of hand.**
**We're not going to out you or, whatever.**

Jack sat, trapped in a mental spin cycle that wouldn't quit. Finally, he did the only thing that made sense.

**You know what, kid? Forget this. Leave me out of whatever mess the two of you have gotten yourselves into and have a nice life.**

He clicked Send, then picked up his computer and threw it against the wall. He didn't have to think about those kids for one more second.

The sound of the glass shattering was incredible. It rang in the air like rain. Drops of rain on the concrete in the middle of a steamy afternoon. He wanted more—and he did it again. This time, a beer bottle. Then another. Then his plate with half a piece of pizza still left on it. And his water glass.

He would've thrown himself through a window if he could have managed it.

The sound of the glass wasn't enough anymore, so he scanned the room for something bigger. Something heavy. Something he'd have to dig deep to manage. He considered his kitchen chairs, two pieces of mismatched seventies crap he'd scooped off the street corner on trash day. But they'd only hit the wall with a thud.

Jack wanted more.

Looking around, he finally saw his tiny apartment for the shit hole it was. Cracked linoleum and a wobbly table covered in maps and manuals and bills. A stained couch he slept on most nights without bothering to pull it open for the bed inside. The only things worth stealing in the whole place were his TV and VCR and they hadn't been worth stealing since sometime back in the nineties.

And now glass and broken shit everywhere.

He picked up the burled oak coffee table he'd bought at a yard sale for two dollars, wrangled it over his head and threw it. Hard. Gave it everything he could, because he was pissed off, and because it was the only thing he had left to destroy. The table smashed a hole the size of a garbage can into the bathroom door and crashed to the floor. If he'd been thinking, he would have thrown that through the front window, instead.

One more regret to add to his list.

# TWENTY-FIVE

## SAVANNAH

The interviews went on the same way for three hours, the whole morning show lineup. Into the station, up the elevator, into makeup for a touch-up, and into the greenroom to wait. Thankfully, other than his weird, deer-in-the-headlights moment during the first interview, Thomas was mostly holding up his half of the work.

At nine-thirty, they all took a brief food break. Thomas swallowed two whole bagels with cream cheese and Savannah debated whether to try lox, but ultimately thought better of stuffing her face with fish just before going on TV. She was exhausted, ready to crawl into a hole and not come out.

That didn't stop her phone from buzzing.

OMG!!!!!! I've totally been watching you all morning!! YOU ARE KILLING IT!!

Tell them to put better lipstick on you

Savannah was about to ask what color when Saj swept them into the elevator and out of the building.

As soon as they reached the street, Sam Tamblin announced he had an appointment across town and wouldn't be going along to their final appearance. "Make me proud," he told them. Then he ushered the four of them into a waiting town car and waved goodbye from the sidewalk.

Saj barely seemed to notice his absence and carried on talking, unabated. She described the last interview as a chatty midmorning panel show aimed at stay-at-home moms and retired women.

"This one is a good way to end, energy-wise," she said. "I know you're getting tired of the same questions. But this is a panel. Which means more interplay between the panelists, and you won't have to be on, on, on. You can relax and enjoy it. Laugh at their jokes. Be your kid-next-door selves."

Savannah sort of knew this show, in that she'd accidentally watched it on days she was home sick from school. Saj said she booked it because she knew the panel was likely to lean heavily on the "innocent kids stuck in a mess they didn't create" angle, and that the sympathy it generated would play well with the mostly female audience.

"Moms love you," she said.

"Not all moms love us," Savannah argued. "Brynn's a mom. And she hates us."

"Actually, Brynn's had quite a bit of radio exposure, thanks to this. I would venture she loves you a lot more than she lets on."

Saj leaned over and smoothed a stray hair on Savannah's head. The morning's initial round of *hair up or hair down* debate was settled when her stylist added a few easy waves around her face.

"Well, even if I don't learn anything else from this whole experience," Savannah said, "I know that wearing my hair up makes me look like a corporate attorney. Yech."

Thomas and Maggie laughed, but not Saj, who said, "Actually, with hair as thick as yours, you'd be best off with a blunt-cut bob for a corporate attorney look."

The correction should have stung, but Savannah's heart was full—from the adrenaline, from surviving all but one last interview, from her mother's visit, still glowing through.

It just felt so good to talk about her. To have permission. It didn't take long for Savannah to learn that when your mom dies, nobody wants to acknowledge her ever again. Maggie and Thomas, of course. Nadine sometimes. But not other people. Not friends. They all had living parents who signed permission slips and attended softball games and annoyed their kids by yelling, "Love you!" out the car window in the school drop-off lane.

But once you lost your mom, you were in the Dead Parents Club, which meant nobody wanted to talk about their own parents because then they would remember your mom is dead.

"I have my mom's hair," Savannah told Saj. "You can probably tell from looking at Maggie."

Saj smiled. "You're like Kanga and Roo, the two of you."

"Except the cleft in my chin," said Savannah. "That's all mine."

Saj turned to Thomas and examined him. "You should keep your hair at a length where the wave just begins to curl. Any longer and it will look like a helmet. Any shorter and it will look unkempt. Where do you get your strawberry blond from?"

He shrugged. "We're not sure. Could be one of the missing links to my dad. My mom was tall, though, unlike Maggie and Savannah. I might get my height from her."

Saj tilted her head and considered the two of them. "You two amaze me. So alike and so different all at once."

The car pulled to a stop in front of the studio and they all piled out.

"A quick touch-up in makeup," said Saj, "and we're on. We're B block, I believe, unless something has changed."

The crash course in TV-speak taught them that "B block" meant they were appearing during the second segment. That meant no sitting around waiting—done and out.

*Finally.*

Savannah could hear the warm-up comedian preparing

the audience as they walked down the hallway at the back of the set. The makeup woman only needed to layer a little bit of concealer under Thomas's eyes, and a touch of gloss to Savannah's lips. As soon as she spun their chairs around and declared them ready, the segment producer appeared and announced they were up next.

"One quick change to today's panel," she said. "Our scheduled guest panelist canceled, so, seat five is Eaton Holmes today. She's a blogger and YouTube personality."

Savannah looked to Saj for a reaction, but she was buried face-first in her phone. By the time she looked up, the producer was leading them onstage.

The segment started just like all the others, but with a lighter midmorning touch. There were a few brief audio clips from the podcast and a mostly vanilla introduction.

Savannah was actually familiar with the panelist taking lead on the interview. Sasha Greer was a former reporter turned globe-trotting children's rights advocate with an incredible smile and an ability to make the khaki field jacket she was wearing look chic. She opened by saying, "Welcome, Savannah and Thomas. Tell us *everything*."

They laughed, just like they'd done four times already that morning. "Where do we begin?"

But they knew exactly where, and that was by talking about their wonderful mother.

Then they talked about striving for grace and professionalism in their search.

They asked the public to respect their father's privacy.

They accepted a few compliments about their bravery and maturity.

Then, they got their first question from Eaton Holmes.

"How do you address the evidence that you have, in fact, been in touch with your biological father but continue acting as if you have not? Anyone with a curious brain would be left wondering who's funding you."

*What?* The transition was so abrupt, Savannah didn't think she'd heard what she thought she'd just heard. There's no way Thomas would be in touch with their dad and not tell her. She looked at Thomas, but he was looking back at her with exactly the same confusion.

"No one is funding us," Savannah started. "I mean, it's a Guava Media podcast sure, but—"

Eaton didn't wait. "So, you deny your grandmother Maggie's connection to the feminist and antimen's rights activist, Lonya Day."

*Who the hell was Lonya Day?*

"I don't know who that is—"

"Because she was featured on your previous podcast, the *McClair Dinner Salon,* episode eight. The episode in which you discussed castrating men for sexual harassment. For even minor allegations."

"I—*what?*"

"It's online. People can listen to it right now if they want. They can also listen to episode twelve during which you argue for the complete feminist takeover of all media."

"I never—"

"Is that your goal, Savannah? A systematic dismantling of men's rights? But disguised as a personal quest for connection and family?"

Syllables. Suddenly, that's all there was. No words or sentences or thoughts. Just disjointed groups of syllables. And a woman snarling at Savannah through white teeth. And Thomas saying, "Whoa, hey, whoa."

Nothing real. Nothing to make sense of. Just jumbles and jumbles of sound.

And that knot in her stomach, twisting, twisting, twisting.

Finally, Sasha Greer broke in. "Easy there, Eaton. Let's not get off track—"

Okay, yeah. All right. Savannah could understand Sasha Greer. She'd get everyone to make sense again. She looked at the other panelists. The black woman with the gorgeously perfect skin. The Asian woman with purple tips in her hair. The Hispanic woman who looked like America Ferrera. They were all looking at Sasha Greer, too. This was going to be fine.

Everything was going to be fine.

Savannah looked at the studio audience. They were smiling. There was a woman in the front row wearing a #McClair-WonderTwins T-shirt.

She was laughing.

Then, Eaton again. "I'm asking honest questions of two people who, themselves, have built a public platform on doing the same. Asking honest questions. So, why won't you tell us who John James Thorson is?"

*Oh my god.* Those syllables added up to a very clear and understandable name.

She'd just said his name.

John James Thorson.

On air. For the whole world to hear.

But maybe Sasha Greer would move on. Distract. Maybe if they moved on right this second, they could salvage it. No one really heard what they thought they'd heard, and they'd forget it all and move on.

Yes, everyone would forget. She was sure. They just had to move on. Right now.

But then, Thomas. "How did you—"

# TWENTY-SIX

## JACK

The next day, Jack stopped off on his way home to see Ford's assistant, Janie Tyson. He'd sobered up enough by morning to make his charters, but by the time he rolled off the water, he was spent, every ounce of energy gone to ignoring the hurricane inside his head. He felt pummeled—not just with beer and bad clients, but with regret. He couldn't believe he'd slammed the door on those kids with a drunken, half-assed excuse. *I'm out.* Such a coward.

Heading to Janie's was the only option he could think of.

Janie managed Ford's website and bookings during high season from an office tacked onto her garage. She peeked through the window, smirked and cracked the door open. "Thought I might see you today," she said, clearing a piece of dinner from her teeth with a long, orange fingernail.

Jack had come loaded with a weak excuse about not having kept his antivirus program up to date.

"A computer virus, huh? That why you trashed yer place last night?" People liked to say there were no secrets on an island, but that wasn't true. There were plenty. And Janie Tyson knew Jack had one.

She pushed the door open to him and walked the few feet to her computer. It lit up as soon as she touched it. "You know Ford'd rather have you come clean with whatever is going on than have you string him along. No one I talk to thinks you have it in for him, but no one thinks you have the money to help him retire none, either."

Jack ignored the inquisition. "Who's taking Ford's charters while he's in Atlanta?"

"Threw a few to Slush. But mostly he's just had me telling people we're booked up."

He opened his email but didn't find anything except spam and late-night forwards from his mother. If Janie weren't hovering, he'd have taken a minute to decide what the radio silence from Thomas meant, and what he ought to do about it. Stupidly, he hadn't even considered that the kid wouldn't have replied, wouldn't have called him out for being a sorry excuse for a human being.

But he hadn't. And Jack knew that could mean one of two things: he either had a narrow window of opportunity in which to apologize, or something had gone very wrong.

He made the uncharacteristic choice to remain optimistic.

Hey, T, he wrote.

Please ignore that last email. I'm not proud of it. Mostly, I'm getting worried. Everything ok there?

He clicked Send.

"You might be careful, Jack." Janie came around from where she'd been looking over his shoulder and sat down on the edge of the desk. She'd lived her whole life on Tybee and still looked like she could manage a bikini as well as anyone twenty years younger. Even so, she'd had a bad marriage at too young an age, and while she was happy now with a decent boyfriend and a good business, a person could still read those years on her face if they knew where to look.

She leaned in to make sure she had Jack's attention. "I think Ford might be talking to a lawyer."

"Of course, he's talking to a lawyer." The good thing about not hearing back from Thomas, he realized, was not having to explain it to Janie. "How do you think he's handling the sale?"

"No, I mean besides that. For options. If you try to screw him."

"I'm not."

"Not intentionally," she said, with whatever kindness that sort of charge deserved. "But you might end up doing it anyway."

Not *might*, he wanted to say. It was guaranteed.

He closed out his email without letting Janie catch his eye again and said goodbye.

Wouldn't you know, Carter Allman was on Jack's porch when he pulled into his driveway.

Carter was wearing a T-shirt with the sleeves cut off that said Check Your Girls Every Month in curlicue pink lettering, a breast cancer ribbon in the middle. It was either a handout from the Goodwill, or that kid had guts.

"Sandra Beals over at the daiquiri stand says she was walkin' home past yer place last night and you were in here havin' a fight with the devil hisself."

He eyed the bandage on Jack's wrist.

"That why yer bleedin'?"

"You're not old enough to be hanging out at the daiquiri stand." Tybee, and most of this part of Georgia, had a tradition of frozen daiquiri bars and open carry laws, meaning, you didn't have to go anywhere in low country without a drink in your hand and a gun on your hip.

"Ain't no crime if I don' buy."

He had him there. Jack pulled his tools from the truck with his good arm.

"Who were you fightin' with, anyhow? Cap'n Slush says you avoidin' Cap'n Ford like a scaredy lil' kitten. But I said I never seen you run from anybody. So, which is it? You fightin' with Cap'n Ford?"

Jack shooed past him, like always, and unlocked the door. He stopped at the threshold. The disaster on the other side was worse than he'd remembered it.

"Whoa—" said Carter, peering in from behind. "Sandra Beals ain't tellin' no lie."

"Nope." Wasn't any point in denying the evidence.

Most of the wreckage fell along the northeast wall where two cement pillars stood like bookends, one at each end, drywall in the middle. Whoever built the place hadn't bothered to plaster, just slathered the drywall with cheap yellow paint the color of mouse pee. Compared to that, the dreary gray of the pillars looked almost stylish.

For Jack, the cement also proved to be impressively destructive.

"Someone sucker punch you, Jack? That how you done yer place up so good?"

"You could say that."

"Was it Cap'n Ford?"

"Nah. Not exactly."

"Cap'n Slush?"

"Nope."

"Randy Stripe from over at the Pig 'n' Whistle?"

"Not him, either."

"You sure? 'Cuz Randy got my brother Cal real good in the face one Fourth of July even though Cal said he weren't payin' him no mind. Randy'll sucker punch you, all right."

"Wasn't Randy."

"Well, who then? I'm sick o' guessing."

Jack brushed a few shards of glass away from the floor near the doorjamb with the toe of his boot. He hadn't set foot in the apartment and already he felt tired enough to drop right down on the front lawn and sleep.

*I thought I'd let you know that we're going to do a bunch of TV interviews on Friday.*

"You still looking to earn some money?" He didn't even turn around, knowing without looking at the kid that Carter would take him up on what he was about to offer.

"What you got?"

"You know how to operate a VCR? Make sure it records and all that?"

"'Course."

"You know where you can still buy a new tape? A blank one? To record on?"

"Sure. I saw 'em at Sara Chen's shop last week. Behind the register."

He looked down at Carter's bare toes and thin rubber flip-flops. "You got a pair of sneakers to wear? Or something to protect your feet?"

"Yeah."

He ran through a quick list in his head. That was probably everything.

"All right. You come back here first thing tomorrow morning. Like first thing—before I leave, even. Wear your sneakers and bring a brand-new tape with you. I'll give you a few bucks to buy one tonight. I'll leave you a list of shows to record all morning. And while you're recording them, you can sweep up all the glass. You get it done by the time I come back home, and I'll pay you twenty dollars."

"Twenty-five," he said.

"Twenty. And I'll let you stay and watch TV until I get back."

Carter nodded. They had a deal.

By the time Jack got back to his apartment the next evening, Carter had swept the place clean and was on the couch watching an old Warren Miller bootleg with a box of Froot Loops on his lap. No one who grew up in Colorado ever dared start the ski season without watching Warren Miller's latest film. Especially not Jack.

"You ever skied like that? Like off a cliff an' such?"

Jack smiled, unable to resist the nostalgia, then lowered his toolbox to the floor and headed for the fridge, where he found one last beer.

"Ever cause an avalanche and let it chase you down the mountain?"

"You know those are professional skiers in those films, right?" He cracked open the beer and sat down next to Carter on the couch. The scene unfolding featured a montage of skiers carving deep, swooping lines down a mountain of fresh powder. He pointed his beer at it. "That I can do."

He hadn't done it for over a decade, but his legs remembered, feeling suddenly restless and eager to move.

"Makes me cold jes lookin' at it."

"Notice the jackets?"

"Still."

They watched a few minutes more. He hadn't kept in touch with anyone from his Breckenridge days. Or his Colorado life, really. He wondered where they'd all ended up. Most of his resort buddies had been Kiwis. The ones he'd planned to stay with when he traveled. On the trip Bess had encouraged him to take.

"Life is short, Jack," she'd said. "Go live it."

His list of failures seemed to be getting longer by the second. "You tape those shows I listed?" he asked.

Carter nodded. "You know those two kids on them there shows?"

"Sort of. I knew their mom."

"Well that short girl got beat up pretty good on one show. I thought she was gon' cry. Or hit her brother. Or maybe both."

The kid's blunt assessment sent Jack's head ringing, a near-constant state for him now. He looked at Carter, expecting more info, but his attention was back on the skiers. Jack dug into his pocket for a twenty and shooed Carter out, making sure he took the cereal with him.

He rewound the tape in the VCR but sat there without pressing Play. He knew he was going to watch. Only he had to do it on his terms. Paying Carter to clean up his mess had been easy. A convenience. Getting him to record the interviews a cheap add-on.

These past few days, though, Jack had started to wake up to the fact that he had dues to pay—and it was a lot more than what he already owed Ford. He was forty and his life could be reduced to a single moment. The one he was in right there, alone, pissed off and sitting in a mess of his own making. He'd spent years flinging himself from one distraction to another. Home to college. College to Breck. Breck to Tybee. He thought he'd been living the carefree life. Staying unburdened. He didn't ask for any extravagances and he didn't make promises he couldn't keep.

Except that he had.

He'd promised Ford a retirement he couldn't give. And he'd connected himself to two kids wanting a father.

If he had even a trace of decency left in him, he was going to have to do something that qualified, at a minimum, as not shitty.

He pressed Play.

The tape opened on a shot of Savannah laughing, and it was all Jack could do to sit, staring at her. The thick brown hair, the matching eyes. He didn't know the whole face, but he recognized the likeness. Bess. The woman who'd asked questions with just a squint and called *bullshit* with a tilt of her head.

He rewound to the beginning of the interview and watched again.

It took him a few minutes to place the voices he knew from the podcast with the faces he'd seen in the photos on their website. He'd constructed them differently in his mind, mostly the same but different. And now, here they were, animated and fully functioning people.

The distinctions between the two kids were astounding. Thomas towered over Savannah, Jack knew to expect that, but she practically burst through the TV with her—what— Savannah-ness. More confident than she ought to be at seventeen, but in a way that made you want to tell her everything was going to be okay.

"We should never have lost our mom," she told the interviewer, a woman with perfect hair and chiseled cheekbones. "But we did lose her and it's still awful. A woman in a Toyota Prius is no match for a concrete block falling off an overpass. No kid wants to learn the term *blunt force trauma* the way we did. But the end of her story isn't the end of ours. We are loved. We have a wonderful, loyal, strong grandmother."

Thomas laughed suddenly, and the interviewer shot him a smile that asked *what am I missing?*

He flushed, seeming to catch himself short. "Oh, I—for a second, I thought Savannah was about to say *strange*, a strange grandmother."

Savannah nudged him. "Ha! She's not going to let you forget that."

Jack's eyes went dry he stared so intently at the screen, amazed by every detail. The way Thomas chewed on his lip while he thought. How Savannah nodded constantly and said, *Mmm-hmm… Mmm-hmm* when listening to a question. The way Thomas was large, but Savannah had presence. They seemed to fit, two pieces of a whole. It made Jack feel—he didn't know exactly—more optimistic somehow.

"Anyway, my point is," Savannah continued, "neither of

us is trying to replace our mom. If anything, we're doing exactly what she taught us to do. To be curious. Be open. Support each other."

A guy with silver hair and a tie to match, asked what they were doing with the money they made from the show.

"What money?" Thomas asked in a tone rich with irony.

"Are you familiar with podcasting?" Savannah added, laughing.

"I mean, yeah," continued Thomas. "There will be some. I'll probably buy myself a cup of coffee with it. What about you, Van?"

"I'm thinking doughnuts. But who knows. If the show gets really popular, I might even upgrade to a Danish."

Another asked them why they thought their mother kept their father a secret from them.

"I sort of think it's a mistake to characterize her choices as secrets," said Savannah. "When we asked about our father, she gave us the information she must have considered appropriate at the time. Like, when we were little, she said we were just like the bean plants we'd sprouted in a cup on our windowsill—there was a seed and it grew and as long as someone cared for it, watered it and gave it plenty of room to grow, it flourished. Then when we were older, she talked about how every creature raised their babies a little bit differently, that penguins cared for their young differently than the robins in our yard, but that didn't make one creature any better than the other."

Jack watched every segment—sometimes rewinding two or three times, trying to take it all in, every laugh and *Hmm*. The sky outside was just turning pink when the tape cut to the kids seated in the middle of five women. He'd never seen this show, but he assumed the women served collectively as its hosts; each held a coffee mug with her name in gold.

Except for the woman at the end of the table. Her mug was blank. Her cohosts called her Eaton.

"Is that your goal, Savannah?"

Jack recoiled at the sneer on the woman's face. She reminded him of the murdering wife in one of the last movies he'd seen. *Beautifully Deadly*, if he remembered the title right.

"A systematic dismantling of men's rights?" Eaton went on. "But disguised as a personal quest for connection and family?"

*What the hell was this?*

On screen, Jack watched as Savannah changed before his eyes, her confidence vanishing, replaced by the face of a frightened little girl. Thomas, too. He looked like he was preparing to dash, to grab his sister's hand and make a run for it.

And then.

"Why won't you tell us who John James Thorson is?"

The alarm in Jack's head began to scream. Not just ringing now, but wailing. An air raid in his brain. His name on national television.

*We're not going to out you or, whatever.*

He knew it. Knew he'd be right. The choice to keep his identity confidential hadn't been theirs to make. It had been Eaton, a woman he wouldn't otherwise have crossed paths with in a million lifetimes and who didn't care what her choices meant to anyone except her own arrogant self.

And that wasn't even the whole of the problem. It was worse. It was worse because Jack saw the last look on Savannah's face. And he knew—again. Knew they were his. Knew he wasn't the only one keeping a secret.

Thomas hadn't told his sister about Jack.

**Trigg:**
OMG Savannah wtf????? [face screaming in fear emoji] [angry red-face emoji] [crying emoji]

**Trigg:**
I googled that Eaton chick [devil emoji] and she's pure evil [flames emoji]

**Trigg:**
Snapchat is totally blowing up [bomb emoji] [collision emoji]

**Trigg:**
No one can believe she outed you [ghost emoji] [flashlight emoji] [devil emoji]

**Trigg:**
Is that guy really your dad? I won't tell. Promise.

# TWENTY-SEVEN

## SAVANNAH

Maggie said five words after the interview. "Get us to the airport."

Sam argued and Saj begged apologies, but Maggie had said what she meant. And when Maggie quit talking, Savannah and Thomas knew there was no changing her mind.

Not that it mattered. New York or home, it was the same. Savannah's head only had room for two horrors: the sneer stretching across Eaton Holmes's face, and the guilt plastered all over Thomas's.

"I'm so sorry, Van." They were in a car again, heading back to LaGuardia, and this time, she didn't care what was outside her window. Thomas had been apologizing to her since they'd walked off the set. Trailing behind her every step with four words of his own.

"I'm so sorry, Van."

"I'm so, so, sorry."

Maggie took a window seat and stared out, not talking. Savannah took the middle, desperate for her grandmother's physical warmth, and grabbed Maggie's hand.

Thomas refused to leave her be. "Van, are you okay? You're not talking."

She wasn't, because if she opened her mouth there would be words, and those words would come out with a flood of tears, and once the tears started, they wouldn't stop. So she stayed quiet. Thomas could keep going as long as he needed to. That was his problem. She was going to keep her words all zipped up, keep them from rushing out and knocking her over.

However many hours later, Chef Bart picked them up from the Minneapolis airport in Maggie's car. No one was talking now. Not even Thomas.

They pulled into the alley at the far end and drove the length of the block toward their house. It didn't take long to see the blue lights flashing at the other end. Police. Two officers. And talking to them was their neighbor, Tabby Melby.

"Maggie!" Tabby was wailing at them before they even got out of the car. "I'm just sick about it! If only I hadn't waited until my hair was dry before going out to get the paper this morning, I might have caught them in the act."

Savannah saw it then. Their welcome home gift. The cause of Mrs. Melby's distress.

On the fence, the one dividing the yard from the parkway, hung a large stuffed toy—some sort of cotton-candy-colored bear. With a rope tied around its neck.

Next to it, in unskilled and drip-dried spray paint were the words, *Waaa! I want my daddy.*

Her mother's bedroom door was closed, like always, but Savannah knew she was welcome. Inside, she sat down on the bed, just the edge so as not to mess the covers, and took a deep, filling breath. Her mom was disappearing more and more with every visit, but Savannah could still get a hint of her. Just enough to remember.

"Hi, Mom," she whispered. "We're home."

The emptiness felt like a joke. Like her mom's stuff and her scent and the memories were mocking her, claiming there was magic in this place. That if she kept coming in, she'd feel it. That a miracle might happen.

But even the emptiness was something.

"Things aren't going so great. I know you were trying to reassure me last night. You did. It helped so much. But then—"

Every breath threatened to bring the tears along with it, forcing her to gulp air as she spoke. She looked down at her hands and saw that her knuckles were white from pressing them together so hard.

"I don't know what's happening. Maggie tries to keep the bad stuff from us, but that's impossible. I know crazies are making threats. We thought it was just online, but I guess you know what we just found in the yard.

"Trigg told me even she's getting threats. I guess it wasn't hard to figure out who our friends were. But now her parents are freaking out and taking her phone and threatening to send her to her grandma's house in Nebraska for the rest of the summer. Her dad even unplugged their Google Home because he thinks someone might have hacked it to eavesdrop. Plus, I'm mad. Mostly at Thomas. I'm sorry. I know you love him just as much as me. But I can't help it. He *knew*. He knew who our dad was and he didn't tell me."

Her brain lit with anger as she said the words aloud and felt herself begin to sweat, a fire raging from the inside out.

"Thomas has said he's sorry like a million times—*Oh my god, Van, I'm so sorry! You have to forgive me!*

"Please. I don't even want to hear it. I don't! He wanted this and I did it for him. As if I had a choice! As if I could say, *No! I don't care if it means you never find your biodad, I don't want to put myself out there for everyone to hate on.* Because that's what's been happening, of course. They all love Thomas but they call me every horrible name you can imagine. Like having the whole school hate me wasn't enough. Now the whole world gets to hate me. They're mad at Thomas, but they despise me. Like he's just stupid, but I don't even deserve to live."

And with that, the first tear fell. Nothing she could do to hold it back. Nothing she could do.

Savannah wanted to crawl under the covers and was already putting on her pajamas when Maggie called them down for dinner. She was only half-changed—a misbuttoned pajama shirt on top, shorts on the bottom—and Maggie gave her a curious look when she walked into the kitchen.

"Chef Bart made us a dinner rich in stress busters," Maggie said. "Vitamin K and potassium and magnesium and omega-3 fatty acids."

Thomas came in through the mudroom. "Ugh. Kale."

"Kale *slaw* with pumpkin seeds," Maggie corrected. "Good for stress and inflammation. We'll need our immune systems to be as resilient as possible until this mayhem dies down."

Savannah slid into her chair and burrowed between the table and the wall. She made a not-subtle point of looking only at Maggie and the plate in front of her.

"Did the police take the bear?" Thomas asked.

Maggie nodded. "And I've hired someone to come out and repaint the fence tomorrow."

No one spoke for a few minutes, the silence filled by the sound of utensils on porcelain. Finally, Thomas cracked.

"I mean, think about this, really. Who are we threatening with our search? Like, possibly one man. But all of these thousands of people now are suddenly so concerned with what we're doing. You have to wonder why."

Savannah did wonder. But hearing her brother act as if this were nothing but an intellectual exercise made her want to leap across the table and choke him. "Are you *kidding me*?" She gripped her fork and wondered if she could reach Thomas's hand to stab it in. "You sound as if this is an assignment for ethics class. But I was assaulted today, in case you didn't notice. Bullied and accused by a conspiracy theorist on national TV. Did you not see the noose on our fence?"

She needed him to understand, to share the depth of the fear and humiliation her haters wanted her to feel.

"Van." Thomas reached across the table for her hand. She withdrew, even though his intentions were gentle. Unlike hers had been. "People do crazy things when they're afraid. Maybe if we can convince them not to fear us—"

"Me," she said. "They hate me. They attacked me. But you get to be some sort of saint."

"No, I don't think that's true." Maggie's lip quivered as she spoke, obviously fighting her emotions back. "Eaton Holmes cornered you today, Savannah, but it's because she needed to. It made her feel strong, when really it was the move of a weak person. She decided you were the more vulnerable twin in that moment, and she drew you out. A predator thinning the herd."

Savannah scoffed. "Didn't feel very weak to me."

"Of course not. But if she were stronger, she wouldn't act threatened. What does she gain by attacking a teenager who's looking for her dad? She's a pariah. A false prophet."

Maggie went quiet for a moment, tracing the edge of her plate round and round with her finger. Savannah watched, trying to quiet her mind with the Zen of it. Round and again.

Didn't work.

"As much as I hate to say this, I don't know what's better," Maggie said finally. "To stand up and fight, or to wait them out, to starve Eaton and all her zombies of the attention they need to survive."

"Makes me wish I'd paid closer attention to *The Walking Dead*," Savannah said, allowing the faintest smile to crack.

Thomas leaned in. "Van, I hate that you took the brunt of it this morning. I never would have asked that of you in a million years. But let's not forget what we got into this for. We want to find our father. Simple. We didn't ask to get sucked into a tornado."

"No one asks to get sucked into a tornado."

Thomas smiled, too. "Trust me," he said. "I know in my gut it's going to be worth it."

Savannah wondered how she could hate her brother so much and still want to cry, desperately thankful to have him.

@eaton_alive
BEST TAKEDOWN EVER!! Wah wah bye bye baby mcclairs
#savannahtrample

@eaton_alive
I used to wonder if you had no shame. Not anymore. Now I know
you have no soul.
#wondertwinpowers

@eaton_alive
Have you found John James Thorson yet? WE WANT PICS!!!!!
#savannahtrample

t.mcclair@guavamediausa.com
To: thorJJ1979@gmail.com
Subject: Hi Jack

Jack,

You haven't heard from me in a while. Sorry about that. I got your email, the one where you sounded mad. And the one after where you said to ignore that. I'm trying to do what you asked. I'll ignore it. Especially because I'd like to keep writing to each other, if you're okay with that.

Anyway. You may have heard that one of the interviewers said your name during an interview. I hope it hasn't caused any trouble for you. Honest, we don't know where she found out your name and we didn't tell her.

I understand if you're mad. Just want you to know I'm really sorry.

Regards,
Thomas McClair

*You have six new messages.*

*[BEEP]*

*Hey, Junior. It's your mom. I ran into Mrs. Baca at the Quick Stop and she said she'd heard your name on TV. She said, "Isn't Johnny's full name John James? I thought they were talking about him on the TV the other day." But then, of course she couldn't remember what show or what they were even talking about. And her fingers looked about ready to jump off her hand from need of a cigarette. Serves me right for listening to her, I guess. Anyway, call me, sweetheart. All this has got me curious.*

*[BEEP]*

*Hey, Johnny, it's your mama. Everbody's tellin' me they keep hearin' your name. Are you gonna call me?*

*[BEEP]*

*Johhnnyy. Johhnnnyyy. Where's my famuzz lil' jun'ier? Mama looooves you. Johhnnnnyyyyy.*

*[BEEP]*

*[muffled noise]*

*[Beep]*

*[muffled noise]*

*[BEEP]*

*Johhnnnnnnnyyyy.*

# TWENTY-EIGHT

## JACK

All of Tybee knew about Thomas and Savannah in short order. Jack stopped to put gas in his truck and Artie Hinkle told him not to forget he always had condoms on a rack by the register.

Sandra Beals put a new daiquiri on her menu called the "Who's Your Daddy"—a blend of blue raspberry and pink champagne.

Slush passed him on the landing, laughing and carrying a couple of buckets of bait shrimp. "How many of these babies are yours, you figure?"

Jack ignored him but notched the insult on the tally he'd started keeping in his bones.

When Jack was ten his mom took a job waitressing at the diner out by the highway, mostly lunch shifts while he was at school. He'd assumed she'd have to wear one of those waitress uniforms with the matching hat and pocket name tag like he saw on all the TV reruns of *Alice* and *Happy Days*, but instead she bought a new jean skirt and a couple of almost-too-tight T-shirts and came out looking more Tina Turner than Joanie Cunningham.

Even Jack's fifth-grade gut told him Hartwell, Colorado, wasn't looking for a Tina Turner to call their own.

"How are you going to lean over enough to wipe tables and stuff?"

"It's not that short, silly. Anyway, a lady has her ways."

Jack wasn't convinced, but she'd also promised to use part of her tip money to help him buy the new parts he needed for the dirt bike he'd bought from Telo, one of his dad's farmhands. Telo had tuned the engine and gotten it running for him, but it still needed new tires and one of the rims was shot. Plus, his dad told him he was going to have to pay for the gas himself.

To Jack's ten-year-old brain, he figured as soon as he had the money to get the bike running, he wouldn't have to think about his mom's legs sticking out from that short skirt anymore. And he wouldn't have, if the kids at school hadn't kept reminding him.

"My mom won't let my dad go to the diner for lunch no more. Says your mom's asking for trouble and she's not gonna let my dad be on the other end of it."

Even with that in his face, Jack managed to keep focused on just how much more money he needed. Thirty dollars. Twenty-five. Eighteen. Ten.

He was short just two dollars and change and thinking about heading down to the junkyard to see if they wouldn't let him pay the rest on credit when Snyder Bellus sneaked up to the blackboard and wrote, "Carla Thorson kissing service $5. Under the neck, extra." Then he punched Jack in the arm on his way back to his desk.

If Jack had been a fighter, he would have met Snyder Bellus after school and stomped him bloody. Would have grabbed him by the neck and squeezed until his head felt ready to pop. Then he'd let him go just long enough to lean over and catch his breath, and that's the moment he'd slam his knee into the kid's face. If all that didn't bring him down, he'd grab him by the business and twist until he was gasping on all fours and crying for mercy.

Then Jack would pull five dollars from his pocket, throw it in the kid's face, and walk away.

If he were the fighting type.

But Jack wasn't, and that day at school was the day he knew

for sure. His instinct was set for slow burn. He learned he didn't fight with his fists. He learned he'd been right about his mother's skirt and Hartwell's silent intolerance. And he learned that the worries you think are confined to the space in your head can just as well show up outside it, written in bright letters for all to see.

A few days after the interview revealed his identity, Janie found Jack at the dock. He was bringing in a group of twenty-somethings who'd come to Tybee for a bachelor party and who still stank like last night's beer. They'd met Jack at 7:00 a.m. as instructed, and it wasn't long before he could tell they hadn't even gone to bed. It was the same stunt he'd pulled at their age, moving straight from the slopes to The Mine to a party with the after-work crowd and back onto the slopes in the morning.

All four of the guys eyed Janie's ass in her short shorts as she walked Jack's way. She smiled and gave them a gratuitous shake.

"Your afternoon group just canceled," she said. "Their kid got the flu. I tried some of the other numbers who'd called looking for availability but no takers. Sorry."

Jack grabbed the neck of his T-shirt and wiped a layer of sweat and grime from his forehead. "I could use a shower, anyway."

She nodded. "Go home. Get the stink off. Then come meet Coop and me at the Pig 'n' Whistle."

"Nah," he said, trying to put her off. She didn't budge.

"You ain't got nothing left in that apartment of yours to smash up. And sitting there alone trying to keep the world away isn't gonna help."

That was as close as she came to the mess with Thomas and Savannah, but they both knew what she was saying.

"Coop's leaving in the morning for Tallahassee. Plus, you

and I ain't got nothing better to do until Ford comes back from Atlanta."

Janie's boyfriend, Cooper, was an insurance adjuster for Allstate and went wherever the latest storm or flood left destruction to be cleaned up and insurance claims to be filed. He ran a whole office out of the back of his Honda minivan and could sometimes, depending on the size of the disaster, be gone for a month or so at a time. Janie was always saying Coop was off to somewhere or another in the morning.

"I'll give you until three o'clock." She turned to go. "Then we're coming to get you."

Most of the bars on Tybee were for tourists and catered to vacationers—people who ought to be enjoying a drink in the middle of the day. But the Pig 'n' Whistle was a local bar, a dank room filled with decaying Long John Silver decor. Jack always had the feeling that people went there because they didn't have anywhere better to be. Himself included.

By the time Jack arrived, Janie was on her second margarita and Cooper was making a serious dent on a pitcher of Bud. Jack ordered a Seven and Seven from Belle, the only waitress he'd ever seen at the Pig 'n' Whistle.

He downed his drink in one long drag and ordered another.

Janie said, "You don't have to tell us nothin' if you don't want to, Jack, but what's your plan? You gonna leave Tybee and go meet up with your kids? Find a pot of gold and hand it over to Ford? What?"

The whiskey was just starting to sing, a faint hum in his ears and at the back of his throat.

After a pause Janie said, "'Cuz the way I see it, you got a nice, easy excuse for gettin' out of your deal. Tell Ford you're real sorry, but how were you to see this comin'? You don't have no choice but to deal with it."

Cooper drained the last of his beer. "We doin' food?"

To which Janie told him he could do whatever he damn well pleased, but she wasn't cooking.

Cooper caught Belle's eye and ordered a plate of nachos for the table, a side of onion rings and another pitcher of Bud.

"You better not put any jalapeños on those nachos you just ordered or you're gonna be up all night with indigestion," Janie said.

Coop ignored her and looked at Jack. "I got a kid."

"Yeah?" That was actually news. He lifted his eyes from his glass, ready to hear more.

"Yeah, up in Macon. A girl. She's in her twenties. I don't see her much."

"Did you ever?"

"Didn't even know about her until she was five. Then only when her ma needed money. She'd call and give me the business about not spendin' any time with her and I'd bring cash. Wouldn't hear from her again until she needed more."

"You never called her?" The whiskey had dulled Jack's inhibitions just enough to call him out. "You just waited 'til they punched your ATM code?"

"Pretty much," Coop said. "To be honest, I don't actually know if she is mine. I have my doubts. Doesn't look like me. Doesn't act like me. But the timeline sort of works out. And even if she weren't mine, I hated the idea of her not having what she needed more than I hated taking responsibility."

"More to parental responsibility than sending money," Jack said.

"Maybe."

Though, what did Jack know about good parenting? His alcoholic mother wouldn't leave him alone and his father looked right through him. There'd been more voice mails from his mom reporting more questions in Hartwell—*What have you gotten yourssself messs'd up wth, juuunrr?*—and Tybee was in his business, too. It didn't seem long before all his worlds collided.

"I don't have any money. And I don't have proof those kids are mine. But I can't run. Not now that my name's out there." The whiskey was rushing warm and smooth through his veins, loosening his thoughts and letting them slip out before he could stop them.

Janie shoved her margarita aside and leaned in. "I knew it."

"What?"

"I knew you didn't have the money to buy Ford out."

"Yeah, well, that makes two of us."

"Ford ain't been nothing but good to you. Hiring a mountain boy from Colorado? We all said he was crazy. But he said he knew good and that you were it. And for the most part, he was right."

"You think that's not already tearing me up? Ford's never crossed me once in all my years working for him."

"Then why'd you go and promise?"

He'd have thought that was a hard question to answer, but it wasn't. "Because I wanted it to be true."

The words surprised him, but the logic wasn't hard to follow. If he bought out Ford, he belonged there on Tybee. With a business, he had a reason to stay. And if he was on Tybee, he didn't have to be in Hartwell. It was a long way round, but in the end, buying out Ford was nothing more than an expensive *fuck you* from Jack to his mom and dad.

The fact that he couldn't afford it just gave him another reason to drink.

"Well," Janie said, "I want fairies to come and fix my hair and clean my house every morning, but that ain't happening neither."

"I'll make it right," Jack promised, hoping it was more than the whiskey talking. "Don't know how yet. But I will."

# TWENTY-NINE

## SAVANNAH

A few nights later, Savannah lay awake in bed listening to the grandfather clock in the entryway chime the hours away. Trigg called several times to check on her, but Savannah didn't take the calls. It was too exhausting to explain, and Trigg's greatest skill was exhausting everyone she came into contact with.

"I mean, not to be a bitch about it, Van," she'd said in her last message, "but like, you did sort of get this guy's identity outed on national TV. Maybe if you just went back on air and apologized or something. I mean, I totally know that wasn't what you meant to happen, but—"

It didn't help any that their neighbor Tabby Melby had come by earlier to report on further events.

"You know I love you all," she had said. "But reporters are camping out in vans and have completely jammed up the street. I called the police no fewer than three times after spotting strangers creeping through my yard. Christine McElroy isn't letting her three boys into the yard until the chaos is over. And have you seen Trygve Bane? He's sitting on his front porch with a BB gun across his lap. I'm not a fan of firearms, but I can't say I blame him."

Mrs. Melby had looked across the table at Savannah and Maggie. "Oh, I am sorry. Here I am, going on as if you brought this on yourselves. We'll be just fine." She wiped at the lipstick smudge on the rim of her drink. "But I've put a hold on my newspaper delivery until all this passes. The less

I have to go outside, the better. Yesterday I went out to get the paper and a man wearing a Don't Fiddle with the First Amendment T-shirt stuck a microphone in my face."

Savannah had smirked. Not because she was glad for what happened to Tabby, but because she knew the guy's T-shirt almost certainly said, Don't Fuck with the First Amendment. Nobody put "fiddle" on a shirt.

After a flood of complaints, the police had barricaded their block with signs reading Local Traffic Only. Now, though, the paparazzi just parked their vans around the corner and down the side streets, spreading over a wider area.

The parkway, however, was still open to foot traffic and the sidewalks across from their house had become irresistible to attention seekers. There was the carload of pro-life teenagers holding signs and shouting, "Your mother chose *love* when she chose *life!*" They were followed by the paternity rights activists who stuffed the neighbors' mailboxes full of flyers about the glories of fatherhood.

Earlier that evening, Savannah and Maggie had stood at the living room window and watched a group wearing Arms Around Our Children T-shirts form a human chain, arm in arm, down the block. Judging by the number of backpacks the activists wore, Maggie and Savannah figured the group planned to be there a lot longer than the hour it took for Mr. Melby to get fed up with not being able to pull out of his driveway and chase them away with his garden hose.

The grandfather clock chimed, yet again.

Savannah couldn't lie still any longer. If nothing else, she knew that Chef Bart had baked one of his cheeseless hazelnut-ginger cheesecakes before leaving for the night.

She crawled out of bed and threw on a sweatshirt. Starting down the stairs, the top board creaked under her weight like it always did, but the sound echoed so loudly in the dark house she flinched. Wasn't the first time she thought of the ghosts among them. The row of photographs along the stairwell followed the descent of the McClair family—Maggie and Granddad, Maggie and Granddad and Mom, Maggie and Mom, then Maggie and Mom and Thomas and Savannah.

Then, just Thomas and Savannah.

She flipped on the kitchen light and saw the cheeseless cheesecake in the middle of the table. There was one slice missing, and it was on the plate in front of Maggie.

"Hello, love," Maggie said. "You couldn't sleep, either?"

"Nope." She took a plate and fork for herself out of the cupboards.

"We just need Thomas for the trifecta, I guess." Maggie handed her the spatula she'd used for her slice. Savannah took it and sat down across the table.

"Any more crazies out tonight?"

"There was a candlelight vigil earlier," Maggie said. "Hymns, mostly. I thought about throwing open the windows to accompany them on the piano. You know how I feel about a cappella."

Savannah wasn't sorry she'd missed them.

Maggie took a bite of cheesecake and scowled ever so faintly as she swallowed. She brought a hand up to her chest and kept it there.

Savannah gave her a quizzical look. "Are you all right?"

Maggie waved away the concern. "Oh yes. Just the travel catching up with me, I—"

Her words were interrupted by the sound of crashing glass and Thomas screaming from the basement.

*"What on earth?"* Maggie and Savannah sprang from the table and rushed to the door in the mudroom leading to the basement stairs. She went for the door just as it flew open, and a man Savannah had never seen before rushed past her, nearly knocking her to the floor.

Now Savannah and Maggie were screaming, too.

The guy panicked and ran around the room looking for escape like a trapped squirrel. Maggie grabbed a broom from a hook on the mudroom wall and raised it as high as the ceiling would allow, then brought it down hard onto the square of his back. He yelped and brought his hands up over his head trying to protect himself.

SWAT!

*"Get out of my house!"* she screamed.

SWAT!

*"Who the hell do you think you are?"*

SWAT!

*"Oh, just try to climb through that window, I dare you!"*

Savannah didn't know where to turn or what to do. She thought about grabbing a broom or something of her own, but she'd have to run past the man to do it. She could grab a knife from the kitchen, but—no way. She quickly dialed 911 and told them what was happening.

SWAT! Maggie went on hitting him.

*"Is this fun for you?"*

SWAT!

*"Didn't expect Maggie McClair with a broom, did you?"*

SWAT!

Savannah thought maybe if she closed her eyes and opened them again, she wouldn't see what she was seeing, which was her grandmother, in the mudroom, wearing a kimono, in the middle of the night, hitting a stranger with a plastic broom while hollering.

The intruder kept ping-ponging around the room as Thomas flew up the stairs from the basement wielding a baseball bat. Thomas nearly had the guy cornered when the sound of sirens woke a crucial receptor in the man's tiny, rodent brain, and he was finally smart enough to launch himself through the mudroom door and out into the night.

*"Who in high holy hell was that?"* Maggie screamed.

Thomas took the broom from her hand, and Savannah curled up into a ball in a chair at the table. The tears came silently, without sobs, and Maggie wrapped her in her arms while Thomas opened the door to the police.

"I was working in the basement studio and I thought I saw something move outside, through the window," he told the officers. His words were coming so fast, Savannah couldn't bear to look at his face. She burrowed deeper into Maggie's embrace.

"I stopped and turned the light off, so I could see out. But I didn't see anything, and I figured I was just being paranoid—I mean, it's been sort of crazy around here, right? So, I flipped the light back on."

Savannah felt Maggie tense.

"And then maybe five minutes later I looked up and saw eyes reflecting through the glass."

At this, Savannah let out a desperate, frightened sob, and Maggie pulled her closer. One of the officers took the moment to pause and ask some clarifying questions, which gave Savannah a few seconds to calm down.

"This guy just crashed through the window," Thomas said. "I think he leaned on it so hard he fell through."

They asked Thomas to take them downstairs to the studio and discovered that the man cut himself on the broken glass. There was blood on the window and the sill, enough for the officers to gather several samples. The man also dropped his camera, which the officers took with them in a plastic evidence bag.

A few days later, the detective assigned to the case called Maggie in to the station and showed her the fifty-plus pictures the intruder had taken of Thomas, working in the privacy of his own basement.

There was no safe place for them now.

# THIRTY

## JACK

"Jack!"

He moved to answer, but his head was screaming like it wanted to split in two.

*Shit.*

Every move a tidal wave of pain. He tried to lick his lips. No spit. Bone-dry.

"Jack! Git up! It's seven thirty. If yer takin' people out this mornin' you'll be lucky if Slush ain't poached 'em by now."

"No clients today. Their kid got the flu." Somehow, Jack made the words come out. In an instant, his gut churned from the whiskey.

"This ain't yesterday no more," Carter said. "This here's today an' yer late. Why'd you end up on yer lawn for, anyhow? Ten more steps and you woulda been inside."

That answered one question: he was on the front lawn of his apartment.

Jack screwed his eyes shut against the light and rolled onto his side, so he could pull his knees into his gut and ease the waves of nausea. It didn't work, but he lay there anyway. Mornings on Tybee had a certain smell and his nose caught wind of it—the sea-salt breeze blowing in off the ocean and mixing with the scent of overheated asphalt and deep fat fryer and the marshes' briny tang.

"An' yer lucky nobody took off with yer truck on account o' yer keys were lyin' on the sidewalk o'er there."

Jack had a sketchy recollection of looking for his house keys and not finding them, which meant he must have given up and lain down. Now he was piecing the night together. They had closed out at the Pig 'n' Whistle around ten, Janie saying Coop needed enough time to sober up before he had to get on the road to Tallahassee. They walked one way toward home and Jack walked the other, toward the pier, thinking he might just sit there and watch people fish while the whiskey hummed. Never mind it was already dark.

He did make it to the pier, that much he knew. And he remembered other parts. Flashes of memory. Of making his way to a bench, of watching the tourists under the floodlights, daiquiris in hand, all of them stopping to look down at the dark water. Everyone posing for a round of pictures. So much picture taking.

At one point, someone handed him a camera, asked him to snap one of her and her kids.

"I got kids!" *Oh god.* It was coming back to him now. "Didn't know I had 'em. But I got 'em. And now, seems like maybe they don't want anything to do with me."

The woman changed her mind and grabbed her camera back. She hustled her children away, tucking them under her arm like a mother hen.

"Or maybe they're *dead*," he called after them. "I don't even know."

That awful part he remembered.

"You know there's still a guy with a big fat camera on the island lookin' fer you," Carter said. "Asked me two times yesterday if I knew you and when I said I did he offered me fifty dollars if I could tip him off to where you were. Gave me his cell phone number and everythin'. I didn't tell him nothin'. So as far as I figure, you owe me fifty dollars at least."

"I'm not paying you, Carter."

"Sometimes he's in a blue Chevy, all tourist rental car—

like. Other times he's on foot, askin' anybody who will talk where you at. I was fillin' my tires up at the Citgo and I saw him talkin' to Artie behind the register. He was pointin' out over the bridge in the direction of the landing, so I figure he at least knows where yer boat is."

"Not my boat."

"Cap'n Ford's boat, then. Anyhow, yer double lucky I found you here this mornin' 'cuz he coulda walked right up and snapped as many pictures as he wanted 'fore you even woke up."

He had him there. "Thanks, Carter."

Jack eased himself upright, not ready to stand but at least able to put head above shoulders. His whole body burned in a way he hadn't felt in years. Maybe ever.

"Can you manage to carry a cup of coffee on your bike without spilling it?"

"'Course."

His body had made it clear there wasn't any salvaging his first booking of the day. With any luck, he might be able to stand by the afternoon.

"I'll pay you double whatever it costs to buy me the largest cup of black coffee you can manage. Nothing fancy. Just black."

He felt for his pockets where any cash he had left would've been. "You got any money?"

"I'm gonna puke!" the kid wailed.

They weren't thirty minutes out on his afternoon charter and the kid leaned forward and lost it all over the deck. Not over the side, onto the deck. And his little sister's shoes.

*"Mooommmyyy!"*

She was wailing, too, and covered from the knees down in chunks of sick.

Jack cut the engines, swallowed back every foul word, grabbed a fistful of rags and a bucket, and just as he was heading over, the sister, headlong into hysterics, slipped and fell into her brother's mess. Now she was covered, head to toe, in slime. Bits of the day's lunch hanging in stringy clumps from her hair. She was screaming, her dad trying to clean her with a bottle of water and a towel, and the mom dealing with the brother who was going another round. All four of them, slicked in vomit and baking in the sun.

And Jack so hungover he thought we was going to die.

Just one whiff and he dropped everything and leaned over the side, heaves racking him. He hadn't been able to take food in all day, so his stomach wasn't giving up anything but bitter bile.

Jack was completely useless, and he knew there wasn't going to be any moving him away from the side of that boat until either the wind changed or the sun fell below the horizon. Hours away. Or days. Or maybe he'd just die there.

At one point, he thought about letting the waves carry him away.

t.mcclair@guavamediausa.com
To: thorJJ1979@gmail.com
Re: Hi Jack

Jack,
Not to be a pest or anything, but you hadn't replied to my email and I thought you might just be busy or something. Or, if you didn't even know your name had been on TV, sorry you had to hear about it in an email.

Or, you might be really mad. And I guess you have the right.

I just want to stress again though that there's no way we told the TV people (or anyone at all) your name or who you were or anything. Again, I'm really sorry. We didn't mean to cause trouble for you.

Could you let me know you got this, at least? Even if you are mad.

Thanks,
Thomas McClair

# THIRTY-ONE

## SAVANNAH

Maggie had the basement window replaced the day after the intrusion. Between that, repainting the fence and buying new privacy shades for the house, Savannah hoped Thomas could see how much money this little quest of his had begun to cost their family. Not to mention the intangible costs—like the fact that Savannah could no longer sleep, and that Maggie wandered the house checking on them every five minutes, no matter where they were. Yesterday she heard Maggie knock on the bathroom door and say, "Just making sure it's you in there, Thomas."

Chef Bart and Nadine came over earlier than usual that afternoon and brought along smoked Gouda macaroni and cheese, bacon-wrapped asparagus, pineapple jalapeño corn dogs, kale chips and Jell-O salad stuffed with tiny marshmallows. Maggie's version of comfort food.

"Come, sit," Maggie said, ushering everyone into the dining room. "I mean it. I love every single one of you and I want to be surrounded."

Savannah and Thomas took seats at opposite ends. Chef Bart sat between them. Nadine stopped to give Maggie a long hug. "I'm so, so sorry."

Maggie held her for a long time, then sat at the head of the table.

"Have you considered moving out for a bit?" asked Chef Bart. "At least until this blows over?"

Maggie shut him down. "This is our home. I'm not leaving it."

"But there's no telling—" Chef Bart began.

Maggie held up a hand, stopping him. "Please." She paused. "Everyone. We are together, and that is…" She didn't finish. Savannah knew Maggie was about to say, "enough." Because that was the McClair way. That they always had enough as long as they had each other.

Only, was that enough?

Savannah realized she didn't believe that anymore. Admitting it made her wince, but why keep on lying to herself when the evidence was black-and-white. The McClair bravado was a myth. Her mom and her granddad were dead. Her brother betrayed her. And Maggie was spinning out. Savannah was now one hundred percent alone. On her own to deal with it all—the humiliations, the threats, the invasion.

For a second, she felt her brain try to lull her back into the comfort of believing. *Oh, come on now, Savannah. What about your friends?*

She pushed back. *My friends can't help me.* She'd finally woken up to that fact, too. For starters, Trigg was useless. Trigg only cared about Trigg—always talking about herself, no matter the subject. *I know you're having a tough time but, seriously, you have no idea how bored I am in Nebraska.* Or, *How did I know Mrs. Thornbird was going to read your essay to the class?* Or, *OMG, my best friend is famous!*

Chef Bart and Nadine were around, but they couldn't really do anything to fix the mess she was in. Saj had provided a tiny glimmer of help, but that was before she fed Savannah alive to a wolf named Eaton Holmes. And Sam Tamblin? He was nothing but a joke, a publicity whore who only cared about one thing: *The subscriber numbers are through the roof! Have you seen the download numbers? They're cr-ay-zy!*

Worst of all, she didn't even have Jack. Thomas did, of course. He apparently talked to Jack all the time. They were buddies, their own private club to which Savannah hadn't been invited.

Maggie stood suddenly, breaking Savannah from her thoughts. She walked to the wall where their mom's essay hung and touched the glass. "Bess was mortified that I kept this up for so many years. She'd take it down and try to hide it, but I'd find it and put it back up."

She ran a finger down the side of the frame until it was perfectly straight.

"I know it's a little bit loony to hang your daughter's college entrance essay on the wall. But I didn't ever want my family to forget what it said. That no one ought to ever be excluded from discussion. That silence is often born of fear. That *every voice deserves its place*."

She returned to the table and sat.

"Your grandfather used to say that we have enough when we have each other." Maggie kept her eyes on her place setting as she spoke and was quiet for a moment before looking at the people gathered around her. "But I think he may have missed the point. It's not enough to *be* together. We have to *stick together*.

"I'm sorry I shut you down, Bart. You were voicing your concern and I appreciate that. If we can't talk to each other about this, what do we have?"

*Ironic*, Savannah thought, given what she'd just decided about her own situation. Just a week ago she would have agreed with Maggie, but now, she knew that all this *togetherness* was whitewash. Feel-good sentiment. The truth was, no one understood how Savannah felt. They'd all attempt to help, keep trying to make her feel better, tell her to give it time, that the awfulness would pass. Just like they had when her mom died. But at least then she'd had Thomas to share the experience with. Now she had no one. And she ought to keep reminding herself of that because every time she did, the truth settled in a little bit more.

"It's reasonable to worry, Maggie," Chef Bart said, looking more relieved than when he first arrived. "Strangers have invaded your house twice now. And the police can only do so much. I'm just glad they're making themselves visible around the neighborhood."

This was true. Tabby Melby had called to say she was keeping a tally on a notepad stuck to her refrigerator. She made a tick for every police cruiser and every uniformed officer spotted and so far, she reported herself impressed.

"We'll take it day by day," Maggie said. "And we'll do it together."

Thomas began to flick his fork angrily against the side of his plate. "If they think these scare tactics are going to stop us from having a relationship with Jack, they have another thing coming. After last night, I'm more driven than ever."

Savannah wanted to scream. "Easy for you to say, Thomas," she spat. "Since you seem to be the only one who *does* have a relationship with Jack."

Maggie held up a finger to say *We'll get to that*, and it made Savannah want to leap from her chair—her grandmother was spewing fairy tales about the magic of togetherness, all the while letting her brother get away with acting entirely on his own.

Maggie asked, "Who is *they*, Thomas?"

"You saw the camera the police took away last night," he said. "That's a couple-thousand-bucks camera, which means that guy was taking pictures because he knew someone would pay big for them. They're making money off of us." Thomas pointed his fork around the table. "We need to find a way to beat them at their own game."

Without waiting to hear more, Savannah stood, took her plate into the kitchen and ran upstairs.

"*Van—*" he called after her.

She slammed her bedroom door so hard the pictures on her wall rattled. *Good.* Let the whole bunch of them hear how done she was with all their crap.

# THIRTY-TWO

## JACK

Her voice mails had been coming all day and Jack ignored them. But now, too tired to sleep and too hungover to drink, he was out of excuses.

"Junior, it's Mom. Call home."

"Baby, I really do need to talk to you."

"Are you getting these? Your dad's in the hospital. Do you care enough to even find out why?"

One message was just two minutes of incomprehensible, snot-filled tears.

"Fine. You hate us. We get the message. But if your dad dies before you decide to lower yourself to call home, that's on you. Know that that's on you. Forever."

"Johhnnyy. Where are you? Your mama loooves you." The last message told him everything he needed to know. His dad was going to be okay. If he were in real trouble, his mom wouldn't have been able to go home to satisfy greater priorities.

He pressed Delete.

It was dark out when Ford rattled the screen door, waking him up.

"I know you're in there, Jack. I can see your feet hanging off the end of the couch."

Jack groaned, acknowledging he was alive, though barely. "Since when do you make so many house calls?"

"Open the damn door."

He eased himself upright and waited for equilibrium. His feet were pins and needles and his scalp itched like he hadn't showered in days, because he hadn't.

"You look like hell."

"Feel like it."

"And your AC is sailing right through yer screen door. What's happening with you?"

The linoleum under his feet was sticky with humidity and Jack could feel the temperature change the closer he got to the open screen like weather zones, arctic to tropical. He popped the lock on the door handle and wondered why he'd even bothered locking it.

"You want something to drink? I got water."

Ford shook his head and Jack pulled from the fridge the milk jug he kept filled with tap water, pouring himself a glass.

Ford followed him into the kitchen and leaned against the counter.

"How was Atlanta?" Jack said.

"Crowded."

Jack took a long drink and waited for him to get to the point of his visit.

"You remember I told you we had business to discuss when I got back? I assume you figured out I've been talking to a lawyer."

"Yeah." He hadn't figured it out. Janie had.

"My lawyer in Savannah wants me to sue you. For breach of contract."

"Okay." This shouldn't have been news, but surprise rang through him, nevertheless.

"That's why I went to Atlanta. Get some time to think. Talk to my sister, who's also a lawyer."

Jack said nothing and waited for the hammer to fall.

"I never use her for legal advice. Don't mix business and

personal, all that. She's not the right kind of lawyer, anyhow. But she can dissect a contract as good as I can gut a mackerel. Plus, she knows me better than just about anyone."

Jack wondered what it was like to be able to say that. He didn't have a person who knew him better than anyone else.

Ford pulled a fistful of envelopes from the pocket of his utility pants. "If you were someone else, I would have sued you. It's obvious you either can't buy me out or won't. We had a contract and you broke it."

He flipped the thick pile of envelopes across his palm and went on talking. "I won't say I'm not pissed off."

"I know."

He held up a hand. This was his discussion. "Even if I'd found out about your kids—and, yeah, I've heard, Jack. Even if you'd come to me and said you were stuck, I still might've sued you."

He made sure he had Jack's attention and gave him a good long stare. Jack felt it, a hot wind through his gut.

"Now before you get to thinking you're out of the woods, that I'm about to let you off the hook, you should know that I haven't made up my mind yet." He pulled an envelope from the stack in his hand and tossed it onto the counter. "That's this one."

Jack pulled the envelope toward him and opened the flap. He didn't need to unfold it to see the Notice of Breach of Contract addressed to Mr. John James Thorson at the top.

"I've gone through lawsuits before and there ain't nothing good about 'em. One long headache followed by lawyer's fees and a whole lot of nothing in the end. That's not the way I'd hoped to start my retirement."

He shuffled his deck and threw down the next envelope.

"That brings us to door number two."

Jack pulled it open and looked inside. Again, it didn't take more than a glance. "I thought you said you'd never sell to Slush."

Ford nodded. "I did say that. Only sometimes money speaks for itself."

Knowing Ford must be talking price, Jack pulled the offer out and unfolded it. Slush's offer was for a full fifteen percent higher than the number they'd settled on.

"There's no way I can match this."

Ford laughed from the bottom of his gut, like that was one of the funniest things he'd ever heard. "You can't even match yer own offer, Jack."

A decent man would have felt the shame in that truth. But there in his dingy kitchen, face-to-face with Ford, shame no longer registered. The curtain had been pulled, and they both knew it.

Jack nodded at the last envelope, the thinnest of the stack. "So, what's behind door number three?"

Ford held on to it, refusing to relinquish an inch of control. "I'll get there. But first, you owe me a few things."

Again, the words should have hit him, but all Jack could do in his sorry state was surrender. He put up his hands.

"For starters," Ford said, "I want a straight answer. Did you know you couldn't afford to buy me out when you signed our contract?"

"Probably. Hoped not, though."

The look on Ford's face said the answer hadn't surprised him. "So—just stupid, then. Not both stupid and a jackass."

Jack nodded. "Just stupid."

"Where were you gonna get the money? 'Specially given you never called the bank back about your loan."

Any other town, Ford wouldn't have known anything about Jack's conversation—or lack of it—with the bank. But Tybee wasn't one of those places. Just like Hartwell, news traveled. Even if Ford hadn't made a personal introduction to National Union banker, Josiah Phelps.

Jack paused. It was no more than a second, but he was certain Ford could see that he was about to tell him something no one else knew—on Tybee or anywhere. "I've got land in Colorado. An inheritance. I was thinking about selling."

"Same land your dad still farms?"

"Part of it. This parcel is mostly fallow. Dad can't farm it without me, and I can't bring myself to go back."

"Trade the land for the sea, in other words?"

Right. In so many words.

They were both quiet for a minute, and Jack was thankful for the pause. In fact, Ford's ability to honor silence was one of the things he'd always appreciated. "Without quiet," Ford told him once, "a person is hard-pressed to get to the truth of a situation."

"You know, Jack," Ford started, "if everyone felt at home on the land they were born to, we'd never have explored anyplace other than our own backyards. I don't need to tell you what that would have meant to the history of mankind, let alone your own life."

He rapped his knuckles on the linoleum countertop, hitting the spot where someone's long-ago misplaced hot pan left a bubbled scar. The sound echoed hollow rather than solid, and Jack couldn't help feeling reminded, yet again, of how badly his life was falling short.

"Point is," Ford went on, "some people are meant to stay put, and some people are meant to go. But running is different than going. When you're running, you spend the whole time looking over your shoulder. To go forward, you gotta look forward."

Jack shrugged. "Seems that's how I got myself here to Tybee."

Ford scowled. "Who'd you tell you were comin' to Tybee all those years ago?"

"You. No one else needed to know."

"No one else in the whole world needed to know where you were headed?" The tone made the insinuation obvious.

"I told my parents eventually. They know I'm here."

Ford smirked. Meaning, *exactly*. "You'll know you're going forward when you have the courage to tell people where you're headed." He threw down the last envelope. "Which brings us to door number three."

Jack reached for it, this time without a clue as to what he'd find inside.

"A decent guide knows the importance of a good map." Ford watched him unfold a single sheet of paper. "You get yerself close and that'll get you the rest of the way."

Jack stared at the page, studying the contents without truly taking them in.

Ford let the silence speak for a minute more, then turned to go. "I trust all this'll have you thinking. Just let me know what you decide by close of day tomorrow."

"All right." Reeling, Jack refolded the page. "I can do that."

Ford was at the door and nearly gone before Jack found the words he needed. "They're mine. I don't have proof yet, but I know."

Ford turned to face him again and smiled wryly. "Seems pretty hard to deny, seeing the gap in that kid's teeth. Braces and all."

Jack laughed without even thinking, the release feeling as good as sudden rain on a hot day. "And her. It's not as obvious, but it's there. Neither one of us can wear flip-flops. It's our toes. It's—well…"

"I get the idea, yeah."

"And not just one, but two. Twins. Nearly ready to leave

for college, and I didn't even know they existed." And again, he could see from Ford's face he knew he was about to tell him something he hadn't ever admitted to anyone else. "I don't know if I should be pissed off or happy or—I mean, I didn't even know."

"But there's a part of you that thinks their mom might have been right to leave you out of it," he said, reading Jack's mind.

"I was a mess."

"Sure."

"But not gone. I mean, I could've gotten it together."

"You could've."

"I should be mad. I mean, I should be, right?"

"But what's the point?"

Jack nodded. That was it exactly. What was the point.

"You know," Ford said after a pause, "if having two decent parents were everything, I would've stayed married for more than three miserable years. Unlike you, I did like my old man. My mom's still alive—eighty-seven next month—and we wish she had thirty more years in her. Even so. I was a crap husband and my ex-wife was a quick study. First thing she says to me whenever we bump into each other nowadays is *Thank god I left you.*"

He laughed, and Jack did, too.

"Like I said, Jack. It's hard to move forward when your eyes are on yer six." He pulled open the screen door and stepped onto the dark porch. "Don't forget. Close of day tomorrow. Let me know."

# THIRTY-THREE

## SAVANNAH

Thomas had called it a "game." As if getting attacked on television, on social media, in her own house was *fun*. As if the past week hadn't been one long nightmare.

*For her.* Savannah.

Not Thomas.

Not Maggie.

Not Sam Tamblin. Or Saj. Or Guava Media.

Not even for their father.

*For her.*

The person who hadn't *even wanted to do this in the first place*.

"Savannah?" Nadine knocked on her bedroom door. "I'm out here if you need anything."

Her gut boiled with rage at the intrusion, and Savannah yanked the door open. "Why do you have to be so nice?"

Nadine's face crumpled. "What?"

Savannah felt a nudge in her gut, knowing she'd hurt Nadine's feelings. Even so, she couldn't help going on. "You're too *nice*."

The word came out as the accusation she intended it to be.

"But I'm—"

"You're always following me around. Like a puppy or something. Or a lost duckling looking for her mama." Her every instinct told her to slam the door, to stop the argument before she went too far. She didn't. She wanted the fight.

"I'm just trying to help. To be a good friend." Nadine's voice quivered, but she didn't retreat.

Savannah stared, doing her best to make Nadine see just how much she hated every bit of her. Every perfect blond hair, every precious freckle, every smile and laugh and *nicety*.

"I have my own friends, Nadine. Sorry to break your 'ittle wittle heart, but I don't need you." She watched for the tears to begin rolling down Nadine's pretty cheeks, waited for her to accuse Savannah of being mean, to run downstairs and report every awfulness to Chef Bart and Maggie and Thomas. Savannah would sit in her room, hating herself and licking the wounds until Maggie came up to confirm what a hateful person she was.

But Nadine didn't move. "I don't blame you for being mad."

"Yeah, well—" Savannah started to explain exactly where to shove her opinions when she realized—"What did you say?"

"I mean, I understand why you're mad. You should be. At Eaton, of course. But even more at Thomas. Especially him." Nadine was barely whispering, her voice unsteady, but she'd managed to say the exact words Savannah needed to hear. "He should have told you."

Savannah's knees went soft, like the floor was opening beneath her, and she grabbed the doorjamb. "Thanks," she said. It felt as if her breath had run away.

"I know Maggie can't pick sides. She's in a terrible position. But the way I see it, he kept you in the dark, and then let you take the fall. How is that fair?"

*"Exactly!"* The word felt like it might choke her trying to get out.

Nadine smiled sympathetically. "And now everyone is scared, and that just makes everything worse."

"Yeah." Savannah reached out a hand and Nadine grabbed it, pulling her into a hug. The gesture was enough to make

Savannah lose it, fat sobs racking her all the way down, re-
ducing her to a quaking mess. And still, Nadine stayed put.

They stayed that way for several minutes, Savannah sobbing
and Nadine not letting go. Finally, Savannah pulled free and
walked over to her desk to grab a box of tissues. She plucked
out the first bunch and handed them to Nadine. "Sorry. I
goobered on your shirt."

"That's okay." She took the tissues and looked briefly at
the mess but wiped her face. She'd been crying, too.

"Holy cow." Savannah laughed through her tears. "You're
so nice you don't even care I just snotted all over your shoulder."

"It's washable." Nadine shrugged and the look on her face
said Savannah must be crazy for making a big deal out of
something so small.

Then Nadine started chuckling, and they just stood there,
laughing, trying to talk, sniffling through every word.

"Trigg would totally be freaking out if I did that to her.
*Oh my gawd*," Savannah mimicked. *"You are sooo disgusting!"*

Nadine snorted and tried to cover her nose, but she was
too slow. A long stream of snot came sailing out, catching
the light, and landing with a splat on Savannah's foot. They
looked at each other in shock for one second, then screamed
with laughter and tumbled to the floor, no longer able to
even hold themselves upright.

"I can't believe you just snotted all over my foot!"

"I can't believe you snotted all over my shirt!"

Savannah was rolling on the rug now, clutching her stomach.

"I can't believe I accused you of being *too nice!*"

"I know! What's wrong with being nice?"

Savannah's stomach began to cramp she was laughing so

hard, a stitch all the way up her right side. If only she could catch her breath. Except, then the moment would be over, and that would be awful.

She gulped at the air, almost gaining control when she caught a glimpse of Nadine rolling on the floor beside her and lost it all over again.

"Did you know I'm a Twitter hashtag?"

"Don't forget Instagram!"

"Oh, that's right! People hate me there, too."

"You're such a social media whore!"

"Hey, you're just jealous!"

"Totally jealous! I mean, who doesn't wish they had such a jerk for a brother?"

"Well, you can't get a brother now because your mom is dead!"

"Yours, too!"

They stopped, a moment of morbid realization passing between them. Then, even the subject of dead mothers wasn't too awful, and they laughed and cried and let it all go. The release was the best thing Savannah had ever felt.

Later, when they'd both finally laughed themselves out, they heard Nadine's dad call upstairs that it was time to go home. She stood up to leave.

"Thanks, Nadine," Savannah said. "You're a good friend."

She smiled. "Of course." She grabbed one more tissue from the box and swiped at the dried snot on her shoulder.

Savannah groaned. "Sorry again."

"Seriously. Don't worry about it. One wash and it'll be gone." She tossed the tissue into the garbage can. "Our little outburst reminded me of something, though. Have you been following Sam Tamblin's Twitter feed?"

The mere mention of Twitter turned Savannah's stomach and it must have shown on her face. Nadine waved her question away. "Sorry, of course not. Twitter's a hellscape and the less time you spend there the better. It's just—" She paused. "It could be nothing."

Chef Bart called up the stairs again.

Nadine ran to the door and answered, "Coming!" She turned quickly to Savannah and said, "Never mind. Ignore what I just said. I'm probably just imagining things."

"All right."

When she was gone, Savannah wiped her face on her shirt. It was amazing what a change an hour could bring.

She felt a happy surge of energy and got an idea. She stood up, walked to her desk and rolled a piece of paper into her typewriter.

Renata Covington
Showrunner, Son Showers
American Broadcasting Company


Dear Ms. Covington,


As you may know, I am an aspiring screenwriter and a fan of your show, Son Showers. I also know you have begun to make a name for yourself as a producer, so I thought you might be interested in a concept I have for a new series.
Imagine this:
    A famous conspiracy theorist and blogger is forced to reconcile with her awful past when she loses all but one of her fingers in a freak lawn mower accident.


Savannah tore the paper from the typewriter and crumpled it. Then she rolled in another piece and started again.

Renata Covington
Showrunner, Son Showers
American Broadcasting Company

Dear Ms. Covington,

My name is Savannah McClair and I would like an internship on your show, Son Showers.

You may recall that I've written to you before. I am seventeen years old and am entering my senior year of high school. Like you, I grew up in Minneapolis and I want to make a career for myself in film and television. My twin brother and I lost our mother when we were thirteen and your show explores parental loss better than anything I've ever seen.

On my enclosed résumé, you'll note that my brother and I have a podcast titled "The Kids Are Gonna Ask" in which we search for our biological father. It's proven to be an unexpected hit, and, in the process, we've learned more than I can articulate here.

I did learn this, however: we would not have gotten anywhere in our search if we wouldn't have asked the right questions.

That is the purpose of this letter. I want to work for you and will do what it takes to make that happen. I have already begun applying to several Southern California schools and hope to be there by next fall.

In the meantime, I will send a copy of this letter and my résumé to Fox Studios, ABC, and your production company.

I can be reached at the contact information provided.

Respectfully,
Savannah McClair
Cocreator and Writer, "The Kids Are Gonna Ask"

When she was finished, Savannah tore this sheet of paper from the typewriter, too. But she didn't crumple it. Instead, she pulled an envelope from her drawer, addressed it to California, and set the two pieces aside with a smile.

Then, she pulled even more paper from her drawer. She was on a roll, and it felt terrific. Her fingers flew across the keys as she typed, "The Kids Are Gonna Ask: The Final Episode."

t.mcclair@guavamediausa.com
To: thorJJ1979@gmail.com
Re: Hi Jack

Jack,
Still haven't heard anything, so I guess you are mad. And you're right. We had no idea what was happening and what kind of a mess we might be getting you into. It's our fault. I just hope you don't hate us. But if you do, I hope you won't feel that way forever. I'd still like to meet you someday.

Sorry again,
Thomas McClair

*[BEEP]*

*Maggs! Where you all at? I'm getting thirty-three thousand phone calls a day. These kids are hot. Call me.*

*[BEEP]*

*Maggs. Maggs. Maggs. Pick up! Maggs.*

*[BEEP]*

*Have you figured out yet that I'm just going to keep calling until you answer?*

**Trigg:**
OMG!!! [screaming cat face emoji] So don't kill me but I sort of talked to a reporter about you [oopsies emoji] [finger biting emoji]

**Trigg:**
I didn't tell him anything. I swear. I mean, not really anything. Just like that you aren't super into being a part of the popular crowd but that's cool because you're more about your writing and you've been so sad since your mom died and...

**Trigg:**
That we've been friends for so long I know you better than anyone and there's no way you want all men to get castrated or whatever that Eaton witch said, even though you did sort of make a joke that someone should do that to Nico. But I made the reporter swear not to use that part because you were just mad that Nico always teased you so much and he promised he'd be fair in whatever he wrote...

**Trigg:**
See? Nothing bad. I was just sooo sick of my phone ringing I couldn't stand it anymore.

**Trigg:**
Have you texted Kyle Larson yet???

# THIRTY-FOUR

## SAVANNAH

Savannah came down to dinner with a pile of freshly type-written pages.

"*The Kids Are Gonna Ask: The Final Episode.*" Thomas looked at her. "What's this?"

"We've got to wrap it up sometime."

As he began reading, she knew he wouldn't like what she wrote. Nor did she care.

"You can't blame Sam Tamblin for—" He stopped to find the quote on the page. "For *surrendering to the darkest devils of corporate greed.* And you for sure can't accuse our sponsors of being *eager to endorse the on-air abuse of children by cable news privateers.*"

"Even though they did," she said.

"At best, that's debatable. At worst, that's defamation, and we could get sued."

She shook her head at the assertion. "Let them sue us. I'd gladly pay back the zero cents we've seen in podcast profits."

Thomas kept reading. "Oh my god, Van. It's not Mom's fault, either."

"I don't say it's her fault. I argue the destructive power of family secrets."

Thomas dropped the script to the table. "You're being crazy."

*Oh, he did not just say that—*

"So now I'm *crazy*, huh? Are you sure I'm not being *combative* or *irrational*? Or how about *overly emotional*!" She was hollering, and it felt incredible. "Let me get this straight. I get attacked on national TV for a *massive* secret that *you* were hiding, but I'm not allowed to get upset about it. You, however, get to mope around all day begging me to forgive you." She began to mimic Thomas with the most ridiculous version of him she could muster. *"I'm so sorry, Van! How did I know that could happen?"*

"That's not fair." Thomas's voice was even, but his eyes began to pool, red and wet. It was pitiful.

"Oh, poor widdle Thomas can't handle it when his sister feels her feelings!"

Maggie, who'd been watching silently, suddenly spoke up. "Keep going." She smacked a hand to the table. "You both need to just get it out."

They both shot her *stay out of it* looks.

Savannah went on. "Keeping our father from me? Really, T? I suppose I'm not allowed to be mad about that, either!"

"I *couldn't* tell you because you were always off with *Trigg*!" Two fat tears ran down Thomas's cheeks. "And when you were home you were always like, *Get your own life, Thomas! Go get some friends, Thomas!*"

Savannah felt her throat clamp shut. She hadn't seen him cry since they'd lost Mom. She couldn't stand it. "Oh, for—"

"No!" he screamed. "You wanted to get into this!" He wiped his tears with shaking hands. "You think it's been easy for me? You think I didn't want to tell you about Jack? You—of all people, Van, you're the only one who could even come *close* to understanding what it was like for me to finally find him. Except, every time I wanted to tell you, Trigg was here, or you were mad at me or I don't even know what!"

Now they were both crying. Even Maggie down at the end of the table had to wipe her face with her napkin.

Savannah felt like she'd been turned raw side out, no part safe from pain knifing at her.

"I don't know why we ever did this!" Thomas put his head in his hands and sobbed.

For a long moment, they all simply surrendered, letting the tears come. Katherine Mansfield clicked across the floor and lay down at Maggie's feet.

Eventually, there was nothing but silence.

Savannah's mind was a stew. All at once she was totally alone. Mostly innocent. Partly to blame. Completely confused.

Finally, she said, "I'm sorry if I made you feel alone, T. I didn't mean to. I know how terrible it feels."

He didn't speak, but his tears began to calm.

"I've been mad, obviously," she continued. "But I guess I've been confused, too. This wasn't supposed to be our mystery to figure out. She was supposed to tell us. Mom was supposed to answer our questions."

Thomas ran a hand across his cheeks and shook his head. "She would have, Van. She just died before she could."

"No," Maggie interrupted. "That's not actually true. You both asked. On occasion. Thomas, you asked once when all your friends were joining Cub Scouts and attending meetings with their fathers. Your mom offered to take you and you said no, you wanted a dad, like your friends, and why wouldn't she just tell you who yours was?"

Thomas's gaze fell to a spot on the table and didn't move.

"And, Savannah, you used to leave her notes. Little folded scraps of paper on the breakfast table or under her bedroom door at night. They said things like, *Did he die?* And *Do I look like him?* And *Have I ever seen him?* She'd show them to me and ask my advice and I'd assure her that she'd know what to do when the time came. But then you'd never press her for answers and, essentially, she let the moment pass."

Savannah hadn't thought about those notes in years, but the old anxiety came rushing back. Because that's why she wrote them—that flutter in her stomach she sometimes couldn't shake. The panic that maybe she'd seen *him* somewhere on the street or in the store or at a party, and maybe he knew who she was but didn't say anything. Or worse, maybe he'd passed by like a stranger. "I forgot about those."

Maggie put a hand to her chest and kept it there. "You were young. Always just young enough that she wondered if it was better to tell you something you may not be able to process or wait until she knew you could."

"I hate that." Savannah felt her rage bubble to the surface again. "I hate that she never told us. I hate that she never told you. I hate that she didn't trust us. I hate that she died. I hate that we haven't been thinking about anything except missing her since she left."

Her whole body began to shake. Again.

"You should hate it," Maggie said. "And your mom a little bit, too."

Savannah eyed her.

"I mean it. Your mom died just before you hit the age when you were supposed to start hating her. Teenagers aren't supposed to love their parents. They're supposed to battle them. Those years are your last obstacle on the path to adulthood—it's a time meant to teach you how to stand on your own. You're supposed to vanquish the forces holding you back."

"What is this," Thomas said. *"Game of Thrones?"*

Maggie smiled. "My point is, when a mom dies—especially the way Bess did—it's hard not to think of her as anything but a saint. *The innocent woman who died too young.*

"But you missed out on an important transition. You're

stuck in a *Mommy* holding pattern, when really, you ought to be pissed off at her. Probably for lots of stuff, but most of all that she left you with a big fat wart of a biofather mystery on your backs."

The metaphor gave Savannah a mental hiccup. Biofather wart?

"It wasn't her fault, though," Thomas argued. "It's not like we can do anything to bring her back, no matter how pissed off we get. Believe me." His face flushed and Savannah heard a hitch in his throat as he forced out the last few words. "If it were just a matter of getting mad, I would have made it happen a long time ago."

She closed her eyes. Couldn't look at either of them. "She didn't tell us anything. And I do hate her for that."

At this, Maggie moved to the chair next to Savannah's and put out a hand. "For what it's worth, love, I hate myself for not pushing her more."

Thomas stood up and came around to join them. "I don't think I can hate her yet," he whispered.

"That's okay," Maggie whispered back. "Maybe someday."

They laughed. The ridiculousness of this family. Their situation. All of it.

"Love you, Van," Thomas said. "Love you, Maggie."

"I love you, too, T," Savannah answered. "Love you both."

Maggie gave them a long, luxurious squeeze. "I don't know what's going to happen next. But come what may, we're not going to falter. Deal? We're in this together—the three of us—right up 'til the end."

"Deal," Thomas said.

"Okay," Savannah added, thinking that for the first time in a while, she might actually believe it.

There they sat, the three McClairs, huddled and worn. And for the moment, it was enough.

t.mcclair@guavamediausa.com
To: thorJJ1979@gmail.com
Re: Hi Jack

Jack,
Just one quick note because I was thinking about everything that's happened and I should apologize, too, for not telling Savannah about your emails. I guess I was trying to protect her? Make sure you were legit before she got her hopes up. I don't know. But, I guess I understand if you're angry about that, too.

Thanks,
Thomas McClair

# THIRTY-FIVE

## JACK

In low country, summer brought two things—tourists and storms. Jack tolerated the tourists, since he couldn't make a living without them. But he loved a good storm. Every day about lunchtime he'd start watching the horizon, over where he knew the heat and humidity were just beginning their invisible churn, rising up against the colder skies above.

Funny that was how storms formed, he'd always thought. A dance between opposites. Forces that found each other irresistible, regardless of the consequences.

Jack had been watching the horizon his whole life. Eastern Colorado was flat, a great open stretch of land at the center of the North American Plate. He knew how to read a storm. Sometimes the dance between forces spun itself into towering marshmallowy clouds. Other times, it cut great menacing gashes across the sky.

Today, the clouds had lined up as a squall—a white wall of rain stretching north to south, as far as the horizon could hold. The rain was still miles away, but Jack knew it was time to get off the water.

"Need to head in," he told his charter. His clients, two retired guys he'd taken out countless times, knew what they saw and reeled in their lines without argument.

Jack turned the boat toward shore.

Usually when storms came, Jack used the downtime to plan for the next morning's charter, or even to deal with the pile of laundry in the middle of his apartment. But today, he owed Ford an answer by end-of-business. And he still didn't have one. The only thing he knew for sure was that his intentions had always been good.

"Storm's picking up speed, Jack. Good thing you turned us when you did." One of his clients had stood up and pulled a Coke out of the boat's cooler. "How'd a Yankee like you ever start fishing down here, anyway?"

"My granddad taught me," Jack said. Normally he would have left his answer there, but these guys hadn't given him much trouble over the years. No reason to shut them out. "South Platte River runs straight through Colorado. Bass and crappie mostly. Some catfish."

Summer afternoons when Jack was a kid, his granddad would swing by the farm in his red Chevy truck and holler, "Hop in, Junior. It's too hot to work on a day like this." There'd be a basket of sandwiches from Grandma in the back and two bottles of Mr. Pibb in a cooler on ice. "For when we catch our limit." Then they'd pull away, down the long gravel drive to the road, their cloud of dust never quite thick enough to block the view of Jack's father coming out from the barn to scowl.

"Even a dumb fisherman can be lucky enough to land a fish or two," his granddad had told him. "But to really call yourself a fisherman, you gotta be able to set a hook when the moment is right, and to get to that point, you're going to have to do everything that comes before it right, too."

Standing on a crumbling concrete slab on the banks of the South Platte, Jack's granddad drilled him on the step-by-step: hook, bobber, worm.

"Don't wait 'til that bobber goes under, Junior. Your worm'll be all eaten up if you go that long. You wanna watch it for a nudge. Not the current hitting it or a wave—those are steady. Predictable. You're looking for the unexpected,

like something's interested. And if you're really paying attention, you'll feel it, too. Nothing huge, mind you. Again, like
a nudge. It's subtle, but you'll get a feel for it."

He'd taken his granddad's advice with him all the way to
the coast.

On Tybee, Ford fished rivers, too. Most charter companies
specialized in deep sea fishing, but Ford ran inland charters.
Dozens of channels and creeks flowed south out of Savannah, slicing the Georgia low country into bite-size pieces on
its way to the Atlantic. They were full of redfish and sheepshead and drum.

"When people ask me why I hired a Colorado boy," Ford
said once, "I tell 'em it's because you were raised on the river.
And rivers require a special way of thinkin'."

Jack's first trip on Tybee, Ford took him out on the South
Channel, close to the bridge, under the shadow of Fort Pulaski. The same place he'd been anchored the day he got his
first glimpse of Thomas and Savannah.

"Let's see what you got, Jack. Gonna be fishing for drum
today, and they'll give you a good fight. We'll look for the
black drum, since they're easier. Basically dinosaurs, and a
little bit dumb." He anchored under an overpass and brought
over a bucket of bait. "Nothing a drum loves more than some
good stinkin' shrimp."

Starting that very morning, Ford taught Jack to fish all over
again. Gone were the days of spinners and bobbers. Now he
baited shrimp, squid, mullet and crabs. And for a long while,
he barely caught a thing.

"Reel and then pull," Ford hollered. "Quit doing the
opposite—you're workin' too hard. Reel—faster than that.
Now pull." One trip, they'd gone out for sheepshead and
it'd taken Jack all day to finally get a knack for what it felt
like when they were nibbling on his line.

"They ain't gonna hold up a sign for ya, Jack. You gotta learn the subtleties. These sheepshead here, they bite the back legs off the crab and start to suck the insides out. That's when you wanna pull up. Hard and fast. Don't give them a second to slip away."

Ford pushed the cork handle of Jack's rod deep into his armpit. "Now, Jack! He's gonna fight you with everything he's got. Use your leverage. You got it!"

Jack was soaked from head to toe in spray and sweat. The muscles in his back burned and his arms radiated with heat. He was wasted. Totally spent. But he'd finally recognized all those signals Ford had been telling him to pay attention to, the fish on the line his reward.

Now, here he was, fifteen years older and still on the water. Only this time, no one—not his granddad and not Ford—could step up to tell him what signal to feel for next.

He brought the boat into the landing and helped his clients unload their catch.

"You wanna join us for a beer at The Crab Shack, Jack?" one of them hollered.

"I'm booked this afternoon," he responded. "Thanks, anyway."

"With these clouds coming, Colorado boy?" They laughed and carried on until Jack heard them drop coolers into the bed of their truck. "See you next time, Jack!"

He waved them goodbye.

The storm had taken three giant steps forward, and layers of gray now roiled in the clouds, tumbling over one another as they approached.

The first fat raindrops fell on his windshield as he pulled out of the lot. To his left, the waters of the channel had gone gray and kicked whitecaps against the wind. To his right, the marsh had gone silent, the life within it hunkering down for the storm to come.

Most days, Jack loved the channel, fond of any landscape that looked eager for a fight. Today, though, he looked toward the marsh. More than anything, he needed shelter.

A few minutes later, he found himself at Janie's door.

"I had a feelin'," she said as she answered his knock.

He took a seat on the faded love seat and Janie opened the cooler she kept by her desk. She handed him a bottle of water.

"These are working hours. Nothing stronger until we're off the clock." She pointed a blue-and-white-striped fingernail at him. "Anyway, probably best you have a clear head today."

Jack nodded, adding nothing.

She raised an eyebrow. "You come here to think or to talk? Either one's fine by me. But if you're here to think, I'm gonna get some work done while you're at it."

"Go ahead," he said. He knew he ought to check his email, see if there was word from Thomas. Only, today's decision had to be about Ford. About how to make things right. And he also knew that if Thomas still wasn't answering his apology email, Jack just might not be able to handle it.

Janie turned back to her screen. "Let me know when you're ready."

There were a handful of smaller decisions Jack had to make, too. Loose ends he needed to tie up before he was gone. Here, Janie's tick-tick-ticking keyboard and the pattering of the rain against the metal roof of her garage worked like a talisman on his thoughts, commanding them to shut up, line up and sort themselves into groups.

Janie typed. Jack sat. The storm passed.

Ford was right when he'd told Jack he was looking in his rearview mirror. Jack may have left Hartwell years ago, but he hadn't gone anywhere. Not really. Nor would he until he cut anchor.

He decided, too, he was done living as a stranger in his own town. Maybe as a kid he hadn't chosen to be the odd one, the boy singled out for circumstances beyond his control. But he hadn't been a kid since he left Hartwell. Being the stranger in town was a role he'd gone on to pick for himself.

Students who intend to graduate don't flunk out.

Men who see a future for themselves don't look for it in a transient mountain town.

Yankees who yearn for their roots don't stay in the Old South.

Jack wanted more. He wanted a home. He wanted a family. He wanted a life. And he'd wasted all those years ignoring the subtle signs that would have shown him how to reel it all in.

But at least he could finally point to where he wanted to go.

"Janie," Jack said. "I think I'm ready."

# THIRTY-SIX

## JACK

"Well, well," Janie said. "You're just full of surprises, aren't you, Jack?"

"Guess so." It hadn't taken long to lay out his plan to Janie, who had agreed and said she figured that was the way things had to be.

It was his last request she hadn't expected.

"I'll make sure it happens," she promised. "He'll fuss and tell me what to do with myself, but he'll come around. Ford ain't afraid of Slush and neither am I." She popped up from her desk chair and pulled him up from the couch into a hug. "You're a good man, Jack. Tybee's gonna miss you."

The rain started again, pounding his windshield by the time Jack pulled up at Ford's a few minutes later. Ford heard him coming and had the door open before he'd even stopped.

"My guess is you're coming with your answer." He ushered him in. Ford's house wasn't anything fancy, a painted cement brick rambler with a trim yard and a car park, but it was tidy and had most everything a person needed. "I'd offer you a drink, but I can see on your face you're not stayin'."

Jack shook his head. "I think you probably already know what I've decided."

"Yeah, but I'm gonna make you say it, anyway."

The moment had come. Jack shoved his fists in his pockets and forced out the words. "You ought to take Slush's offer. The money's better and you deserve it."

He wanted to see a change on Ford's face, something to re-assure him that Ford knew he was being sincere. But he didn't.

"I know Slush'll crow and carry on and try to make you feel miserable about handing your business over to him, but he's not going anywhere. Slush's people have been on Tybee as far back as anyone remembers. He's loud, but he's Tybee. And that means he'll take care of what you built."

Ford studied him, his scowl framed by the deep lines of all those years in the sun. Then, finally, he laughed. "I wish I could stand here and say Slush ain't the son of a bitch he seems to be. 'Cept he is. Most days. Give or take a time or two."

Jack chuckled. "He wants your business something awful, though."

"That he does."

"Which is why I have one request." Jack didn't have to read Ford's mind to know he was treading awful close to pissing him off. "I know I don't have the right to ask anything of you. I didn't mean to create such a mess of things, but I did. You deserved better. And I'm sorry."

Ford gave him a small nod, accepting the apology.

"Maybe once you hear what I'm asking, though, it might make accepting Slush's offer just a little bit sweeter."

Jack told him what he had in mind. It wasn't much. Not nearly enough to erase the aggravation he'd caused, but enough to make Ford bark with laughter.

"Janie's promised to help make sure it happens," Jack assured him.

"Oh, I'm sure she has. She's been pushing Slush around since they were riding the school bus together."

He walked over to his kitchen table and picked up a piece of paper from the stacks he must have been working on while waiting for Jack to show.

"I had my lawyer put this together." He handed the paper to Jack. "Had a hunch we'd need it."

The header read Dissolution of Contract. Jack pulled a pen from his pocket and signed. The less he drew this out, the better. He handed Ford his pen, and he did the same.

"I suppose you want to know what I decided on the other," Jack said.

"Would be good."

Jack wished he could give him more than news. "My dad's in tough shape. Like always. But he fell, and it sounds like it was bad. I need to go home and be of some use while I'm there."

"You gonna stay long?"

"Nah." He shook his head. "My family and I aren't made for long."

"Then?"

"Then, forward."

Ford nodded, and this, Jack realized with relief, told him Jack had heard his advice.

"They know you want to meet 'em?" Ford asked.

"Not yet. I'll reach out. Try my best to do it right for once."

"Well. Seems to me like a good first step."

Jack hoped so. "You know I want to thank you for everything, right? For more than the job or for taking the chance on me. I mean it. For everything."

Ford held out his hand and Jack took it. "And you know if you get emotional on me, I'm going to kick you out on your ass in the rain."

Jack grinned. "I may be dumb, but I'm not stupid."

"Didn't think so." He walked over to the door and opened it. "Now go. Before the storm starts again or I change my mind or both."

Jack waved one last time as he drove away, and saw that Ford was smiling.

★ ★ ★

Jack suspected it wouldn't take long to pack up and get on his way. He didn't have many more charters booked and there wasn't much in his apartment worth taking. He'd already had to surrender the security deposit on the place for all the damage he'd done.

Even so, he woke the next morning to a fist pounding on his front door.

"This is getting really old, Carter." He wasn't about to let on to the kid that he was just the person Jack had been hoping to see.

"I'll stop bangin' on yer door soon as you stop sleepin' through yer morning charters. Yer jus' lucky I got nothin' better to do 'til I'm old enough to be a deckhand."

Jack opened the door.

"Same old story, then."

"Yer sleepin' when you should be out on the water and I want to be out on the water but no one'll let me."

"What if I said I took care of that?" He wondered how long it would take before the kid caught on.

Carter eyed him. "You sayin' you got a spot fer me on yer boat?"

Jack shook his head. "Nah. Not me. I'm done with the fishing business. Ford's retiring and I'm moving on. Slush, though. As soon as you turn fifteen, go see him. Tell him you're ready to take your spot on deck."

"Slush ain't never promised me no spot."

"No. But he'll have one for you. As soon as you turn fifteen, you're old enough and he won't have the excuse of having to pay you under the table. If he gives you a hard time, go see Ford or Janie. They'll make sure he follows through."

Carter backed up. "Yer leavin'?"

Jack nodded. "Family stuff."

"Fer good then?"

"Most likely, yeah. But here's the thing. Ford gave me a chance no one else would have. I didn't treat him nearly as well as he treated me, that's for sure. But I figure I ought to at least try to do for someone else what he did for me."

"So, you got me a job with Slush?"

That was the plan. "You want to learn the fishing business, right?"

"'Course."

"Then that's what I did." He waited a few seconds, letting the kid sort everything he was telling him. Then Jack said, "You're driven and you're responsible, Carter. More responsible than me, even. You've earned your shot."

He held out a hand for him to shake, and Carter eyed him again, still wary. But he took Jack's hand and shook it.

"Hold on," Jack told him, walking back inside for something. He found it quick and went back out to the porch. He handed Carter the same packet of maps Ford had handed him all those years ago—laminated, spiral-bound and flecked with the rain, grime and sea spray of their travels. "Any good fisherman knows the importance of a good map."

# BOOK THREE

# THIRTY-SEVEN

## THOMAS

Thomas never called people on the phone if he could text, email or Snapchat instead. This time, he didn't have a choice.

"Thank you for calling Big Tybee Fishing Adventures. Can we book you a charter?"

The mess with Jack and Savannah was his fault, and he was willing to do anything to fix it. He'd already called three other fishing charters and Jack didn't work at any of them.

"Hi, I'm looking for John—um, sorry—Jack Thorson. Does he work for your company?"

The woman on the phone paused. "You're looking for Jack Thorson?"

"Yes." Thomas felt a surge of promise. "I'm trying to get in touch with him. Is he a guide with your company?"

"No, not with Big Tybee."

"All right." He was about to apologize for bothering her when he realized she sounded sort of curious. Everyone else had just hung up at that point, but she was still there. Thomas said, "Do you happen to know what fishing charter he works for on Tybee?"

"Sure do."

When she didn't say any more, he knew he had something. "Could you tell me?"

"Depends. You're gonna have to tell me who you are first."

This, Thomas was prepared for. He and Savannah had done so many cold calls for the podcast they'd developed a strategy. "I'm a friend of the family and I'm trying to reach him, but I don't have his cell phone number."

"Hmm. Funny. Jack's had all kinds of 'family friends' looking for him lately."

"I, uh—are you talking about the podcast?"

"Well, lemme tell ya. I've had a guy offer me two hundred dollars for any pictures I have of Jack. I had a guy offer me fifty dollars to drive him to Jack's house. And I had a guy offer me three hundred dollars to book him on one of Jack's charters."

The woman hesitated just long enough Thomas wondered if she was trying to shake him down for cash. Finally, she said, "I just have a hunch, though. You're not with one of them tabloids, are ya?"

"No." He realized he was shaking his head wildly. "No, I promise I'm not."

"I didn't think so. You sound a little bit too young to get messed up with all their nonsense."

"Yeah, exactly."

"But then again, here you are calling random Tybee fishing charters trying to find him."

"I don't have his cell phone number. And you don't have to give it to me. If you could maybe just pass on a message?"

"Have you emailed him?"

"Yeah. But he stopped answering. I think he might be mad."

The woman let out a long, quiet whistle. "Listen, I'm a friend of Jack's. And a few of us around here feel a certain protection for him, with all that's happened lately. So, here's what I'm gonna propose—I'm gonna tell you a bit about me, then I want you to prove who you are by answering some questions. You good with that?"

"Um, all right."

"Good. Then, my name's Janie. I've known Jack since

he moved to Tybee to work for Inland Fishing Adventures. That's not the company you just called, but I happen to answer the phones for both. I'm sort of a central office to a bunch of companies here on Tybee. Chances are, if you'd kept calling random charters, you'd get me again. So, really, it's sort of your lucky day."

Thomas let out a sigh of relief. "Hope so."

"Okay." Her tone changed like she was smiling. "Now that you know my name, I'm going to guess that your name is Thomas. Am I right?"

He hadn't realized she so obviously knew who he was. "I, uh—"

"No, I know. You shouldn't give yourself up without proof. So, here it is. I know you and Jack had been emailing. I also know you hadn't told your sister about it."

"What?" The conversation had suddenly gone off a cliff and he was in free fall. "Wait, just stop. Who are you?"

"Look, I'm not trying to corner you. But you called looking for a friend of mine who's been in a bit of a pickle lately. And I happen to know that you and Jack were emailing because he told me. Not everything, mind you, but enough to know he suddenly had a lot to think about."

"Okay." Thomas couldn't believe he was standing in his kitchen in Minneapolis talking to a woman in Georgia who actually knew his father. It was almost too much to process. So close to solving the mystery that had upended their lives.

"How do I know you're not going to turn around and tell someone everything I say—like, one of those people offering you money?"

"You don't. But I will tell you something they haven't seemed to figure out yet." She stopped.

"Yeah?"

"Jack is leaving Tybee."

Thomas felt like the breath had been knocked out of him. "What? For good?"

"Well now, Thomas, I can't tell you that until you keep your end of the bargain. I need you to answer a question for me that proves you are who I think you are."

His head was such a mess he surrendered. "Okay. Go ahead."

"All right, true or false. Jack sleeps well during thunderstorms."

He knew this! It wasn't some trick question. It was easy. "False!" He was practically hollering.

"Whoa!" She laughed. "And why is that?"

"Because of the lightning. It makes his ears pop or crackle or something. I can't remember exactly what he said but it happens to me, too, only slightly different. It's one of the reasons he started to believe he might be our dad. Because we mentioned it on one of the podcasts. Not the exact problem, but just that I don't sleep well when there's lightning, and then he emailed and said he thought he knew why I didn't sleep well and told me what happened to him during storms and, like, we knew. Neither one of us had ever met anyone who has that problem."

It was way more than Janie really needed to know, but it felt so good to explain all the amazing coincidences.

"All right!" Janie was laughing even harder now. "Relax. You passed. I believe you, Thomas."

He took a breath to calm down and said, "But Jack left?"

"He did, or he's going to. Family stuff. I'll let him tell you."

"But, see—"

"I know. You're trying to find him."

"Yeah."

"How about I tell him we spoke. It's not my place to give

away his private phone number, but I'll be happy to pass along the message for you. Now that I trust you are who you say."

"Thanks."

He knew the next step was to hang up. To end the call and wait for Jack to get in touch. But he couldn't. He needed her to understand just how important it was for Jack to call him back.

"Can you just, I dunno, tell him—" What? That Thomas was such a screwup he'd possibly destroyed Jack's life and his relationship with Savannah? That he wanted to get to know Jack as their father, even though he wouldn't ever be their dad? That he and Savannah were really more normal than they seemed?

"Just, tell him I'm sorry. For the mess. We really didn't mean for it to happen. And, well…" He tried to make sense of his thoughts but couldn't. "Just tell him that, I guess."

"I will, Thomas. And one more thing?"

"Yeah?"

"Don't you want to leave me your phone number, so he can call you back?"

# THIRTY-EIGHT

## MAGGIE

Maggie smiled and patted herself on the back. She'd just completed the one job she promised herself she'd do today: she made an appointment with a cardiologist. It was in a week. And she was going to show up.

She opened her calendar and wrote the details in pen. *August 4. Dr. Addington. 3 p.m.*

She closed the planner just as the phone rang.

"Hello?" She'd quit answering with *McClair residence* as soon as the reporters started calling. Telling a stranger her name gave too much away.

"Mrs. McClair?"

"Who's speaking?"

"Detective Blegen."

*Oh dear.* Maggie was deeply thankful for the assistance the Minneapolis police had given them, but that didn't mean it was ever good to hear them on the other end of the line.

"I'm calling to let you know that we're planning to remove the blockade on the parkway soon. We haven't had any incidents in two days, and the attention on your family seems to have died down significantly."

"Oh?" Maggie took the phone into the entryway and peeked through the front window. She didn't see anyone. How incredible.

"We plan to keep an officer in the area for a few days, just to monitor. I recommend you call us immediately if you ever have any concerns."

"Of course."

"And Mrs. McClair? Be careful who you let into your house. Who you socialize with. Extra caution is advised for the foreseeable future."

"Thank you, Detective Blegen. I will most certainly do that."

They hung up and Maggie had to take a moment to steady herself. Their world had gone from calm to chaos and back again in less time than it took her accountant to do her taxes.

*See, Mom,* Bess whispered. *I told you it would work out.*

Maggie scoffed. *Easy for you to say. You flit in and out at whim.* She busied herself, wiping the kitchen counters and checking the fullness of the trash bin under the sink. But Bess was still there. She could feel her waiting for Maggie to say the unsaid.

Finally, Maggie could no longer resist. *You said that other situation would work out, too. And you were dead wrong.*

*Ha! Dead. Get it?* Bess laughed.

*You hush,* Maggie scolded. *I don't think your dying is funny at all.*

Maggie carried the teakettle to the sink and ran the water. The kettle slipped through her wet hands and hit the stainless steel basin with a clang.

*He didn't kill me, Mom. The concrete killed me.*

*You can't keep denying it, Bess. It was him. He killed you.*

The phone rang suddenly, interrupting the argument.

*How perfect!* Maggie threw down the towel she'd been using to wipe up her mess. *I suppose this gives you an excuse to disappear again. Just as we're starting to get somewhere.*

Bess didn't reply. Because of course she wouldn't.

Maggie turned toward the phone and scowled. She knew who was calling. He called every day, without fail.

"Hello?"

"Maggs! When will we get this podcast going again?"

"Hello, Sam."

"Did you see the article I just sent? Amaze-bombs, am I right?"

Sam had always been generous with his emails, but recently the subject matter had changed. He used to send links to pieces about Thomas and Savannah—their search, their willingness to take such a public risk, the success of *The Kids Are Gonna Ask*. Now he sent articles about himself—the interviews he'd given, how successful he'd become, how Guava Media was changing the podcast world. All of it self-serving nonsense, and none of it helping to fix the mess he'd made for Savannah and Thomas. If George were around, he would have laid into Sam Tamblin with the ferocity of a German shepherd on an all-vegetable diet.

Maggie took the phone to the kitchen table and sank into a chair. "I'm afraid I haven't checked my email yet today, Mr. Tamblin. Another feature article on Guava Media? Or you, perhaps?" She looked down and noticed a faint stain on her skirt. She rubbed at it.

"You're breakin' my heart, Maggs! You go shimmy open your laptop and read it. Full page. And they mention the kids."

If he only knew how effectively she was managing her surprise. *This man.* It had been nearly two weeks since the fiasco in New York, but had Sam asked about Savannah and Thomas? About how they were faring? Or expressed concern for their well-being? Had Saj called to offer help? Not that Maggie would have accepted. Guava Media's mishandling of events was at the very least irresponsible, and at worst, criminal.

"We need to get moving on the next episode, Maggs. Fans are scuh-ream-ing for it."

Maggie considered making a quip about absence and the fondness of the heart, but she'd learned that Sam Tamblin was allergic to metaphor. Instead, she dipped her finger into her glass of water and dabbed at the stain on her lap. It felt crusty. A dried drip of butter, perhaps?

"I know you said Savannah's working on writing something, but we gotta get a move on. Shake the trees while they're hot. Hey, speaking of which, three new potential show sponsors to consider: Fyrz, which is like part AI tool, part social-media amplifier. Very trend-forward—"

Maggie then noticed she'd dribbled a bit of jam on her shirt. For heaven's sake. She put the phone down and went to the sink to wipe it clean with a cloth. Her hands were sticky, and she took a moment to wash them, too.

Sam Tamblin didn't appear to have noticed her absence.

"—then the last one. You ready for this? It's going to blow your mind. Piper. Cubbins. Piper-effin'-Cubbins, Maggs! Are you hearing me?"

She heard him, yes. Understood him, not at all. "Do you require any immediate action by us, Mr. Tamblin? Savannah and Thomas are still recovering from the events in New York. Speaking of which. Have you given any further thought to following up with Ms. Holmes? Do you think we'll be receiving an apology?"

Sam Tamblin suddenly sounded very distant and muffled.

"What was that, Maggs? I'm headed into an eleva—"

The line went dead.

*That man!* That lying, selfish, conflict-avoiding man.

# THIRTY-NINE

## THOMAS

The next morning, Thomas popped out of bed with a renewed sense of possibility. Jack was going to call. He knew it. He pulled a pair of sweatpants over his boxers, then grabbed a T-shirt off his floor, sniffed it and figured it wasn't too bad for one more day. He threw it on and headed downstairs to grab a bagel.

Nadine was standing in the kitchen.

"Hey," she said. "You look rested. Did you get some sleep last night?"

"Yeah—um, wow." Thomas felt a rush of relief he hadn't come down in his underwear. "Aren't you here early? You usually don't come until after lunch."

"Dad made some excuse about wanting to work in the garden. Really, though, I think it just makes him feel better to stick around. He's still worried about you guys."

"Ah." Thomas felt for the waistband of his sweats, just to make sure he really did have pants on. He didn't mind having Nadine and Chef Bart around so much lately. Usually it made him itchy to have too many extra people in the house. All those nights of coming home to Maggie's new friend from tai chi class, or the woman Maggie met selling goat's milk soap at the farmers market. But Nadine and her dad didn't feel extra. Not anymore.

"Hey," he said. "Did you see any protesters outside when you came? I just looked out the front window and the street was practically empty. I couldn't believe it."

Nadine considered. "No, come to think of it. There was a guy over by the Melbys' place, but he had a trailer full of lawn mowers and stuff."

"They've got a lawn guy." Thomas grabbed the bag of bagels and took one out. He offered one to Nadine, but she declined, so he popped his into the toaster and went to the refrigerator to find the cream cheese. Nadine went into the mudroom and returned holding Katherine Mansfield's leash.

"Want to come with?" she asked. "I've been taking Katherine Mansfield on her walks since you guys haven't been able to. Now that the street's empty, though—"

Thomas felt a shot of panic through his chest. "I'm sort of—" He paused. It wasn't that he was afraid to go out. In fact, he was dying to escape the house. But he didn't want to leave and risk missing Jack's call. Thomas had left the number for the house phone in his message because leaving his cell felt too private, another secret Savannah could accuse him of keeping. Now he kicked himself for not leaving both.

"We can make it a quick one," Nadine said, reading his hesitation. "If that helps."

"Um…" What were the odds that Jack would call in the next twenty minutes? "Sure," he said, even before realizing he'd decided. He plucked his bagel from the toaster and tossed it in the air until it was cool enough to hold. Then he slathered cream cheese across the surface and threw on his shoes.

Nadine grabbed Maggie's oversize sunglasses from the counter. She handed them over and smiled. "Maybe you should put these on. Just in case."

"Funny girl."

They let the mudroom door slam behind them and made for the parkway. They came to the end of the alley and Thomas peeked around the corner from behind Mrs. Tellison's overgrown lilac bush. Nothing. They turned onto the sidewalk.

"Sounds like you and Savannah are getting along again," Nadine said.

"Yeah, sort of. I mean, she's still mad at me, but it's not like she doesn't have a right to be. I should have told her about Jack. I'm trying to fix that."

Nadine asked how.

"By telling her everything I know. Where he lives. Where he grew up. That he takes people out fishing for a living. Really, I don't know all that much. But I just get this feeling he's a good guy. Normal, you know?" Thomas noticed that Maggie had wrapped a scarf with bright yellow suns all over it around Katherine Mansfield's neck. "Like, I doubt he dresses his dog up like a beauty show contestant."

"Aww." Nadine tsked. "I like the scarves. I mean, boy dogs wear bandannas. It's no different."

"Maybe." Thomas decided if he ever owned a pet, it'd be a black Lab with nothing but a plain brown collar. "Thanks for encouraging me to get out, by the way. Feels like forever since I've breathed real air." The past few nights his legs had taken on a life of their own, antsy and refusing to let him settle. They wanted to move. Wanted to run.

"You're welcome."

"And thanks, I guess, for helping us out. Your dad making sure we're eating well and all."

"He loves it."

They walked some more.

"Do you love it?" he asked after a while.

"What?"

"Your dad's job. Coming with him to our house. Helping him in the kitchen." Thomas couldn't imagine. All he ever wanted to do after he got home was eat, go up to his room, shut the door and find some peace and quiet.

"I don't always come with him," Nadine said. "Just when I don't feel like being home alone."

"God, I'd give anything to be home alone once in a while." Last year, he'd returned from track practice to find an entire mariachi band in their backyard. Savannah was nowhere to be found, but Maggie was dancing around the patio holding a rose in her teeth while Chef Bart roasted corn on the grill. Thomas had heard—and smelled—the ruckus blocks away. He'd thought it was a food truck. "Seriously, what's wrong with alone time?"

"Sometimes it reminds me."

"Of what?"

Nadine stayed quiet. "I figured you already knew," she said finally. "From Maggie. Or Savannah."

"No." Hardly the first time he was the last to hear something. "But it's okay. You don't have to tell me if you don't want to talk about it."

"My mom died when I was in sixth grade. A drug overdose."

"*What?*" He definitely had not known.

"She struggled for a long time. That's why my parents divorced. My dad had custody, and my mom was going through all these treatment programs. She was doing well. Looking good. We'd meet her sometimes. Together. Like, out for ice cream or something.

"But then, she disappeared. One day we were supposed to meet her at the park and she never came."

Thomas didn't realize they'd stopped walking until a mom with a stroller had to squeeze past them on the sidewalk. "What happened?"

"We didn't know for a long time. Dad filed a missing person's report, asked her friends. She didn't have much family.

My grandparents both died before I was born, so—" She let the story end there.

"Holy shit, Nadine." They were the only words Thomas could find.

"I know."

"I really had no idea."

She nodded and readjusted Katherine Mansfield's leash around her hand. "It's okay. I mean, it's terrible, but I see a counselor, and he's great. And my dad, of course. He and I have always been close. But there was a whole year we didn't know where she was. I used to go to bed at night thinking that my dad secretly went out looking for her while I was asleep, like I'd wake up in the morning and there she'd be, eating breakfast in the kitchen. Or, for school events—concerts and stuff. I'd spend my whole time on stage searching the crowd for her face, convinced she was there."

Nadine kept her thoughts to herself for a moment. "Do you sometimes wonder if it was your fault somehow? I mean, I know it wasn't. My dad and my counselor love to remind me of that. But what if she had to go out for diapers some night, and she met someone while she was out and that's how she got started with the drugs. Or maybe I cried too much for her to handle, or—"

Thomas knew the questions exactly. "Or maybe if she hadn't been going where she was going that day, everything would have been different."

"Yeah." Nadine glanced at him and winced. "Maybe all that stuff."

Thomas had run every *if only* scenario a thousand times in his head. Sometimes, he did it to prove that there was nothing he could have done, that his mom's accident was totally random. Sometimes, though, he did it to torture himself.

Because at least when he was mad at himself, he didn't have to miss his mom.

"How did you find out what happened to her?" Thomas wasn't sure he actually wanted to know, but it felt wrong not to ask.

"The police called. About a year later. Like I said, she'd struggled for a long time."

Thomas did the mental math. Nadine would have been in sixth grade, meaning she'd lost her mom a full year before he lost his, and she'd never even mentioned it. Two years counting her disappearance.

"I'm sorry," he said. "All we've been talking about is our crazy McClair family. Seems kind of selfish now."

"Nah. I mean, yeah, you've all been pretty amped up lately. But shouldn't you be? It's a lot." She paused. "I've never understood, anyhow, why people think they can't feel bad just because someone else has it worse off. It's not really a competition. At least, not one I'm interested in."

"You'd win, though." He meant it as a joke, to lighten the moment. But he knew as soon as it came out how badly he'd aimed.

Nadine lost her hint of a smile. "That's what I'm saying. I don't want to win. I don't want to be the girl who always has the awful story attached to her. Do you like being the kid whose mom died when the overpass crumbled?"

"No." He didn't like being that kid at all.

"Savannah and I have talked about this. You guys didn't have a choice—everybody heard about your mom's accident. Me? At least I get to decide who to tell."

There was no world Thomas could imagine in which having your mom die wouldn't feel awful. "How is that better?"

"Because I only tell people as much as I trust them with the truth." She stopped and adjusted Katherine Mansfield's scarf where it had begun to bunch against the leash. "I don't want to be secretive, but it's also my story to share. You know?"

He thought he did.

"I think that's made your search for your dad more difficult," she said. "It's so public. Everyone has an opinion."

"But without going public—" Thomas held up a finger. "You know what? How about we change the subject?" He couldn't help it. He didn't want to debate the very personal choices he and Savannah had been forced to make. Not with Nadine. Not with anyone.

"Sorry," Nadine said, and Thomas could barely handle the hurt in her voice.

"No, no, it's just… No offense. Anyway, new topic, okay?"

Nadine held out a hand to shake. "Okay."

Thomas walked a few more steps, gathering his thoughts. "So… I've been trying to figure something out lately. Normally, I'd talk to Nico, but he wouldn't get it."

Nadine shot him a look and let out the kind of chuckle that said she didn't think Nico got much of anything.

"Have you been following the whole McClair Twin mess on Twitter?"

Nadine stopped. "Are you talking about the weird stuff on Sam Tamblin's account?"

He was. Though, something told him not to show his cards yet. Like making her say it without prodding was some kind of proof. "What weird stuff on Sam Tamblin's account?"

"Okay." Nadine handed him Katherine Mansfield's leash and pulled out her phone. She scrolled for a few seconds, then leaned in, showing him her screen. "This was the first thing that caught my eye. He tweeted this on June 10—that's before your first NPR interview, even." She read the tweet aloud. "'Those McClairs are hadly innocent children. More like overprivileged white kids. #paternallivesmatter.' At first,

I assumed it was a retweet, but even that would be strange. Why would your producer be retweeting something so mean? Then I noticed it's not a retweet."

Thomas reached for her phone. "Can I see?" He knew the tweet she was talking about—it had been one of the first about them to go viral. It was still making the rounds, though now it was amended with a whole lot more hashtags like #McClairCryBabies and #IWantMySpermDaddy. "Are you saying you think Sam Tamblin wrote this tweet?"

"Not sure." Nadine reached for her phone and scrolled some more. "I can't seem to find it right now, but at one point I thought I was able to trace its origins back to the very first retweet. It got picked up by what looked like a bot, but it went crazy from there."

"*Whoa.*" This hadn't been what he was talking about at all. He'd been talking about the increasingly graphic links Sam Tamblin had been sending for the Guava Media podcast, *It's Only Murder*. Most were so gory they came with an Explicit Content warning.

Nadine went on. "There are one or two others that caught my eye, too, but I'd probably have more luck finding them on a computer. My screen's too small for all this scrolling."

Thomas suddenly couldn't get back home fast enough.

**NICO:**

DUDE! I know you're home. Come over

**NICO:**

I'm level 54 on RedZoneSix

**NICO:**

It's pretty much all I have to do this summer since you got famous

**NICO:**

You know cross-country practice starts next week, right?

**NICO:**

If you're not there, I'll know you're too fat to run

# FORTY

## THOMAS

Thomas and Nadine made it back from their walk just before lunch. Chef Bart was out at the farmers market, and Savannah and Maggie were nowhere to be seen. Nadine took Katherine Mansfield into the mudroom to clean her paws and get her fresh water, and Thomas offered to make sandwiches.

First, he checked the phone for voice mails. Nothing.

"I make a decent turkey and cheese," he called to Nadine. "Anything fancier and it'd probably turn into a mess."

Nadine said turkey and cheese would be great.

He had his head in the refrigerator when the home phone rang.

All thoughts of investigating Sam Tamblin's social media fled from Thomas's mind.

He ran to the phone, leaving the fridge open, the cold air rushing his legs. "McClair residence," he said. His hand was shaking, and he didn't even know who he was talking to yet. Could be a reporter. Could be an obscene call. Could be Jack.

"Yeah, um, I'm returning a call from Thomas? He left a message at my office. And I'm returning it. The call, that is."

The voice on the line paused, and Thomas realized with a jolt who it had to be.

"Sorry," the man said. "I've never done this before. I mean, not make a phone call. I've done that, obviously. Just, this situation…"

"Jack?" His voice came out like a croak. "This is Thomas." Talking to him was like an out-of-body experience. He had this average-guy voice. A total surprise. Thomas always imagined a deep, Ten Commandments-ish voice. Like James Earl Jones as Darth Vader, without the freakish wheezing and death threats. But Jack sounded just like Jack. He didn't have any sort of an accent despite living in Georgia, and for a minute Thomas panicked that he wouldn't recognize his voice if he ever got to talk to him again.

He got ahold of himself enough to tell Jack why he'd reached out. "I'm really sorry we got you into this mess. Did you get my emails? And—I'm sorry I didn't tell Savannah. I'm sorry you didn't know about us... I guess I'm just sorry for everything."

"Seems like that's an awful lot for a seventeen-year-old kid to be sorry for," Jack said.

"That's not even the half of it. And when I stopped getting emails from you, I just assumed you were mad at me."

"I didn't get your emails. Long story. But you don't have to worry. I'm not mad."

Thomas felt a weight lift from his shoulders he hadn't realized was there. He took a deep breath. "A lot's happened, Jack."

"Sounds like. That why you called?"

Thomas told him all of it—Savannah getting ambushed on national TV and the whole world after them and the neighborhood on lockdown.

About Thomas feeling pissed off and awful and helpless about all of it.

"I take it you're a fixer, huh?" Jack said.

Thomas wanted to say, *No, I'm not.* But then, maybe he was. Or wanted to be, at least. After all, if you can't fix something when it breaks, what's the point of having it?

That's when Jack told him where he was headed. "My family is in Colorado. Wheat farmers. Unlike you, I haven't been trying to fix anything with my folks for years. So, I've got some work to do. But after that—"

He stopped, and Thomas knew what he was going to say. At least he hoped he knew, and the adrenaline kicked in so hard he thought he was going to punch Jack through the phone if he didn't.

"Well, this isn't something I should ask you. I really ought to talk to your grandmother, first."

That, well, made sense.

Jack, as a person, just made sense to Thomas.

This call could have gone so wrong. He could have been an asshole—screamed at Thomas or hired a lawyer or gone crying to the media like Brynn. But Thomas never even considered the possibility that he would. Why?

"In the meantime," Jack said, "I was thinking I'd reach out to Savannah directly. Send her a letter. Just wanted you to know, so you're not surprised."

"Yeah. Of course. I mean, whatever you want to do." He paused and gave him the address. "Be nice to her, Jack. Not that I think you wouldn't be… It's just—" He looked down at the table and, for the first time, saw the turkey sandwich in front of him. He hadn't made it. Which meant Nadine had, even though now she was nowhere to be seen. "It's just that I've been sort of amazed at how mean people can be, and it's better to be around decent people."

"Well, if my life is any indication, decent people tend to pop up when you need them. Even sometimes when you don't deserve them."

Thomas was still thinking about those words when Jack sounded ready to hang up.

"Wait—Jack. I've been trying to tell Savannah everything I know about you. Where you're from, all that stuff you told me. And she keeps asking me if you and Mom kept in touch.

I said I didn't think so because you were going to New Zealand or whatever. Right?"

Jack cleared his throat and Thomas was afraid he'd crossed some sort of line. After a beat of silence, he asked again, anyway. "Right, Jack?"

"No, that's right," Jack finally answered. "I wanted to travel, and your mom encouraged me to. So, yeah, that was part of the reason. But also, your mom was in love with someone else. She told me before she left, and I wasn't about to break that up."

Thomas fell into his chair. Stars began to dance in front of his eyes, blurring his vision. "She *what*?"

Jack blew out a heavy breath. "Geez, Thomas. I never... I shouldn't have—"

"No, right. We knew that." They didn't, of course. Not even close. "He and Mom didn't get married. Mom was too busy with us to date and all that." Thomas was seeing double.

"You okay, Thomas?"

"Yeah!" His voice sounded like somebody else's. "Of course! So great to talk to you, Jack. Thanks for calling. For sure write that letter to Savannah. She'd love it."

Then, for the first time in his whole life, Thomas hung up on his father.

# FORTY-ONE

## MAGGIE

Maggie lay in bed, not sleeping. She'd gone to bed hours ago and still, not even a wink of rest. She sat up, turned on the lamp and pulled her dog-eared copy of *Zorba the Greek* from the bedside table.

But that only made her hungry for spanakopita.

She slammed the book shut and grabbed her journal. There was so much she hadn't been able to bring herself to think about, much less record, and perhaps this was why sleep eluded her.

She put pen to page. "RE: PODCAST." She always wrote her headlines in block letters. "IMPORTANT CONSIDERATIONS…"

And that's when she heard them—voices in the kitchen. She threw on her kimono and hustled downstairs before her brain got smart enough to stop her. She flipped on the kitchen light and startled. "Oh!"

Thomas and Savannah huddled together at the table.

"Hey, Maggie," they said.

"Apparently I wasn't the only one who couldn't sleep." She kissed the top of Thomas's curls and ran a hand across Savannah's shoulders, sitting down next to her. "What has the two of you awake tonight?"

Thomas shrugged and bobbed his head, acknowledging her question while giving nothing of substance away in return.

Maggie suddenly understood. "Ah. You weren't expecting me."

Savannah sighed and shot her brother a look. "We may as
well get to it."

Thomas glared back, unblinking, until he surrendered and
spit out the news. "I spoke to Jack Thorson today. I was just
telling Van about our conversation."

Maggie flushed. "As in, John James Thorson?"

"Yeah."

"On the phone?"

"Yep." There was an edge to Thomas's voice. A tone that said
*Are you sure you want to start this?* He went on, anyway. "We'd
been emailing, you know. But after Savannah got so upset, I
felt like I had to do something. So, I tracked him down."

Maggie's breath stalled in her throat and she had to get
herself a glass of water to push it down.

Thomas said, "You look surprised."

She took a long drink and returned to her chair. "I ought
to be angry. You took things to a whole new level without
my knowledge."

She wasn't mad at them, of course. Not really. She just
had this sinking feeling that they *knew* now. That her grandchildren knew the same thing Jack Thorson knew and that
Maggie had never told. Because they were still children, and
because children didn't need to know that about their mother.

*It's not that big of a deal, Mom*, Bess whispered.

Maggie shushed her with a flick of the wrist. "Never mind
me. If I'm mad at anyone, I'm mad at myself. I wanted to
give you both your independence, to let you do this search in
your own way. But I'm not sure you were ready. That any of
us were." She fiddled with her robe, cinching it tight. Then
tighter again. "Let's just say that this whole affair has forced
me to face certain realities that are…uncomfortable."

Thomas nodded, acting as if he understood, even though
Maggie knew there was no way he could.

"Like what?" Savannah asked.

Maggie gave her a tight smile. "Oh, nothing." She picked up her glass and held it at the ready. "Let's talk about Jack. Tell me everything." She took a pointedly long drink.

Thomas started at the beginning. He told her about their early emails and how he'd hunted Jack down on Tybee Island until he found someone who could pass along his phone number.

"It was amazing to actually hear him on the other end of the line," he said. "I mean, it's like it was—" He stopped, wide-eyed.

"Fate?" Maggie said. Her throat was thick with anxiety and it came out more of a croak.

Thomas and Savannah exchanged smiles, and the light on their faces made Maggie's heart dance—literally. The rhythm pounding her chest was "Zip-a-Dee-Doo-Dah."

Thomas's expression darkened. "He also told me that Mom was in love with someone else when they met. It's part of the reason why they didn't keep in touch."

At this, Savannah looked Maggie directly in the eye. "Is that true?"

"Oh." Maggie was lucky she was no longer swallowing, or she would have choked. She scolded herself for being surprised. *Good grief.* She'd known where this conversation was going. And was it such a terrible thing? Their mother had fallen in love with a man who was in no way her equal. A man named Tad. Who names their son Tad, anyhow?

*Just tell them,* whispered Bess.

*Let me do this my way.* Maggie cleared her throat with another sip of water. "Yes. It didn't work out."

Savannah snickered. "Obviously."

It wasn't nearly as obvious as Savannah imagined.

"They went to high school together," Maggie continued.

"Head over heels for each other their whole senior year. But when college came, he went off to California and she stayed here in Minnesota. Bess was brokenhearted about the breakup. But your grandfather and I assured her that if they were really meant to be together, they'd still be in love after they graduated." Her body shuddered at the memory of that conversation. Bess, positively distraught, convinced she'd never love anyone again the way she loved Tad.

"Was he nice?" Thomas asked.

Maggie closed her eyes quickly, before he could see her reaction. *Nice* wasn't the issue. Tad was weak. Weak and dishonest, a man who tried to account for his lack of spine by calling it "moral character."

"They…were…just not right for each other." That was as much as she planned to say about dear old Tad.

But there was something else. One more thing they needed to know. She opened her eyes. "He was *not* your father. I asked your mother explicitly and she was very clear."

Of course she'd asked.

*"Mother,"* Bess had scolded. As if this weren't a perfectly appropriate question, considering the situation. "Not that I should have to prove anything, but Tad and I have lived two thousand miles apart for four years."

"Are you certain?" Maggie urged her to be one hundred percent sure.

But Bess had only gotten more upset. "Are you suggesting he FedEx'd me his sperm?"

Maggie searched her grandchildren's faces, desperate to understand what they needed to hear. What would make this not so confusing for them. "Your mother never hesitated in her decision to keep you. Not once. You were the loves of her life."

"I know," Thomas said, sounding like he meant it, and

Maggie softened at the calm in his voice. He was handling this, processing it in his Thomas-like way.

Then Savannah. "It's just… I can't help but feel like it's our fault. Like, if she wouldn't have made the mistake with us, she would have had a husband and a whole other family."

Maggie's mouth fell open, shocked. The hair on the back of her neck stood up and she had to stop herself from leaping out of her chair. "*No!* Your mother got pregnant unexpectedly, but the two of you were never a mistake!" Behavior was a mistake. Choices, a mistake. The only mistake Bess made was to love a weak boy like Tad.

Because she had still loved him. Even after four years apart. Even after other boyfriends, and travel, and a life of her own. She was planning to move to San Francisco as soon as she graduated, and Tad was planning to meet her there. They were going to try to pick up where they left off, see if they'd survived the test. "It's like you and Dad promised," Bess had said, calling to share the news with Maggie. "If it's meant to be, it's meant to be."

Only, Bess discovered she was pregnant only a few weeks before graduation. And Tad suddenly discovered a latent moral compass in his soul that would "never allow" him to look at Bess the same way again. He wanted nothing to do with her once he found out she was going to be a mother, refused to raise another man's child.

Later, when she said she wanted to keep the baby, Maggie wasn't about to argue. That "mistake" pregnancy rescued Bess from a life with a man who didn't deserve her, or her children.

Friends used to *tsk* quietly and shake their heads when Maggie told them about Bess's pregnancy. "No father?" they'd whisper. And Maggie would do her best to disguise her delight when answering, "No. Bess is going to raise them on her own. With my help."

Now, sitting in their quiet kitchen, in the very room where Bess had told her about the pregnancy that led to these two wonderful human beings, Maggie felt suddenly desperate. To instill in Thomas and Savannah every ounce of their mother's love. To ensure they believed in themselves with the same ferocity that Bess had. She had chosen them over him for a reason.

"I have this memory," Maggie said, "of standing over your crib when you were newborns. You were so tiny that you slept side by side in the same bed. We'd put you down every night and then just stand there, marveling." She felt her eyes glisten. "Bess would say, 'Look at them, Mom. They're perfect. Absolutely perfect.'"

Savannah snorted. "You tell that story a lot."

Did she? "Funny, I worry I don't tell you enough about your mom. That I'm your last connection, and that I'm failing."

"I wish you wouldn't." Thomas pushed back from the table and his chair screeched across the floor, wood on wood. "I mean, I know you want us to remember her and everything, but sometimes we just want to forget. Except you won't let us. I'll finally get to a point where I'm not thinking about her constantly, and then you tell some story about something that happened when we were little and it's like—*argh!*" He shoved his hands into his hair and pulled. The edge in his voice was razor sharp. "You want us to hate Mom. That's what you said, right? You said we had to hate her in order to grow up. So we didn't get stuck." He pointed at Maggie. "But how can we do that when you constantly live in the good old days?"

"That's not my intention, Thomas."

"I know. But it's like, give me a break, Maggie. The house is either full of strangers or it's full of ghosts. We're either eating dinner with someone we've never met before, or you're telling us stories about things that happened *forever* ago."

"I—" Maggie stood, no longer able to stay still. She got

up and paced back and forth before spinning back to Thomas and Savannah and saying, "I love to be around people, is all. And I want you to know your family. To know your history. To have a rich community of friends."

Thomas pounded a fist on the table. "Then why didn't you tell us about Mom? Why did we have to hear it from a man we've *never even met*?"

"Because there are some things that are better not to know!" There, she'd said it. There was no taking it back now.

Savannah asked, "What else are you keeping from us? Are you dying? Is that why you keep grabbing your chest?"

"No!" Maggie rushed to her and wrapped Savannah in her arms. "Oh my heavens, no. I feel fine. In fact, I have an appointment at the doctor just to make absolutely sure."

"Okay, good." Savannah was muffled against Maggie's robe, but neither of them let go.

"We need to be able to trust you." Thomas's voice was tight, and Maggie could hear the tears coming. "I want to come home and feel safe, not stuck in a house full of strangers. I want to be able to tell you about my day. And I want you to listen. Everything I say doesn't have to lead to some story about Granddad when he was young."

His first tear fell, and he wiped it away quickly. "We're our own people."

"Is that why you wanted so badly to find Jack? Because he's all yours?"

Thomas grabbed a napkin and wiped his face dry. "Part of it, yeah."

"Ours and Mom's, actually," Savannah said. "He was Mom's, first."

An unexpected chuckle escaped Maggie's throat. "I guess it's funny, then. That it was Jack, not me, who told you the first new thing you'd heard in a long time."

"That's what I've been trying to say." Thomas's voice was still wobbly with emotion.

Maggie promised to try and do better.

"Maybe it's not all bad." Savannah released Maggie from their embrace and sat up, wiping her eyes with her sleeve. "I wanted to meet our biodad. But I really wanted to learn as much as I could about Mom." She wiped her nose. "Good news is, we're doing both."

In Maggie's mind, Bess giggled suddenly, and whispered, *She's right. My fabulous daughter is right.*

**Trigg:**

My parents just called and they're not picking me up until next week! I'm going to die!!! [skull emoji] [praying hands emoji] [sobbing emoji]

**Trigg:**

My grandma just told me she was going to Target and asked if I needed any maxi pads!!! OMG

**Trigg:**

At least Kyle Larson is a Cornhuskers fan, tho [football emoji]

**Trigg:**

We've been texting [football emoji] [corn emoji] [football emoji] [corn emoji]

**Trigg:**

OMG I think I might like Kyle. Don't be mad!!! Are you mad???

**Trigg:**

ARE YOU EVER GOING TO ANSWER ME?????

# FORTY-TWO

## SAVANNAH

Savannah slept in. All the late-night emotion of the past several days had taken its toll, and she was officially exhausted.

It was sometime past noon when she finally crawled out of bed. She'd heard the mailman, who never came before lunch, and the sound of him opening the slot in the front door made her stomach growl. She headed downstairs in search of food.

She grabbed the scattered pieces of mail from the floor in the entryway and flipped through on her way to the kitchen. Most of it was college brochures, until she saw a fat white envelope addressed to Savannah McClair.

The return address was "Tybee Inland Fishing Adventures."

*Whoa.*

Savannah clutched the envelope and ran upstairs to her room. She sat on her bed for a long time, looking at the envelope. The handwriting was masculine and square. The postmark was from Tybee Island, Georgia. Obviously, Jack. Or a hoax from some hater with just enough smarts to think about postmarks.

It could be bad.

It could be from Jack.

She ripped it open.

Two envelopes lay inside. One read *open first*. The second read *open the other letter first*. Both in the same boxy penmanship.

Obviously, the juicy stuff was hiding in that second envelope. The sender may as well have written, "The contents of this envelope are so incredible, they may burn your eyeballs right out of your head."

She went straight for it. He had to have known she would.

*Then again*—if Jack really was her dad, this was a pivotal moment. She was only going to get to open these letters once. She had an idea.

A minute later, Nadine was knocking on her bedroom door. "Savannah? I got your text."

She hurried Nadine inside. "I need a favor. I got these in the mail. I think they're from Jack."

"Whoa," Nadine said.

"I know. You're not the only one." The surprise was definitely mutual. "Thing is, I need you to hold them up to the light and tell me if you can see anything that shows what order I should open them in." She held up the second envelope. "I mean, I'm thinking the good stuff is probably in here. But context is everything. Like, will I understand what's in the second envelope if I don't read this one first?"

Nadine took them both and walked to the window. She held them up, one at a time, and peered inside as best she could. Finally, she turned back. "I think you ought to open them in order."

Of course, Nadine would say that. Any sane person would.

"Did you see anything? Like, something terrible that makes you think maybe I shouldn't even open them at all?"

"No. I just think he had his reasons, you know?"

Savannah nodded. "Will you sit with me while I read the first one? Just in case?"

"Sure, but wouldn't you rather do this with Trigg?"

"She's in Nebraska." It was an excuse. Even a few weeks ago, Savannah would have called Trigg, and she would have come right over, and they would have spent hours speculating on what the letters might say and spinning scenarios on every single *what if* they could imagine. Then Trigg would tell Savannah what to do and she'd do it.

That was back then.

"All right." Nadine sat down on the rug with her back against the bed. Savannah joined her. She told herself to quit thinking so hard and eased the first envelope open.

It was a letter in the same handwriting.

*Dear Savannah,*
*My name is John James Thorson and I knew your mother.*

She realized she was shaking. "I can't read it."

Nadine looked at her, confused.

"I'm trying to read the words, but it's like I can't absorb them. My brain is running too hard to take them in, like I'm on overload."

"Okay." Nadine took the letter but refused to look at it. "Don't you think that's sort of private? Something you should read with Thomas, or even Maggie?"

Savannah shook her head. "It's not addressed to them. It's addressed to me." She could have called Thomas, but something in her screamed *no*. She wanted this moment for herself. Thomas had gotten plenty already.

"Plus," she told Nadine, "you're so calm. My brain won't have any choice but to settle down and listen."

"You're sure?" Nadine and her lovely eyebrows begged an honest response.

"Positive." Then, "No. Wait."

Savannah stood, grabbed a pillow from her bed, and tucked it behind her spine where the bed frame hit. "Okay. Now I'm ready."

Nadine began.

Just as she'd hoped, Savannah's brain settled down and listened.

*Dear Savannah,*

*My name is John James Thorson and I knew your mother.*

*I think you already know about me, but I assumed you knew about me before and I was wrong. So I'd like to introduce myself in my own words.*

*Most people these days call me Jack. I'm 40 and I live in Georgia as a fishing guide on an island off the coast called Tybee. This is going to sound like I'm lying, but Tybee is just 20 minutes from Savannah, GA and highway 80 runs all the way there, connecting the two. It's just a coincidence, I know. But also cool.*

At this, Savannah stopped Nadine. "He's talking about my name, right? That's the coincidence he thinks is cool?"

"Must be," she said.

Savannah smiled. "Okay. Go ahead."

*As I write this, I'm actually getting ready to move out of Georgia. I'm going to drive to Colorado and spend time with my parents. They own a wheat farm in Hartwell in the eastern part of the state. I haven't been the greatest son and I haven't helped much with the farm or with my parents as they've gotten older. That's a long story I'll tell you sometime (if you want to hear it). My dad fell recently and anyway—I'm heading out to CO for a while.*

*I listen to a lot of podcasts, but I heard about yours from a kid who was on my boat one day. The show is great—I want to tell you that. You have a lot of talent and even if I didn't think I might be the guy you're looking for, I would have kept listening. I know you want to become a producer someday and I hope you do.*

This time, Nadine stopped to say, "That's really nice."

But Savannah couldn't take in the compliment, not from a stranger. "Mmm. Keep going."

*When I saw the picture of Thomas on your website it was pretty shocking. I looked exactly like him at that age. I even have the gap in my teeth and I never got braces so mine is still there, too. If I had a picture with me I'd send it to you, but I don't, so I'll just tell you that I'm tall—6'1"—and I'm still pretty thin even though I don't eat great, being a bachelor (which is NOT to say I expect a woman to cook for me but just that I work late and it's not all that easy to cook for one). Anyway, I've always had wavy hair and freckles like Thomas does, too.*

"Wait. Don't you think it's strange he doesn't have any pictures of himself? I mean, who doesn't have pictures? He could snap a selfie right now and text it to us."

"Does he have your cell number?"

"No. But I mean, there are options."

Nadine bobbed her head. "Yeah. But maybe he's just not that into technology, spending his time on the boat and all."

"He listens to podcasts."

"You could ask for one," said Nadine, of course, being the totally logical person she was.

"True."

Nadine went back to reading.

*I began emailing Thomas after I'd heard enough clues that I knew (at least believed) this had to be more than coincidence. I honestly thought I was emailing with both of you and I guess now I should have asked why it was always Thomas who replied but maybe you were busy with the show or something. I'm really sorry, Savannah. I feel responsible for coming between you and your brother and that was never my intention.*

Savannah put a hand on Nadine's arm and said, "It's good that he's a guy who can apologize, right? I don't trust people who can't apologize."

Nadine agreed.

*If it turns out that I am your biodad, I want you to know that I never knew about you and Thomas. Not that I blame your mom, either. She was really smart and had plans for her future and I was sort of a ski bum who didn't know what I wanted to do. So, I'm glad you and Thomas both seem to have inherited her smarts. I'm not dumb, I just haven't always taken advantage of the opportunities I had in front of me. Your mom probably saw that in me and knew I wasn't ready to be a father. At least, that's my best guess.*

*I would like to meet you and Thomas someday, if you're interested. I'd be willing to do a paternity test and answer whatever other questions you have. I don't know what sort of relationship you'd like from me, if any. I didn't ever expect to be in this situation. But I feel like, most of all, I want you to know that if I am your biodad, I'm not ashamed. You've been treated pretty awful by some people and even I had people trying to find me on Tybee. That's why I want you to know these things. You're both really impressive and inspiring. If you don't want any sort of a relationship, I will understand.*

*Anyway, you're probably wondering about the second envelope. Inside you'll find the story of how I met your mom and the week we spent together. I want to give you something I never told anyone. Maybe it will even the score—though I realize that's the wrong word because this isn't a game. I guess I'm just trying to be fair. But I also realize you may not want to know that story. So, you can do whatever you want with that envelope. Read it or not—it's up to you. If you choose to name me in the podcast or use the story there, I won't deny it.*

*I just want to say, do what you think is best. I won't reach out again unless I hear from you. I'll put my cell number at the bottom of this letter (Thomas has my email address, but my computer is broken).*

*Best regards,*
*Jack (Thor) Thorson*

Nadine waited for Savannah to say something.

"I can't feel my hands. I think I've gone completely numb."

"Should I get you a glass of water?"

Savannah shook her head. "I'll be okay."

They sat quietly for a few more minutes.

"Thanks, Nadine. Seriously. You were really nice to do that."

She smiled. "It's a lot. You sure you're okay?"

"Yeah. I'm good. Really good." She took the letter back and looked again at its precision. "It's funny. From his handwriting you'd expect him to sound like a professor—all business. But he's not. He's just normal."

"Seems like it."

They both looked up, hearing what sounded like a whiffling on the other side of the bedroom door.

"I think Katherine Mansfield's getting desperate for her walk," Nadine said.

"Go." Savannah smiled. "I'll stay here and read this eighty-seven more times."

Which she did. Or at least portions of it. At least long enough to delay the decision she had to make.

Did she want to open the second letter, or not?

It wasn't that she didn't want to know the story of how her mom and Jack met, because she did. Eventually. But she didn't feel ready. Right now, it was enough to take in the fact they might have found him—their biodad. The guy Savannah had thought of in fictional terms her entire life.

Until she could process the fact that he was real, flesh and blood and walking the earth, she knew she wasn't prepared for her and Thomas's origin story.

Savannah lay down on her bed and tucked the second envelope under her pillow.

It could stay there until she knew what to do.

# FORTY-THREE

## JACK

Jack was finally packed up and ready to hit the road. He'd stuck around Tybee just long enough to tie up loose ends. Ford and Slush finalized the sale and Jack threw away everything but his cell phone, his tools and a couple of boxes of clothes he couldn't justify getting rid of.

His belongings didn't even fill the bed of his truck.

On his way out of town, he stopped at Janie's to say goodbye.

"This island is gonna miss you, Jack," she said. "But if there's any bunch of people who understand the need to sail on, it's us." She gave him a long hug.

"Say goodbye to Coop for me, will you?" Jack said. "Whenever he's done chasing hurricanes or floods or whatever."

"Will do." She gave him one last squeeze. Then said, "Did you call the number I gave you?"

"Yeah. Talked to him. It was wild."

Janie winked. "I bet it was."

He left Janie's and pulled out onto the highway, past Fort Pulaski, over the causeway, into the marshes. One more bridge and he'd be within Savannah city limits. Off the island. On the mainland and on his way back to Colorado.

At the last minute, he decided to make a final stop. He swerved onto the exit for the boat landing and pulled his truck into the parking lot.

There were a few cars that likely belonged to tourists out on morning charters. The door to the guides' shack was locked, and even the wind was low, blowing thin curls across the surface of the water.

Jack walked one last time to the end of the dock and stood, watching an egret fishing at the edge of the marsh, its stick legs barely discernible among the salt meadow and its white, swan-like body sitting atop a nest of green. It was just the two of them, the egret and Jack. The bird gave him barely a look before scooping its next bite from the water.

Tybee hadn't been perfect, but it had been good. His whole life, Jack and the water had managed to find a way to get along.

Footsteps on the dock broke the quiet. Startled, Jack turned to look behind him.

"You wouldn't happen to be John Thorson, would you?"

The man wore an inconspicuous outfit—jeans and a plain blue T-shirt. The expensive camera in his hand, however, was a dead giveaway.

*Aw, hell.* If only he'd just kept driving, not stopped for a last farewell. "You know they call me Jack now, right?"

"I do." The man held up his camera and fired off a few clicks.

"Didn't see you in your car back there," Jack said, jutting his chin back toward the lot. "How long you been waiting?"

"Didn't have to." Camera guy fired off a few more clicks. "Just followed your truck out of town."

And to think Jack had been so careful these past few weeks, watching his rearview mirror, checking his tail. Today, though, his attention had been squarely focused on the road ahead. He considered where he stood now, the water on all sides, a guy with a camera between him and the land. He couldn't help but laugh. "Well then, good work. You got me."

Again with the clicking camera shutter.

"How would you like me?" Jack said. "Smiling? Angry? Putting up a fight?" He winked, showing the guy he planned to be a good sport. "Seeing as I'm pretty much cornered, like you said."

The guy let his camera answer for him. *Click click click.* Jack could tell he was working with an expensive kit. The lens itself probably cost more than Jack's truck, and there was a rectangular digital screen on the back where he could get a sneak peek at the pictures.

Jack said, "Hey, if you're going to make money off of me, let me at least see a few of the shots."

Camera guy smiled, shaking his head. "Nah. I get too close, you'll shove me into the water. Not happening."

Jack gave him an appreciative grin. "Hadn't thought of that, but good for you. Playing it safe." He let the guy fire off a few more shots. "How much you figure you'll get for these pictures, anyway?"

The man scowled. "If I'd found you last week, a couple of thousand, easy. But you're not as hot this week. So maybe five hundred."

Jack hadn't expected that. "Sick of us already?"

"News moves fast."

That gave Jack an idea.

"In that case, let's give 'em something to talk about." He faked as if he were going to attack the guy, who startled, but fired off a few action shots in the process.

"Shit, Jack. You scared me."

Jack laughed. "Let me see those."

Camera guy shook his head.

"Seriously? I probably just doubled your money. Let me look."

Camera guy hesitated.

"Maybe I can do even better, get you even more money," Jack said.

After a second or two, the guy nodded. "All right. But

don't fool with anything. Just press the arrow buttons. They control the preview screen." He handed the camera over.

Jack did just as he'd been advised. He flipped through twenty or so shots, most of them boring—him standing at the edge of the dock not doing much. The fake attack shots, though, made him laugh. "See? These are good!" He flipped through a few more.

When he was satisfied, he looked at camera guy and smiled. "Thanks, man. Even for a scum-of-the-earth paparazzi, you're a decent guy."

Camera guy scowled. "Funny."

Jack reached out to hand the camera back. And just as camera guy went to take it, Jack flicked it over his shoulder and off the dock.

"Oops!" he said. "I can be so clumsy around water."

Then he walked up the dock and back to his truck, finally ready to go home.

# Is Sam Tamblin the Podcasting World's Yoda, or its Jar Jar Binks?

## The Guava Media Founder Is Just as Quotable, and Just as Divisive

By Coco Beans

Podscape.com

Sam Tamblin walks through the door of the coffee shop where we've agreed to meet in a shirt that says, "I murdered a thousand cotton plants, and all I got was this lousy T-shirt." It's Tuesday afternoon. Not typically a popular time for coffee, but the place is packed. Sam's face is glued so tightly to his phone, he doesn't even notice the mother holding the door open for her toddler daughter. He walks right through. The toddler waits her turn.

The obliviousness piques my curiosity, so instead of calling his name, I decide to sit back. I check my watch; it's two minutes past three. Sam is scrolling on his phone.

At three-oh-four, a woman says loudly, "Excuse me." Sam's blocking the path to the register. He takes two steps to the right without looking up.

Five minutes pass by. The barista announces "Double-shot cappuccino, bone-dry," and places a fresh drink on the pickup counter. At this, Tamblin looks up, grabs the cup and notices me, the woman in the zebra-striped shirt, waving at him from three feet away. He's unshaven. Not in a hip, beard grease and electric trimmer sort of way. More like he can't find his razor and *who cares*.

He wanders over.

"I didn't see you order a drink," I say by way of introduction.

"Have you ever tried their steamed cold-brew? Lip. Smacking. Licious."

I try to write that down—colleagues alerted me to Sam's quotability—when I encounter a new curiosity: how to spell his unusual word combinations. And how to punctuate them.

I say, "Three hit podcasts in less than a year. That's Crooked Media and Earwolf territory. Congrats."

"What I think you mean," he corrects me, "is that Crooked Media and Earwolf are in Guava Media territory. Am I right, Coco? Is that your real name, b-t-dubs?"

I explain that my dad was inspired by the actor, Rip Torn. Then I say, "I watched you after you came in. You scrolled for nine minutes without looking up. What's so interesting?"

"Are you being serious with me right now? Social media is at the heart of everything. Has no one explained this to you?"

He scrolls again. My phone beeps. I look down to find a text with more links than can fit on my screen.

"I just sent you the latest discussions on the future intersections of micromedia, social media and traditional broadcasting. The last one practically gave me hives I loved it so much."

Tamblin is passionate to the extreme.

As best as I can gather (no definitive numbers exist) Sam Tamblin has produced or participated in the production of more than forty podcasts. That's not episodes; that's show runs. Not all shows, however, are of equal quality or impact. The show *Sam and Mike Talk Movies*, which he and his best friend made in Tamblin's bedroom when they were thirteen, had a sporadic, two-year run, releasing only six episodes and only when they felt like it. Others, like the latest Guava Media production, *The Kids Are Gonna Ask*, have become megahits; that show had also released just six episodes. But fans are clamoring for more.

"I've got a screen rights agent shopping *Kids* as we spea-

zak. Did you see the TV production of the *Dirty John* podcast? We're talkin' double-dirty numbers for *Kids*."

Which of course is just the latest controversy in this industry of ours: Will all this courting of television and movie money dilute podcasting's rising influence? I ask Sam.

"Mark my words. *Kids* broke the broadcasting world. Move their next chapter to the screen, and we're talking an industry change of epic proportion. Like, the Death-Star-vaporizing-Alderaan proportions."

After he says this, I can't help but remember the horrified look on Obi-Wan's face in *Star Wars* as the planet Alderaan explodes, our hero realizing that the galaxy is now and forever changed. Then I think, *A great disturbance in the force, indeed.*

Sam doesn't agree. "Look, you can stick with the old world order and die, but I'm gonna go with the new rules of the game and thrive."

# FORTY-FOUR

## THOMAS

A few days after the phone call from Jack, Thomas was busy running endless mental circles about his mom and Jack and everything else. His mom had been in love with another man. A man who wasn't their father. She'd almost had an entirely different life.

Then Nadine walked into his room with her laptop open. Ever since confessing her suspicions about Sam Tamblin, she'd been on a mission. "I think I figured it out," she said excitedly.

A few minutes later, Maggie, Savannah, Chef Bart and Thomas clustered at the red table around Nadine's screen.

"So, here's what I suspect," she said. "Sam Tamblin has been planting fake and intentionally provocative stories about Thomas and Savannah on Twitter."

"Oh fabulous," said Savannah. "More Twitter drama." Maggie and Chef Bart *hmm*'d sympathetically.

"Unfortunately, yes." Nadine brought up a screenshot of the tweet she'd shown to Thomas a few days earlier.

Those McClairs are hadly innocent children. More like overprivileged white kids. #paternallivesmatter

"This was the first tweet that got me curious. See how Sam misspells the word *hardly*? I know it seems like a simple typo, but the tweet that went viral didn't include it. Here—" She pulled up an account for @Prddad_AmrcnDad69. She scrolled until she found the identical tweet. It was time-stamped with the same date as Sam's tweet, but it was sent one minute later. It also had over half a million likes and had been retweeted several thousand times.

"See?" Nadine explained. "Same exact words. Same hashtag. No typo."

Maggie straightened. "What does that mean, dear? In layman's terms. Proud American Dad elicited more of a response than Mr. Tamblin?"

Nadine shook her head. "Sort of, but not quite. Notice the picture @Prddad_AmrcnDad69 uses for his bio? It looks like him and his young son, right? I did an image search on it. It's actually a stock photo you can download for free. I found the same picture used in an ad for bug repellent and for an insurance agency in Tulsa."

"So, this man lives in Tulsa?" asked Maggie.

"No," said Nadine. "The man doesn't *live* at all. It's a fake account. And I think Sam created it. That's why the second tweet doesn't have a typo. He goofed. He was logged in to the wrong account—his own—when he wrote the tweet, and he didn't realize his mistake until he'd sent it. I bet he then logged in to @Prddad_AmrcnDad69, rewrote the tweet and sent it again."

"Okay…" Savannah said slowly. "But why didn't Sam delete the original tweet from his real account?"

"Several possibilities," Nadine answered. "He might have *thought* he did. Or maybe he thought no one would notice. I mean, he tweets like eighty times an hour." She paused for dramatic effect. "Or—he wanted the tweet to get picked up and promoted by a bot."

"What on earth?" said Maggie.

"A bot," Nadine explained. "It's an automated account designed to generate new tweets and boost the visibility of existing ones. Something like two-thirds of the accounts on Twitter these days are bots. There's a whole long study on them from Pew Research. I'll send it if you're curious."

No, Maggie said that wouldn't be necessary.

"Then Sam Tamblin's a bot?" Chef Bart asked.

Nadine snorted. "No, Dad! Sam is a real person posting to his own account. At least, some of the time. What I suspect he's done is created a bunch of fake accounts—like @Prddad_AmrcnDad69. And he's also created a bunch of automated bots to help the tweets from his fake accounts gain attention. It's not that hard."

She flipped her browser back to Twitter and pulled up an account called @PeekabooSammyTammy. There was no profile picture, and no biographical information. Where a user's name would be listed, the screen read, "Me."

Even as generic as @PeekabooSammyTammy was, though, the profile screen showed that it had generated over two hundred tweets and gained nearly twelve hundred followers.

"This is my bot," said Nadine. "I created it yesterday. It's programmed to find tweets featuring the term *ice cream*. Then it automatically likes and forwards them."

"You coded that?" said Savannah.

Nadine smiled. "Trust me. You can find instructions for just about anything on Google."

Chef Bart patted her shoulder. "Well done, my young hacker."

Nadine rolled her eyes. "Anyway, I think Sam created fake accounts where he posts intentionally provocative tweets. Then he has a bunch of bots promote them. For publicity. That's how he managed to generate so much debate and attention so quickly."

"All press is good press," said Chef Bart.

Maggie scoffed. "Hardly."

It made sense to Thomas, though. In fact, Sam's strategy was so simple it was nearly genius. It was so simple that— "Wait. I thought Twitter was onto this sort of scam. They've been purging fake accounts recently, right?"

Nadine bobbed her head. "Yes and no. It takes time to weed them out. And new fakes go up as quickly as the old ones get taken down. Eventually, the Twitter stream gets so mixed up, users don't know which tweets are real and which are fake. Because all users can see is how much a tweet has been liked and retweeted—and sadly, that's evidence enough for most people. Anything with six thousand retweets must be important!"

Maggie clapped her hands together in disbelief. "How is this even legal?"

"It's not always fake," answered Nadine. "In the end, bots are just plain old promotional tools. Visibility on social media is determined by algorithms—the more attention something gets, the more the algorithm promotes it. Bots just help beat the odds, fake or not."

Savannah was not having it. "That hardly excuses him! Sam Tamblin fed me to the Twitter dogs in exchange for free publicity—in what, five minutes or less?"

Thomas winced. That sounded exactly like what had happened. "What about Saj? Was she in on this, too?"

"I'm not sure." Nadine brought up Saj's account and scrolled. "I haven't been able to find anything suspicious. But you'd be surprised how long this sort of research takes. It's like trying to trace a spiderweb back to its center."

"Did someone say black widow?" Chef Bart snickered at his own joke. Maggie joined him.

*"It's not funny!"* Savannah sounded close to tears now. "Have you all forgotten the horrible things being said about us online? About *me*, in particular? This has been hell—and it's Sam Tamblin's fault." She sank into the closest chair and dropped her head into her arms on the table.

Thomas sat down in the chair next to her. "Van?" He put his hand on her back.

"I'm not crying." Her voice was muffled by her arms, but not by tears. "I'm too fed up to cry."

Maggie motioned to Chef Bart to take a seat, then took one herself. Nadine closed her laptop.

Maggie took a deep breath. "All right. Nadine has given us ample reason to suspect Mr. Tamblin of some very serious and questionable activity."

She thanked Nadine, who nodded solemnly. Chef Bart gave her a side hug and kissed her cheek.

"The question is," Maggie went on, "what do we do now?"

Savannah lifted her head. "Easy. Hang him up by that stringy beard of his. Then cut him loose and let the squirrels eat him."

Maggie redirected, tapping her fingers on the table. "While I believe everything you showed us, Nadine, I don't think it's definitive. Correct me if I'm wrong, but Sam could easily brush our accusations aside."

"It's definitely suspicious, but no, what we have isn't indisputable," Thomas agreed.

Nadine sagged. "Sorry, guys."

"Heavens." Maggie waved away Nadine's disappointment. "You've done far more to prove my suspicions than I have. I can only judge Sam by the annoying pit in my stomach every time the phone rings. You did some real sleuthing, my dear."

Chef Bart stood and went into the kitchen, reappearing with a pitcher of iced tea. "We're going to need some caffeine."

Thomas jumped up to retrieve glasses. Nadine went for the ice.

Savannah finally lifted her head. "Does Sam still think I'm working on writing the next episode?"

Maggie said he did.

"Good. I wonder if that would be enough to get him to fly into town."

"To discuss the draft?" Thomas doubted Sam Tamblin would leave the ci-*tay*, as he called it, for script revisions.

"No." Maggie held up her hand, thinking. "But he might come if I were able to convince him that his being here would make for the quickest path forward."

"Who's ready for tea?" Chef Bart held up the pitcher and began to pour.

"Hopefully Sam is ready to spill the tea," Maggie said ominously.

# ITINERARY

Sam Tamblin Visit to the McClair House
Tuesday, August 18

**TRANSPORTATION**
Delta Airlines #725 from LaGuardia arriving 2:59 pm

**ACCOMMODATIONS**
Hotel Ivy-Minneapolis

**ARRIVAL AT MCCLAIR HOUSE**
5 o'clock Central Daylight Time via car service

**COCKTAIL HOUR**
Upon arrival at McClair house

> *Purple Dragon cocktails*
> *Pan-fried butter beans*
> *Farm-fresh goat cheese with molasses blackberry syrup*
> *Pâté with caramelized onions*
> *Handmade 12-grain crackers*

**Dinner**
7 o'clock

> *Chilled watermelon mint soup*
> *Brandy-soaked apricots with crème fraîche drizzle*
>
> *Falafel with sweet cream tzatziki sauce*
> *Roasted garlic hummus*
> *Pistachio lentil couscous*
> *Fermented red cabbage salad*
> *Fresh baked pita*
>
> *Farm-fresh cheese plate*
> *Lemon-curd custard with vine-ripened raspberry swirl*

# FORTY-FIVE

## MAGGIE

Sam Tamblin showed up wearing a vineyard vines whale T-shirt that had a coffee stain and sneakers so white they made Maggie squint.

"Hey," he said. "I thought I'd find you guys all tan and chillin' by the lake."

Maggie couldn't even begin to count the levels of asinine. He could have started by inquiring about their health. Or about their general well-being. Or by saying, *I've been thinking about you all,* or *I've been worried about you,* or *Hey, just so you think I'm not a complete imbecile, let me say it's nice to be here.*

But he didn't say any of that. Instead, he made fun of her family for being pale. Which was quite something coming from a man who, judging from the divot in his mustache, looked like he'd sneezed while trimming it that morning.

"I loved the cookies and milk you left for me at the hotel, by the way. Just like Grandma!"

"Don't you know how to charm a hostess, calling her a pale grandma?" Maggie smiled, dulling the reprimand. "I take it you received the itinerary I left at the hotel?"

"Totally impressive, Maggs. One question. When's bedtime?" He laughed at his own joke so hard he snorted.

"I expect you'll be back at the hotel by ten o'clock." She refused to surrender even a hint of sarcasm. "But now, come and enjoy a Purple Dragon. We're lucky enough to have Chef Bart cook for us, and every once in a while, I'm able to cajole him into fashioning a cocktail or two." Maggie led Sam into the family room and poured him a martini glass full of a deep purple concoction. Savannah and Thomas followed.

"Whoa." Sam dipped a finger into the glass to examine a drop on his skin. "Looks almost radioactive."

"Sour-plum nectar, lime juice, vodka and just a shot of sweetness," Maggie explained. "It's the plum that gives it color."

Sam took a tentative sip, then must have liked what he tasted because he took another, and then nearly drained the glass. "That goes down too easy. And you know what they say—easy peasy makes you sleazy."

"Is that right?" She refilled his glass and offered him first crack at the hors d'oeuvres spread out on the sideboard. "I recall you talking about the farm-to-table movement in New York, so I've asked Chef Bart to give you a sample of what we enjoy here in Minnesota. Nearly everything we're eating tonight either comes from our garden or from local farmers."

Sam filled a cocktail napkin with one of everything. "There's a restaurant in the city that serves a three-hundred-dollar burger. S'posed to be this incredible beef that they, like, hand massage and then mix with truffles. Something like that. Anyhow, I know I'll have made it when I can order that burger whenever I want."

"Absolutely," said Maggie. "I'm quite a believer in food, and if a delicacy burger is on your list, I say, *cheers to that*." She lifted her glass and toasted him. Thomas and Savannah lifted their sodas in return.

"Hear, hear!" said Sam. "Here's to big, beefy success."

The room was quiet for a bit. Savannah stood and took a few crackers. Thomas wiped the condensation from his Pepsi can with a napkin. Sam crunched on his food.

Maggie presumed Thomas and Savannah expected her to keep the conversation on track, and she had a very specific timeline to her work. She was following the map they'd devised over iced tea with Nadine and Chef Bart. The goal was to get Sam Tamblin to admit what he'd done. Some variety of, "Yep. I drummed up publicity for your podcast by igniting fake controversies on social media."

Maggie knew it wouldn't be easy. But she'd get it done.

With Sam, the secret would be to unfold the subjects carefully. First, they had to make him feel welcome—that they couldn't be more pleased to see him. Next, they were to praise his work and make him feel like the master of the podcasting kingdom. And when both of those goals had been accomplished, they needed to convince him they couldn't possibly move forward without his skills and insights.

Therein would lie their trap.

"I notice you've taken a liking to the pan-fried butter beans, Mr. Tamblin. I'm so glad." Maggie stood and moved the bowl to the side table next to his chair. "Help yourself. Dinner, as you saw on the itinerary, will be ready at seven."

It was now five-thirty.

"Good. Great," said Sam.

"There's plenty of time to discuss the future of the podcast tonight," Maggie went on. "We've kept our whole evening free. Just for you."

Sam grabbed a handful of beans, ignoring the serving spoon. "Awesome. The sponsors are itching to get started again. The download numbers are incredible. You'd think they'd slow down, given your hiatus, but they haven't. The show's like a zombie. It—just—keeps—going."

"Have we lost any sponsors?" Savannah asked. "Because of the break?"

Maggie quickly brought a hand up to her ear and pulled, a signal for Savannah, reminding her to maintain her enthusiasm. Follow the map.

"Um!" Savannah had seen it. "I mean, how exciting. *Yay.* People still love the show!" She pumped a meek fist into the air.

Sam chewed and pumped his fist in response. "For reals. We've got new sponsors lining up. That luggage company— Fleetway? They're begging for spots. And I'm working on closing sponsorship from this startup that makes sustainable fiber pants. Right Leg, they're called. Horrible product, super itchy. But an awesome millennial draw."

"Even given the tenuous future of the show?" Maggie caught the question too late and mentally kicked herself.

"*Tenuous?*" said Sam. "Sure, we still need to find the biodad. Which, hey, I know all about Jack Thorson out in Georgia. I mean, I'm cool y'all didn't tell me about him right away, but we have to make hay with all that sunshine. Go big on the reunion. Major splash. Then we've got a whole second season, if not a third and a fourth, on all of you getting to know each other. Do you know if he has other kids? That could be a totally untapped stream."

"No," Thomas answered. "He didn't even know about us."

"Cool," Sam said.

"Oh—" Maggie forced a chuckle, trying her best to make it sound breezy "—you have such vision, Sam."

"My whole life's been a vision quest. From the day I was born."

*Aren't donkeys born blind?* Bess whispered.

*Not now!* Maggie scolded.

"Sam," Savannah said. "It's just so great to have you here in person. I mean, we haven't left the house much lately. Not since New York, anyway. And we won't be going back there anytime soon, am I right? Not after the interviews Saj lined up."

Maggie began to pull desperately at her ear, though Savannah refused to look at her.

"Van?" Thomas said, voice dripping with caution.

"Okay. Okay." Sam held up a hand, and Maggie saw bits of soggy bean crumbs fall to the floor. "Super not cool what happened. And, rest assured, we are probably going to let Saj go as a publicist."

"Rest assured probably?" Savannah said.

"Oh yeah. Totally. Probably soon, even. Way unacceptable for her to put you in that position."

Maggie's ear was now ringing with pain. Even so, she saw Savannah shoot Thomas a look as if to say, *are you hearing this?*

Thankfully for the sake of Maggie's ear, he was. "Geez. Forget it, Sam." Thomas flushed crimson and waved a dismissive hand. "We can talk about fault some other time—"

"No way. Easy call," said Sam. "Totally Saj's fault. Ab-so-tute-ly. Serious ostrich move on her part."

Maggie jumped from her chair and pointed to the clock on the mantel. "Look at the time! I'd hoped to take Sam on a tour of the neighborhood before dinner. Stretch the legs and get some fresh air. Savannah? Thomas?" She gave them exacting looks. "Chef Bart and Nadine could use some help in the kitchen."

There was a reason Maggie had scheduled two full hours for cocktails, and the evening, though a bit rocky—Sam Tamblin had talked nonstop during their walk about nothing relatable or relevant—was unfolding more or less on schedule.

At seven, Chef Bart called, "Dinner's ready!" and they all took their seats in the dining room.

"What is this?" Savannah had spotted the starter course, a highball glass filled with what appeared to be pink bile. From the look on her face, she planned to have no part in it. Not that Maggie could blame her.

"Chilled watermelon mint soup," Maggie explained. "The watermelon is from the Melbys' garden. Drink up!"

Sam shot his back in a single swallow. Thomas sipped. Savannah scowled.

"Is it good?" she whispered at Thomas.

"Actually, yeah. Try it."

Maggie watched as Savannah stuck the tip of her tongue into the brain-like puree. She recoiled. *"Pass."*

Maggie changed the subject. "Sam and I had an interesting discussion on our walk. In fact, I asked him how we ought to wrap up. Since you've likely met the original goals of the podcast."

"Whoa there, Maggs." Sam wiped away a watermelon soup mustache. "I didn't hear you say the words *wrap up*. We've got momentum on our side. Mo-mentum, mo-money, after all." He grinned, and Maggie saw a splotch of pink goo in his teeth.

"I marvel at your insight, Sam," she said, pulling back. She needed to redirect. Stay effusive. "Certainly, that's why we asked you here. To discuss the future. Given that the goal of finding Thomas and Savannah's father is very close to having been accomplished."

"Nowhere close until we get a DNA match," said Sam. "You're on the hook to use GenePuul for genetic testing, don't forget."

Maggie had forgotten. But that was fine. She wanted the certainty of DNA.

Chef Bart arrived to sweep the soup course away and replaced it with falafel and hummus.

"I made a special, lactose-free tzatziki sauce for you, Savannah." He leaned in as he spoke, not quite whispering, but presumably sensitive to the fact that she may not want Sam Tamblin to know about her propensity for indigestion. "And

I'll have aged cheeses for you on the next course, and a fresh raspberry sorbet for you for dessert."

"Thanks," she whispered.

He gave the table a friendly wink and disappeared back into the kitchen.

"Man, I may have to change what I said earlier," said Sam. "Forget the truffle burger. This food is amazing. I'll know I've made it when I can hire Bert as my personal chef."

Maggie couldn't bear to look up, lest she risk losing her cool.

"But seriously, Maggs. Let me tell you what I know about podcasting. It's the future. And it's already here. On-demand audio programming for everyone. I've been in this a long time—the first podcast I hit really big with was six years ago. That's like, the Ice Age in podcasting years. I made eighteen thousand dollars on that one, which doesn't seem like much, but back then it was phe-nom-i-nal. Every show since has at least tripled the subscriber numbers. And this podcast, *The Kids Are Gonna Ask*, it's already done five times as well as any other show I've ever done. Five times. Fivefold. Five hundred percent. Five a-roony."

"Yes, I understand."

"So, you get it, then, that to stop now would be criminal. Heinous. Stick-a-knife-in-my-back, bad."

Chef Bart appeared from the kitchen. "More falafel? More hummus?"

"Please. Thanks," Sam said without looking at him.

"Simply enjoy your dinner, Sam," said Maggie. "We'll discuss the nitty-gritty over the cheese course."

Thomas, she noticed then, had begun to push the falafel balls around his plate rather than into his mouth.

"Thomas?" Maggie pulled on her earlobe as soon as he looked up. She was careful to target the opposite ear this time. "Something on your mind?"

"Oh, uh, yeah." He cleared his throat. "Sam, how can we be sure listeners don't get tired of our story? You're so savvy about the promotional stuff. Won't the interview requests slow down eventually?"

Maggie noticed that Thomas slowed precipitously when saying "interview requests." She needed them to be careful not to overplay.

"We keep the story fresh," Sam answered. "Ain't no better script magic than an unexpected surprise."

"What sorts of surprises aren't unexpected?" asked Savannah.

"Savannah," Maggie scolded.

"You're a smart one, Van-tangelo. Love that big brain of yours." Sam lifted his plate and craned his neck, trying to see into the kitchen. "Is there any more of this cabbage? You should try it in the pita with the hummus. I'll smell like garlic for days, but it'll be worth it."

Chef Bart reappeared with a full dish, and Maggie breathed a sigh of relief. Sam was nonplussed. She shot a warning at Savannah, anyway. *Settle down*, she mouthed.

Savannah smirked. "But how do you keep it fresh, Sam? After we've met our father and everything. Is it like, more interviews or more social media...?"

"Man, I don't know if I can do another course." Sam leaned back in his chair and rubbed his belly like a caveman. "I think I overdid it with the Mediterranean bonanza. How many pita-fuls of cabbage did I eat? Two? Three?"

By Maggie's count, five. Plus falafel and hummus and the watermelon soup.

"Ha!" He laughed at his own joke. "Pita-ful. Pitiful. Get it? I'm a pitiful mess from all those pita-fuls of cabbage."

"I'm pleased you enjoyed it." Maggie felt her smile beginning to strain, but saw Savannah and Thomas silently connect, recommitting to pushing Sam where they needed him to go.

"I'm just curious," Thomas said. "We never did much promotion for the *McClair Dinner Salon*, so this is new territory for us. What sort of big surprise are you planning for *Kids?*"

Sam Tamblin snorted. "Have you forgotten what you started this for? To meet your big-ee-o dad-ee-o!"

"Right, of course, but—"

Maggie saw Thomas shoot Savannah a lost look, two innocents unsure of where to go next. It gave her an idea.

"Sam," Maggie said. "Here's a crazy thought. Given how much Thomas and Savannah have been attacked on social media, what if we staged a counterassault? You know, delete all the show's social media accounts. Make a very public stand of *not* promoting the show there. Like a reverse psychology move?"

Sam Tamblin shook his head and continued rubbing his belly. "Would never work. Have to be on social."

"Yes," Savannah jumped in. "But what if we didn't? Wouldn't our *quitting* social media get just as much attention?"

Maggie suspected they'd just turned a rhetorical corner. If Sam was forced to drop all social media promotion, he'd be left with a one-sided controversy. And trolls, as far as she could tell, were uninterested in singing for the same choir. Agreeing with each other was boring, and they'd move on to other controversies. But if Sam Tamblin insisted on sticking to his social media strategy, Nadine's findings might hold more leverage—a man so clearly dependent on one outlet would never want to be outed there as a fraud.

"I'd really love for you to consider the idea," she said.

Sam blew a long steady breath. "I'm pretty loathe to—" He stood suddenly. "May I use your bathroom?"

Surprised, and yet, not—this was Sam Tamblin, after all—Maggie pointed the way. "Just down the hall on the left."

As soon as he was out of earshot, she leaned in, whispering. "We're closing in, and I think he knows it. Just hang in there. Savannah, I think your trauma is our best argument. Use it."

Savannah nodded.

"Have you noticed he never answers questions directly?" Thomas said. "It's like, he talks around the edges. Just enough so you think he's answering you, but you realize later he's told you basically nothing."

"The man is vacuous," agreed Savannah.

"That's what I'm saying," said Thomas. "Talking to him is like trying to get ahold of Jell-O."

Sam reappeared then, and the table went silent.

"Sorry 'bout that," he said.

Maggie smiled and passed him the cheese platter. "May I recommend the Brie with apricot glaze. It's not a French Brie. We buy it from a farm just across the border in Wisconsin."

Sam took a slice, spinning the cheese on his fork to examine it.

"Sam—" Savannah started, then fell silent.

"Yeah?"

Maggie shot Savannah an eager look and touched her ear. Both sides were now too sore to pull.

"I've been trying to get my thoughts together about what I experienced, being attacked by so many people online," Savannah said. "It really would mean a lot to me if we could boycott social media. At least for now. It would save me an awful lot of pain. Plus, Thomas and Maggie and I all think it's an important statement."

Every one of the McClairs turned their eyes on Sam. What he said next was crucial. Proof he was either their friend. Or, as Maggie increasingly suspected, their foe.

"Uh…" He dropped the piece of Brie to his plate.

"Yeah—" Then he stood abruptly, knocking his chair over backward. "Be right back." The McClairs exchanged looks, watching him flee back down the hall.

*"What was that?"* Savannah whispered. Then a horrified look came over her face. "You don't think he's in there live tweeting the dinner, do you?"

Thomas pulled out his phone and began to scroll.

"He wouldn't dare." Maggie leaned over to get a glimpse of the hallway.

"Nothing on Twitter," Thomas said. "At least not on Sam's account. The hashtags look clear."

They sat in silence for several more minutes. It's awkward to carry on when one of your guests disappears for extended periods. Especially into the restroom.

"We need to find out what he's doing." Savannah looked at Maggie, pleading with her to understand that this was clearly not a teenager's job.

"Just a minute more," Maggie said.

They gave him several minutes more.

Finally, Maggie stood, walked down the hall and knocked gently on the bathroom door. "Sam? Is there anything I can do for you?"

Sam's singular reply came as an agonized groan.

"Oh dear," Maggie said through the door.

At that, Thomas and Savannah stood to clear the table. Chef Bart and Nadine joined them.

"Think he's all right?" Thomas asked.

"He ate like a whole bowl of those beans," Savannah said.

"Plus cabbage. And hummus is made of garbanzo beans," added Nadine.

"And the Purple Dragon has a prune juice base," Chef Bart said. "Sour plum equals prune."

Maggie returned. "He's going to be in there all night."

★ ★ ★

A few hours later, Maggie and Chef Bart managed to convince Sam to at least transition from sitting on the toilet to lying on the cool tile of the bathroom floor. Maggie wet a washcloth and laid it across his forehead. "Eventually, we'll need to get some liquids in you. To rehydrate."

The remainder of the party migrated to the den, and Chef Bart turned on the Twins game just loud enough to mask the sounds coming from the other side of the wall.

They'd been watching for a few innings when Savannah said, "Well, this evening has already gone to *shit*, so—" She waited for the laugh, but the best she got was Thomas rolling his eyes and Nadine smirking. "All right. Too obvious. Anyway, I may as well tell you. I got a letter from Jack Thorson."

Thomas smiled, finally giving Savannah his attention. "And?"

"And it was nice. Really nice. He apologized for what happened. Explained. Introduced himself. Said he wants to meet us, if we're interested."

"And are you?" Maggie said.

"Possibly. Probably. I don't know."

"I'd meet him," said Thomas. "I mean, yeah, I want to know for sure. Eventually. But it seems like there are too many factors pointing to him being the correct match."

"Hang on. Don't move." Savannah jumped up and ran for the stairs. "There's something I want us all to open together."

# Envelope #2

*Dear Savannah,*

*If you're reading this, it means you want to know the story of the time your mom and I spent together.*

*NOTE: If you cheated :-) and opened this letter first, be aware of what you're getting into.*

*But, if you're still reading and you want to know the story, here it is…*

*I met Bess while I was working as a bartender at The Mine in Breckenridge, Colorado. I worked there for a few years, but I'll always remember meeting your mom because the first thing she ever ordered from me was a white wine spritzer. I said, "A summer drink with all this snow?" And she said, "I'm a Minnesota girl. This is like July for me!" Then she laughed and I noticed her teeth were all perfectly straight except for one tooth that twisted, like it wanted to stand out.*

*Plus, she was pretty. I noticed that right away, too.*

*The bar must not have been busy the first time your mom and her friends came in because I think I talked to them for a few hours at least. Especially Bess. I was fascinated by her. The way she could laugh at herself without putting herself down. Too many women do that. It's like they can't be funny and be smart, both. I was a bartender, so I saw it all the time. Don't ever fall into that trap, Savannah. Your mom didn't, and I hope you inherited her smart sense of humor.*

*Anyway, Bess and her friends came in again, I think. To be honest, it's gotten sort of fuzzy over the years. But I know for sure that I ran into her on my night off. I was with friends and the two of us eventually ditched everyone else and hung out at a table in the corner. Your mom was so funny. Not like a stand-up comedian, but it was like she could talk about any-*

*thing without getting too heavy. Keep in mind this was 2002 and the whole country was dealing with 9/11 and the Taliban and Bush talking about WMDs in Iraq. It was crazy. The economy had tanked and no one was traveling so all the resort bums like me were trying to get by on less cash but sort of happy we had more days off to ski. I know that sounds bad, that the country had just been attacked and I was just happy to have more time on the slopes. I don't mean it like that. It's just, when you don't know what you want to do with your life, it can be pretty convenient to have an excuse—that there aren't any decent jobs even if you wanted one.*

*Sorry, I think I've gotten off the subject. The point is, your mom had a way of sounding optimistic even in the middle of all that. It's contagious, being around a happy person. She made me feel good. Made me feel even a ski bum like me could do something cool. I hope she was the same for you as a mom.*

*At some point I told her I was thinking about going to New Zealand for the summer. Their seasons are the opposite of ours—summer is winter and winter is summer—so the "Kiwi Crew," that's what we called them, all came over to the US to work the resorts and ski during their off months. I'd gotten to know a few of them pretty well and they invited me to come visit. Said they'd give me places to stay and hook me up with friends I could crash with when I traveled. Your mom encouraged me to do it, too. She said I'd never get a chance to do something so adventurous for so cheap again. I remember she said, "It's just money." And I was like, "Yeah, coming from someone who has plenty." Because it was pretty obvious. I'd just flunked out of a state school and lost whatever financial aid I'd been given, and she was about to graduate with no loans and a job waiting for her (to be fair, I don't remember if that was true—as in, something she told me—or if it was just how I saw things back then).*

*We talked about the future a lot. She played this game called, "Let's Imagine." She'd say something like, "Let's imagine you go to New Zealand and fall in love with a Kiwi ski bunny. What would life be like?" And then we'd talk about what life would be like if that happened. One time I said, "Let's imagine you quit school and stay here with me in Breck." She just laughed and said, "Not gonna happen, sport."*

*I wanted you to know that story because ever since this whole thing has unfolded, I've felt bad that maybe you guys would think you were the result of some one-night stand. But you weren't. I really liked Bess. It's not like we were going to get married or anything, but it wasn't sleazy like that. I admired your mom. We had fun together. I knew she was going to live a good life.*

*Obviously, I didn't have any idea that would include raising the two of you.*

*Okay, so I guess I'd better get to the point. Yes, we slept together. A lot (sorry—TMI). We were careful. I was always careful. So as to how the two of you STILL happened, I don't know. But I guess if you play the law of averages?? Ugh—this is getting awkward. Sorry, again.*

*We did exchange info when she left. I had her cell phone number and her email address. But back then you lost your cell number every time you changed call plans or companies and I think I had like four different numbers when I was living in Breck. So maybe she tried to call but the number didn't work anymore? Maybe she figured I'd gone to New Zealand? She had other reasons, too. Other people in her life. I won't get into all that because I don't know much. Only to say that I think if she'd really wanted to find me, she could have tried. You guys found me, after all. But, like I've told both of you, I think she knew I wasn't in any shape to become a dad. Maybe she thought you'd be better off just having a stable mom and home life. As far as I'm concerned, we met, things happened, and when she found out she was pregnant she decided to raise the two of you the way she felt was best. She believed she could do it on her own. And in the end, I'm really glad she did.*

*I guess that's it. If you want to know more, I'll be happy to tell you whatever I can. Mainly, Savannah, I want you to know that your mom made me feel decent about myself for the first time in a long time. That's why I remember her. I want you to know, too, that if I do turn out to be your biological father, I'll be really proud and amazed. You and Thomas are already way more "together" than I've ever been and you have your mom to thank for that.*

*Best wishes, as always,*
*John James (Jack/Thor) Thorson*

# FORTY-SIX

## THOMAS

Thomas's first instinct after hearing Jack's letter was to hug Savannah.

"Oh my god, what is happening to you?" She laughed and hugged him back.

"It has to be him," he said. "It has to be."

"She called you 'sport,' too," Savannah said.

"And the 'Let's Imagine' game—how many times did we play that?"

"A thousand."

"It was her favorite." The falter in Maggie's voice cut through the revelry, and Thomas saw tears dangling on her eyelashes. "Even as a little girl. She'd say, 'Let's imagine I grow up to be a famous ballet dancer and get to wear tutus every day.' One time—" and then she laughed, remembering "—she said to your granddad, 'Let's imagine I turn into a dog and bite you on the leg.' And then she did! I just about wet my pants I laughed so hard."

Thomas took the letter and read the opening again. He could hear it in Jack's voice now. *Dear Savannah, If you're reading this, it means you want to know the story of the time your mom and I spent together.* He wondered if it would ever feel real.

"It's not gonna feel real until we meet him," Savannah said.

Thomas drew back, shocked. "Did you read my mind? I was just thinking that."

"Seriously? I never thought we were *those* kinds of twins,

but who knows? Maybe the father quotient changes something."

"It definitely changes something." Thomas looked back down at the letter in his shaking hands. "Every time I feel like I've got a handle on this father thing, something new comes up and I have to start all over again."

"I know what you mean. I'm still processing Mom being a cheat."

Maggie reached over and took Savannah's hand. "She didn't cheat, love—she was single when she met Jack. But it was good she didn't marry that man. She chose you over him. I want to be sure you understand that."

"Oh, I know," Savannah said. "If she chose to raise twins *by herself* rather than marry him? That's a sign. Watching Trigg's parents stay miserable together is all the proof I need."

Maggie noted that Bess had most certainly *not* raised twins by herself, but she bit her tongue.

Everyone fell silent for a moment. Thomas looked at Jack's handwriting. It was precise, not anything like his sloppy penmanship and bad spelling. It surprised him.

"I love how she encouraged him to travel, you know?" Nadine said quietly, barely audible over the baseball game on TV. "It's exactly the opposite of what would happen in a movie where the woman always falls in love and tries to get the man to settle down."

"Counternarrative," said Savannah. "I love that part, too."

Thomas turned to his sister, the realization coming quick and true. "Our mom was sort of a badass."

She squeezed his shoulder. "I think so, too."

It was enough to make them both tear up. Then, before anyone knew, all of them were hugging and crying—including Nadine and Chef Bart, who hadn't even known their mom.

And then, from the other side of the wall, *"Uuunnnggghhh."*

"Good lord." Maggie ended the hug, the spell broken.

"He's hurtin'," said Chef Bart.

Van waved away the concern. "Serves him right."

"Bet your ass, it does," Thomas said.

"More like, his ass," agreed Van, and they lost it, all five of them, laughing and crying and falling into an exhausted, hysterical heap.

Finally, Maggie sat back and gathered herself. "Since we're having show-and-tell, I may as well come clean. This whole evening was designed under false pretenses."

"You mean like, you lured Sam here to get revenge? Is that why he's being held toilet prisoner? You poisoned him?" Savannah laughed like it was a joke, but Thomas suddenly wondered if she might be onto something.

"No!" Maggie protested. "I simply thought I might gain a few concessions from him if I had the upper hand. Gastro-intestinally speaking."

"Oh, his intestines are speaking, all right," Chef Bart re-marked.

"So, you poisoned him?" Savannah looked angry and astonished at once.

"Absolutely not! I would never. I simply took advantage of his weaknesses." Maggie sighed and gathered her thoughts. "The man eats nothing but white bread and red meat. You saw him as well as I did in New York. Roast beef sandwich on potato bread. And his fascination with burgers. He prob-ably has one bowel movement a week."

Thomas groaned, but couldn't help laughing. This was such a typical McClair conversation.

"The menu was rich in FODMAPs—that is, foods known to engage the bowels. I don't remember what all the acronym stands for, fermentable something something. Anyway, it's a long list of foods. Garlic, beans, sugar alcohols, fiber, fresh cheeses, dense fruits. At the very most, I thought he would feel uncomfortably bloated. And uncomfortable people are quicker to tell the truth." She swung an arm toward the wall between the den and the bathroom. "I never imagined *this*."

"That's why you left cookies and milk at his hotel?" Thomas said. "And had so many appetizers? Served him prune juice? Took him for a walk, all that?" The pieces were coming together.

Goat cheese, Brie, caramelized onions, garlic, cabbage, beans, beans and beans.

"I admit I may have taken it a step too far."

"But, to be absolutely clear, you did *not* poison him, correct?" Savannah was obviously having a hard time getting past the possibility.

"We didn't poison him," said Chef Bart.

Savannah spun on him. "*You* were in on this, too?"

He answered her with a slow nod.

"*Dad!*"

Thomas couldn't believe what he was hearing. Except, of course he could. Nothing was ever normal in this house.

Chef Bart held up his hands in surrender. "I told her about FODMAPs and suggested the menu. But we *didn't* poison him. He was just the victim of too much, too fast."

"Gluttony." Savannah grinned. "One of the seven vices."

As if on cue, Sam Tamblin moaned. Through the wall, they heard the toilet flush.

"We need to get some fluids in him." Maggie stood and gestured to Chef Bart. "And maybe some ginger, to settle the roiling."

"Right behind you." The two of them disappeared toward the kitchen.

"This is way too awesome for words," said Savannah. "I couldn't write a script this good."

"An innocent man trapped in our bathroom, in agony, by our grandmother's hands?" Thomas said.

"Maggie's hands, nothing! She put the food in front of him, but he ate it. We all ate it—except for me and the dairy, of course. You ate it. And Maggie. And Nadine and her dad. Nobody forced it down his throat. And none of us are running to the bathroom. Not even lactose-intolerant me."

"Don't you feel at all guilty that he's in such bad shape?" Thomas was no Sam Tamblin fan, but it was hard not to feel some sympathy for the guy. At least until he could peel himself off the floor.

"If he had taken even the tiniest bit of responsibility for everything we've been through, maybe. But you said so yourself. The guy is as slick as Jell-O. Let him wallow. Maybe he'll learn something."

"Well," Nadine laughed, "Sam's never going to forget you guys. That's for sure."

"Maybe we should record him moaning," said Savannah. "Just in case we need it as blackmail."

# FORTY-SEVEN

## JACK

Jack made it to Colorado to find his folks in tough shape. His mom was drinking more than he knew, and according to the doctors, his dad's hip was shot.

He also hadn't been aware of just how much of the day-to-day work his dad had surrendered. His farmhand, Telo, was still there every day, as well as Jack's cousins, Todd and Greg. He didn't know if they were getting paid, but it didn't take more than a few minutes to see that those three men were the whole reason the family still had a farm at all.

As soon as he pulled up, his mom ran out of the house and threw her arms around him. "Junior!"

He could smell it, the alcohol. On her breath and seeping out her pores.

"Mom." He was about to lay into her—about the farm looking one step away from fallow, and the drinking and the fact his dad wasn't in any shape to handle it.

It was the skin bagging over her kneecaps that ultimately stopped him. Not baggy in the way that happens to older people, but in the way that happens when a person's body is falling apart.

His mom was falling apart.

His dad was falling apart.

And neither one of them wanted to do anything to stop it. They'd shown Jack their intentions ever since he'd been a child—they were going to live like they lived and die like they died. The trajectory of his parents' lives was set.

So, Jack shut his mouth and returned her embrace. Maybe it was Ford's good sense rubbing off on him.

It took him about a week to work up the courage to say something about his concerns. Up until that point, he'd shown his family loyalty by helping his cousins and Telo with the day-to-day work. Helped repair an irrigation hose. Spent a day spreading gravel over the ruts in the road behind the implement barn. All while his dad stood back, correcting his every move.

One morning, he said, "I'd like you to quit drinking, Mom." They were at the kitchen table. Jack was nursing a cup of coffee, his mother a hangover. "It would be better for your health, help you live longer. I think you know that."

She patted his face. "I love you, Junior. I've missed you."

At any other time in Jack's life, his mother's evasion would have angered him enough to leave. Abandon his parents to their own misery. But what was the point? If his parents had been the ones to set the paths of their lives, Jack was the one who got to set his.

His mom fussed with a strand of hair that kept falling across her face. "Did you see those nasty curtains Todd's wife wants to hang up in my house? I made those curtains myself. With my own hands." She pointed to the curtains that had been up as long as Jack could remember, a nightmare of feverish orange and green dots. "You were a baby and I was practically dead from no sleep and still, I wanted to make a nice house for my family. I had pride. And what happens? She has the nerve to suggest I need to brighten the place up and hands me a pile of cheap made-in-China crap. We'll probably get bugs."

Jack looked past her to the land beyond the windows, the road toward town. "You think you'll ever move off the farm?"

"When I'm ready." Which he knew meant probably never. And which also told him, his business in Hartwell was as good as done.

# FORTY-EIGHT

## MAGGIE

Maggie never imagined the menu she planned would have any more impact on Sam Tamblin than to make him feel uncomfortably full. Perhaps bloated. Frankly, she'd doubted it would even work at all. Digestion isn't something humans can flip with a switch, it typically takes hours, and every human body tolerates foods in its own unique ways.

She just had no idea Sam Tamblin would tolerate her food so uniquely.

He never made it to his hotel that night. He emptied out, so to speak, within a few hours, but Chef Bart and Maggie sat up with him all night, keeping him hydrated and making sure he stayed warm. She couldn't help but feel sorry for him.

But responsible? That was a stretch. Sam Tamblin himself chose to eat that whole bowl of pan-fried beans. As well as the triple-quadruple helping of hummus and falafel and purple cabbage.

Eventually, Maggie coaxed Sam out of the bathroom and onto the couch. He slept well into the next morning and by the time he woke up, he was looking much better. She timed his morning restroom visit and found no reason for concern.

He joined them in the kitchen, and she put a glass of water in front of him first thing. Chef Bart was there, too, cleaning up from the night before.

"So," Sam said, "that was mortifying."

"Stomachs can be very unpredictable." Because really, Maggie thought, hadn't he just proven that?

"How are you feeling now?"

"Good. Fine. Well, not hungry. That's for sure." He blushed.

"You're going to need your rest," Maggie said. "I called the hotel and extended your reservation by a day. We'll have a car bring you over as soon as you feel up to it." She pushed the glass of water toward him. "Hydration is going to be your best friend for the next few days."

"Yeah. All right." He took a conciliatory sip.

Maggie saw her opening. "Before you go back to the hotel to rest, perhaps it's best we get the issue of the podcast settled?"

He answered her with a glare that said *Don't push it, lady.*

"Yes. Of course." Maggie wished she'd been pumping him full of Gatorade and rehydration salts to speed his recovery. "Sam," she started again. "I do hope you don't blame us for anything that happened last night."

He drained the last of his water and looked at his watch. "Any chance you can call me that car?"

Maggie fought a crushing sense of defeat. They hadn't gotten Sam to admit anything.

They'd have to come up with a Plan B.

After Sam Tamblin left, Maggie closed the door behind him and surrendered to the shortcomings of the past twenty-four hours. She was losing her touch.

She stood in the empty entryway and surveyed the moment. Bart had left for groceries, Thomas was out with Nadine and Katherine Mansfield, and Savannah was upstairs in her room, the sound of her Underwood striking letters into words into pages.

As for Maggie, she figured she had one more apology to deliver.

She closed Bess's door behind her and sat down on the bed.

"Well, Bess, you know how your old mom feels about regret. *Keep looking backward and you're likely to smack into a tree. Isn't that what I used to say?*

"This time, though, I almost screwed up horribly. Letting Thomas and Savannah loose on this journey. What was I thinking? I let myself believe they were ready for so much more than they were."

She waited a moment but was met with silence.

"Wonderful. Now you're quiet."

She tapped her fingers on her leg, piecing together her thoughts. She didn't know if there was even any reason to be in this room. Bess didn't live here any more than she lived in Maggie's head. Only, how would Maggie survive if she let her daughter go?

Maggie took a deep breath and continued. "My point is, I should have been smarter. There was a teddy bear hanging from a noose on our fence. A noose, Bess! Who does something like that? I should have stopped the whole thing the first time we talked to Sam Tamblin. But I was thinking of Savannah and Thomas. These amazing, driven, bright, shining children of yours.

"And you know me. I just couldn't let myself think that anything bad would happen. They're McClairs, for Pete's sake! McClairs don't shy away from the hard stuff. As if I didn't know better. I lost my husband before I turned sixty and my daughter before I'd even hit retirement. It's like, *Hello! Are you awake, Maggie? Terrible, horrible, awful things happen.*"

She felt the first tears beginning to knot behind her eyes.

"If you can hear me, baby, I need to say I'm sorry. I'm so, so, desperately sorry. I can't promise I won't ever screw up again because we both know I will. I'm probably always going to be one to let out too much rope. But I won't turn my back again. I know better. I owe you more."

She blew out a long, tear-laden breath. She didn't want to

cry. Emotions were just too exhausting—and she was wrung dry. In the silence, she felt her heart begin to play. Was that… the Bee Gees? *Ah, ah, ah, ah…*

"Very funny, Bess!" Her tears had all but stopped. "'Stayin' Alive.' Did you do that? Is that your idea of a joke? I'm sitting here apologizing to you and—" She pointed to the ceiling and scowled. "You know what? I just realized something. I'm mad at you—if you even care, wherever you are. But I am. Because this wasn't all my fault."

After everything the McClairs had been through, Maggie finally felt brave enough to begin this long-overdue conversation.

"Why didn't you tell them, Bess? Why didn't you at least tell me? That's what you do when you're a single parent. You make plans for *In Case of Emergency, Break Glass* scenarios. And you didn't.

"You know what's worse? You left your kids. And yes, yes, I know, you didn't plan to die. But that afternoon, we both know where you were going. You were going to see *him*."

Maggie rested her head in her hands and rubbed her thumbs across her eyebrows. She felt thoroughly exhausted. Drained. Even her toenails hurt.

"The kids still think you were headed to the funeral. But someday, when they're ready, I'm going to have to tell them that to go from your office to that church, you don't go under the 46th Avenue bridge, which is on the way downtown. Where the fancy hotels are. And where I can only assume Tad was waiting for you."

She sat up straight and took a deep breath. "You know what? Let's play a game. Your favorite. Let's imagine you didn't reconnect with that man. That you hadn't said to me, 'What can I do? There's an electricity between us.'

"You know you sounded like a cliché, don't you? I think I

said as much. In fact, I know I said, 'You've been fine without him for thirteen years, Bess. You'll survive without him again.'

"Ha!" She couldn't help but laugh. "*Survive*. The irony." Bitter bile rose in her throat and sorrow spread like a poison into every bone and muscle. She flopped back onto Bess's bed. The comforter used to smell like her, of Bess's elderflower shampoo. The same bottle Maggie had thrown away just last year when the plastic finally crumbled into pieces on the shower floor.

Maggie inhaled, putting her nose deep into the fabric. All she smelled was dust.

"You know what he did after you died? He sent me a card. Mailed it all the way from California. He let Hallmark do the talking and signed his name to the bottom. As if that was enough. As if signing his name to a card could make up for what he'd taken. Where's the moral character in *that*, I'd like to know?"

She waited for Bess to reply. But there was nothing. All that came were Maggie's tears. Running down her face until there was nothing else to do but welcome them.

She cried for Bess.

She cried for George.

She cried for all the nights she wanted to laugh with them, and hold their hands, and have their assurances that all was good. That they were there, and they were family.

She cried for Savannah and Thomas. That they were growing up with Maggie instead of Bess. That she'd be gone long before they were done needing a mother or a grandmother or someone, anyone, who loved them so desperately.

She couldn't control her tears.

She couldn't control anything.

She lay down on her daughter's pillow and let it all go.

[BEEP]

*Hello, McClairs. This is Saj in New York. Don't worry, I'm not calling on Sam's behalf. Or anyone at Guava Media, for that matter. I'm calling to let you know, in fact, that I've been fired. Sam called my work with you "unprofessional" and "failing to meet Guava Media standards of excellence." I'll let you decide if that's true or not. But before you make that judgment, I'd like you to consider one more piece of information. I think you may also find it pertinent to your future working relationship with Mr. Tamblin. And it is this: I have irrefutable proof it was no accident that Eaton Holmes stood in as the last-minute replacement for your final interview in New York. Sam secretly recruited her, himself. And somehow—I suspect a bribe but cannot prove that piece of the puzzle—he also convinced the show's producer to swap Ms. Holmes for their previously scheduled guest host. Mr. Tamblin, it seems, has developed quite a reputation for himself in our industry as being willing to do just about anything to gin up publicity. I have confronted Sam about this, and he denies it, of course. But I am willing to provide you with my evidence, should you decide you want to know more. You have my cell number. Again, this is Saj in NYC.*

[BEEP]

# FORTY-NINE

## JACK

Given the mess he'd made of things on Tybee, Jack wanted to do right by whatever move he made next. He helped some on the farm, made sure his dad got back and forth to his hospital visits and watched carefully for the subtle signs it was time to go.

One afternoon, over a chicken salad sandwich his mom was busy complaining had too much mayo, he found an interesting listing on a real estate website.

FOR SALE
Fishing guide business. St. Vrain. House/office, website, client list. Work-to-own offers OK.

St. Vrain, Colorado, was known for its fishing. It sat farther on down into the heart of the state, near the bottom of the Rocky Mountains' eastern slope, where the creeks spilled and swelled, forming tributaries into the South Platte—the southern branch of the very same river his granddad taught him to fish all those years ago.

He could already see the sign he was going to hang: St. Vrain Fishing Expeditions. Right then, he reached out and scheduled a visit.

The next day, he drove down. He was standing on the porch of his could-be home when he took the call about recording a final podcast episode. They wanted him in Minneapolis.

"I'm not much of a talker," he said. "Not sure if I'm comfortable being broadcast."

Right. But would he reconsider? They had a plan. It allowed him to stay anonymous.

There wasn't any question in Jack's mind that he wanted to meet Thomas and Savannah. He was ready to take a paternity test, answer any questions, go where they wanted him. But doing that in private versus doing it for the world to hear were entirely different requests.

He did promise, however, to think on the offer.

"Trouble at home?" Lou, the woman showing him the St. Vrain property, came around the corner. She'd given him a moment of privacy to take his call. Lou reminded him immediately of Janie, not so much in appearance, but in that Jack could tell she belonged right where she was. Janie, with her painted nails and bikini body, looked like Tybee. Lou, on the other hand, had sun-specked freckles and pink-gray dust at the hem of her jeans—all Colorado.

"Nah. Not the end of the world." He tucked the phone back into his pocket. "Just something I wasn't ready to think about is all."

Lou's eyes sparkled in the sun as she smiled and climbed the porch steps to unlock the door.

**Trigg:**
OMG!!!!! [screaming cat face emoji] I made out with Kyle Larson [kiss emoji] [lipstick lips emoji]

**Trigg:**
He came over after I got home from the airport and we went for a walk and well…

**Trigg:**
Are you EVER GOING TO ANSWER MY TEXTS?????

**Savannah:**
I'm here. Congrats. You and Kyle will be great together.

**Trigg:**
I know, right? Are you mad? You're not mad, are you? [praying hands emoji] [lipstick kiss emoji]

**Savannah:**
Not about Kyle.

**Savannah:**
I'm mad because I don't feel like you really care or understand what I've been going through.

**Savannah:**
I'm mad because I think you like that I let you tell me what to do.

**Savannah:**
I'm mad because you always talk but hardly ever listen.

**Savannah:**

I'm mad because I don't think you'll even understand why I'm mad.

**Trigg:**

Seriously???? Text me when you're not jealous [green heart emoji] [red-face emoji] [green heart emoji] [red-face emoji] [green heart emoji]

# FIFTY

## SAVANNAH

Savannah was a nervous wreck. She'd barely left her house since the humiliation in New York, and now here she was, on the verge of altering her entire life.

They were going to record the final podcast.

With Jack.

It was quite possible she might throw up all over his shoes.

This wasn't going to be the final episode she and Thomas and Maggie had originally hoped for. She'd written four drafts, every one of which Sam Tamblin rejected.

"You have to meet live. In the broadcast. Pure, immediate emotion." Every argument was the same.

Savannah wrote an episode where they met first, off mic, then came together to discuss the experience.

Sam Tamblin hated it.

She wrote an episode where they wrote letters back and forth to get to know each other. They'd read those during the podcast, and then meet.

Sam Tamblin said it muted the immediacy.

She wrote an episode where they called each other on the phone and put that on the podcast. "Let us at least dip our toes into the relationship before jumping in cold."

"Not a chance."

Finally, after a particularly tense negotiation, Savannah had a stroke of genius.

"He's always wanted this to feel like a reality show. So, let's give him one. A prefinale reunion special. Like they do on *Survivor*, or whatever. Those shows always make the final episode a two-hour special. The first hour is all the contestants who got ejected. They get together to gossip and talk about the behind-the-scenes experience. The second hour is when the reveal happens."

The three of them were sitting at the kitchen table, Savannah and Thomas and Maggie.

Thomas played with the pencil in his hand, spinning it on his thumb as he considered. "Could work. Except, that still doesn't solve the problem of the big reveal. Which is the part we all want to avoid until the right moment."

"Oh, but we can avoid revealing too much!" Savannah swept her hand in the air. "If we play our cards right."

She described the last bit of her plan.

"Brilliant," Maggie said.

"Yeah," Thomas agreed. "Let's do it."

In one last act of negotiating prowess, Maggie convinced Sam to record the final episode at their house. "Give the kids the comfort of home, at least."

"Fine," he said. "Whatever it takes."

That was already a month ago. Now Savannah put on her best jeans and the new white shirt Nadine helped her pick out at J. Crew. They'd just gotten word that the flight from LaGuardia landed ten minutes early, and Sam Tamblin was on his way from the airport.

She stepped into the bathroom for her final, zero hour preparations. She smoothed her hair—though, who was she kidding, her waves never lay flat—and brushed her teeth.

"Hey." Thomas joined her at the sink and drew his toothbrush from the holder. "You ready?"

Savannah bobbed her head—not yes, not no. "Why do I feel like this is going to blow up in our faces?"

"Because it probably will." He flashed her a freshly white

smile. He'd gotten his braces off a few days ago and the gap that had so clearly connected him to Jack was nowhere to be seen.

"Your teeth look great," she said. "But I do sort of miss your gappy smile."

Thomas laughed. "Oh well. At least the DNA speaks for itself."

# FIFTY-ONE

## THOMAS

Sam Tamblin arrived holding a Styrofoam cooler. "Brought my own food this time. Don't want to take any chances." He handed it to Thomas as he welcomed himself into the house.

"Good to see you, too, Sam." Thomas followed him into the dining room and placed the cooler under a buffet table loaded with appetizers. There were no pan-fried butter beans.

He and Sam had already consulted on the audio setup, and though the dining room had never been ideal for recording, they'd minimize the room's inherent noise with clip-on microphones and a rented overhead boom mic. Sam Tamblin agreed to dual task as both audio tech and producer.

"Pretty choice setup, dude." He ran his fingers along Thomas's soundboard. "Good old Maggs has some money, huh? Your granddad must've been loaded."

"*Good old George* had an eye for investments." Maggie stepped in from the kitchen just in time to hear. "He left us in good financial standing, yes."

Thomas watched the color drain from Sam's face. Not unlike how he looked the last time he visited.

"Uh, hey, Maggs," said Sam. Then, as if trying to level their social standing, he pointed to the cooler under the table. "Brought my own provisions this time."

"I see that," she said, and excused herself back to the kitchen.

"All right." Clearly relieved Maggie was out of the room,

Sam clapped his hands together. "Here's the plan. We'll have you, Savannah and Maggie mic'd before the guests arrive. Who's confirmed, again?"

"My mom's friends, Kristen and Elise, plus Abe, the guy who runs The Mine."

"Can't believe he's coming all the way from Colorado."

Thomas did his best to maintain a neutral face. "Well, uh, yeah. It helped that you paid his airfare."

Sam rubbed his thumb and forefinger together. "Cha-*ching*! Happy to. Guava Media is rolling in some mad cash thanks to you kids."

He walked across the room and surveyed the red table. Maggie had set it earlier in the afternoon. There were six place settings, plus one. At the seventh stood an elegant candle, surrounded by white roses. "What's this?"

"A reminder that our mom is with us, tonight," Thomas explained. "Maggie suggested it."

"Spooky." Sam wiggled his fingers in the air à la Shaggy from *Scooby-Doo*. The resemblance hit Thomas like a slap. *So that's who Sam Tamblin reminded him of!* He'd been trying to figure it out for months.

"No Brynn, huh? Couldn't get her to come? I've been calling her house 25-8 for days but think she might be screening my calls."

*25-8?* Was that Sam's exaggerated version of 24-7? Thomas couldn't wait for the moment he didn't have to waste any more brain cells trying to sort out Sam Tamblin's nonsense. He wiped his palms on his pants and his brain flashed to all the normal things other teenagers were doing right now. He knew Pete and Ro were in Nico's basement blasting sand mongrels because they'd been texting him their scores all day. Nadine was at the DMV taking her driver's test.

Thomas was running with the cross-country team now

that school had started. He'd given Nico a few weeks of the silent treatment, and eventually the kid wizened up enough to focus on other targets. And anyway, having to tolerate a few stupid Nico comments wasn't a good enough reason to quit running. One summer off the pavement had been enough to teach Thomas that.

Since the start of the season, Thomas'd had one first-place finish, after Jack had agreed to come to Minneapolis to meet them. The adrenaline from the news had given him wings for days. The next week, though, he dropped to fourth place. That race he spent criticizing himself, convinced that every footfall was wrong, every breath was out of sync with his pace, that a real runner wouldn't make the mistakes he made.

Except, he also knew better than to give up this time.

"You've created a whole picture in your head you don't even know is true." Savannah was with him for vanilla shakes at Burger Mania that night. Pete and Ro were out with the team celebrating, but she'd driven to the finish line and waited for Thomas to cross. "Did you even ask Jack if he was a runner?"

"No. I didn't get the chance."

"Oh, then of course it's totally logical to construct a world in which you're a complete disappointment to him."

"Shut up, Van." He hip-checked her, landing the shot more at elbow range.

"Watch it." She took a long pull on her straw, then flicked her head toward the parking lot.

Thomas obliged, walking in the direction of the car. "Don't you ever wonder, though, if he's going to like us?"

"Who, me?" She gave him a smug look. "Why would I worry?"

"Oh right, I forgot. You're invincible."

"Mmm." Savannah took another long pull. "So invincible, even Trigg doesn't bother me anymore."

"Yeah, sorry about that." Trigg and Savannah were on the outs now that Trigg was dating Kyle Larson. "You know he's a total pothead, right?"

She laughed. "We're not fighting over Kyle Larson. We're fighting because I sent her a couple of bitchy texts. But good bitchy, though. Not Carrie Westlund bitchy."

Thomas smirked. "There's a difference?"

"Of course. The difference is, I finally decided to quit letting people tell me what to do. And that's what I told Trigg. It's okay to be bitchy if you're doing it to stick up for yourself."

"Uh-huh." Thomas didn't have the energy to try to understand.

"You're the one who's always telling me to speak for myself." Savannah opened her car door and paused before getting in. "Anyway, let's go pick up Nadine. I told her we'd meet up when you were done."

Now, here they were. The moment of reckoning. If only Sam Tamblin knew that the reckoning wasn't theirs, it was for him. After all, Thomas and Savannah had already met Jack. And he was amazing.

# FIFTY-TWO

## SAVANNAH

Sitting there at the red table, surrounded by people who loved her mom, Savannah closed her eyes and let the moments fall around her like rain. Onto her shoulders, her hair, her hands. Into her skin and her pores. Into her deepest, most Savannah self. She didn't want to forget a single second.

"I hung up the phone after our first conversation and cried like a baby." Their mom's friend Elise sat across the table, next to her friend Kristen. Elise had been dabbing her eyes with her napkin all evening. "I kept thinking *What if these were my kids?* I'd always felt so sad that Bess died. That you lost her so young. But I don't think it really struck me until that day. These are big questions, and you're on your own."

Elise wiped her nose and whipped around, turning to Maggie. "I don't mean—"

"No, no." Maggie held up her hand. "My sentiments exactly."

Sam Tamblin, at the soundboard wearing fat black studio headphones, gave the moment a thumbs-up.

Dinner was nearly over. Chef Bart had just cleared the cheese boards and Nadine was handing out dishes of sorbet. Earlier, she and Savannah had celebrated Nadine's successful driver's test with sample bowls. Chocolate mint. Their mom would have loved it.

Savannah surveyed the faces around the dining room table, her heart full and her head torn, all at once. She'd just spent an entire dinner listening to stories about her mom and she didn't want it to end. They did, however, have one last important item of business to attend to.

"Remember that awful batik wall hanging Bess kept in her apartment?" Elise sniffled, laughing through tears. "It looked ridiculous—all orange and black. So un-Bess. I always thought she liked it because it confused people. Everyone expected her to act like an uptight rich girl, but then they'd walk into her apartment and be like *What is that?*"

Kristen covered her face with her hand and howled with laughter. "That's not why Bess kept that wall hanging! There were pockets on the back. It's where she stashed her—" She flashed eyes at Savannah and Thomas, catching herself. "Never mind."

Savannah and Thomas both answered her with knowing smirks.

"Your mother was a teeny bit of a rebel," said Kristen. "But she was brilliant, too. You know that, right?"

"Yeah," Thomas assured her. "Maggie reminds us every day."

"About the brilliant part," Savannah clarified. "We're just starting to learn about the rebel part." She made a mental note. Someday she ought to write a book titled *Badass Bess*. Maybe she could even make it a children's book. Little girls needed more role models.

Maggie cleared her throat, more loudly than necessary. "So, Abe," she said. "Tell us what's new in Colorado."

Sam Tamblin nodded wildly from beneath his headphones and threw her a thumbs-up.

"Uh, well—" Abe started. Two words was about the extent of what the poor man had said all night. Nobody had thrown many questions at him, but Savannah knew they were going to have to get around to it eventually.

She prompted, "Hired any handsome bartenders in Breckenridge lately?"

The guy's whole face flushed bright red. "Heh. Well. Hmm." He brought his hand to his chin, striking *The Thinker* pose.

Thomas switched tack, turning back to Kristen and Elise. "It's a shame Brynn couldn't join us tonight. Did she talk to you guys about why?"

"Actually..." Kristen caught Elise's eye. They shared a second of mental simpatico, and Elise picked up where Kristen had left off.

"She's keeping a low profile these days. Not doing any more *interviews*, even."

"Yeah," Kristen continued. "She never could understand how those radio shows all started calling so quickly."

"Almost overnight, wouldn't you say, Kristen?"

"Yes, Elise. I would. So unexpectedly sudden."

The entire table turned and looked at Sam Tamblin. He grinned, then made a rolling motion with his hand. *Keep going.*

Savannah closed her eyes again. *Don't forget even a second of this.*

"Wow," Thomas went on. "Must have been *so strange* for Brynn to get sucked into our controversy like she did."

"Oh certainly." Elise nodded with keen interest. "She's always had strong opinions, of course. But she'd never even heard of those radio shows."

"And she's not even on social media," added Kristen. "Not Facebook."

"Nope," Elise confirmed. "Not on Twitter or Instagram."

There was a lull in the conversation and Savannah looked to see if Sam Tamblin was picking up on any of this. But he was playing with the knobs and dials on Thomas's soundboard.

"No idea where the radio programs got her name?" Savannah couldn't believe Sam wasn't picking up on this. Her voice was practically dripping with innuendo.

"Nope," answered Elise. "It's just the most confounding mystery."

And again, the six faces at the red table all turned to look at Sam Tamblin.

*What?* he mouthed.

Maggie couldn't stand it anymore. "Mr. Tamblin. Do you honestly mean to be so dense?"

Sam made repeated cutting motions at his throat and pointed to the soundboard. He wanted Maggie to limit her conversation to the people at the table. To quit talking. Even though, Savannah could say with one hundred percent certainty that nobody at the table actually wanted Maggie to quit talking at all.

Maggie ignored Sam's admonitions. "In case it has managed to escape your attention, Mr. Tamblin, we are well aware of what you've been up to." She began to tick items off on her fingers. "The fake Twitter accounts. The bots."

She paused, as if waiting for Sam to catch on, but he had his face so close to Thomas's soundboard he may as well have been sniffing it.

"We got a call from Saj." Maggie ticked off another finger. "Certainly, you remember the Guava Media publicist. The one you fired on our behalf? Even though, we now quite clearly know that you masterminded the whole Eaton Holmes sabotage yourself."

At this, she had him. Sam turned and gave Maggie a look so barren of emotion it almost made Savannah want to cry. *What was wrong with him?*

"So, what, you're disappointed the podcast caught fire?"

Sam said coldly. "Disappointed the kids' father is in the kitchen right now, waiting to meet them?"

"Ha!" Savannah couldn't contain herself. Thomas shot her a look and his eyes screamed *WAIT*.

Savannah crossed her arms and squeezed her eyes shut. Thomas was right. This was just getting good.

Maggie continued, undeterred and impressively zen, given the moment Savannah knew was about to unfold. "Have you actually met Jack Thorson, Mr. Tamblin?"

"Of course!" Sam spat. "Whad'you think, I'm a complete moron?"

Savannah squeezed her arms tight across her chest. *Do not spoil it. Do NOT, Savannah.*

"What," Maggie asked Sam, "does he look like?"

The room went silent. Savannah couldn't even hear herself breathe. And she certainly wasn't going to open her eyes to see what was happening, given how close she was to losing it this very second.

"He's—" Sam started. "You know. He's like, a guy. Like an older version of Thomas."

"Yes, Mr. Tamblin!" Maggie sounded like she was talking to a kindergartner, even though she kept calling him mister. "He does. It's just astounding how much they look alike. Don't you think?"

"Yeah. I mean, it's what I said, right?"

"Oh, forgive me. That is what you said, isn't it?" Maggie paused for a second. Savannah, against her better judgment, peeked out of one eye. Thomas was smiling directly at Sam.

Abe's mouth was cemented shut.

"I'm so thrilled with the results Thomas's orthodontist was able to achieve. The gap in his front teeth measured three-eighths of an inch wide before we fixed it. But just look at him now—would you even know he'd ever had it."

Oh, this was just too good. Maggie'd always said she was good at this—luring fools into unfriendly waters, she'd called it. But Thomas and Savannah had never really seen her do it this well. Never, ever like this. At last, Savannah let herself open both eyes.

Thomas flashed Sam Tamblin a bright, white smile.

"Yeah," Sam confirmed. "Looks great, T. Totally impressive orthodontia."

Thomas grinned and nodded.

No one said a word.

Until Maggie said, "Abe? We're just so thrilled to have you with us tonight. What an absolute honor to meet you."

Abe turned to Maggie and smiled. A giant, gap-toothed smile that filled his whole face.

"Oh!" Maggie clapped her hands together like a little girl. "What a lovely smile you have, yourself, Abe. Why don't you show the table? Yes, please. Show everyone!"

Abe smiled for the whole table. For at least a whole minute.

Sam Tamblin sat. Not moving. He saw. His face wasn't in the knobs of the soundboard. He was looking. He just didn't want to admit that he'd been had.

Even so, Maggie gave him a chance to respond.

All six of them waited, all eyes on Sam Tamblin. And Sam, predictably, sat in cowardly silence.

"You, Mr. Tamblin, are a liar," Maggie said. "Jack's sitting right here." She motioned toward the man they'd been calling Abe all evening. "Right *here*. And you didn't even notice, yet you claimed to have met him. Even worse, you thought we actually believed your lies. The lies you just did such a wonderful job of recording for us." She pointed to the soundboard.

"You're crazy, lady!" Sam Tamblin stood up and threw his

headphones to the floor. "I don't have to stay here and take this, you know!"

Maggie tossed her arms in the air, triumphant at last. "Marvelous! I'll show you out!"

She crossed the dining room toward the front door. Only, she didn't see the cord for the boom mic snaking along the floor at her feet. She hooked it with the heel of her shoe, tripped and fell, all arms and legs in the air.

She hit the buffet on the way down with a sickening sound—the same indestructible, wrought iron table their grandfather had bought for her on their first trip to Italy. She didn't move.

"Maggie!" Thomas and Savannah shot out of their seats. Kristen and Elise, too. Chef Bart and Nadine ran in from the kitchen.

"Are you all right? Can you speak?"

Maggie was silent. Her eyes were open, locked in pain and shock, but they didn't move. No part of her moved.

"Maggie?" Savannah reached for her grandmother's hand. She wanted to touch her, to let her know they were there. That Maggie wasn't alone. Savannah reached out—and froze.

Maggie had closed her eyes.

"*Thomas!*" Savannah screamed. "Someone call an ambulance!"

"Already on its way!" Chef Bart stood next to Savannah, his phone to his ear. "She tripped and hit the buffet on her way down," he said. "Yes, her eyes are open. Or, they were. Um, I—I don't know. Let me check—

"Where is the pain? In your chest? Your head?"

Maggie groaned. "My arm. I think I broke my arm!"

Chef Bart relayed the information to the person on the other end of the line. "Don't move, Maggie," he told her. "Ambulance is three minutes away."

Savannah sank to her knees at Maggie's side. "Oh my god, Maggie! You scared me."

Maggie grimaced, trying to catch her breath after her outburst. "Sorry, love. Not what I'd planned, obviously."

Thomas knelt down next to them. "Ambulance is almost here, Maggie. I can hear the sirens."

She gave him a weak smile.

Savannah could hear the sirens now, too. "We'll follow you in the car," she said. "Is there anything you need me to bring?"

"No," Maggie said, wincing. Every breath seemed to bring her pain. "Just don't forget Jack."

Savannah laughed. Couldn't stop herself. "If we haven't scared him away yet."

The ambulance pulled up outside the house and Chef Bart ran to the front door, ushering in the EMTs and all their equipment. Savannah and Thomas got out of their way, clearing a path to Maggie. Nadine, too, began to shove chairs aside in order to make more room for the EMTs to work.

Sam Tamblin flew through the front door and sprinted down the sidewalk to his car.

But Savannah also saw Jack. He hadn't fled, despite Maggie's cries, despite the sirens. Despite Sam Tamblin's ham-fisted meddling. And Thomas's secrets. And Savannah's anger.

Jack was here. Right next to them.

Savannah and Thomas. And Jack.

Savannah threw herself into his arms and didn't let go.

# FIFTY-THREE
## THE THORSON TRIO

What sealed Jack's commitment to the podcast was Maggie's promise that he'd meet the kids first. Just Savannah and Thomas. And Maggie. But no Sam, no microphones, no anything else.

The plane from Denver touched down in Minneapolis a full twenty-four hours before Sam Tamblin arrived from New York. Chef Bart met him at baggage claim with a sign that said, Jack. Then they drove straight to Maggie's house, where she opened the front door and welcomed him in.

"They've been waiting to meet you." Her smile stole the breath from Jack's chest. Hints of Bess all over Maggie's face.

"I—" he started. "It's so nice—"

Maggie took his hand. "I know. Later." She led him inside and turned the corner.

And there they were, standing in front of him, for real. Thomas and Savannah. Bess's kids. His kids. He didn't know if he should offer a hand or a hug or shove his fists in his pockets.

He was on his own.

To do his best to not completely screw this up.

To do what a biological father was supposed to do in this situation. Which was, *what*, exactly?

Savannah answered by throwing her arms around his neck. She hadn't thought about what she was doing until her face was buried in his chest, one of his buttons digging into her cheek. She winced, and for a flash she allowed herself to think about how strangely intimate this was. In the arms of a stranger. The feel of his muscles under her fingers. But she closed her eyes, shutting it all out. He smelled like laundry sheets and airport cinnamon rolls.

Jack squeezed her back. It felt incredible.

"I'm Thomas. You must be Jack."

Thomas stepped in and offered his hand. He didn't really want to interrupt Jack and Savannah's moment but—well, it was getting a little awkward just standing there.

Jack reached across Savannah's shoulder and took it. "Nice to meet you. Finally, I guess. In person." God, he wished he'd practiced so this kid wouldn't remember his first words as the jumble that had just come tumbling out.

Thomas looked down at Jack's hand in his. The long, narrow fingers. The flat knuckles. His hands, the ones he'd never seen on anyone else. Thomas suddenly felt like a stranger in his own body. Bound to this guy he'd never met in a way that couldn't be described. Jack wasn't McClair-ish at all. And still, Thomas didn't want to let his hand go.

"Wow," Jack said. "You got the Thorson hands."

Thomas looked up to see Jack examining his hand just as closely. "What are the Thorson hands?"

"You see how flat your thumbnail is?" Jack held his up by way of example and, sure enough, Thomas had the same. "My dad and granddad both have the flat thumbs." He made a fist. "And the flat knuckles. That's a giveaway, too."

Jack felt like a kid again. How many afternoons had he stood on the water, watching his grandfather's hands at work, only to see them again, here, in a place he'd never even been. "Wild, huh?"

"Yeah, wild."

Savannah, still buried in Jack's chest, gave him one last squeeze and let go. "We are so glad you're here."

# FIFTY-FOUR

## MAGGIE

Maggie sat on the bed of her ER exam room, with Bart beside her. Nadine stayed back at the house with Elise and Kristen, who'd offered to clean up. Sam Tamblin left the scene before Maggie was even in the ambulance. Thomas, Savannah and Jack were together in the waiting room, a few doors down.

The doctor suspected a broken collarbone, but they were waiting on her X-rays for a final verdict. It was going on two hours since Maggie fell.

"Mrs. McClair?" The doctor appeared, this time seeming even younger than when he'd first examined her. Maggie wondered what age she'd been when doctors went from looking like her parents to looking like her children.

"The X-rays confirm a clavicle fracture. A broken collarbone, in other words."

He walked to the sink and washed his hands. "Good news is, it's not a complicated break so you won't need surgery." He pulled her robe back from her shoulder and gently examined her one more time. "Bad news is that we're still basically treating clavicle fractures the old-fashioned way—six weeks in a sling and lots of Tylenol and ibuprofen."

His hands were a tiny bit cold, but the pain was still so red-hot, Maggie welcomed the cool.

"All right." He stood back up and walked to the computer where the nurse had entered all of her health information earlier. "When was your A-fib diagnosed?"

Maggie cocked an ear toward him. "My what?"

"Your A-fib. Atrial fibrillation." The doctor adjusted the angle of the monitor displaying her vital signs. He pointed to several points along the peaks and valleys representing her heartbeat. "These here indicate atrial fibrillation."

Maggie shot a sidelong glance at Bart. "Yes, I'm aware. I was diagnosed about a month ago."

Chef Bart gasped. *"What?"*

Bess whispered, *Mother...*

Maggie held up a hand to shush them both, only to feel a shot of pain in her arm hot enough to make her think she might throw up on the floor.

"Easy there, Mrs. McClair." The doctor pulled the stethoscope from his neck and gingerly placed it against her chest. He listened several long minutes, moving it carefully as necessary.

When satisfied he'd heard enough, he pulled the buds from his ears.

"Are you seeing a cardiologist for treatment? A-fib is pretty common, but left untreated it can have serious complications. Including stroke."

Bart looked furious enough to cry. Maggie looked directly at him, even while answering the doctor.

"I do have a cardiologist and he's monitoring me closely. We're in the process of finding the correct dose of medication."

The doctor cocked his head, considering. "Well, the shock of your accident must have thrown you out of rhythm. It's possible your heart may reregulate on its own when the pain subsides. But even so, I'd like you to make an appointment with your cardiologist within the next day or so. Just as a precaution."

Maggie promised she would.

When he'd gone, Chef Bart turned on her. "I told you to go see a doctor."

Maggie scowled. "Didn't you just hear me? I did go."

"He said you could have a stroke!"

"*Could* have. Not *did* have."

"Margaret McClair." Bart only used her formal name when he wanted her attention. "You have two grandchildren who need you healthy."

She held up her good hand, stopping him. "You think I don't know? I'm stuck in here like Brenda Brittle Bones when I'm supposed to be out there, keeping them safe." She nodded toward the waiting room and it was all she could do to swallow back the pain.

"Why didn't you tell me?" The look on his face a mix of anger and worry.

"Because it's humiliating."

"A heart condition? *Please*."

"Not that. Everything." Maggie's mind flashed with all the fears she'd been holding in as long as she could remember. "I'm the only one left for Thomas and Savannah. And ever since Bess died, I've been trying to be enough. Fun enough they didn't dread coming home. Encouraging enough they grew up knowing they could do anything. Flexible enough that I don't hold them back from actually doing it all."

She motioned at the box of tissues on the counter across the room. Bart grabbed it and came back, offering her one. She took it and blew her nose. "It's just awful trying to raise grandchildren with such talent and potential."

Bart snorted. "Oh, the burden."

Maggie laughed, then flinched. "*Ow!* How am I going to survive the next six weeks if I can't laugh?" She let out a heavy breath. "Anyway, *that's* the embarrassing part. The other part is—" She stopped. This was Bess's business. And Maggie hadn't ever told anyone precisely because it wasn't her story to share.

*Need I remind you I can't speak anymore?* Bess whispered.

Maggie ignored her and let go of a long, decades-old breath. "Everything that's happened has also forced me to deal with—" No, that wasn't right. She hadn't fully dealt with it yet. "Forced me to *acknowledge* some anger I've been holding on to since Bess died."

Bart looked at her, calm but attentive. His unflinching composure was just one of the hundreds of things Maggie cherished in her friend.

"I won't go into it all, but Bess and I had a disagreement before she died. About a man from her past. We never got to resolve it." Maggie steadied herself before looking at Bart. "That's terrible, isn't it?"

She'd found out the truth about Tad the night before Bess died. He'd stayed in California after college, after all, but at some point, they'd reconnected. That night, Maggie came down to get a glass of water and Bess was just coming home. Her shoes were in her hand and her blouse was misbuttoned, and Maggie knew that even if Bess had been working until 2:00 a.m., she wouldn't have come home with her blouse on wrong. She'd said, "Bess, I don't care if you're sleeping with someone. But can you at least let me know you'll be late, so I don't have to worry?"

Bess answered, "I slept with Tad." Just blurted it out like that. "He's here. He came to say he still loves me. That he's never forgiven himself for deserting me." And then she'd died the next day, on her way to see him again.

Maggie felt suddenly so drained from the memory she couldn't hold herself upright, and she slumped, carefully, against Bart's side. He held still and let her.

"So," Bart said finally, "who are you really mad at? Bess, or the guy?"

Maggie sighed. "That's the worst part. For a long time, I convinced myself I was mad at him. But what I've learned is that I think I'm actually mad at Bess."

She sat up and turned her face to Bart's. "I loved my daughter. I don't want to be mad at her."

He squeezed her hand. "I know. It's the worst part of grieving."

"Are you still mad at your ex-wife?" Maggie asked.

"Not anymore," Bart said. "But I'm glad I was angry for a while. It was a necessary part of moving forward."

"That's exactly what I told Thomas and Savannah a few months ago. That they had to get mad at their mother so they could love her more fully." Maggie rolled her eyes. "I wish I knew how to take my own advice."

Bart chuckled. "One step at a time." He poked Maggie gently on the top of her head. "Maybe you should start by cleaning out Bess's old room."

She sat up and pointed at her injured arm. "Why do you think I did this to myself?"

Bart laughed. "Ah, yes. Quite the excuse you've created for yourself." He tapped a finger to his chin, grinning, but also studying her as he spoke. "I think I may have finally figured you out, Maggie McClair. Let me see if I've got this right. You didn't want to get in the way of the kids' mission to find their biodad, so you let them do the podcast, despite the risk. Then the whole time they were busy turning over every stone, you sat and worried yourself sick over what they might discover. But instead of going to the doctor like a rational person, you convinced yourself that your heart could match itself to music." Bart looked at her. "You really prefer your own version of reality, don't you?"

She felt suddenly sheepish. "Magical thinking can be a very good distraction, my friend."

Bart chuckled. "So is delusion."

The nurse walked in holding a more heavy-duty-looking sling and a stack of paper. "You ready to go home and get some rest, Miss Maggie?"

"Yes, please," she whispered.

# FIFTY-FIVE

## JACK

If Jack could have sat and watched the two of them forever, he would have.

Savannah reminded him of Bess in all the little ways—how she tucked her chin into her chest when she giggled or had the vocabulary of a PhD linguist. At one point, Savannah laughed so hard she snorted, which of course he knew was common—it's just that she did it in such a Bess-like way.

He didn't see quite as much Bess in Thomas. But what he did see amazed him. Pictures hadn't done Thomas justice. He looked exactly the way Jack had felt at that age—all restless energy and limbs that couldn't quite stop moving. He'd been shaking his left leg since the moment they got to the hospital, hours ago.

All the little things. So many, many small wonders.

The big things, though. That's where he felt he didn't know these kids at all. He hadn't been there for any of their memories, or to help make the choices that now stood to shape their futures, or to listen to any of the questions now long answered.

He didn't know Thomas or Savannah. Not really. But he wanted to. He very, very much did.

"When did you switch your name?" Savannah handed him the can of Pepsi they were all sharing, having had to pool the spare change in their pockets to have enough for a single trip to the waiting room vending machine.

"Well, I went by John growing up. That's what my family still calls me. One of my fraternity brothers nicknamed me Thor in college, and I liked it, so I brought it with me to Breckenridge."

He left out the part that Thor was a drinker's name, earned after a particularly raucous night. The Norse god of thunder, more strength than brains.

Since waking up on the lawn back on Tybee, he hadn't had a single drink. He didn't know if he intended that to become a permanent thing, but the sight of his mom's decaying drinker's body was still fresh enough in his mind to turn him off anything stronger than the Pepsi in his hand right now.

"When I started guiding, Jack just sounded like a better name for a captain."

He thought about the postcard he sent to the resort where he'd been hired in Oregon, announcing his change of plans. So many years ago. And thank god he'd done it.

"My boss on Tybee, Ford, was sort of a mentor. He said the name Jack belonged on the water. Captain Jack Morgan, and all that pirate stuff."

Instinctively, he reached up and felt for the piece of paper folded up in his breast pocket. It went with him everywhere. Ford's map. The one of Minneapolis he'd printed for Jack. He'd circled the McClairs' house and written HERE at the top of the page. It had been in the third envelope.

"What about now?" Thomas said. "Are you going to change your name again since you're not on the water anymore?"

Jack smiled, happy—relieved, even—to have good news for once. "Actually, I'm staying on the water. I just arranged to take over a small fishing business in St. Vrain, Colorado."

The words hit him. They were so permanent. So decisive. And yet, suddenly, he couldn't help but wonder if his good news wasn't good at all for Thomas and Savannah. Had they thought he'd move to Minnesota? Were they hoping to be closer to him? Even move to Colorado?

"I—" He wasn't sure how to begin to approach a subject as foreign to him as this. "I'm from Colorado, you know. I guess I just feel like I belong there. And, fishing—of course."

Savannah leaned in and nudged him with her shoulder.

A singular, meaningful nudge.

"Of course!" Her voice beamed. Happy for him. Bright with enthusiasm. "Like we McClairs say, *Follow your instincts!*"

# FIFTY-SIX

## SAVANNAH

Savannah couldn't believe she was sitting there without a notebook. *Of all things.* Her dad was right next to her. A pivotal moment, and she wasn't going to be able to remember the half of it.

"Jack, we have *got* to make a movie out of this."

He grinned. "You think after what we all just went through with the podcast, I'm gonna let you put me in a movie?"

"Yes." Savannah grabbed his arm with both hands. "I know for certain that someday, we are all going to make a movie. The whole *world* is going to want to know how our story ends."

Because that was the greatest thing about meeting Jack. She knew almost immediately this wasn't the end of their story. It was just the beginning. He didn't freak out when he got outed on national television. He made good when he found out Thomas hadn't told her about his emails. He even went along with her idea for salvaging the last episode.

The net of all their summer's worth of chaos was one, crucial fact: their father was a decent human being. He wasn't going to sweep in like a white knight or try to borrow money or even try to sell their story for money.

She didn't think so, at least.

As far as she could tell, Jack Thorson was a nice, decent guy. And she liked him.

"Hey, Jack." It was getting dark outside, which always reminded her of her favorite pastime. "What's the best movie you've ever seen?"

He thought for a minute. "Well, to be honest, I don't think I've seen one in a while. I watched a lot of Warren Miller films growing up in Colorado, though."

Savannah had never heard of the guy.

"I watch TV some." Jack snapped his fingers. "What's that show? About the boys who lost their mom, except it's sort of a comedy?"

Savannah knew that one. Not a second's hesitation.

*"Son Showers."*

"Yeah!" Jack was beaming. "That's a great show. Sad, but funny. You know?"

"I know exactly. In fact, I've written so many letters to one of the producers, she might think I'm stalking her."

Jack laughed. "Well, whatever works, right?"

"I'm trying to learn how to speak my mind." She didn't mind admitting this to Jack. It felt safe. "I mean, I have a lot to say, but sometimes I don't know the best way to express it. I'm either too meek or too—" She wanted to use the word *bitchy*, but she'd recently promised to stop using it to describe herself or anyone else. Unless they really deserved it.

"Let's just say, I'd like to feel I can say what I need to say without having to apologize for it." That felt right. She had to remember that.

"Well," Jack said, "I'm trying to learn that, too. Wish I was your age when I learned it, but better late than never, I guess."

Savannah wanted to hug him. But that would have been about the eightieth time and eighty-one hugs felt excessive. Instead, she turned and caught Thomas's eye, wanting to say the only thing on her heart. *Thank you*, she mouthed.

*Thank you back*, he said.

# FIFTY-SEVEN

## THOMAS

Thomas studied Jack's every move. When he drummed his fingers on his knees, there was a rhythm. It wasn't random. It was anxious, but it wasn't random.

And his fingernails. Like they'd talked about, wide and flat. Trim. Just like Thomas's.

They were the same height, too. Six foot one. They'd even stood back-to-back while Savannah measured. Jack had smaller feet, though. Size ten and a half. Thomas wore elevens.

Jack sort of nodded when he thought, not speaking until he'd put the words together in his head. Thomas did that.

Not like Savannah, who constructed complete paragraphs on a single breath.

More than anything, Thomas just couldn't get used to looking at someone and seeing his own face looking back.

Okay, so it wasn't exactly his face. Jack had a wide, square jaw and Thomas's was long and narrow. Jack had a lot more freckles—probably all that time in the sun. But they definitely had the same, fairish skin. And the gap in Jack's teeth. Thomas brought his tongue up to where his had been, even just months ago. Would he have wanted to leave it there, if he'd known?

Probably not.

Not that it was ugly, of course.

"I can't imagine what you were thinking, sitting there at the table tonight."

That's all Thomas had been able to think about during dinner—that Sam Tamblin was going to uncover the whole scheme. Sam had seen Jack's pictures. And how could he possibly think that Abe, who'd owned The Mine for decades, looked the same age as the guy sitting at dinner?

"I'm really sorry, Jack. We didn't know we'd end up in the ER tonight."

Jack scratched at his chin. "Well, if there's one thing I ought to know about the McClairs by now, it's that you're never predictable." He smiled his gap-toothed smile at Thomas. "Your mom gave me twins, after all."

Thomas missed his mom so badly all of a sudden, it was as if they'd just lost her again.

Everything they'd done to find Jack would have gone so much better if she'd been alive. More supervised. Less Maggie-esque. Savannah wouldn't have gotten ambushed and their whole life wouldn't have shut down while they hid.

Everything would be different. If their mom hadn't died.

He took a long breath, hoping to calm the emotion that threatened to come screaming out.

The woman in the chair across from him was holding her toddler daughter across her lap, rocking her and singing. She was asleep now, but the little girl woke every few minutes to cry and squirm. Her hair was plastered down with sweat and she hadn't let go of the nubby pink blanket in her fist the whole time they'd been there.

"She's supposed to be here." The words came out aloud.

Jack drummed his fingers slowly on his knee. Purposefully, not random. "Yeah," he said. "She is."

They sat without speaking a few minutes more. Quiet. But there. The three of them. Finally. Together.

Renata Covington
Showrunner, Son Showers
American Broadcasting Company

Dear Savannah,

It appears you are quite the fan of our show, Son Showers.

I received your résumé and (multiple) letters. Your doggedness is admirable. Even more, you're an insightful woman and our production team is always in need of sharp young minds like yours.

Plus, we Minnesotans look out for our own, no?

I've passed on your information to the producer who leads our team of interns, Alison Bloom. Please reach out to her when you've settled college and your plans for next year.

I look forward to working with you.

Respectfully,
Renata Covington

*[BEEP]*

*Good afternoon. This is Theodore Brown calling for Thomas McClair and family. Thomas, I'm one of the track-and-field coaches at the University of Chicago and we received the recruit questionnaire you completed online. You're an accomplished young man, and so first let me say, congratulations. As you probably already know, we're a Division Three school here at the university. Meaning, we focus on providing each of our student athletes with a well-rounded educational experience. You'll work hard and you'll train hard, but you won't be asked to sacrifice your academics for your sport. Which, since it looks like you intend to study genetics or engineering, is a good thing. Anyway, we'd love to talk to you. See if University of Chicago is a good fit and what we can do to help you in your decision making. Maybe bring you down from Minneapolis for a visit. I've taken the liberty of mailing you a few materials you might find interesting, and I'll reach out again soon to try to catch you in person. Take care. And, Thomas, keep running.*

*[BEEP]*

<<EXCERPT>>

The Kids Are Gonna Ask
*No Longer a Guava Media Podcast*
Finale

OPEN

**SAVANNAH**
Here's what we knew when we started: Bess McClair had just
turned twenty-two when she and three friends—Brynn, Kristen
and Elise—flew from Minneapolis to Colorado. It was spring
break, March 2002. The four women were college seniors, due to
graduate in two months. It was their last vacation before they'd
be on to the next chapter in their lives.

**THOMAS**
Here's what we know now: Our biodad is alive and healthy. He's
a year older than our mom would have been. He remembers her
well. DNA tests showed a near-certain match. Last month, he
flew to Minneapolis to meet us. We spent three days together.

**SAVANNAH**
Sorry, folks. As much as our *previous* producer wanted to record
our meeting for this podcast, we had other ideas.

**THOMAS**
Not to mention our *previous* producer is currently very busy. His
business partners sent him on an extended *involuntary* vacation.

**SAVANNAH**
Delicious, no?

[pause]

Anyway. As tempting as it is to tell you all the sordid details
about *that*, let's get back to our story.

**THOMAS**
The better story.

**SAVANNAH**
One teeny problem before we get into it, though. We're not going to tell you much. The first meeting with our biological father was just too personal. I mean, it was totally crazy. Cray-zee. Believe me. But we decided there are some things that are better left private.

**THOMAS**
Yeah, you're just going to have to trust us when we say, it was pretty amazing.

[pause]

So, do you feel different now?

**SAVANNAH**
Only in about a thousand ways.

**THOMAS**
Ha, yeah. I guess what I mean is, I feel different in ways I didn't expect. We got answers to questions I didn't even know I had.

**SAVANNAH**
Like what?

**THOMAS**
Like, I knew Maggie missed Mom. But I always thought about Mom's death in terms of what it meant to you and me. But it changed Maggie's life, too. She's lonely. And I think that helped me understand her better.

**SAVANNAH**
You know how I feel different? I'm not so worried about the future. Like I have a clearer picture of where I'm going now.

**THOMAS**
But you've always known where you were going.

**SAVANNAH**
No, I knew where I wanted to go. Now I feel like I *can* go.

**THOMAS**
Plus, it's nice to know we won't be alone if anything happens to Maggie.

**SAVANNAH**
You'll always have me, dummy.

**THOMAS**
And you'll always have me. But now we have Jack, too.

**SAVANNAH**
Now we have Jack.

**THOMAS**
I want to tell Mom thanks for picking so well.

**SAVANNAH**
You know what I wish I could tell her?

**THOMAS**
What?

**SAVANNAH**
That I'm so glad we discovered she was a badass. I'm still going to miss her every day, but now I'm inspired by her. She always did what she wanted to do, what she believed was right. And I'm going to honor that by carrying her badass-ness forward. Always.

<<END EXCERPT>>

★ ★ ★ ★ ★

# ACKNOWLEDGMENTS

The characters in this book are fictional, but the choice to understand one's history and biology is a very real and deeply personal decision for millions of people. I haven't faced the reunion journey in my own life, but in writing this book, I gained a profound respect for the emotional and logistical tangles such a decision requires of individuals and families. As much as possible, I tried to reflect the very real questions, concerns, hopes, fears, dreams and heartaches that can come with any biological search. I also recognize, however, that every journey is as unique as the person who undertakes it. There is no single, definitive story about finding one's biological family, and in recognition of that, I did not set out to write one.

I would, most importantly, like to extend my sincere thanks to those who shared their origin, adoption, search and reunion stories with me—some who chose to search, and some who chose not to. Special thanks to K.S., J.O. and V.L. for being willing to answer my questions. Also, many, many thanks to Karen, who not only shared the story of her search and ongoing journey with me, but who also took the time to read an early, messy draft of this book. I hope I did your feedback justice, Karen, and that I extended to these kids the same generosity you showed me.

I will not presume to give advice to anyone considering finding their birth parents. I will, however, share several resources that proved valuable to me in researching and writing Savannah and Thomas's story.

The Child Welfare Information Gateway on Searching for Birth Relatives is an online resource maintained by the US Department of Health and Human Services. The gateway provides access to reunion registries, support groups and a variety of resources for conducting domestic and international searches. https://www.childwelfare.gov/topics/adoption/search/searching/

*Who Am I...Really?* Podcast. Real stories about adoption, searching, biological reunions and the emotions throughout. http://www.whoamireallypodcast.com/

Adoptees On. A podcast and online community of adopted people willing to share their stories and experiences. http://www.adopteeson.com/

As for the day-to-day writing of this book, there are more thanks to be given.

To Josh Moehling and Laska Nygaard, two-thirds of the Monday Night Go Go's, this book would not, could not, exist without you. For real. I will attempt to repay you every week from here until the end of our writing lives.

To my editor at Park Row Books, Natalie Hallak, you give one heck of a pep talk, and I needed so many. Thank you for keeping my chin up and your editorial flashlight fully charged. There was a lot of dark, but we made it.

To my agent, Holly Root, because all writers should be so lucky as to have her.

To every independent bookseller, librarian and reader who loved, talked up and hand sold my first book, *Evergreen Tidings from the Baumgartners.* I thought I was a lucky woman the day I held the finished book in my hands. Boy, was I wrong. As a writer, nothing beats the feeling of learning that your book meant enough to a person that they're willing to evangelize on its behalf. The experience is magical, humbling and, sometimes, on the hard days, the only reason to get back to the keyboard. Thank you, thank you, thank you.

On a related note: SUPPORT YOUR INDEPENDENT BOOKSTORES AND PUBLIC LIBRARIES! [red-face emoji, laughing-through-tears emoji, flag emoji, cheerleader emoji]

And finally, to my family, you're crazy, and I love ya.

My mother, to whom this book is dedicated, actually did spend an afternoon in 1962 helping my grandmother paint her antique table bright red. Like the table in this story, ours passed from my grandmother's house to my mother's and now to mine, where my husband and I eat with our three boys every night. There's something magical about that table, and may we be forever thankful for the blessings it grants to those around it.

To our boys, you're already incredible young men. Just keep going.

To Chad, all of it would mean so much less without you.

With heartfelt thanks,
*Gretchen Anthony*

# THE KIDS ARE GONNA ASK

## GRETCHEN ANTHONY

Reader's Guide

PARK
ROW
BOOKS

1. Throughout the book, Maggie worries about the potential dangers of doing a podcast for Guava Media, yet she allows her grandchildren to pursue it anyway. Why? Does this contradict the McClair family motto, "Listen to your instincts"? Would you have let your children or grandchildren pursue a similar public endeavor?

2. The McClair household is figuratively haunted by the memories of George and Bess. What effects do you think these "ghosts" have on each character? Does Maggie think she's really talking to her daughter? Does Savannah believe her mother visits her in her dreams? If so, what does that say about each of them?

3. Maggie engages in magical thinking throughout the book: she believes her heart can match its beat to music and she engages in conversation with Bess. Why? How does magical thinking benefit Maggie? Are there ways it's not helpful?

4. Thomas and Savannah's sibling relationship changes throughout the book; it's sometimes volatile and sometimes tender. How did the external pressures of school and the podcast affect their relationship? How did it evolve with time? Did the podcast harm their relationship or strengthen it?

5. Maggie describes Thomas and Savannah as trying to avoid falling into a "quicksand pit of emotion" during their podcast journey. How did the kids display this

"quicksand"? How did their internal and external emotional responses evolve as the podcast went on?

6. Thomas keeps his email relationship with Jack a secret from everyone, including Savannah. Why? How did it benefit him? Do you think he had a right to do so?

7. George McClair used to say, "We will always have enough, as long as we have each other." But at different points throughout the book, Maggie, Savannah, Thomas and Jack each express feelings of loneliness. How does loneliness affect the choices they make? How does it affect the way they interact with others? How is it possible to be surrounded by people who love you and still feel alone?

8. Savannah is a smart and outspoken young woman but is often ridiculed for it. At one point she says, "Like having the whole school hate me wasn't enough. Now the whole world gets to hate me." Have you experienced this conflict in your own life? Have you watched other girls or women experience the same? Do you believe Thomas was treated differently? If so, was it because of his gender?

9. Jack recognizes that his boss, Ford, became more of a father figure to him than his own dad. Even so, Jack betrays his promise to buy Ford's business. Why did Jack make a promise he couldn't keep, especially to someone like Ford? At what point did Jack decide to "make it right"? What does his relationship with young Carter say about Jack's character?

10. The podcast earns decent ratings when it's a happy story about two kids searching for their father, but it goes viral when it becomes the subject of hate and fear. What examples of this "hater" phenomenon do you see in the world today? Is there a way to beat it, or is the "hater" culture simply a fact of human nature?